CATCH
KID CURRY

Center Point
Large Print

Also by W. R. Garwood and available from
Center Point Large Print:

Kill Him, Again
Ringo's Tombstone

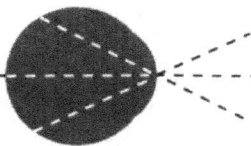

**This Large Print Book carries the
Seal of Approval of N.A.V.H.**

CATCH KID CURRY

W. R. GARWOOD

CENTER POINT LARGE PRINT
THORNDIKE, MAINE

This Center Point Large Print edition
is published in the year 2023 by arrangement with
Golden West Inc.

Originally published in the US by Bath Street Press.

The text of this Large Print edition is unabridged.
In other aspects, this book may vary
from the original edition.
Printed in the United States of America
on permanent paper sourced using
environmentally responsible foresting methods.
Set in 16-point Times New Roman type.

ISBN 978-1-63808-597-3 (hardcover)
ISBN 978-1-63808-601-7 (paperback)

The Library of Congress has cataloged this record
under Library of Congress Control Number: 2022946048

To Shirley,
Alice and John
Gracias Compadres!

CHAPTER ONE

Christmas is a time of peace, with pine trees and big stars, but two nights past that Christmas of '96 all hell broke loose!

When my brother Lonny Logan, Jim Thornhill, our foreman, and myself rode our buckboard into Landusky, Wyoming to the holiday dance, I had me a feeling I couldn't shake. Call it foreboding, if you go for big words. But in spite of the crisp, snowy-cold air and the tang of whiskey and the reek of cigar smoke inside Cripple Jake's Saloon—I smelled more trouble than anything else.

I didn't know where it was coming from until I spotted the man the little burg was named after. Deputy United States Marshal Pike Landusky, himself, was leaning against the rough, wooden bar, bawling out a string of dirty words to a Christmas song. Three saddle-tramps, who served Pike as deputies, from time to time, were stretched out along the bar with Pike.

"There's th' old buffalo," Lonny clipped. "He's probably spoutin' his big medicine, as usual, how he's gonna run us Logans clean out of th' country, and just because our little horse spread's makin' money, while his mangy cow-ranch can't cut th' mustard."

Lonny was right. Ever since we Logans moved in on Crimson Creek, west of the Little Rockies, just to the north of Pike, there'd been bad blood. Our 4-T Brand had been slapped on the hides of some mighty fine horses, all raised on the 4-T, and sold honest and above board.

We'd been brought up, as shirt-tail young'uns, back in Missouri, with right proper horse sense, as the saying goes. So we were making it while Pike was forced to take on extra jobs, like a Tin Star, to help keep his wife and four grown daughters in grub and duds.

But Lonny was wrong about the real burr under old Pike's saddle. It was Lonny—*himself!*

Lonny was a tall, good-looking young man. And Pike's oldest girl, Elfie, had taken a great shine to him. This seemed to heap coals on Pike's head, and he'd done his level damndest to brand our own Logan hides as rustlers and horse thieves.

Back in November he'd hauled both Johnny, my older brother, and me into town on some trumped-up charges. Lonny would have been grabbed also, but he was away on a trading trip at the time.

When Johnny slipped away, while being taken to the out-house by one of Pike's hoosegow gun-hands, Old Pike sobered up enough to larrup me with his pistol barrel, before they stopped him.

Johnny, like a fool, lit out for the safety of Hole

in the Wall, down near the middle of Wyoming Territory, but I was released on bond the following morning to stand trial in January at the next court session. For the following two months I'd stayed put on our ranch, but it sometimes seemed that I couldn't wait out the time until I could get my name cleared—and show up Pike for the tricky devil he was.

All this was running through my head as I crossed the uneven, plank flooring toward Pike and his bunch.

He wasn't taking any notice as he swilled down his Old Crow and pounded on the bar-top to hurry up Cripple Jake for another round.

I could have walked down to the far end of the bar, but it was seven weeks since I'd been near Pike, and I had a lot of eyes on me.

Lonny, for some reason, better sense likely, hung back with Jim. Pike seemed to be minding his own business, so I pulled my horns in a mite and ordered a drink from Jake, the one-legged bartender and owner of the saloon.

Turning, I waved Lonny and Jim up to join me. The pair of fiddlers, Ike Jacobs and Hank Macomber, both bar-flies and summertime cowboys, but good fellows, struck up another break-down. And as they sawed away, the dozen or so couples in the long, log room began to sashay around the floor.

Lonny, with a big grin on his face, took a

rancher's daughter and plunged into the fray, but Jim lounged back against the door.

Jim, always even-tempered and cool-blooded, seemed glad that things had settled down. But he was in for a disappointment.

Pike wheeled toward me like a lowering, old mossy bull. He'd been studying me in the smudged bar mirror, though I hadn't noticed until the instant before he moved.

"Goddam you Logans!" he bellowed out above the noise of the dance and the fiddlers' "Devil's Dream." And he sure looked the Devil, himself, with wide, scarred face and wicked, little red eyes. "You Goddam cow thieves! What's a man to do to keep you out'a his town?" He whacked his big fist down on the zinc-topped bar, rolling bottles and glasses.

The dance stopped right dead in its tracks, folks scattering like stirred-up quail.

"No need to make a fool of yourself, Pike, when it's just the whiskey mouthing," I said. I could see the old buck was stone drunk, but not too drunk to move his hand toward his coat. For he wore a bulky, floor-length buffalo coat in spite of the steamy saloon air.

"I'll fool you!" Pike, cursing and damning, was ripping away at his coat, trying to get at a pistol.

"Cut that!" I gave him a shove. I've always been mighty strong for my build, and I shoved hard. Pike bounced off the bar, and fell sprawling among the broken glass with a grunt.

He came up bleeding and howling for my own blood.

I backed off, afraid the old lobo would start heaving broken bottles and hit some of the folks in the room. His deputies tried to hold him, but he jerked away and, head down, charged straight for me.

There was nothing to do, but stop him. I let him have a real haymaker straight to the jaw, but it only slowed him a bit. He shook his shaggy head and was square on top of me.

It was my turn to hit the floor, and I thought the roof timbers had caved in. Pike must have thought he had me then, for instead of pounding away at me, he reared up to kick my face in with his big, nail-studded boots. That was his mistake! Outweighed by a hundred pounds, I rolled out of the way and kicked back, myself. I connected with his ribs. He cursed and reaching out, flailed a long arm that landed a fist aside my head with the punch of a mustang's hoof.

Lonny and Jim were shouting, and I caught a glimpse of them from the corner of my eye, where they stood, with drawn pistols, keeping the crowd and Pike's deputies out of the way.

By now my Logan dander was up and red-hot, and in spite of the difference in our sizes, I was fighting mad. I wouldn't have cared if Pike had been seven feet tall, and was packing two law badges, I'd have tried to half-choke the life from him.

"Beat th' hell out of him!" Lonny called, but I didn't need any prodding. I butted Pike in the belly with my head, and as he sailed over backward, I was on top of him.

When Pike found me astride, he tried to roll me off, but his head thudded against the iron bar-rail, and he yelped like a mad wolf.

"Take it back, you old rattler," I grunted between punches. I was pounding him in the face and chest, a glare of red smoke bobbing before my eyes. "Take your lies back—you damned lying old devil!"

Pike bucked and reared, but I stuck a'top his heaving carcass until he grunted out an admission that he'd tried to crowd us Logans off the good range near his spread, and that the indictment against Johnny and myself was a pure lie. He even owned up to using his office to frame us on false cattle theft charges.

When the crowd heard that last, they sucked in their breaths. That was a fact many suspected, but few dared talk about openly.

"If you weren't such an old man, I'd really beat hell out of you," I gritted. "But if you've had enough, we'll call it square and you can go on your way."

Bleeding from cuts and blows, Pike nodded

sullenly, and the saloon full of folks let breaths out loud enough to hear. I got up and scooped my Smith and Wesson .38 Russian pistol from the floor, jamming it back into its holster.

Wiping the sweat and sawdust from my face, I turned away from Pike. He was all through. I felt sort of sorry for him. He'd lose his tin star, and probably his ranch before the law was done with him.

"Let's go back to the place," I started to say to the boys, who'd also holstered their guns. "This isn't my idea of Christmas spirits."

"Look out Kid! He's goin' to shoot!" Jim yelled, as the crowd ducked and scrambled again.

A gun boomed out behind me, before I could turn, and the bullet seared the side of my neck like a white-hot branding iron. I jerked around and pulled my .38. Pike had his fur coat yanked open, and was cocking his Colt .45 to shoot again—but I let him have it!

He staggered back toward the bar, but had enough brute strength to fire back, smashing out the saloon's only window.

I shot again, and this time he stumbled and fell headlong like a gunned-down buffalo.

"Let's go, you crazy wildcat," Lonny yelled from where he and Jim, guns out, were covering the crowd and deputies, none of which were making much of a move to stop me.

"Lookit Cripple Jake!" Hank Macomber shouted. And there went the old duffer on his crutch, flying out the door, so locoed with fright that he burst right between Lonny and Jim to tumble head-first into a snowbank.

Jim let off a couple of shots into the roof as we backed out.

A small bunch of townfolk and ranchers were standing outside, surrounding the one-legged bartender, where he lay in the snow, all positive he was the victim.

I felt mighty roused up and bad about the fight, but couldn't help laughing at Jake as we piled into the buckboard.

"You'll laugh on the other side of your chin when they get around to come looking for you," Jim growled, whipping up the black mare.

"Then they'll have to travel a hell of a trail," I said, as we went rocking away up the one street of Landusky, heading out the snow-covered river road to our ranch.

The stars were still blazing with the same cold fire that seemed to burn inside me. Low over the silvery-blue streak of the Southern horizon, one star glowed, pulsing deep red, in the direction of the only safe haven for a man in trouble with the law—Hole in the Wall.

CHAPTER TWO

We scratched gravel when we got back to our ranch.

As I'd made up my mind to leave before first light, Lonny and Jim grabbed provisions and ammunition while I went out to the log barn, and putting up the buckboard, stabled and fed the mare. I saddled my black riding horse Dan Patch and shook out some feed for Dan and Pot Belly, our little pack-mare, waiting in the warm barn while they ate.

Sleet slapped me in the face as I led both horses back to the house, tying them to the hitching rail under the shelter of the overhanging roof. The weather had taken a turn for the worse, and the thermometer was showing a drop.

Inside the ranch house, I stood by the kitchen table and loaded the bone-handled Colt .44 that Johnny left when he made his dash for the wide open. The rising wind was humming and whistling down the chimney. But that was the only music in the house.

"Takin' Johnny's Colt?" Jim asked as he stuffed a side of bacon into the pack-mare's gunny sack. Lonny looked up from oiling my Winchester '76 carbine saddle-gun.

"I've had enough of pop guns," I said, pulling

off my Smith and Wesson .38 and heaving it onto the table. "It took two shots to take Pike out of action. If I ever have to shoot another man, I want him to stay down."

Switching pistol belts and buckling on the .44, I sat down to drink a cup of coffee, but Jim, who'd gone outside with a sack for the pack-mare, eased back inside with his head cocked to one side. "Company!"

"Where?" Lonny jumped up with the Winchester, jacking a shell into the chamber.

"Horses heard something," Jim answered. "I heard a horse whickerin' back at Pot Belly."

Dan Patch wasn't very sociable, so I knew he'd not been carrying on. "Catch sight of anyone?"

"Nope, but there's someone out there." Jim rubbed the barrel of his six-shooter alongside his hawk nose.

"Probably Pike's egg-suckin' deputies," muttered Lonny. He poked the Winchester out the crack of the doorway.

"Hold it!" I blew out the lamp and peered into the billowing whiteness of the storm. As the blinding sheet sagged, with a pause in the wind, I caught sight of three horsemen, sitting reined-in by the lee side of the log barn.

I didn't know if they'd spotted the lamp go out, due to the swirling sleet and snow, but right then I decided to make my move. "Give me the extra grub in that sack and the Winchester," I said.

"I'm not waiting for light. And I can't travel with that slow pack horse. There's at least three of them out there—maybe getting up enough sand to come over. When they do, I don't want you both getting mixed up in this."

Lonny handed over the saddle-gun, saying nothing. He could see I was right, and that someone had to stay and tend the ranch with Jim.

I got into my old, green-checked mackinaw and stuffed the pockets with .45-60 cartridges from a box on the mantle of the fireplace. In the flickering yellow fire-glow I could just make out Jim's long-jawed face and Lonny's handsome phiz—both mighty sober.

"No need to act like you both lost your last dollar," I grinned. "I'll lay low until I see how Pike made out."

"Pike's a goner, certain. You hit him too square," drawled Jim.

"Oh—maybe he's just stove-up good," Lonny ventured. "An old he bear like Pike can take a cupful of lead and not cash in—just too damned mean!"

"Those jaspers out by the barn aren't here to hand out holiday greetings." I bundled up, wrapping a long muffler of Jim's around my neck. "Send word down to the Hole."

"The Hole?" Jim edged the door open with his left hand, with his Colt at the ready in his right.

17

"You gonna ride a hull territory off before you stop?"

"Well, th' Hole's a damn smart place to head for," Lonny said. "Lots of good cowboys layin' low there, I expect, may be even Johnny."

Looking past Jim's big shoulders, I could see little but feathery snow and the hazy outlines of Dan Patch where he stood drooped over the hitch rail. Down by the barn all was just white emptiness. The outbuildings and the strangers were completely hidden. But, I reckoned so was the ranch house from the unknown visitors.

I shook Lonny's hand, trying to get a last look at his boyish face, then turned to pump Jim's horny paw. "If those fellows don't try to start anything—don't you—Lonny! Watch him, Jim. And let me know—somehow—what's going on here. And maybe when Pike's back on his feet, things could clear up somehow."

They stood in the dim light nodding without speaking. After taking a last look at the pair, I turned away and went out to the hitching rack with my sack of grub and the Winchester. I listened for some sound from the barn, but all was wind hum and the clabbery whisper of fast-falling snow.

I stuffed the rifle into the saddle boot, and slinging the sack behind, unhitched Dan. Swinging into the snowy saddle, I nudged him into an easy walk. He went mighty unwilling—

probably feeling that I was a blamed fool to set out on such a night. Pot Belly, at the far end of the hitch rack, whickered once, but Dan was too riled to answer back.

Circling the west side of the ranch house, I rode cautiously through the whipping snowfall and pulled up just in time before the vague streaks of fencing by our cottonwood grove. I dismounted and guiding Dan along the line fence for about sixty paces came to the break gate in our west horse pasture. By now the storm was petering out enough to give me a glimpse of the old 4-T. One of the boys had relit a lamp. That small orange square of window light looked mighty good to me about then. There didn't seem to be anything going on back there. And I certainly hoped those three riders had returned to town.

I replaced the rickety gate and, remounting, struck off across the five acres toward the river road and on due south. My mouth tasted bitter and dry, and ached from one side to the other from that fool Pike's fists. Behind me the light at the 4-T was twinkling out like a fading star. Ahead, the stars over Hole in the Wall, a hundred and fifty miles off, were hidden for a moment by the drifting storm.

I yanked my fleece-lined mackinaw around my ears, pulled the scarf up over my nose and settled down in the saddle for a ten-mile haul. If I could stay awake and keep the hulking horns of the

Little Rockies at my back, and if Dan didn't let me down, I'd fetch up at John Coburn's Circle-C Ranch on Crimson Creek. Coburn was a friend of us Logans. We'd sold him more than one string of fine horseflesh. I was sure of a hearty welcome at his place and could thaw out and lay over for a day.

"Huddup, Dan!" I booted him a good one to keep him alert. He grunted once and perked up his gait, seeming to know that we were headed out of the storm as soon as we could get there.

CHAPTER THREE

For half an hour after leaving the 4-T, I'd ridden back and forth along the river road in the whipping snow squalls, listening for any gunshots, but there'd not been a sound. Once as the wind picked up from the north, I heard a horse coming full tilt through the storm, and pulled off in a hurry into a small stand of timber. The rider went on by in a hurry. After waiting a spell, I set off down the road myself, but never came up with him.

By the time I'd loped Dan as far as the wooden bridge over the first bend of the Crimson, near the start of Coburn's Circle-C range, I was pretty well frozen up. The storm was over, and the stars overhead were glittering away like chips of blue ice, but the evil wind still kept up its blustering. Right about then I'd have given fifty dollars for a good shot of Old Crow.

Dan Patch just creaked along, and I knew the horse was feeling the bitter cold. Reining in, I dismounted and stumped ahead on half-frozen feet, batting at my chest and shoulders to keep warm. I soon found it hard going through the drifts over the road and was forced to remount.

Three miles from Coburn's layout, the range-land dipped into a gradually deepening valley where another bend of the Crimson curved in from the northwest. I knew there was a line shack on the far side of the creek that was bound to be empty this time of the season.

The road continued along the ridge toward another bridge at Big Tree Crossing, but I headed down the snow filled slopes into the bottoms. The snow was deeper here and Dan grunted and heaved through the drifts until we came out among a string of willow thickets at the creek's edge.

I rode along the rim of the ice, searching the opposite white bulk of the hills for some sign of the cabin. While the valley held off the bite of the wind, the cold was still growing. I had it figured for zero or below. The brittle willow branches snapped and slashed at my face, but Jim's old scarf gave me some protection. Dan was getting his share and shook his head doggedly.

The moon, down for most of the night, commenced to throw a weak, silver stain over the valley as it edged up from the west. Shadows began to stretch out thin black streaks.

When I guided the horse around a pile of snow-covered rocks at a gap in the willows, I saw a large blot of shadow about fifty yards away on the far side of the creek. It was the line shack.

Crossing the frozen surface of the Crimson and up the hillside to the cabin. I stiffly dismounted to find the door nailed shut. I pulled the saddle gun from its boot and knocking out the shack's boarded-up window, managed to slip through the opening into the dark interior without cutting myself. Lighting a match, I saw the place was completely empty except for a small stone fireplace at the far end of the shack.

I was beginning to grow stiff with the bitter cold and desperate at my fix. If I tried to sleep without a fire, I'd never get up with the morning sun.

The hut was old and the planking on the door and two of the walls was dry and half-rotten. The other walls, set into the hillside, were rough-hewn logs—so I tackled the door. In a few minutes I'd battered it down and kicked enough apart to fill the fireplace.

Throughout the rest of the night, with Dan close-tied near a corner of the hut, I huddled by the fire, feeding the roaring blaze with pieces of planking. Out beyond the orange circle of firelight, the cold wind still shrilled from time to time, but we were fairly protected. I wasn't much bothered by the thought of anyone coming out this way on such a hell of a night. Even the casual passer-by would hardly ride over from the road to peer down into the valley.

About once an hour I'd rouse up, knock apart more planking, stoke up the fire and cast an eye on the snowy, silent, moonlit ridges. But all was still.

During my uneasy dozes I had odd, mixed-up dreams . . . of fighting Pike . . . and of my old Aunt Lee in Missouri, and at last that sad day our Mother had died along the Missouri trail. It came as clearly as if it were happening again—her last day . . .

. . . "Lonny, stop the horse. This is a good place to cook supper," I told my ten-year-old brother, as I walked along beside our ramshackle wagon. It would be a good place to stop. We were near a small cottonwood shaded river, close to the Missouri line. We'd come all the way from our poor, red-dirt farm in the north of old Virginia. Our Pa had died ten years back, ten years to the month he laid down his weapons along with the rest of General Lee's soldiers. Mother stuck it out till the next spring of 1876, and then sold the whole place, lock, stock and barrel, except for our old wagon and horse, for the sum of two hundred dollars hard cash money. And now here we were three hundred miles off and ready to camp.

"Harve! I can't rouse Maw," Lonny called out in his high, childish voice, while wide-eyed Johnny, our older brother, ran back from the horse's head. She'd been poorly since leaving our High Bridge farm, but had hoped to gain back her strength on the way west. She'd told us that the trip out to her older sister's place at Dodson, Missouri would make her "chipper and full of ginger, again." But it wasn't so. For the past week it had been up to us three boys to light the fire and cook up our corn meal and slab pork. Winter Sickness, that had taken a lot of folks bad the past fall, seemed to get a'hold of Maw and wouldn't let go.

Now as I ran to the wagon I could see both Johnny and Lonny standing on the wagon seat, looking wild-eyed and scared. Lonny, who had always been timid at times, began to cry.

"Maw's dead, Harve," Johnny said, wiping at his eyes with his hickory shirt sleeve.

"Aw, no!" I climbed up to peek into the shadowy interior of our canvas-covered wagon—but it was true. She was dead. And we boys were alone—a long way from Virginia and home.

Though I was the middling boy, I was always the most sober-sided, except when my terrible temper cut loose. Generally, I was the one to buckle into any job that had to be done. And now, I went to the back of the wagon and clawed out a shovel.

We buried our mother by the little, silvery, bubbling stream near to a wide-spread cotton-wood, with a split trunk. Patting down the last shovelful, I saw the first star break out in the deep blue of the evening sky.

As we'd wrapped her in the beautiful old Cherokee Star quilt of her mother's, with its points of orange, red, yellow and a dozen other colors, the only words I could think of to say was the one's she'd taught us as toddlers:

"Star bright. Star bright. First star we seen tonight. Wish we may—wish we might."

Lonny cried and Johnny, though he was oldest, he cried too—but I was now in charge of our layout, so I gritted my teeth and got to work building up a fire for our supper. It was certain dark and lonesome. And it seemed, as I worked at keeping that blaze going, Lonny, or someone, kept telling me to heave on more wood.

The harder I worked at keeping that fire up, the colder it got along that river bank in Missouri. I could, somehow, no longer see my two brothers—only the darkening river, and tall cottonwoods swaying and shivering in the cold wind from the west. And over them, one lonesome star in all of that cold night sky . . .

I woke up with such a start that I whacked my elbow against the stone fireplace of the line shack, reaching for my gun. But there was no one in the half-demolished building but myself. The fire had burned down to a few feeble coals. The cold was strong as ever, and poor old Dan was halfway into the shack, with hanging head, trying to get out of the weather.

I stood up in the chilly darkness and rubbed my horse's nose. There was a light in the east about the same shade as the fire-streaked embers. Morning was ready to break through the cloud-patched night sky. It was time to get moving.

After feeding Dan a handful of grain, I tightened his cinch and leading him out of the battered shack, mounted up. We crossed the frozen creek and made for the road at the top of the ridge. I was still cold, stiff and hungry, and wanted to be out of the valley before anyone coming down from Landusky could box me in.

I put the steel to old Dan, who snorted with disgust and humped himself into a lope for a short spell. But drifts had mounded so deeply across the narrow road that Dan was forced to come back down to a plunging walk.

About the time I pulled up to let Dan blow, I saw we were within a hailing piece of Coburn's. Coming into the Montana Territory in the days of the Indian troubles, old Bob Coburn had picked an easily defended site. The ranch buildings sat upon a small, round hill with a good stand of timber to the west for a wind-break. A branch of the Crimson cut between the buildings and the grove, making it pretty hard to be rushed. Anyone at the ranch had a good view of whoever came along—but it worked both ways.

In the grey-white light I caught sight of something that decided me to keep riding. At least two strange buckboards were parked out by the long, log ranch house, and there seemed to be a half-dozen extra saddle horses in the corral that opened out of the main barn. Whoever they were, I wasn't about to stop by and pass the time of day.

The drifts were lighter on this stretch of road and I spurred Dan up again. As we went by the ranch in a cloud of snow, I turned in the saddle and saw a head sticking out of the open ranch house door. It could have been old man Coburn, or one of his sons, but hungry as I was there was no stopping for breakfast.

It just wouldn't do to mix with people, friends or strangers, until I saw how this fight with Pike was going to come out.

As I rode down the snow-covered road that wound away to the southwest, I remembered what our old Aunt Lee, back in Missouri, used to say to me: "You've just got an extra streak of the Old Nick in you." And though folks all said I was the steadiest and hardest-working of my brothers, I did have a certain restlessness deep under my hide. Jim Thornhill once said I was like a kettle "always just about at the boil." Well, this time I'd boiled over for sure, and forced myself to high-tail it for some robbers' roost like Hole in the Wall.

Cursing my Logan temper, and old Pike for a fool, and ploughing into another sudden snow-squall, I came near riding dead into a horseman coming up from the south.

Before I could rein in, the stranger whipped out a Winchester and covered me. "Where you goin'? Oh, hell's fire!" He lowered the saddle-gun and squirted out a stream of tobacco juice that would have drowned a ground-squirrel. "Hell's fire. Ain't that Harvey Logan?"

It was Arapaho Brown, an old frontiersman and Deputy to Sheriff "Red" Angus in Johnson County, Wyoming. We Logans had run into him several times when delivering strings of horses into that territory.

"Just heading down your way to pick up some mounts," I answered, watching him jam that Winchester back into its saddle scabbard. "What fetches you up here?"

"Same thing." He shook the snowflakes from his broad, silver-streaked beard. "Lookin' fer horses, 'cept these partikaleer cayuses been cajoled off by some light-fingered hoss-fancier without money changin' hands. Th' trail of some of 'em, out of Hole in th' Wall, led up this way."

I told him, quiet like, that I hadn't seen a thing since starting out from our ranch, which was just about the truth. But it made my neck burn to hear the Hole mentioned. The Hole might not be the safest place in the world to land, if they were using it for rustling operations. But it was the only place I knew, and Johnny was there—from his letter of a month back.

Arapaho waved his high-crowned sombrero, with its Indian bead-work on the band, and went pounding on toward Landusky, looking for his horse thieves, and spraying tobacco juice against the wind.

I waited until he'd dipped out of sight and then put the spurs to Dan Patch. I didn't want to be around while any posses were being formed.

I rode along steadily for most of the morning, seeing nothing but a few deer and one elk. About noon, I pulled into a pine grove, about a pistol shot off the road, and unsaddling Dan, fed him some of his grain. I hauled out the coffee pot and small skillet from my gunny sack and soon had a good mess of bacon and plenty of Arbuckle cooked up on the small, but hot fire I'd started from dead pine branches.

I cleared off a couple of logs that lay half in the sun, behind some junipers, and putting down my saddle, slicker and blanket, dozed away until well into the afternoon.

Once a rider, leading a good-looking pair of bay horses, went by on the road, but he poked along heading toward Landusky, so I forgot about him.

I figured that if I had no more bad weather, I'd fetch up at Ab Winters' Ranch on the Broken Bow about dark.

At four o'clock I resaddled Dan, kicked out the fire and we headed southwest again.

CHAPTER FOUR

It was well past sundown when I caught the welcome sight of Ab Winters' ranch lights gleaming like yellow stars in the deep blue night.

Twice I'd gone astray and ridden off the road, which wasn't much more than a glorified buggy track anyway. I didn't care as long as I was able to dismount and stagger into the warm kitchen of the house, while a ranch hand put up Dan in a good warm stall.

All through supper Ab kept pestering me with small talk, but his young, dark-haired wife sat a right smart table, so I kept up a polite mumble while I tackled the beef-steak, boiled potatoes and side-dishes.

Winters, a gangling, gander-eyed jasper with a stringy yellow beard, was from Texas, and as tight-fisted as a down-east Yankee. He was mighty industrious though and had built up one of the nicest cattle spreads in Montana since he'd arrived ten years back. He'd also built himself a reputation as a mighty hard man with a dollar.

Johnny'd had a run-in with him a couple of years back when Winters had tried to outsmart him in a horse-buying deal.

So now all Winters could harp on was Johnny and his "trouble with the law." He really meant Johnny's jail-break out of old Pike Landusky's

31

hoosegow and was mealy-mouthed about it, making out to sympathize with me, but I could see he was really mighty glad. I wondered if he'd swallowed my story about being on a trip south on 4-T ranch business.

The food was beginning to stick in my craw, but I kept on eating. Several times, his wife, with a hesitant look at Ab, put in her oar to try and change the talk. We talked over the weather, the chances of telephones coming into the Territory, a story she'd just read by some man named Wister about a cowboy in a magazine called Harpers, and a dozen other things.

When Ab, with a scowl at his wife, switched the talk away from mail-order catalogues and back on to Johnny, I rose, and excusing myself, went into the back lean-to for my hat and mackinaw— heading for the bunkhouse.

I heard a commotion behind, sounds of a scuffle and Winters' woman came through the door after me, holding together a rip in the bosom of her cheap, red gingham dress. Her eyes were over-red and there was the fresh imprint of a hand on the side of her face.

I'd heard Ab Winters was as rough on his Missus as on his working help so I wasn't surprised. But in spite of myself, my dander started to rise at the thought of that long drink of water striking this girl, who was at least fifteen years younger than himself.

"Mister Logan—we really don't want you to go out to that bunkhouse. There's extra room here and you're welcome to it," she said, extending her hand to me.

"I shouldn't want you to put yourself to any trouble," I said as I gave her a hurried hand shake, and was as surprised as if I grabbed hold of a hot branding iron—the shock of it ran through my arm like a jolt. "I shouldn't want to put you to any trouble," I repeated foolishly, still holding her little, slim fingers.

"No!" Winters had come through the door after his wife. "No, we don't treat a fellow rancher that way. You're still half froze-up." He glared black as a thunder cloud as I let go of her hand. "I'll bed you down for the night. We're full up at the bunkhouse anyway. Just took on an extra hand."

What he was doing hiring in the middle of bad weather when there wasn't half-enough work for a regular bunch was beyond me. I followed him through the large but sparsely-furnished rooms while his missus brought up the rear with a big coal-oil lamp.

My room was in an ell off the ranch house and must have been added some time after the place was first built. There was a comfortable, spool-bed with a thick shuck mattress covered with three blankets. It was cold in the room, but that bed was mighty inviting.

Mrs. Winters, without speaking or looking at

me, placed the lamp on a small, rough table by the window and went out.

"Sleep in as long as you like, Logan." Winters gave me a smile that was only half-thawed. "Presume you ain't anxious to mix up with any more Blue Northers on your way." He went out shutting the door slow and easy.

I peeled down to my flannels. Sticking my pistol under the pillow, I blew out the lamp and turned in.

For a spell I lay there all keyed up from the events of the night before and the day just ended. I couldn't for the life of me, figure why Winters' woman had put such a funny feeling in me. Then I grunted and rolled over. She was Ab's wife, and it was none of my business.

After a while, it might have been an hour, I was roused by some small noise. I'd been sleeping so heavy that it was a minute or so before I could get my bearings. The moon was up, lighting the snow to near daylight and the room was flooded with a pale silver.

By bending over and craning my neck I could get a view of the bunkhouse. There didn't seem to be anything going on down there, not a light.

I was just sinking back onto the mattress when I felt a hand over my mouth . . . and heard a woman's low voice—"Hush, Mister Logan, hush!"

I sat bolt upright, and peering into the shadows

saw the moonlight faintly silvering the jutting breasts and rounded curves of Ab's wife, where she crouched at the edge of my bed. Her flannel night dress lay crumpled on the floor beside her.

"Mrs. Winters," I whispered with suddenly dry lips. "What are you thinking—coming in here?" Sweat stood out on my forehead in spite of the cold room. I tried to look away, but her shadowy eyes held me like a jack-lighted deer.

She got to her feet in the silvery glow and throwing her arms above her long hair, turned slowly and silently on her tip-toes, like a dancer, letting the moonlight flow over every part of her. She circled and circled, reminding me of one of the beautiful slave girls in Lonny's Diamond Dick novels.

I sat up in bed, motionless and hardly breathing—afraid to move. There had been few females in my life, so far, and those mainly nester's daughters—plump prairie chickens, all looking for husbands. The only others were a couple of saloon girls, who showed me what women were—for a price.

And now the girl stopped her graceful, silent little dance and took a step toward the bed, beginning to tremble as though chilled.

As she began to shake, I began to burn.

"Let me—get warm, Harvey." Her quiet voice was odd sounding, and choked in her throat. "Let me—"

Suddenly I found I could move. I flung open the blankets and reaching out, pulled her to me.

"Your husband?" I muttered later as we rolled over like two drowning people coming to the surface for a split instant before sinking again into delirium.

From a thousand miles off I heard soft laughter. "He always sleeps at night—every night." And I felt her urgent and demanding against me.

Sometime during that night, I'm not sure just when, peaceful slumber finally came to us.

When I awoke in the pale red light of earliest sunup, she was gone.

A strange hunch settled on me like a hundred-pound pack saddle. Climbing out, I pulled on my clothes as fast as I could. Just as I was yanking on my second boot the door opened and she came in—completely dressed, though her long, dark hair was still in a snarl about her face.

"Harvey, hurry!" She was wringing her hands and brushing strands of hair away from her great brown eyes, now wide with excitement or fear.

"Hurry?" I stood up and holstered my Colt. "Your husband found out about our—visiting?"

"No," she grabbed my arm and tugged me toward the bedroom window. "Look! See that!"

That turned out to be a pair of horsemen, reined in by the bunkhouse, talking to Ab Winters and a rough looking cowboy in a green mackinaw.

Both Ab and the cowboy carried Winchesters. Every so often all glanced at the ranch house, but I didn't think they could see me at the window. The sun was full in their eyes.

"Who're those folks?"

"That's my husband's foreman and his two riders."

"What're they up to?"

"They know you've been in trouble back in town, and Ab is sending out his hands to round up a law officer."

"How'd they know about—?"

"The shooting?" She pulled me away from the window as the pair of cowhands galloped off to the east, and Ab and the other man came toward the house, passing out of sight as they neared the corrals. "The foreman was in Landusky and rode down ahead of you yesterday."

"I didn't see anyone and I was watching the road."

"Hurry!" She pushed me out of the bedroom, handing me my hat and mackinaw as we went up the hallway and into the kitchen. "The foreman came around by the Three-Bar range and down Red Creek road to our place."

I waited by the door, six-shooter in hand, for Ab and his man. Outside the house, I could hear the drip of melting ice along the roof. A thaw had set in.

"Where are the rest of the men?"

"Ab lied. We've only the foreman and the two ranch hands, but be careful."

Her eyes were still large with excitement, but now they reminded me of last night. I couldn't help admiring the look of her. She was a mighty handsome filly—all of her.

"You'll get in Dutch for tipping me off."

"I don't care." Her large brown eyes fairly burned. "It'll serve Ab right!"

"You don't like your husband much?"

"I hate him!" She passed a narrow hand over her eyes. "Three years ago he returned to Texas and to the town I lived in. He was from the same county, and knew my family for years. He bragged around so much about being a successful rancher up here that my folks made up their minds to snare him." She smiled sullenly. "I know now, all right, who was snared."

I cocked my Colt and listened for Winters' footsteps. "Here's one hombre he's not snaring." Then a thought came keen-edged, like a knife in the ribs. "You knew about me—last night?"

"Yes."

"And you still came to the bedroom?" In spite of the bind I was in, I felt a glow shoot through me, like a double belt of rye whiskey, and then I got another knife in the ribs.

"I'd have come to the Devil himself to spite that old fool!"

The front door of the ranch house creaked open,

but there were two rooms and a hall between us, and I couldn't tell who'd entered. A moment later I knew. They both, it seemed, still thought me in bed.

The kitchen door opened, and Ab walked in, blinking from the strong daylight, Winchester cradled in his arm.

"Morning!" I jammed my Colt into his broad breadbasket so hard he came near to dropping his rifle.

"What?—" His face was dirty white under his beard.

"Tell your gossipy foreman to toss his Winchester, and any other shooting-irons, out here—and follow 'em or you're going to be mighty sorry . . . both of you!"

My Logan blood was up and it was all I could do to keep from pistol-whipping the yellow hound where he stood.

Winters quavered out a command at the hallway, and a rifle and a six-shooter thumped the floor, sliding up to my feet. The foreman, who I recognized as an ex-drunk by the name of Upton, followed his weapons into the kitchen with upraised hands.

Within five minutes both men were sitting on the floor, lashed back-to-back with pieces of a lariat that had been hanging from a peg in the hallway. I gagged them with their dirty pocket handkerchiefs. Placing Mrs. Winters on a kitchen chair, I tied her up snug but didn't gag her.

After I drank some coffee, I took all the shells from the guns and stuffed them into my mackinaw pockets. It began to look like I'd need all the ammunition I could get my hands on.

Mrs. Winters kept her eyes turned on me, not giving Ab a single glance. I was sure she was afraid I'd give her away. And I felt like it—but she had warned me in time.

"Thanks for your hospitality, Ab," I said, with my hand on the door latch. "You sure know how to make a man feel wanted. And thank you Mrs. Winters for the night's—lodging. Sorry I had to take you all unawares. It's not in me, generally, to return good with bad."

She opened her red, ripe mouth. "You go to Hell!"

I closed the door behind me, running for the ranch barn and Dan Patch. The fat was really in the fire now. No matter what I did, things seemed to get worse.

And I wasn't staying around to argue with any posse—even if Ab and his woman, for different reasons, would try to lie my reputation black.

CHAPTER FIVE

Hole in the Wall didn't look like I thought it would.

With a week and a half of cold, hard riding behind me, I reined in Dan, and stared at the bulk of the snow-covered red wall where it loomed up through the sunset a mile away.

From my vantage point I could see more than one gap in the rocky-faced ridge, giving access to riders, or teams of wagons for that matter. The small frozen stream, where I sat Dan, was another avenue of entrance angling off to cut through the hulking sandstone barrier.

A good part of the Hole's defense seemed to be the wild and open land, itself, stretching away into the distance. The nearest settlement, Kaycee, lay over fifty barren miles to the northeast. There wasn't any kind of house or even a line shack in all that expanse of empty space—nothing but wind-whipped plains.

When I'd hit Kaycee, two days back, I'd been about all-in from the long, grinding miles of narrow trails and just-about-roads that often petered out into snowy wastelands. Nobody had seemed interested in me or my arrival, and after a good soaking in a hot tub in the back of the Grand Hotel, a ten-room, clapboard building, I'd slept the clock around in room number nine.

I lounged around for a day, and the following morning picked up Dan from the nearby livery, and pushed on for the Hole. There had been no secret about its location. A casual talk with the barkeep at the Bird-in-Hand Saloon, the night before, was all I needed to get exact directions.

It seemed the little cow-town of Kaycee often played host to "the boys from the Hole." And though no names were mentioned, it appeared "Hole in the Wall Ranch" was mighty nigh as respectable, in Kaycee as any of the other Johnson County spreads—especially since the Johnson County "War" back in '92.

Game had been pretty scarce on the two-hundred-and-ninety-mile down trip, because of the many snows. I'd had a chance, just twice, to get a shot at a stray deer, but it had seemed a waste as long as my grub-sack held out.

Now as I sat resting Dan, a large, prong-horned elk came up over a rise of ground and stood snuffing the cold, sunny air of late after-noon.

I slowly pulled out my saddle-gun and drawing a bead just back of the branching spread of antlers, squeezed off a shot. My aim was good. The animal gave a wild leap, stumbled about ten yards, slowly knelt into a snow bank, and toppled onto its side. There'd be some haunches of meat to fetch in for the Hole in the Wall "ranchers."

Sort of an overdue Christmas present for my brother Johnny.

Hardly had the echoes of my shot rippled away when a bullet kicked up snow and gravel in front of Dan's nose. He suddenly sunfished sideways. Taken unawares, as I was about to jam the Winchester back into its saddle boot, I dropped the carbine and fought to keep from being heaved headfirst from the frightened horse.

Spurring Dan into a gallop, we high-tailed it for the downed elk. The animal had come up from a dry wash, and I headed straight for that wash's safety.

Before we were half-way there, two more shots cracked out, the balls slamming into the frozen ground with little explosions of snow.

I pulled up short about a rod from the elk, and gentling Dan, raised both my hands, waiting for whatever—or whoever was coming. There was no use in being chased away from this place. I'd ridden too far and too long to get here. I sat still and waited.

"Hey! You there!" a voice hailed me, but I could see no one. "You on that hoss—you want to keep teasin' my trigger finger, or do you wanta ride back th' way you come and keep on breathin'?"

From the sound, I figured the marksman was somewhere near the edge of the frozen river, just where it curved past a clump of ice-covered willows and headed directly through one of the openings into the rocky cliffs.

I was about to shout at the willows, naming myself and asking for Johnny, when that hidden rifle cracked again—the ball whirring past my head.

I threw a leg over Dan's back and hit the ground. My Logan dander was up, and I'd had all the pushing I was going to take. The Winchester was out of reach back in the snow so I pulled my Colt and wriggled up behind the elk.

Another slug pounded into the ground near Dan Patch making him shy-off and trot away a piece. The rifle cracked again, the bullet clipping through Dan's mane.

That anyone would deliberately fire at a horse was mighty close to being a sneaking Indian trick. I had a chunk of Indian in me too, but that was too much. I meant to call his hand!

I dived past the elk, and scrambling down the shallow ravine, rolled to the edge of the frozen creek. I couldn't see the rifleman, but I was able to inch along the icy rim, picking my way over snow-slick sandstone boulders until I was about twenty feet from the willows. I'd lost my gauntlets from my belt when I dropped the Winchester and my hands were getting numb from the cold steel of the Colt, but I ground my teeth and crawled forward.

As I squatted on the very edge of the thicket, I

44

heard a stick crack, and a man with a rifle rose up within rock-heaving distance.

Clawing up a small, three-corned chunk of loose sandstone, I waited until the figure in a buffalo coat turned away to level his rifle at Dan, and heaved the dornick directly at him.

It struck his back dead-center with a hollow thump, causing him to stumble and drop the rifle. When he bounded back up, snow-covered and cursing, he turned to find my Colt covering him.

"—Th' hell is this?" His jaw gaped open. He licked his bearded lips and held out one dirty hand in front of him as I moved forward, cocked .44 in my fist. "Watch out! You wanta shoot someone?"

"That's the idea," I answered, tight and angry. "Put that dirty paw back up there with the other, or I'll let you have it right now, you damned dirty dry-gulcher!"

It seemed just about the last straw . . . the fight with Pike, the long and grinding ride after Ab Winters' tricky play—and now, fired on like a skulking coyote—when I thought I'd found a place of safety.

I don't know what I was about to do, but the bearded man in the buffalo coat seemed to think I was going to shoot him where he stood. His knees buckled and he sank down like a pole-axed steer, bellowing in a slobbering fit.

I lifted my foot in a blind rage and gave him

a good boot in the ribs. His howls covered the sound of advancing riders behind us until a loose pebble, sliding down the bank, roused me to my own danger. Giving him another hard kick in the side, I whirled around to face two horsemen, who were pulled up a dozen feet away.

"Harvey? For Christ sake, what're you doin' here?" The voice shouting at me was Johnny's, but I had to blink twice to recognize the man on the flaxen-maned sorrel. He sat his saddle with the old familiar stance, leg cocked up over the pommel, white teeth gleaming in a sandy beard.

"Yeah?" The other rider, a tall, broad-shouldered man, with black eyes that glittered at me from a broad, brick-red face, spoke again. "Yeah? And what're you doin'—usin' Bronco here fer a football?" A long, dark mustache curled slightly under a flattened nose as his knife-slit of a mouth twitched.

The man at my feet was groaning and cursing a steady stream of filth as he staggered up, grabbing at his ribs.

I holstered my pistol and spoke up to the dark-looking man. "I just don't like some son-of-a-bitch trying to shoot me and my horse full of holes." Somehow I felt angry at Johnny also, as if he were to blame for me being where I was. I was glad to see him, but it still peeved me at the way he sat all slouched over on his horse, grinning at my troubles.

"This here's George Curry, Kid." Johnny nodded at the man on the bay. "He's boss of th' Hole." I don't know what made Johnny tag me with a name he'd called me from time to time when we were youngsters—but it proved to be a handle that stuck like a burr.

"Kid," Curry growled through his wide mouth, barely opening it, but making himself understood mighty clear. "I'd take it kindly if'n you'd let this galoot catch up that horse of his over in that thicket, and git back in to th' Hole. I promise he's gonna be more careful in th' future just who he takes snap-shots at." He spurred his mount down the incline between the man in the buffalo coat and myself.

Bronco picked up his Winchester and went stomping off to lead out a hefty sorrel. He mounted and turning the horse's head with a yank, rode up out of the snow-filled river bottom without a backward glance.

"Now let's take a look at your game bag." Curry headed toward the downed elk.

As I followed on foot, Johnny rode beside me, talking about the Hole, and starting to quiz me about my sudden appearance. He bent down and placed a hand on my shoulder. "That Bronco there sure has been ornery ever since I came and even before, from what I hear. He was part of Teton Jackson's horse thieves. Got run out of Colorado a year or so ago. He's always lookin' for trouble. That's why he likes to do sentry duty out here—plain mean."

"Well, I've tangled with a couple of mean ones myself." And I went into the particulars about the scrap with old Pike, mentioning for the first time, Ab Winters' attempt to corral me for the Landusky law.

Johnny shook his head, knowing Pike's cantankerous disposition, and having felt Pike's fist, himself, didn't seem much upset over the shooting. But he turned white with anger over Winters' treachery. "He's just plain got it in for us Logans, like that damned Pike, ain't he? And for no good reason except I outsmarted him on a horse deal, th' Texas lunkhead!"

I went on ahead and gathered the reins dangling down from Dan's neck, gentling him where he stood near my half-buried rifle.

Curry straightened up from the elk and swung back onto his horse. "Well, come on Kid." He spat a brown hole in the snow. "Let's see if we can git you th' right kind of welcome for a change. We'll send out and have your elk toted in."

I picked up my saddle-gun, blew snow out of its barrel, shoved it back into its boot and mounted Dan. I'd kicked around in the snow, but couldn't find my gauntlets. That was one more thing I still owed that Bronco Jack, even though I'd done my level best to try to even the score with my toe.

Riding into the Hole, we veered away from the river as it took a different course through a narrow canyon, and passing around great, scattered boulders, entered a deep gorge of black rock. In spite of the snow blanketing the towering walls with pure white, I could see the formations changing—within a few dozen feet—into a brilliant red. The way narrowed until it seemed we had ridden into a box canyon, but I noticed horse tracks leading off at a sharp angle, almost into the left-hand cliff. Turning the outthrust rock cropping, we were suddenly behind the Red Wall.

The valley stretched away for miles, both north and south. To the west were rolling badlands—a mighty tough place to get into without the right welcome.

Everything was snow-covered, but I could see the thick grass under the snow. Hole in the Wall, from the inside, was a huge, grassy valley. And yet, according to Johnny, it had never harbored more than a few stolen herds.

As we sat looking over the peaceful scene, for some reason, I felt downright sad. It was just something I couldn't put into words. In spite of my rough and ready life, I always had an eye for the beautiful . . . though I'd never spoken of such things to anyone, except some that night to the Winters woman.

"Really hits you, don't it?" George Curry turned sideways on his saddle after pointing out the Hole in the Wall Ranch—a group of cabins about a mile north up the valley. "Enough room here to build up an army, and y'can hold it with a couple men." He gave a sharp bark of a laugh. "Nossir, Kid, you'll learn, just like your brother, that th' only law out here is th' gun. And th' smartest gun, at that. And that should make a gun-hawk like you real valuable to a law-and-order-man like me."

CHAPTER SIX

The first few weeks after coming into the Hole, I spent most of my time loafing around a small cabin, about ten rods from the main Hole in the Wall ranch house.

Johnny shared the cabin with a fellow called Peep O'Day, whose proper name was Tom, and now the three of us bunked there. O'Day, who hailed from Texas, seemed a happy-go-lucky sort who didn't care if school kept or not.

Bronco Jack, who'd chummed up with O'Day, in spite of their different makeups, came around once in a while. But we ignored each other—until the end of the third week when we got into that card game.

Jack was still a tough-looking object. His long, black whiskers, and hair, needed a curry-combing, and he had a wild look in the eyes.

All through the game he kept grumbling and fault-finding over the fall of the cards: "There, lookit that! You, Peep, you play like you was a tin-horn dealer. No need to tell how you left Texas—two jumps ahead of th' last man you cold-decked. There, you, Johnny . . . it's your deal, and mebbe we'll have a square hand for a change. Nope! Lookit this . . . worse'n before. What—Peep? You're out? Best if you never got in! I'm gonna lose my shirt and saddle on this one. Nope—no more cards for me, I'm holdin' onter these beauties all right. And lookit old lucky Johnny there. Standin' pat too, eh? Well, I might as well lose my spurs and saddle bags. Here's where I raise. Ten dollars in gold! This time we'll see who's th' big buck around here. Oh, you call? Well, how's this for a look at luck? Three big Jacks—jest like you three, three slab-sided Jacks . . . and thanks fer th'—! Aw . . . God a'mighty, what's th' use?"

While Johnny was raking in the thirty-dollar pot, Bronco picked up the three Queens and was scowling at them when the cabin door creaked open, tattering the orange-yellow bloom of the kerosene lamp as George Curry and another man entered.

Curry and the stranger stood in the shadows where I couldn't get a good look at them.

Bronco Jack, intent on the cards, paid no attention, until bluffing to three treys, he lost again to Johnny.

"Hey there, Bronco! Lucky as ever?" The little man walked around into the light.

Bronco's face, flushed with bad-temper and too much liquor, went grey-white, while his dark eyes suddenly narrowed at the sight of the stranger. With a curse, he reared up, clawing at his six-shooter and tipping over the rough log bench. "Goddam, my luck's bad enough without the likes of you around!"

Bronco Jack was able to get off just one shot before I thumbed two back at him. My first bullet went wild, ricocheting off the wall, but the second hit Bronco in the hip, bringing him down with a crash.

As he lay writhing on the floor, Johnny ran around the table and kicked the Smith and Wesson pistol out of his fist.

Curry and I bent over the little stranger, where he lay half-insensible from the shock of the bullet. Several of Curry's bunch, including Walt Punteny, came bursting through the door. Punteny, a round-faced young hellion, who'd worked at one time for a horse-doc, knew what was up at the sound of the gunshots. He carried several clean shirts and a tea-kettle of water grabbed up from the main bunkhouse.

The stranger, Curry called Jackson, and Bronco Jack, were both attended to shortly. Of the two, Bronco seemed in the worse condition, the ball from my pistol having hit a bone in his hip. He was lugged off to a cabin on the other side of the main bunkhouse, while the wounded Jackson was bedded down in an empty bunk in our own cabin.

Coming around after several slugs of rye-whiskey, old Jackson lay with a patched-up shoulder chattering like a mountain jay. Waving an undamaged right arm, he regaled Johnny, O'Day and myself with one tall tale after another.

Alongside Blacky Jackson and his partner, Sam Bass from Texas, Jesse James and his bunch were fit only to hold up oyster socials. Old Blacky even claimed to have invented train robbery, and to have put some new twists to stage-coach hold-ups, though he modestly gave his departed partner a piece of the credit.

I stared at the old fellow. He might have been the stout-hearted Frank Jackson, the man who single-handedly stood off an entire pack of Rangers at Round Rock, Texas until his friend Sam Bass could ride out of town. Bass, I'd read, somewhere, didn't get far as he was sore wounded and Jackson had to leave him and ride for his own life. He'd ridden long and far, I could see, since that day in 1878. And now here he was, still on the run—and filled with lead . . . yet not done for, yet.

After two hours of Jackson's windy brags, Johnny was ready to heave a boot at him where he lay propped up in his bunk, grizzled mustache stretching from ear to ear and reeling off one wild, joke-filled tale after another. I thought, as I winked at Johnny to lay off, that this could be myself years later—a worn-out fugitive—if I lived that long. It was a pretty dismal thought.

Finally the liquor did its business, and Jackson shut up for the night.

"Damned blow-hard," Johnny growled, while we got into our bunks and rolled up in our blankets for the night. "All he's done is to get you into some real trouble."

"Bronco Jack?"

"Yeah, Bronco Jack. One of Curry's right-hand men—even if he's a regular skunk."

"We may not be here much longer," I said, thinking of our chances back in Landusky, now that Pike had publicly admitted to being a damned crook.

"Don't bank on it," Johnny mumbled. "I got a feeling that things are going to get worse before they ever get better."

In spite of the ruckus and the thought of Bronco Jack, I drifted off to sleep, accompanied by the blending snores of Old Blacky and Peep O'Day, and drowsily considering the soft curves of that Winters woman.

When? I wondered. Probably never!

CHAPTER SEVEN

For a day or so after the shoot-out, things went along as usual, and none of the bunch seemed to fault me for the gunplay. Bronco and Jackson were still bedded down in different cabins. There'd been a big snow the evening that Jackson arrived, so Johnny and I kept pretty close to the cabin, even though he grumbled at me, from behind his hand, at times, at the almost non-stop flow of yarns and brags from old Frank.

"You'd thought that bullet would have let a little hot air out of him," Johnny growled. "The only way he'll run out of words is when he cashes in his chips."

Four days after the shooting my brother slipped away and went off on a hunting trip down the Hole with George Curry and a young horse thief from Sundance, Wyoming named Longabaugh.

The same afternoon, with Johnny gone, old Frank kept up a string of yarns. But for a man with so much to tell, I noticed one thing, never did he say a word about any family, or where he first sprung up from in Texas, or where he thought he was going to wind up.

I talked about him with Walt Punteny and others of Curry's bunch outside the cabin.

"Yeah, Frank raised a lot of sand in his day,

even after he hightailed it out of Texas after that old Sam Bass Gang got riddled, but he's all through ridin' th' high trails," said Punteny, who seemed to know some things about Blacky Jackson that the old rascal never spilled. "Bronco was with old Frank and another jasper about three years ago. They hit a little mountain town in Colorado, cracked th' bank and lit out for th' tall timber, but it kinda mis-fired. The third man got blasted out of th' saddle, and Bronco took a slug in th' shoulder. Seems like he's always gettin' punctured.

"When they tallied up th' take, it just about was enough to pay for th' doctor bill and horse feed. Old Frank raised hell, sendin' notes into town threatenin' the feller who pulled triggers on 'em. But th' man, who run the local gunshop and hardware, just sent a playin' card out to th' camp where Frank and Bronco was layin' up. It was th' ace of spades with three bullet holes in it—drilled dead center.

"Accordin' to Bronco, Frank Jackson folded up and faded out into th' night while Bronco was asleep' takin' what loot there was and th' best horses. Naturally Bronco was plenty riled."

And that was what sparked the explosion in our cabin when the feisty little bandit chief appeared out of the winter night.

That same afternoon that Punteny filled me in on Frank "Blacky" Jackson, I could see the old outlaw was starting to slide out of this world, despite the constant attention given him by young Walt Punteny. As Jackson's fever mounted, with the passing hours, he commenced to rave and rant in earnest, and I discovered another fact about the man. He could keep his mouth shut when it suited him.

Not only had Blacky Jackson been in Landusky the day after I left, he'd stopped by Winters' place and lifted a pair of his best saddle horses. Thinking back to the afternoon that I had hid out in the stand of timber on my way south, I recognized Jackson as the rider who'd gone down the road with a string of horses after I met up with Arapaho Brown. How he'd got away with it in tracking snow, I couldn't imagine, but there were tricks to every trade.

While ghosting around the Winters' spread, he'd picked up some talk about my brother Johnny and me. It appeared "horse thief" was the easiest handle Ab Winters had been yelling about . . . so it served Winters good and proper that Blacky had relieved him of his horses.

A big change seemed to come over Jackson around dark. The cabin was empty save for Blacky and myself. I sat by his bunk, wiping his face with a bandana. He seemed to come to himself at last, and I thought the fever was breaking, and he was going to pull through.

"Oh, ho," he mumbled, "still at th' same

address." He lifted his undamaged arm and laid a hand on my shoulder. "Young feller," he muttered, and it seemed his breath was going again, but he kept at it. "Y'been right good to me—since I blew back in here, and got you into a ruckus with that damned Bronco. Cain't say I blame him much . . . but he'll always be a cheap penny-ante crook." He stared vaguely around the cabin, and a thought seemed to come to him. "Now, when you was out a few times, I heered from one of th' boys that both you and that brother of yours . . . he don't cotton much to me . . . that th' both of you ain't real owl-hoots. Y'best head on south, because you cain't go back to your own range."

Answering the look on my face, he muttered— "Y'done fer him."

"Done for who?"

He painfully raised up on an elbow and fished into his vest pocket, taking out a silver badge. "Got this," he gasped, "th' day I was in th' great metropoleus of Landusky. When th' deppity wasn't lookin' I hooked it off'n th' late Pike Landusky. They had'm laid out in th' bar in a pine box, ready for plantin' when th' ground thawed out a mite. Yep." He sank back down into his rumpled bunk.

For a while he lay there motionless and then began to pitch around, mumbling with the increase of fever. At last he roused up again and feebly motioned me closer. "Family went to hell a long time ago, leastwise so I heered. Never went back to Texas to find out. Really got a lot to be proud about—I don't think . . . except for Starr."

I looked at the object in my hand. The star of Pike Landusky. There was a bullet hole spang in the middle of the bent silver badge. I had put Pike out of action and for good. And myself, what had I done to myself?

"Starr, she's my little gal," old Frank whispered hoarsely. "I up and left her years ago when things sorta went to hell fer me. Left her with some folks a'runnin' a tin-horn newspaper up in Montanny."

He sank back down, and I tried to get him quiet, but he gave a shudder and clawed his way back up to a sitting position and started in again. "Give my horse to Bronco. Least I can do. Run out on'm and he's got a proper grudge. Ain't got nothin' to leave you though, 'cept that star there and some advice." He tried to laugh, but choked. "Oh, I know you young bucks ain't much fer any damned advice—I was th' same way back with my pore pard Sam Bass. But lissen . . . there's a map in my saddle bag over there that'll put you into a hide-out that'd make this place or Robbers' Roost look like a pair of plugged nickels. Ain't more'n half-a-dozen long-riders in th' hull West knows of it. Could come in handy to you some time. Now—that ain't my advice, though. It's this. Git out of this life before it's too late . . . like me . . . look—" But Frank Jackson had finally run out of words. He was dead.

I went out to the other cabins, looking for Walt Punteny and found him with O'Day who grinned at me, and Bronco Jack who stared at his cards. Walt tossed in his hand and followed me out into the gently falling snow.

"We lost our patient."

Punteny pushed up his Stetson and batted off a few snowflakes, squinting at me in the ruddy glow of the wintery sunset. "Thought you knew."

"What?"

"That bullet was a .44 calibre, from your Colt—not a 38.40 Smith and Wesson. Must've ricocheted off'n th' wall."

CHAPTER EIGHT

We had barely got old Frank Jackson buried, chipping away at a hole with a mattock until it was deep enough to lay him down, wrapped in his blanket, when the heaviest snow of the season blew in over the Red Wall . . . blew in and blotted out the boulders over his grave.

It was a good thing my brother Johnny, George Curry and Harry Longabaugh came back that morning, before the storm hit, with enough venison to last for a good long spell.

For over three weeks we were completely snowed-in. Johnny bunked with me, as usual, and Longabaugh, the kid from Sundance, Wyoming, moved in because he said he couldn't stand all that caterwauling down at Bronco's cabin where he was nursing his game leg.

For myself, when we weren't playing those everlasting games of cards, I sat and stared at the bullet-dented star of Pike Landusky, turning it over and over in my hand.

Johnny was also down-in-the-mouth, and I knew what was eating him, but never said a word until he brought it up himself.

"You hadn't oughta pay that jasper any heed," Sundance snorted after listening to Johnny cursing Winters to a fare-thee-well. "Hell, I got run plumb out of Wyoming Territory. And all I done was borry a couple saddle broncs to take my best gal to a dance. They up and called me a blamed horse thief. Tossed me into th' Sundance calaboose, and left me there 'til mornin'. But that cheese box wouldn't hold a blind hobo. And now they got a warrant out for a horse thief—me! I don't pay it no mind though. Felt like driftin' down this way. Like they say, it kinda moved me."

Johnny grinned, though I knew he was still bitter.

"What do you care, Johnny?" I said. "What do you care what some no account up there says about you—or me, for that matter?"

"I ain't about to let some chunk-head like that gander-eyed Winters go makin' bad medicine about us. That's all there is to it!" Johnny got one of his bull-headed Logan looks and spat into the fire. "I was hopin' to go back after this Pike Landusky thing blew over, and I still aim to do it— . . ."

"I got us all up the brush, fighting that damned Pike. You go back there now, and they'll be laying for you. And even if you do button Winters up somehow, it won't do any good. We just can't go back to the Four—Tee for a spell." I looked at the star in my fist. "Let's just be thankful that Jim and Lonny are still on the spread and keeping the place running."

Though Johnny was older than I, he usually followed my lead, and so he grudgingly nodded and began to talk to Sundance about some wild high-binder Longabaugh knew as Cassidy. This was the first I'd heard of Butch Cassidy, but it wasn't the last by a long shot. I listened while Sundance yarned about that young Mormon Cassidy and his shenanigans with a pair of rough-riders called Matt Warner and Elsworth Lay. They just weren't plain horse thieves and rustlers. Three banks in less than six months! That was their score. This included the bank at Castle Gate, Utah, where they took over eight thousand dollars. According to Longabaugh, the Castle Gate posse was so jim-jammed that they nearly shot into each other before they got on the gang's trail out of town toward Robbers' Roost. But Butch and his pals left them away in the dust.

"Sounds like a real wild bunch," I said.

"Wanta know somethin'?" Sundance asked. "Soon as it gets on toward warm weather, that's just what George Curry'd like to pull."

"Hell, we ain't no crooks!" Johnny said.

"No, you ain't—except the Kid here has got himself on a murder warrant. And I guess, from what I hear there's a warrant still out for you for skippin' out of th' Landusky hoosegow." Sundance shrugged. "Wouldn't say either of you is on th' rosy right side of th' Law."

"Things will work out," I said.

"You better hope so," Sundance went out the door toward the cook shack.

"He's right, darn him," Johnny said somberly after we were alone. "Maybe after the weather clears and I went up to th' ranch—maybe we could get to the right people. Old Charley Peck's there in town. Charley has got a lot of pull . . . owns plenty of land. Maybe, as the banker, Charley could say th' right things to th' right people. We always played square with him, like with everybody else. We can't hole up in this owl-hoot nest forever!"

"Yeah, but Landusky?" I took the star out of my pocket and tossed it into the air and caught it. "What about Pike Landusky?"

"It was a fair fight. You told me so, and I believe you. All them other folks'd say it too," said Johnny. "Maybe when this weather lets off I can ride up there and get old Charley or somebody to bat for us. And if th' worst comes to worst, why then we could sell off our spread. Charley always wanted it, and he'd be fair about buyin' th' shebang. Then we could move on someplace else. We still got our health, which is more'n old Pike's got—and that's somethin' to be grateful for, at least."

I noticed that Johnny hadn't got around to cussing out Winters again, and I was glad. Lord knows we had enough trouble to handle.

• • •

One day in the Hole was just about any other day. And one week was pretty much like another. In spite of the knee-deep snow in the valley, the really wicked storms stayed on the other side of the Red Wall, raising Cain with ten-foot-high drifts and higher. It could have been a completely lazy, carefree life—if those Landusky troubles could have been wiped from our minds as easy as the gentle winds of the Hole rubbed out our own foot-tracks.

George Curry was out of the Hole for days on end, off on business at his own ranch near Kay Cee, leaving The Sundance Kid, Tom O'Day, Walt Punteny, Bronco, Johnny and myself to hold down the camp.

As with any spread in the field, my week as cook or "old lady" came along and I got by except for the fact that we had ran out of baking powder and Old Crow. There was some grumbling about my sour-dough biscuits, usually from Bronco Jack, who hobbled down to the rude, log mess-cabin on his make-shift crutch. But then I'd never claimed to be any great shakes with a skillet. Lonny was the one for that, from hanging around our Aunt Lee's kitchen back in Missouri as a young'un.

By the fourth day of my stint, George Curry was back with a full gunny sack that included whiskey and baking powder. The weather had now begun to clear up and a February thaw or Chinook had set in the morning after Curry returned.

While I was up to my elbows in baking powder dough and gabbing with Walt Punteny about steel-dust horses in the kitchen lean-to, Johnny saddled up and rode out of camp without a word to anybody.

At first I thought he'd gone down the valley on a hunting scout as he'd taken a Winchester '66 and a box of shells from the cabin. But that night as I was sitting on my bunk, pulling off my boots, I spotted a note tacked to the upright post.

It was short: *"Looks like the Chinook is going to hold. Should make good time. Will give your best to Charley Peck, Lonny, Jim, and even Ab Winters, if I should run into him."*

There was nothing for it. Sundance was down at the main cabin, playing cards with Curry and the bunch, so I stoked up the mud-and-rock fireplace, blew out the candle in the Old Crow bottle and piled into my bunk.

I dozed off to the drip, drip of ice melting from the roof of our lonesome little cabin.

Next night Sundance propped himself in our best chair, a rickety three-legged affair, shucked his boots and warmed himself at the fire. "Looks like this weather'll keep on for a spell. Shouldn't worry about brother John. He's bound to come sloggin' in here shortly with a couple of deers."

I knew that Sundance, like the rest, had a good idea as to where Johnny had gone. "You know," I told him. "Johnny didn't go out to track down deer."

"Well," Sundance wriggled his toes, looking over one that stuck out of a hole in his sock, "I put him down for a gent that can keep his eyes open, and not go lettin' himself be pushed into some fool play." He grinned up at me from under a thatch of coarse, black hair.

"Meaning that I'm the kind that would?"

"Don't go gettin' riled up. I was just thinkin' that nobody'd be able to pull anything on your brother. Too level headed." He grinned and spat in the fire. "Now you—if you'll pardon me . . ."

"Yeah, me?"

"I'd say that you're both from th' same flock, no doubt. Nobody'd best try to cross you, either—but . . ." He wriggled his toes at the fire. "You're th' kind that wouldn't only not back down from trouble, but might go tryin' to stir it up, somewhat. Only a guess, mind you."

I fingered the star in my pocket, but didn't answer.

Time kept drifting along, with life in the Hole the same easy-going monotony it had been—with the exception of my run-in with Bronco Jack and old Frank Jackson's death. But Bronco stayed away from me, and I never looked his way twice.

Long-riders came in to the Hole in the Wall Ranch, hung around for a few days, and when the weather changed for the better, rode on out—no telling where and for what purpose.

It had been that way as far back as when Sang Thompson's cattle-rustlers camped there, later to be followed by Nate Champion's Red Sash Gang. Others had used the Hole from time to time as a temporary hide-out. Some of the names mentioned by Curry included Dutch Henry, Teton Jackson, Persimmon Bill and Big Nose George Parrot. Punteny told me that both Frank and Jesse James had been in the Hole as early as 1877, but it may have just been some tall tale.

All I knew was that Harvey Logan, *myself,* was sweating it out at Hole in the Wall, and wishing I could get back to my ranch and pick up the pieces. Maybe when Johnny got back from Landusky—.

The weather seemed to be thinning out, with each day more pleasant than the last. Brooks cutting through the Hole ran nearly free of ice, and the blue and white of the drifting skies overhead rippled on the glinting surface of the Powder. The early canyon wrens hunted nesting sites along the red cliffs, while the snow's surface was pitted with the bright green spikes of the balsam roots. And the white-tail ptarmigan, feeding along the willow thickets slowly turned from snow-white to rock-brown.

Restlessness was in the air we breathed. It was in the sky that whispered with the circling wings of returning jays, swallows, kingfishers and blackbirds. And I was getting restless, waiting for Johnny's own return, waiting to see what might happen to our ranch—and ourselves.

CHAPTER NINE

For a spell I lay in my bunk staring at a pale lemon square of light pasted on the wall, then knew it for the gleam of earliest dawn streaming in through the cabin's one window.

Something had roused me, and I listened . . . wondering what day it was. That sound came again, threading through the shouting of voices—the clopping approach of a horse.

Before I could rouse completely, the cabin door burst open and Walt Punteny stuck his head in. "Hey, Logan! Y'got someone here to see you!"

Sundance in the opposite bunk, groaned and burrowed down into his nest of blankets.

"Johnny!" I was on the floor in a moment and to the door in my long-johns. In the rose-hued light I saw a figure dismounting by the mess cabin. Before I could make out the stranger, I spotted the familiar, barrel-shaped outline of the pack-mare, Pot Belly.

Dashing back to the bunk, I collided with Sundance, who was wrapped in a pair of blankets and hopping around on the cold floor looking for his boots.

I tugged on my clothing and was out the door before Sundance had his first boot on. "Johnny!" I shouted. But it *wasn't* Johnny!

"Hello, Harve." Lonny stood looking at me, leaning against his black horse. I must have stared stupidly around, only half-awake, while I asked, "Where's Johnny? He's coming in later?"

"Johnny's not coming in later, Harve." Lonny began to loosen the saddle girth on his black horse, Velvet. "Johnny's dead! Killed a week ago by that damned Ab Winters. Shot in the back on the main street of Landusky!"

Later as Lonny and I sat in my cabin, with a mightly subdued Sundance, I heard how Johnny'd got it.

"Johnny come by th' ranch and spent a couple days, talkin' over plans with us. He was all for goin' into town to try and sell our spread to Charley Peck, but we kept tellin' him that he had a warrant hangin' over his head for that break out at old Pike's jail. But you know Johnny—as bull-headed as—."

"You or me!"

"Anyways, he rode out one mornin' early and was in town when he and that damned Winters bumped into each other on th' street. Ab just up and shot him outa th' saddle as he rode by. Johnny wasn't goin' to do a thing—I guess, but it didn't make no difference. Talk is that Charley Peck set him up to it, as a way of tryin' to get our ranch."

"And Winters?"

"Oh, he weaseled out of it. Claimed Johnny

was a fugitive and all that sort of thing, and he was doin' his duty as a civic-minded citizen."

"They swallowed that?" I was seeing blood red now, but kept my voice as calm and easy as I could.

"Yeah. And smooth as goose-grease, he let his woman bring flowers to th' funeral, when we buried Johnny out at th' cemetery north of town."

"She came to the ceremony?" All at once I felt my neck burning, with a different sort of fever. That damned she-cat! Why did she have to come into the conversation, at all. Now I could see her silhouetted in the moonlight of that bedroom back at Winters' place . . . feel her softness, smell her perfume. Damn her!

"Yeah, she seemed all right. Folks say Ab sure treats her mean."

"Ab treats everybody damned mean." And I told Lonny about that night—and morning at Winters' ranch—or most of it.

"Yeah. Johnny said Winters had sure tried to roust you good." He gave a short laugh. "Guess that's why I'm here. I took a couple of shots, long-range at Ab. Missed him, but sure gave him somethin' to think about. Then I got to havin' th' fidgits about it. Knew Winters would come gunnin' for me—when he had it figured out . . . so I up and pulled freight for you and th' Hole."

"What about Jim Thornhill?" I asked, to get Winters and his woman out of my mind.

73

"Oh Jim's cut from a different piece of cloth. Jim ain't gonna run from anyone. Besides he's a great man for straddlin' a fence. Not that he ain't got sand enough for a dozen ranch hands. Jim'll sit it out, hold down the ranch, until we get things squared up proper with th' law."

Sundance, who hadn't said a word, cleared his throat, gave me an odd look, and rising, went out to breakfast.

I just sat and looked at Lonny, with a lump in my craw at what I'd done to get him into this bog-mire of trouble. And I thought about Johnny back in his grave in Landusky. Buried in the same cemetery as old Pike—and neither of them caring one damn about it all. That was left to us—the living. And I also thought about that grave, not a hundred yards away, where Frank Jackson lay and no one caring about him, except that girl of his up in Montana. And she didn't even know he'd died in an outlaw camp—a victim as much to my hair-trigger temper as Pike Landusky. It would be better if she never knew.

Lonny fitted into the easy-going life of the Hole. He played cards, sawed away on a fiddle an owl-hoot had left with Curry, and went out on hunting scouts when his turn came.

And Spring slipped into the Hole, lazed around—until, at last, early Summer eased in over the Red Wall. Then the valley fair burned with the golden blaze of rabbit brush and fire wheel. Along the small creeks, and the Powder, itself, the mountain laurel dressed itself with hundreds of pink flowers, while the mountain ash greenery was spangled with snow-white blossoms. And always the humming, busy breeze rippled the countless acres of prime grass.

The restlessness, I'd felt with the coming of earliest Spring, grew ever stronger, until I, for one, had to be somewhere. Anywhere.

As it was, Bronco Jack was the cause of my move. The thing happened so fast that I was still trying to put the pieces together as I saddled up Dan Patch.

O'Day and Bronco had been sitting out on a split log in front of the mess cabin with a bottle when Lonny and I sauntered past on the way to look at our horses in the corral east of Bronco's log shack.

Lonny, who'd heard the details of the shooting of Frank Jackson, glared at Bronco, but gave him a wide berth as we went around a corner of the cabin toward the corral. But Jack, who hadn't more than nodded at me in the past weeks, called out some nonsense, spiked with a filthy curse.

I ignored him, but Lonny spun and rushed back around the cabin with a drawn six-gun. Before I could make a move, one shot cracked out, followed by another.

By the time I got there, Lonny was on the

dead run, headed for our own cabin. "Put it up, Bronco!" I covered him, until his six-shooter wavered and dropped.

"Hell, you Logans're all th' same—can't take any funnin' at all." He waved an arm at O'Day, who still sat on the log bench with a frozen grin on his face. "Peep here'll tell ya I didn't fire until your crazy brother pulled down on me—and fer what? All I said was somethin' about Johnny's luck. Y'know he cleaned me out th' night that damned old Frank—" He stopped and licked his lips, staring at me. "That damned old fool sure got me into a world of trouble."

"No more than you deserve." I watched him closely, but he shoved his six-shooter back into its holster, and sank down on the bench, easing his stiff leg with a grunt.

"Jack, here, is up to his old tricks," I told George Curry, who'd come on the run along with Sundance and the rest.

"That young brother of yours is at th' cabin a'loadin' his Winchester and yellin' for Bronco's blood," Sundance announced.

"There ain't gonna be any more shootin'," Curry bellowed, yanking off his Stetson and heaving it away. " 'Cause if there is—I up and wash my hands of the hull damned lot of you. You can all git and find another hide-out to squat in!"

"There be no more shooting," I said. "Because

if there is, I'm going to kill that sage rat—where ever I find him." I spoke, quiet-like, but for a long minute there wasn't any noise, except breathing.

"Hell, Kid," George put an arm around my shoulder, "ain't no need to rile-up over this. I know damned well Bronco's not about to pull anythin'—that is, if your fire-cracker of a brother'll simmer down." Behind him, both Bronco and O'Day looked at each other.

"I know Bronco won't," I spoke quiet again.

By the time I'd got back up to our cabin, Lonny was leaning in the doorway, with an egg-sucking grin on his face. It didn't take long to lay down the law, then I was back at the corral, with my bed-roll and a gunny sack full of grub, saddling up Dan Patch.

"If I don't get out of here for a spell, I just might kill that damned Bronco," I told George, as I rode out. "So, if you want me, I'll be camped down near the Powder."

And there I camped for a week on a bend of the Powder, where the river flared, throwing out a wide bed of gravel and willows, before curving on through the Red Wall.

On Wednesday morning, June 23, I'd just got around and had coffee boiling when I saw a horseman loping toward my make-shift camp from the direction of Hole in the Wall Ranch.

One long look at the loose-jointed rider on the black mare, and I knew him for Lonny.

"Well, did Bronco put you on the run?"

"Harve!" Lonny swung down, with the same look on his face he'd had as a young'un when he'd had to fess up some dido. "Thought I'd let you know that George and a couple of th' bunch are ridin' over th' line to Dakota. Me, I'm ridin' along with 'em!"

It didn't take long to find out that George Curry, deep in debt to the banks, planned making a six-shooter raise on the Belle Fourche Bank to shift some funds his way. O'Day, Longabaugh, Punteny and Lonny were riding with him.

"Not on your life. You're locoed!"

"But we all gave George our word. He needs us bad."

When we rode up to the Hole cabins, the bunch was saddled and on horseback. Bronco was limping around turning the air to brimstone blue—as usual.

"Won't do you no good, Bronco," Curry growled, his hand resting on his hip, near his pistol. "We need whole men for this job, and that sure don't fit either your leg or your head."

Bronco whirled around on his whittled-out cottonwood crutch, glaring at Lonny. "Yeah? I'm as sure as good as that there skinny saddle-tramp!"

I could see Lonny getting the fidgets, his face

draining of color. I swung Dan Patch in front of him.

"Lonny's not going anywhere." I stared hard at George Curry.

"Hell! We need every man we can git," Curry complained. "And you ain't helpin' matters any."

"Maybe, but you didn't ask me anything about this damned fool deal!"

"Thought you wouldn't want to take a hand, Kid. You're still in dutch with th' law up at Landusky, ain't you?"

"Maybe, but Lonny's not wanted for a damned thing yet—and I aim to keep it that way. I'll go, and he can stay here."

"Harve," Lonny turned in his saddle, "there's still a chance you can square matters—especially after th' way Winters back-shot Johnny. Th' townfolk, and th' rest, they're fed up with th' way Pike handled things—"

"Shut up and get off that horse."

"George's been good to all of us."

"George'll get his debt paid!" I grabbed Lonny's reins, holding tight, until he dismounted with a thin-mouthed look.

So, without any more talk, George Curry led out, with Sundance, Tom O'Day, Walt Punteny and myself following. We'd left Lonny, standing by his Velvet mare, along with a scowling Bronco, and a trio of recently arrived long-riders—a half-Mex kid named Billy Rogers and two saddle-tramps who claimed to be wanted for horse theft in Idaho.

I had some qualms about leaving Lonny with Bronco, but I figured they would just have to watch each other.

We rode east up the trail, heading for the main chink in the Red Wall. George Curry forked a big, wild-eyed black stallion with a blaze-face, while Tom O'Day and Sundance were mounted on chestnut mares. I rode Dan, and led Pot Belly the little pack horse.

"Watch me fetch that jay!" O'Day called, hauling out his six-gun and banging away at a black-billed magpie, perched in a squaw bush.

The bird flew off minus a couple of tail feathers, but the damage was done. Curry's black stallion reared up, spooking our pack horse. She tore out of my grasp and went charging through O'Day, Punteny and Sundance, scattering them. Curry's black got out of control, pitching, pin-wheeling, and finally dumping him headfirst into some scrub trees.

Punteny chased and headed off the stampeding Pot Belly, while I dropped a loop over the black, bring him to a fighting standstill.

"That's it for George," Sundance called out as he rode back to a battered George Curry.

He was right. Flat Nose George Curry was in no shape for his big raid.

An hour later, with Lonny getting his wish, as

80

George's replacement, and in spite of plenty of argument from me, we started out again.

This time I was riding the point. Curry had saddled the scout onto me, along with his map and ideas on the strike. "Kid you're th' only one that'll pull it off. Th' others are O.K., but you've got th' real sand. Y'gotta lead 'em. I'm plumb down-and-out at that damned ranch of mine, and I need some ready cash bad to keep'r afloat. But with his swole up knee of mine, I couldn't ride ten mile."

Passing the heap of boulders marking old Frank Jackson's grave, I felt a chill creeping along my backbone in spite of the bright June sun. That was the way most outlaws wound up. But I guess we did owe it to George Curry, as Lonny had said.

Much as I didn't want to pull a gun on anybody and take their money like a regular outlaw—this was one time that I had to go ahead and bite the bullet . . . get it over with. And if we pulled it right, then Lonny and I could drift away, maybe for the southwest. We could hit for New Mexico or Arizona where nobody knew us or our names. Later on we'd get in touch with Jim Thornhill and see what the word was.

Once outside the Hole, we settled the horses down to a steady trot. It was 200 crow-flight miles to Belle Fourche. The bank, picked out by George Curry, was in the heart of the Belle

Fourche River cattle country and close to Deadwood. It was reported to be full of blood-money, drained away in overdue mortgages and promissory notes from ranchers who were unable to come up to scratch because of bad times and poor beef prices.

"You ride on point a hundred yards or so," I told O'Day. "Stay out there and keep your eyes open."

"Yeah, and if you start another stampede, back y'go to th' Hole with th' rest of th' cripples," yelped Sundance.

"O.K. Kid Logan," O'Day kicked up his chestnut. "I mean—*Kid . . . Curry!* If you're reppin' fer Curry, y'might as well lift his handle."

I waved him out front. "That damned rattle-brain's half-right, for once," I told Lonny—speaking to him for the first time since leaving the Hole. "If I have to get roped in on George's loco stunt, I might as well use his name. I'm not going to bring any more law down on us Logans!"

"O.K. *Kid Curry!*" Lonny and Sundance spurred ahead with Walt Punteny, leaving me in the rear with the pack horse, eating their dust.

CHAPTER TEN

We rolled out of our blankets early on Monday, June 26, 1897. Five days on the trail had put us in the hills, just north of the Belle Fourche River Valley. The town of Belle Fourche lay beyond those hills, two miles away.

"What's Belle Fourche named after?" asked Sundance, hunkered down by the fire, taking his turn as cook.

"That's old French mountain man talk for good pickin's," O'Day sounded off from his bedroll.

"Means Pleasant Valley," I said. "And it also means you rouse out, hit the pike for town, and check out the bank and get back here fast, seeing you're our scout."

O'Day had bent our ears all the way from the Hole about his savvy of the lay-of-the-land around Belle Fourche, having once been through the place on a cattle drive. Now he took his time getting around, but was finally mounted and cantering south down the narrow dirt trail toward the valley by seven a.m.

Come nine o'clock we were still saddled up and waiting.

"That gol-darned chunk-head has gone and got himself picked up or somethin'," Sundance gritted, kicking out the embers of our fire and getting back aboard his buckskin.

"There ain't been any shots," Lonny answered.

"Somebody might have recognized him though," Walt Punteny said. "You know he was around these parts—could have stoled 'em blind, knowin' him!"

"Come on!" I spurred Dan out of the oak grove. "We won't know until we get there—then we'll worry about it." But I was worried right then and there. O'Day was a chunk-head, as Sundance said. And George Curry had picked him to scout out the town and bank. The whole thing was crazy. Here I was leading a bunch of hard-cases, myself included, on a downright lawless errand. But Lonny had been bound-and-determined to try and help George out of his bind with the money-men, and get his two-by-four ranch in the clear. And I'd gone along, because I couldn't let my brother down.

We strung out, riding along stands of spruce and aspen, until we came to the old Deadwood Trail. This was a good wagon road and led down into the Belle Fourche River bottoms. Here we picketed Pot Belly, my little pack horse, in a small stand of trees with the intention of picking her up on the way back out.

Riding on, we passed several small ranches and outbuildings near the river, but saw nobody.

"So, there ain't no welcome committees

around," Lonny grinned, kicking his chestnut mare into a lope, pulling ahead of us and onto the long, iron bridge spanning the river. "Come on, *Kid Curry!*"

We clattered across the planks and rode past the first houses of the town. Folks were about, poking at scrubby gardens, or walking along the wooden sidewalks, but they didn't seem to find anything out of the way about a party of dusty horsemen.

It was just nine-thirty when we hitched up behind the Belle Fourche Saloon and swung down in the alley, two doors away from the Clay Robinson and Company Bank.

Leaving Punteny in the alley with the horses, Lonny, Sundance and I walked into the bank by a side door. We had scarcely got inside when Tom O'Day, half-full of "Brave Maker," staggered in the front door, waving his six-shooter.

Sundance, Lonny and I, along with four customers, just stood flatfooted and stared at O'Day as he came whooping up to the bank's counter.

I jumped forward and knocked O'Day's Colt down, but it was too late!

A crabby-faced old clerk, behind the wicket window, ducked and came up with a rusty Smith and Wesson Russian, snapping a shot at Tom. The explosion whacked like a thunderclap, the bullet singing out through the open doorway.

"Hold-up there!" Sundance yelled, yanking out his Peacemaker and firing at the old gent at the same time as O'Day and Lonny. It began to sound like a pitched battle.

The other two behind the bank's counter dove for safety as the old battler folder up beside them, minus part of an ear.

"Nobody'll get hurt—if you stay put," I shouted, my head ringing with the racketing echoes. "Keep 'em up and stand still!" I pulled my own six-shooter and covered the townfolk, where they stood with hands high.

Lonny kicked the side door back open and waved Walt Punteny on with the horses, while Sundance hopped the counter and scooped up all the greenbacks in sight, stuffing them into his shirt. We hadn't ever fetched along a proper sack for the loot—not that we needed one.

"Shell out—you rabbits!" O'Day was waving his pistol under the noses of the four customers.

"Let 'em alone, and get out of here while we can get!" Gunshots began to crack out near the bank as I gave him a good boot in the rear end that started him for the front door.

"My horse! My damned horse has got loose!" And O'Day's horse was in the middle of the street, shying and dragging its reins every time a bullet kicked up dust or thudded into the front of the bank.

At least two townspeople were firing at the

bank from a hardware store across the street, and from the sound it was with high-powered rifles.

"Mount up! Mount up!" I led the retreat out the side door of the bank. I wasn't about to risk our hides for any handful of paper money.

We climbed into the saddles in the alley, while the slugs from those rifles across the street kept slamming into the bank's front.

"Come on, we've got to get out of here fast!" As the alley, behind the bank, was narrow and jammed up with boxes and wagons, I took a chance and rode around into the street. O'Day was still trying to get aboard his horse, and not making a go of it. We rode up to him, and Sundance made a grab for the mount's bridle. Catching it, he trailed us up the street, away from the hardware, where a hot-lead blockade was forcing us to head for a different escape route.

"Grab on!" I shouted at O'Day, riding back to where he was holed-up behind a wooden horse trough. Just then a slug knocked his hat off and gave him a bath of water. Another whistled over my head.

"That ought'a sober you up some." I made another grab at O'Day, but he broke loose and made a run for a mule that was tied in front of a barber shop. Splinters from the barber pole stung Dan Patch and he bucked off up the street after Lonny and the rest.

Sundance jumped from his buckskin and hitched O'Day's horse by a drygoods store, nearly getting himself a bullet from a pudgy, white-faced clerk, who'd run out with a dinky Derringer and shot off both barrels at him point-blank.

The rest of our bunch was up the inclined street at the south end of town, firing back down over our heads at the sharpshooters in the hardware. More people were coming out on the street with pistols and rifles. We either had to fight the whole gang or light a shuck.

"Let th' damned fool go!" Sundance was beside me and riding toward Lonny and Punteny, who were whooping and shooting at everything that moved.

We hit the pike south out of town, away from the bridge, as fast as we could belt along, firing a shot over our shoulders from time to time to slow down any one who tried to trail us.

"What do you think of your welcome committee?" Walt Punteny shouted at Lonny, as we halted at the top of a rise over-looking the town and river bottoms, to let our horses blow.

"Wouldn't have been any if that fool O'Day hadn't got so liquored up that he botched th' works," Lonny muttered.

"Don't worry about him. They've probably stretched his neck by now," I said. "We've got to cipher ourselves a way out of this country."

"We certain can't go back th' way we come," Lonny said, gawking toward town. There was no one in sight—yet!

"For all that powder smoke, nobody could hit the broadside of a bull calf," Sundance grinned, reloading his Winchester '73 carbine from his saddle bags. "And that includes them Buffalo Bills down there."

"Don't sell 'em short," I said. "We're not out of it yet, by a damned sight." I took out the field glasses George Curry had given me. It was still a good two hours until noontime. "Ride on up that way," I motioned Lonny ahead toward the long, swelling reaches to the southeast. "See what's there and where we can make a stand—if we have to."

I could see the northwest end of Belle Fourche through the glasses, with its small green and white houses and grey barns, also the river as far as the iron bridge. Nothing was moving, but I knew the law would be stirring up a posse way before noon.

"Well, what're we gonna do, Kid?" Sundance and Walt had dismounted and were rubbing down their horses. Punteny, the ex-veterinary helper, looked over a cut in Dan Patch's foreleg.

I swept the countryside again with the glasses. A flock of king-fishers were circling over the rippling sparkle of the Belle Fourche River, grey and white flecks in the sunshine. And to the north, a small eagle or some sort of hawk was hovering a stand of cedars.

Belle Fourche, with its painted stores and trim looking homes, was a mighty thrifty and peaceful-looking place, but mighty unfriendly to owl-hoots.

Lonny and his chestnut mare were small, black figures on the rim of table-land stretching forty miles to Deadwood. Bringing the glasses to bear on him, I saw he was waving us to follow.

"Let's go," I said.

"You ain't goin' very far on that there horse till he gets this taken care of." Walt pointed to the splinter gash in Dan's foreleg.

"Ride or walk," clipped Sundance, "you'd better do one or th' other."

I looked back down the road toward town, and there came a knot of horsemen—at least a dozen—all riding hell-for-leather up the hill.

We mounted up, except for Sundance. He yanked his Winchester from its boot and began to pump shots at the posse. "I'll slow them river rats down to a crawl. Get a'goin', and I'll catch up with you!"

I looked back as we rode for the top of the rise. Sundance was still cracking down on the posse, which had halted in the middle of the road and begun to fire back. Several near shots whistled overhead, and one screamed off from a ricochet on a roadside boulder. He wouldn't be able to hold them off for very long. We had to fort-up somewhere. They were close, and Dan Patch's leg was too lame.

It was a good half mile to where Lonny sat waiting, Winchester held on a stranger. "This puncher says he was on his way to the Three Vee Ranch up th' line when he heard th' ruckus. Came down, and now we got ourselves a hostage."

My brother was all white in the face, and when the cowboy's horse made a sudden move, being loose-reined, I thought Lonny was going to pull the trigger of his saddle-gun.

"Ease off, Lonny! Let's get on the way. Here comes Sundance."

Sundance loped up, with a hole in his hat, but grinning, as usual, like a wildcat. "Slowed 'em down some, but they'll be comin' again. Are you hittin' fer th' high timber now?"

"You may make it far as that Three Vee place, but your horse ain't goin' much farther unless I get a chance at that foreleg," said Punteny.

According to the cowboy, a skinny fellow with a droopy mustache, the Three Vee Ranch was six miles on east. And, if we could believe him, the only folks on it was Mr. Clay, the banker's brother and his family.

"I got th' polecat ready to ride," Lonny indicated the cowpuncher, all neatly lashed to his saddle horn with his stake rope. My brother seized the man's reins and hit the pike with the rest of us following.

We never did sight the posse until we pulled up in front of the Three Vee Ranch House, where it stood on a swelling piece of land, surrounded by a small track of timber. Like Coburn's place back on the Crimson, it had been built with an eye for defense against Indians.

"Get back in there if you don't want a hell of a lot of trouble," Lonny yelled at Clay and his wife as they both came out into the door-yard to see what the commotion was about. "And you come on with us, duckbill!" Lonny whacked the defenseless puncher with the barrel of his Winchester.

Sundance got behind one of the big pines with his rifle and began to squeeze off shots at the posse, now halted about a quarter of a mile off. Punteny and I put up the horses in a log barn built close to the ranch house, Walt going to work right away on Dan Patch's foreleg with a knife and some turpentine he'd uncovered in the barn. It had been a mighty near thing, for Dan had been favoring his leg badly by the time we arrived. The posse would have overhauled me in another mile or so.

Over the whip-cracking of Sundance's weapon, Walt Punteny put into words just what I'd been thinking. "Looks like Lonny is—ah—sorta frazzled around th' edges don't it?"

"Yeah. How's Dan going to turn out?"

"Oh, that plug of your'n is good for a big long ride . . . anytime we can get out of this rat trap, and ride. Y'think Lonny is—?"

"Lonny is what?" Lonny had come around into the shed with his Winchester in hand. "Lonny is what?"

"Lonny's gonna get the hell knocked out of him—if he goes off and lets those folks in the house bust loose." I bristled up to my brother. I'd had just about enough of his damned greenhorn foolishness. He was bringing shame on us Logans with all his mouth and no backbone.

"Hell, Kid! Y'think I'm addled by some gunshots? Hell . . . go inside and take a look!"

Once inside the cabin, I whipped out my clasp knife. Mr. Clay, his wife, the puncher and a little girl, about ten, were hog-tied, and stretched up on their toes, ropes binding their wrists, slung over the roof pole.

"Ma'am, I've got to apologize for my brother. He's all wrought up, with that posse and the shooting."

The woman, a nice-looking strawberry blonde, a bit on the plump side, never looked at me, but went right to her little girl the moment I released them. "Never mind, Viola, this man is nicer than the others. He'll keep them from hurting us anymore."

"You bet!" I was sweating under my Stetson,

and asking myself how I got into such a fix . . . shoving helpless folks around, like a rough-neck in some damned Beadles Dime Library yellowback.

I called Walt, Lonny and Sundance in and gave them their orders. My brother was to come out with Sundance and myself, while Walt would guard the puncher, Mr. and Mrs. Clay and their daughter. Clay, to give him credit, hadn't said a word since we arrived.

All through the afternoon, we kept up a long-range fire-fight with the posse, which seemed to be made up of about a dozen men. They never came any nearer than a clump of hemlock about fifty yards from the south-end of the ranch house. They stayed bunched up and hadn't seemed to know enough to fan out and surround us—but I knew they'd figure that out for themselves sooner or later. Sundance nailed a couple of the possemen with shots that sent them limping back into the trees. And no one else got close after that, having nothing but open ground to cross. To give them credit, they seemed to keep from firing right at the ranch house. As Lonny said, we had *hostages.*

By dark, I had Lonny, Sundance and Punteny spaced around the outbuildings and waiting for the posse's next move.

At ten o'clock, while I was drinking a third cup of Arbuckle's and full as a tick from supper, for

Mrs. Clay had fed us proper, as well as her folks, the back door opened and Lonny stalked in.

"They're gettin' closer, Kid! They got fires all around us now." He still looked mighty wild in the eyes—not the old free-and-easy Lonny.

"All right. The more fires the better." I told him, under my breath, that as soon as things settled down, we'd made a break through the posse's lines.

"Won't that be chancey?"

"You want to stay here until they wear us down, and then give us what they probably gave O'Day?"

He went back out to pass the word along to Sundance and Punteny, while I got up and checked the ankle ropes on Mr. Clay and the cowpuncher. I also kept a close eye on Mrs. Clay and tossed her kitchen knives up on top of the pie safe.

The little girl, Viola, and her ma were sitting at the kitchen table playing with a deck of cards, while Clay and the puncher stayed lashed down in a couple of chairs.

"Ain't you got any dolls or gimcracks to play with," I asked the girl Viola.

"Had a dollie, but she got stepped on in the horse lot. Mama says Saint Nick might fetch me one come Christmas time," she smiled at me. "Ain't you afraid Saint Nick'll forget you— seeing you're such a bad man?"

"Hush, Vi," her mother held a hand over her mouth, giving me a troubled look. "Viola's Pa there was bad sick a year back, and hasn't been able to work much since—or talk. We just about lost this place because Viola's uncle in town at the bank won't give Mr. Clay credit—so you see . . ." Her voice trailed off.

"Yeah, I see. Well, I'm just sorry that we didn't take that flea-bitten coyote for more than we did." There was nothing more to say, but I did some hard thinking.

I moved my chair over to the table and let the little girl tell my fortune with the tattered deck of cards, all the while listening for any movement out of the ordinary, inside or out.

"This here King of Spades mean that it's you, and you are going to meet some surprises—that's these hearts and diamonds." She shuffled the cards with her little fingers and turned up some more. "And this Queen of Clubs is a lady coming back into your life . . . and, oh, another Queen—a Queen of Hearts. Well, that means another lady is coming into your life. And this Ace of Clubs— that means . . ."

"That you are going to bed, right now." Her mother laid aside the cards, and lifted her up to her breast. "Can I tuck her in? You know, I don't want her around . . . if . . . there's any more trouble."

I went over to the window and turned up a

corner of the frayed, green blind. Fires were still burning around the outskirts of the place, hemming us in tight until morning.

But—we weren't going to wait until morning.

"Put her to bed, Mrs. Clay. There won't be any more trouble." I went to the back door and whistled for Punteny. He came up and slipped inside to watch, while I rounded up Sundance and Lonny and had words with them.

The sky, which had been pretty overcast all evening, was clotted up completely by eleven. And that's when we made our move.

Scouting around earlier, along the back of the horse barn, I found a ravine, or wash, that ran off at right angles from the buildings. I hadn't dared give it the once-over, while it was light, but with nightfall had let Sundance follow it to its end.

All horses had their hooves wrapped with gunny sacks from the barn, as we moved out. They made little noise in the rising wind that blew the posse's fires into whirls of smoke and sparks.

We were out of the wash and miles down the Pierre, Dakota Territory road by daylight. We'd hit a fork in the Deadwood trail an hour after leaving the Three Vee Ranch, and recrossed the river at another bridge, ten miles to the east. All posses would be trying to cut our trail to the westward . . . so we'd keep on east for a spell.

Sundance pulled up beside me, where I was

riding point. "Did you have to hand over that much cash to th' lady at th' ranch?"

"We've still got twenty dollars for supplies," I said.

"It's one hell of a way to run a business," he shouted at my back as I kicked Dan into a gallop.

CHAPTER ELEVEN

On Saturday, the First of July, 1897, we were camped out in a pine woods near Miles City, Montana Territory. We were a long way from Belle Fourche and its posses—but right up against it for grub. We'd shot a stray young sheep, near a sheep camp on the Little Missouri and ate right well for a day, but that was on Wednesday.

For three days, as we doubled back into Montana, skirting all ranches and settlements, the pickings had been mighty slim. Sundance knocked over a pair of blue grouse, and I'd hit a couple of white-tailed jack rabbits on Thursday, but it just wasn't enough fare for four half-starved long-riders.

"I don't give two damns in a bucket if they got out dodgers on us or not, we got to get some grub!" Sundance pulled up his belt another notch.

"If Harvey had brought th' pack-mare along instead of turnin' her loose when we went into Belle Fourche, we could be eatin' our heads off," grumbled Lonny.

"Which would be better than complaining yours off," I told him. "But seeing we probably wouldn't have got away, dragging that load, it's better to be here in one piece—hungry or not."

"They surely won't be lookin' for us around

here?" Punteny raised up from looking at Dan Patch's foreleg, voicing all our thoughts.

"Maybe yes, maybe no." Sundance stared at the afternoon sky. "I say we go into town and get some supplies." He glanced at me. "What say, Kid?"

"We've got to eat, that's certain." My backbone was getting closer to my front with each hour. Sundance hadn't spilled the fact that I'd left eighty dollars with the rancher's wife when we slipped away from the Three Vee place—so I owed him something.

I was getting almighty fed up with Lonny's complaining, and didn't need any more. It made me feel down in the mouth that my brother was getting thorny as a cactus. He'd got me into this crazy campaign, trading lead with the law and on the run because George Curry was such a damned poor businessman that he'd let some banker rope and hog-tie him. And here we were away up in Montana with no sign of a stake for George.

"Well?" Lonny stalked out and stared up the road. "It's gettin' on for evening. We could be up to town and back in time to cook us a good meal—or maybe even eat at one of them restaurants."

"Give him th' grub money, Kid." Sundance winked at me. "Let your brother do th' marketin' and sass buyin'."

"Meaning what?" Lonny had his Colt out and

covering Sundance before we could bat an eye.

"Put it up, Lonny. You're getting too damned jumpy!" I stepped between the two, while Punteny sauntered around the other side of his horse.

"Leave him alone, Kid! He's more'n a yearlin' now. He can make his own play." Sundance was in a crouch, hand near his ivory-handled six-gun, face split with that wild-cat grin.

"Everybody's jumpy. Ease off all of you. If anyone does the marketing, it'll be me." I mounted Dan, warning Walt Punteny to try and keep a little peace in camp.

"Let me go in, Harve!" Lonny, still tight-faced, came and ran a hand over Dan's shoulder. "Any chance they're lookin' for us, I'd rather you let me take care of it. You had to up and fight Pike Landusky just because I'd been sparkin' his daughter. Belle Fourche was as much my fault as that loco O'Day's . . . for you came along to keep me in one piece. But we'll still get that money for George, won't we?"

"No matter how?"

"Well we owe George Curry quite a lot."

"But we can't repay him by shooting up half the lawmen and bankers in the territories, can we?"

Lonny just stood there, his jaw clamped rock-shut, his Logan stubbornness showing.

"What," I asked, "happened to our plans about going down to Arizona or Texas, and earning money to law our way into the clear back home?"

"We can still do that. Just one good raise."

I rode off for Miles City, without answering their farewells. Sundance was getting hair-triggered, and Lonny wasn't any better, though he still had a mighty healthy respect for his own hide. With those two firebombs ready to explode at any time, there was no telling what might happen if we tried another strike.

It was a two-hour jaunt on Dan, with his stiffened leg, to the outskirts of Miles City, Montana. I passed a couple of punchers heading back in the direction I'd come from, but they only gave me a wave of the hand and kept on their way.

Staked out twenty years before by an army general, named Miles, the town, like Belle Fourche, rambled along a river, in this case, the Tongue. I crossed over on the Main Street Bridge, reining up in front of a large frame building bearing the name of the Macqueen House.

On a hunch, that there would be an ordinance against gun-toting within the city limits, I'd taken off my gunbelt and rolled it up in my slicker, retying both—behind my saddle. The six-shooter under my coat was out of sight, but where I could get it in a hurry, if I needed it.

Looking up and down the street, I spotted a big clock on a pole in front of a store. It stood at right on to five o'clock.

Though there were plenty of people around on the board sidewalks, coming and going out of the stores and saloons, nobody paid me a might of notice. I, actually, had to stop a man on the street to find out the way to the local vet.

When I left Dan Patch with the veterinarian, who had an office next door to the livery on Fifth around the corner from Main Street, I also had directions to the town's paper—The Yellowstone Journal.

I'd thought that if the Belle Fourche fight had hit the telegraph wires, the local newspaper might have some mention. It was easier to look over the papers than to saunter into a lawman's office trying to get a gander at the reward posters.

When I entered the office of the Yellowstone Journal, I had to stop and blink until my eyes got used to the darker interior. The door had an overhanging bell that tripped when anyone came into the place. This was still jingling when a girl at a desk in the room's corner spoke to me.

"Couldn't catch that, Miss, with your old cow-bell clanking in my ears," I answered, blinking away.

"I said it was almost closing time. We shut up the office at five, and I really should ask you to come back Monday, unless you have a short item, or a classified for the next issue."

"Won't be around this neck of the woods on Monday, I certainly hope." Now that I could make out her face, I wasn't exactly sure what I was saying. I had a feeling—like I'd stepped into quicksand, or maybe hooked with a horn. Right then I didn't know how to get out of there, or for that matter exactly why I was there. Her face and those blue eyes—they downright dazzled me.

"Well," she smiled, "if I can't sell you any advertising, maybe I could sell you a copy of our paper."

"Papers? Yes, that's it. I want papers."

"How many?" She rose from the desk, and taking a light, wooden crutch I hadn't noticed, from the corner, came slowly over to the counter.

"Papers? Oh, this week and last week ought to do fine."

"Here you are." She shuffled through a stack under the counter and spread out the Yellowstone Journal for the week before and the present week. "Will these be enough?"

I could feel those deep blue eyes on me, even as I took the papers and stared at the front pages. It seemed she was looking right through me with those eyes . . . eyes that I could swear I'd seen before. And then it came to me. I knew, without knowing how I knew—and recalled old Frank Jackson's voice, "Starr is with some folks a'runnin' a tin-horn noose-paper up in Montanny."

"Will these do? I really have to close the office now."

"Oh? You bet." I laid down the ten cents for the copies.

"Thank you, Mister," and she whisked a gay-looking little straw bonnet from under the counter, tied the blue ribbon under her chin and, balancing on the crutch, came around the end of the counter and waited for me to open the door.

When I'd closed the door behind us, she took a key from her dress pocket and locked up. "There!" She smiled at me. "Now, I suppose you have a lot of reading to do . . . and there are certainly some wild doings down in Dakota, and over in the Oklahoma Territory. It just seems that the West doesn't want to settle down and behave like the rest of the country, does it?"

"No, Miss." I'd got a glimpse of the issue describing the Belle Fourche attempt . . . and was wondering if this lovely, young girl suspected the stranger beside her . . . or had any idea of the last days of her father.

"Well, good night." The blonde girl, who had to be Starr Jackson, turned and went along the boardwalk toward the east end of town, away from the business district.

I stood there, watching her go, and wondering if she really was Frank Jackson's daughter, and wishing I'd had gumption enough to ask her name.

As she crossed the second block, she turned the corner, and looking back, waved to me.

I wig-wagged my papers, and then unrolled

them and took a good, long look at the news from Belle Fourche. It was right on the front page: *"Belle Fourche Bank Attempt!"* That was the headline. It went on to describe the fight as the reporter saw it (from a distance). *"This morning, June 28, 1897, shortly after 9 o'clock, six (?) men rode into town on horseback. They rode up to the side entrance of the Butte County Bank, dismounted and entered. The officers of the bank and customers were covered with revolvers and ordered 'hands up.' At first Arthur Marble, assistant cashier, snapped his revolver in the face of one of the robbers. The weapon failed to explode and was thrown aside, and Mr. Marble obeyed the order of 'hands up.' The gang then cleaned out the money in sight . . . One robber failed to mount. His horse shied and he was not able to catch up with the others. He made frantic efforts to secure a mount, and in the excitement he rushed around the crowd and tried to cut a mule out of harness. He was then captured. He gave his name as Tom O'Day. He had in his possession $392."*

Where O'Day, who'd not been lynched, but stuck in jail, got that money, I didn't have any idea. He might have picked somebody's pocket while loafing around that Belle Fourche barroom before we got into town—or it could have been cash he'd socked in his pocket before we left the Hole.

The story in the Journal went on to give a pretty good rundown on all of us, including Sundance's habit of grinning, Lonny's pointed nose, Walt Punteny's wide mouth and big ears, and my own black eyes and dark *Cherokee* features.

The piece wound up with a brief mention of the tangle with the Belle Fourche posse out at the Three Vee Ranch, and the fact that we had come over from Hole in the Wall, and were *"desperate members of the Curry Gang."* They had got that from O'Day and his loose jaw. The reward for us was up to $250 each—which didn't seem enough to get any amateur bounty hunters on our tracks.

I stepped wary on my way back uptown, just the same. That Peacemaker felt mighty good under by belt.

Holding out enough to pay the veterinarian, I went into the Diamond R Store and bought bacon, beans, Arbuckle coffee, tinned peaches, several cans of Blue Hen tomatoes, and such other oddments as a fry-pan, kettle, coffee pot and some tin dishes. I toted this stuff away in a gunny sack.

It had been over forty-eight hours since I'd had anything in my insides but branch water, and I was getting wobbly. Even though the boys were waiting, I walked into a small restaurant on a side street and ordered up a quick meal of steak and potatoes.

As I worked my way through the grub, I dug

into the two issues of the Journal. Starr, if that was who she was, was about right concerning trouble filling the printed page—only it wasn't just in the West. Hell was busting loose all over the place.

Besides our efforts at Belle Fourche, there was *"Unrest in Cuba."* Over in Europe, in the Balkans, the Turks and Greeks were just getting around to hold a peace pow-wow. A hired-killer named Jim Miller was on trial for a job down in Texas. They were still trying to turn up leads on the murder of Colonel Fountain and his little son in New Mexico. Yellow Fever was killing off the ditch-diggers down on the Panama Canal. A renegade lawyer, named Jennings, was leading a gang of third-rate train robbers over in the Indian Territory. And even New York City was having its troubles with crooked police on the take and labor *"Anarchists"* trying to stir up riots. There was more, but I folded up the sheets and went back to the livery stable to get my horse.

When I walked by a mirror mounted on a store front, advertising clothes, I got a good look at myself. With a four-day growth of beard, dusty Levi's, patched and mended, dirty-brown coat, and shabby boots and Stetson, it wasn't any wonder that Starr wanted to get me out of the newspaper office as quick as she could. I'd never been a dandy-dude like Lonny or some other punchers, but now I looked like a perfect tramp.

I hustled along, glancing around for the town marshal or police. Though I hadn't noticed any law about, if any of them got a look at me, they'd be bound to run me in for vagrancy.

The sun was burning up the western sky with big streaks of red and purple when I got my horse from the vet's, paying two dollars for the doctoring. He'd found and pulled out a long, narrow sliver that had been poisoning Dan's foreleg.

There wasn't anyone on the road south to the pine woods, but it took me almost as long to get back from Miles City as it had to ride there.

The evening was peaceful and every so often a killdeer would answer another with its lonesome, anxious call. The moon was up long before it was full dark, lighting herds of silvery-humped summer clouds, moving along so slow and calm-like, until, to my overworked imagination, it seemed the sky was filled with snowy-white buffalo, wandering on forever.

And as I rode, looking at the wide-spreading plains and small hills, with their moon-touched shrubs and trees, I kept thinking what the little girl at the Three Vee Ranch had tried to tell me with her cards. *"This Queen's coming into your life . . . "* Or had she said *a lady coming into your life?* Well, it seemed a hell of a life for anyone.

Back at the camp in the woods, I found all peaceful as a church. Sundance was asleep in his blankets, and Lonny, who seemed more easy, was yarning with Walt Punteny over a small, protected fire. Both swore the other was on guard, but neither had hailed me until I'd dismounted and was within ten feet of them.

I gave them some hell, but I had a full belly, and they hadn't. So after they'd cooked up and polished off their grub, and gone over newspapers, particularly the reports of the Belle Fourche scrap, they followed me into the blankets. This time, Sundance stood first watch— as there was no use getting jumped by someone who might have followed me.

Drowsing off, I was thinking of Starr, and how young she must have been when old Frank Jackson left her, probably, with the people at the paper. He hadn't mentioned her lameness, and that got me to wondering how it had happened, and if it could be helped. She was too pretty a little lady to be in such a fix . . . and when I thought the word *lady,* all of a sudden—that Winters Woman came into my mind.

I hadn't thought of her for days on end, with all the high-binding going on. But there she was—bold and brassy, and I could smell her musky-sweet hair, and again recalled the yielding but firm feel of her body against mine that long night. And when I thought of the Winters Woman, I got Johnny back into my mind. I owed Ab Winters plenty, in a lot of ways.

CHAPTER TWELVE

"If you want to hit the trail, then you'd better do it," I told Lonny. "It makes sense to split up now, especially with those rewards."

We'd spent all of Sunday out in the woods, chewing over the best way to get on with our business—that of making enough of a raise to take back to George Curry. I'd been against more trouble, in fact was still against it, but a promise was a promise.

It seemed the best way out of our jam was to have Lonny and Walt, who seemed to hit it off, take a separate route, and let Sundance and I go a different way, all meeting up later.

I could keep Sundance, more or less, tight-reined. And I had kept my Logan temper under the lid since we started out from the Hole. I'd had to. With hotheads like Lonny and Sundance along, someone had needed to keep his wits working.

Two hours after daybreak, Lonny and Walt Punteny rode down the road in the direction of Deadwood. I didn't know what they might run into, and was uneasy-like about my brother. But as Sundance said, Lonny wasn't a yearling any more.

Lonny and Walt were to scout around, without getting themselves into trouble, and join up with us around the third week of August, just north of Sheridan, Wyoming, where Punteny had relation running a saloon on the Little Goose Creek.

"We goin' into town?" Sundance quizzed me as we saddled up.

"If we want any supplies." I'd turned over most of our grub to Walt and Lonny.

"Them reeward dodgers out where anybody can see'm?"

"I didn't see any around. Of course I didn't go down to the marshal's office and ask to look, either. But what's bothering me most is not being able to buy much grub. I've only got five dollars left."

Sundance toed at a rock, grinning sly-like. "I might dig up a little." He hauled out two twenties from his vest.

"Where'd that come from?"

"Maybe, from down the road apiece."

"Maybe from Belle Fourche? Well, it's a good thing you're sticky-fingered."

On the way to Miles City, I couldn't help thinking about the way things kept going. Here we'd got into a hell of a scrape, trying to rob that bank—and getting damned little but bullets . . . and we were still on the scout, with rewards out for Lonny and me. All this on top of the Pike Landusky shooting. Things seemed to keep piling up so fast there was only one thing to do—get out of the country.

But we couldn't . . . until we made that raise for George.

There was some traffic on the road. We must have met a good dozen horsemen, mostly cowpokes, coming from town, as well several buckboards with ranch families and nesters going back home with supplies. Most looked us over casual-like, but one rider, going toward town, overtook us and tried to strike up a confab.

This gabby stranger had a long, narrow face, narrow eyes and a slouchy grizzled mustache. "You fellows new around here?"

I didn't trust him much. He was packing a six-shooter and a long needle gun in a scabbard on the side of a big sorrel bearing a III brand.

"Just passin' through." Sundance spurred up his buckskin and left me riding beside this nuisance.

"Saw where you camped back there," he drawled in a Texas brogue. "Must have been more of you?"

"Was, but they've gone," I answered, spurring Dan forward to get up with Sundance. Looking back, I saw the stranger had halted his big sorrel in the road and was watching us go.

We were in town around noon, eating at the same restaurant where I'd laid on the grub Saturday. The name on its front window branded it as *The Can Can.*

"I can tell you why they call it th' *Can Can,*" Sundance commented, after lunch as he leaned against the building's front, chewing at a tooth-pick.

"Yeah?" I was looking down the street toward the Yellowstone Journal, and keeping an eye out for that curious rider with the needle gun.

"Because all that so-called food has just got to come out'a cans."

"And that slouch-hatted jasper on the wall-eyed sorrel comes out of a posse, or else he's a lawman."

"Well, let's go for our stuff and git." Sundance tossed his toothpick and headed for the big general store.

"Get what you think we need—and don't forget a coffee pot, skillet and ammunition," I said. "Don't run into any law or trouble—remember our pistols are in the bedrolls! I'll be up there in a few minutes. I want a couple more newspapers."

"Gettin' to be a real reader, ain't you? Well, maybe there might be more in th' papers about us."

A hardware and a drygoods store stood to the town-side of the paper office, with a vacant lot between. To the south of the Yellowstone Journal was another vacant lot, grown up with a big grape arbor. I took all this in as I sauntered up to the steps leading into the office.

When that blamed cowbell had stopped jingling, I could hear the sound of a machine chugging away in the back of the building. I took it to be some kind of printing machine, though I'd never seen one.

In about a minute or so a big, bald-headed man, with ink-smeared apron and side whiskers came out of the back room. "Too late for this issue, friend, if you're thinking to put in an ad or an item," he rumbled. "Got some good items on a sale at the clothing store, though. Wait a minute, I'll send out a copy—fresh off the press."

I'm damned if that blonde girl didn't come back out, with a copy of the paper. And there I stood in the same old torn coat and dusty trousers. But at least I'd scraped my beard off back at camp and was half-way clean.

"Starr your name?" was all I could think to say as she handed me the inky-smelling sheets.

"Why, yes." She looked over her shoulder at the inner room, with its clink-clanking racket. "Did Uncle Sam Gordon tell you?"

"No. Someone else did." I couldn't take my eyes off her crutch.

"Oh? And you were so interested in a three-legged girl that you had to come back and ask her name?" She had caught me staring, and her eyes, clear and friendly, were all at once—remote.

"No such damned—beg your pardon—thing!" I didn't know to back out of my fix. I could feel my ears burning. I'd come back to the paper in hopes of seeking this girl again. And now I was bogged down like an old muley cow in mud.

"I'm sorry," she smiled suddenly, and her face glowed. "Here I go at you, a stranger, and for no reason."

"That's all right, Miss Starr." I folded up the paper and took a nickel from my pocket. "Here, I got to get on back up the street."

"Wait—you said someone told you my name." She reached out a slim, ink-smudged hand. "You see, I go by my middle name of—, well it doesn't matter. You can call me Starr. But who are you? and who told you?"

I thought fast, and a name came to me that I'd read in the papers. "My name's Bob Nelson—and I think it was your father who told me." I hadn't meant to say that, but this girl's straight-shooting look and manner brought out part of the truth— and just my luck I told her the wrong part.

"Father?" Her blue eyes widened and she stood motionless, not breathing for a moment and then went into the newspaper's press room.

I stood stock-still, wondering if I hadn't best leave before anything more came out of my jabber-jaws.

Starr was back almost at once, smiling, her apron off and a brown-striped paper sack in her hand. "I usually go home to Aunt Sue Gordon's at noontimes, but press day, I fetch my lunch in a little poke." She headed for the door.

I followed her out onto the wooden steps.

"There's a nice shady bench in our grape

arbor next door, where we can sit and talk, if you don't mind." Her eyes were puzzled, but pleasant.

Ten minutes after we'd seated ourselves under the shifting gold and green shadows of the wind-turned grape leaves, Starr had every bit of the story of Frank Jackson. Every bit that is, except that he'd died an outlaw in an outlaw camp. I'd made out that old Frank was standing up for his rights against the gunmen of the big ranchers—protecting his small spread, and had died doing just that. I told her all this and stuck to it. It was rather like reciting the Johnson County War all over again—but on a smaller scale.

She went at me like a regular little lawyer or newsman. "And he got a Christian burial, Mister Nelson?" There were tears on her cheeks and her lunch was untouched.

"Yes. We had a regular minister come from town," I lied, trying to look over her head and getting my eyes caught with hers.

"I'd always hoped he'd come back ever since that night four years ago when he left me here with the doctor after our horse fell and hurt my leg. I figured that he'd been in trouble with some other folks that he'd stood up to. He was always that kind of man . . . ever since Mother died at our ranch in Oregon, when I was small. His letters, sending money to Uncle Sam Gordon, who took me in, didn't say much, but I knew he was splendid and brave. And that someday he'd come back, as he said."

"You hurt your leg when you were four years younger? Why didn't they try to do something about it?" I asked, trying to get away from old Frank Jackson's *goodness*.

She turned on me with a frown, then looked away. "Yes," her voice was low. "Our horse fell and rolled on me—because Father was in a great hurry. The bones in my ankle were injured, and the doctor didn't set them properly . . . and now it's too late."

"Why should that be?"

"Because it would cost a great deal. And Uncle Sam Gordon here doesn't make that sort of money. Half the subscribers to the Journal pay him in vegetables and other produce. Besides he's just a kind man who agreed to take care of me. Letters came addressed from Father, with some money from time to time, but not enough. That's why I work here." She rose and picked up her crutch. "We help as much as we can, I and my wooden friend."

Now—why I said what I did, I haven't any idea, but I heard myself rattling on about old Frank's ranch, and the money coming from it when the estate was settled up. "And that should go a long way toward getting a good doctor to fix things up proper and right."

She stood there, leaning on her crutch, staring

at me, her lovely young face filled with a mixture of sadness and surprised hope. "Do you really think there is a chance it could happen, and there would be money truly coming? From what Father wrote, the big ranchers down in Wyoming Territory were always trying to cause trouble for him."

"Well, I'm sure it will work out." Just how I couldn't even figure for myself. But, something, somehow, had to be done for this girl. Queer as it seemed, I'd had one of the most peaceful half-hours in the past weeks . . . even with my stretching the truth way past the breaking point over old Frank, the noble ranchman.

"Is that man looking for you?" Starr pointed out at the road, where Sundance sat on his horse, Stetson tipped down over his nose, and with a gunny sack strapped to the saddle.

"Yes, he's riding herd on a small bunch of stock with me." I didn't want to lie any more, but I didn't want any more questions either.

"Will—you be coming back this way, soon?"

"Maybe . . . as soon as I can." From the way Sundance was jerking a thumb in the air, I got the idea he'd spotted a lawman, or a lawman had spotted him.

"Let me tell Uncle Sam about your news." And before I could say a word, Starr was out of the arbor and making her way toward the back door of the newspaper building.

"Come on, Kid!" Sundance clipped when I got out to the street. "You called th' turn. That was nobody but Frank Canton back on th' road to town. It come to me all at once."

"Canton?"

"Yeah, th' curly wolf of th' Powder River War back in '93. Th' killer lawdog who's already dry-gulched half a dozen cowpunchers, and led th' raid on poor old Nate Champion and Nick Ray!"

"What's he doing around here?"

"Good question. I heered he was killin' behind a badge over in Oklahoma Territory. He's th' sidewinder what wiped out what was left of th' Daltons!" He twisted in his saddle, peering up and down the street. "Come on! I don't know what you think you're doin' tryin' to spark a little gal on a crutch—but we oughta make tracks before that son of a gun shows up."

I'd started to walk beside Sundance's buckskin, heading for the livery barn, when the front door of the Yellowstone Journal opened and the big man with the inky mutton-chop whiskers hurried toward us.

"Mister Nelson! Mister Nelson, wait up a bit!"

"Don't tip the hand," I told Sundance and waved him on.

"Mister Nelson, our little girl has just informed me as to her unfortunate father." Old Gordon came up and wiped his sweating head, getting ink on the bald spot. "Now, just between us, and

I don't know exactly how much you know about Mister Jackson, or where you met him but I was not unaware of the business he was actually in." The old man looked sharply at me from under bushy eyebrows, and moved closer, lowering his voice. "Understand?"

I made an involuntary movement for my six-shooter, but it was out of reach in my bedroll at the livery.

"Mister Gordon, I only met Frank Jackson once, and he died soon after that—not by my doing," I said.

"What's this cock-and-bull story about Jackson's ranch and money coming from its sale?"

"Sort of a white lie, I guess."

"It's a lie that can hurt badly. Starr, as you call her, is a fine young lady and she's going to stay just that way." He stuck out his whiskers at me, like a proddy old bull buffalo. "In fact," and his voice sank, "the money just isn't here to help her. And that's why I don't want anyone coming around with such talk—lifting up her hopes."

"You knew Frank Jackson before," I asked to change the subject.

"Yes. Back years ago, when he first came out to this country from down in Texas. He did maintain a little ranch, first at a place in Oregon and then down in a corner of Wyoming. But he was always shifty, and met his Waterloo robbing a bank in Colorado about four years ago. He lost his nerve then and brought his daughter up here to me for safekeeping. But he destroyed a horse and nearly killed Starr in the accident."

"She doesn't seem to know anything but good about him?"

"Yes, I've always kept his name and his many aliases out of our paper, and watched our exchange papers as well, so she suspected nothing. As far as she knows, Frank Jackson was an honest rancher—and died one."

Sundance, who'd ridden on up the street, was back now, leading Dan Patch, and itching to get out of town.

"Well, Mister Gordon," I said, taking the reins off Sundance, and mounting Dan Patch, "thanks to you, I'm sure—from Frank Jackson. He spoke good of you. And don't be surprised if some of his money comes this way . . . sometime."

When we cantered past the Journal office, Starr came to the doorway and waved, blue eyes sparkling, and face glowing with a light that seemed to come from deep within herself.

"Pretty as a spotted pup under a red wagon," Sundance yelped as we both pulled off our Stetsons and waved them in the air—heading for the east river road that ran toward the Dakotas.

Two miles out of town Sundance pulled up and motioned me to haul-in. "Just what was that talk back there about Frank Jackson's money? You been holdin' out on us?"

122

"Like you?" I swung down and ran a hand over Dan's leg. It seemed to be coming along, with all swelling down, and fever out of the pastern.

"Don't go changin' th' subject. What about old Frank's money?"

"I was just joshing that newspaper fellow."

"I'd say he'd be the exact man *not* to bamboozle—him or a lawman."

We both stopped and looked at each other, then pulled our six-guns and belts out of our blanket rolls and strapped them on again.

I stepped out into the middle of the road with the field glasses. There was nobody in sight, in either direction, but I had a feeling.

"Canton," said Sundance, "is sure to come this way, with or without a posse, for he's bound to have quizzed half of Miles City to cut our trail. And knowin' a bit about him, I'd say he's on his way right now—playin' th' lone hand as usual. It makes less reward to split."

"I don't know much about him," I answered, getting out my saddle-gun and refilling its magazine with the extra ammunition Sundance had bought. "And I don't want to, but I do know I'm not about to let him spring any traps on us— when we can spring a better one on him."

I went over my plan with Sundance. He swallowed it and was soon riding ahead into a piece of timber, about a mile onward, while I stood beside the Fort Keogh-Bismark Road, rubbing down Dan and waiting for a distant rider on a rangy sorrel horse.

Sundance had been gone nigh onto an hour when my glasses picked out a horseman coming over a rise of prairie to the west. The man, Canton, rode slowly, looking around the country, but keeping his eye on the road from time to time.

I put away the glasses and mounting Dan, kept ahead of the rider. In a minute or so he seemed to spot me and began spurring up.

I stayed out about a hundred yards in front, until I reached the grove where Sundance was holed-up. I tried to get a glimpse of him but he was too well hidden, so I went on down the road like the greenest tenderfoot in the world.

Shortly came the rattle of hooves coming along fast, and my backbone began to freeze—expecting anything from a stock whip to a bullet. It took plenty of sweat not to turn around and tip my hand.

By now we were well ahead of Sundance and nearing a small, iron bridge that crossed a branch of the Yellowstone. Over to the north, the hazy-blue smears of the Mountain Sheep Bluffs reared up but all else was rolling country, all the way into the Dakotas.

The man behind was closing and I could hear him shouting as we pounded over the bridge, our hoof-beats rippling like drumfire. "Hold up there! Hold up there, Curry!"

Hitting the dirt road off the bridge, I turned in my saddle and stared back. Canton had a long-barreled six-shooter out and was waving it over his head. And right behind him came Sundance flailing the air with his own six-gun.

I pulled up short and the man on the sorrel was on top of me before he could stop.

"Get 'em up—Curry!" Canton went to throw down on me, but his wall-eyed sorrel slammed into the side of Dan Patch, and both horses reared up.

I kicked Dan around and tried to pull my own six-shooter, but Sundance, right behind, was quicker. His shot took Canton in the shoulder, knocking him half out of the saddle.

"You get'm up, Curly Wolf!" And Sundance poked his cocked pistol into Canton's face. "Hoist 'em and keep 'em hoisted!"

Canton dropped his pistol and held his hands high. He was groaning from the wound, but his eyes glittered with pure hatred. "You two-bit black legs. Go ahead and shoot. You'll never plug a gamer rooster!"

"Who's going to shoot you?" I dismounted and taking him by the elbow, yanked him off his horse. "Stand over there and let's take a good look at the polecat who dry-gulches cowpokes from behind a badge."

"I took a good look at you too, *Kid Curry*. And I ain't gonna forget it, you can bet!" Sweat beaded out on Canton's forehead and dripped from his frazzled mustache. The splotch of blood on his sleeve was spreading.

"Why're you chawin' at him?" Sundance dismounted and came over to where the gaunt lawman stood swaying at the head of his sorrel. "I'm th' boy who put th' cork in your bottle."

"Yeah, and you'll be grinnin' on th' other side of your face too, Sundance Kid," Canton growled, wagging his head like an mossy horn steer in a pen.

"Here!" I pulled off his long-tailed coat and looked at the bullet hole. It was little more than a good, clean flesh wound. I went to my saddle bag and taking a spare shirt, tore it and plugged Canton's arm until the blood stopped dripping. Then I bound it up, and getting a bottle of Old Crow from our gunny sack of supplies, gave him a good belt.

"Regular Good Samaritan, ain't you?" Sundance stood with his hands on his hips. "And th' next time this old panther gets on your trail, I suppose you'll patch him up again."

Canton glared at him. "Next time I'll call th' turn! I never forget and I never stop once I'm on th' trail. Believe me there's going to be a next time. And maybe soon!"

"This is one time you're gonna stop . . . and lucky for you I'm a damned good shot, or you'd be stoppin' permanent like." Sundance pulled

Canton's stake rope from the sorrel and shoved the old lawman ahead of him back to the middle of the bridge and hog-tied him to a girder.

"How'd you come up with our names?" I asked Canton.

"Reward posters from th' Sheriff at Belle Fourche," Canton snarled.

"I knew it," Sundance groaned. "But what're you doin' over here, you old devil? Ain't you a marshal in Oklahoma Territory?"

"Ran out of road agents and came back. My ranch is in Johnson County, Wyoming."

Thunder mumbled back in the west, where it had clouded up and was starting to come on with a rain.

"Let's get on our way," I told Sundance and mounted Dan, then swung back down and taking Canton's slicker from his saddle, tossed it over the man.

"That's another favor you can chalk up for Harvey—ah, Kid Curry," Sundance called from where he was stripping the sorrel of saddle bags and needle gun. "That and th' fact he set th' trap for you, and played bait to boot!"

"I ain't forgettin'," Canton answered with a regular volley of cuss words. "That and th' fact he done dirt to my relation—Ab Winters!"

I was going to answer and quiz him about Winters, but the rain was beginning to come down hard and stinging, and along with the rain here came the Medora stage, larruping toward us—not half a mile off.

We struggled into our yellow slickers and turned toward the north, heading over the open country toward the dim outlines of the bluffs.

Within twenty yards we were out of sight of the bridge, Canton, and the oncoming stage-wagon; the rain covering all with its grey sheet.

"Looks like you got into a regular Texas-style feud," Sundance yelled through the rain and thunder.

"Winters has got a lot to answer for," I shouted, wiping the rain from my face, "including his relations."

CHAPTER THIRTEEN

For the next month we drifted along, heading first this way and then that. Sometimes we rode into a cattle camp and had ourselves a square meal. The XIT was one of the outfits that fed us well and asked no questions.

Sundance, who'd been mildly curious over Frank Jackson's daughter, Starr, back in Miles City, finally gave up joshing at me about getting old Frank's money to her, and settled down to improve his "eddication" by panning-out chunks of information from a battered copy of *The New Home and Library Gazetteer and Indexed Atlas of the World.* He'd found that jaw-breaker in Canton's saddle bag.

So while we lay out in the shade of some cottonwood or pine grove, or holed up under the shelter of a cutbank, we debated the information from the book. And in between gabbing about the number of Chinamen in San Francisco, or the distance between Florida and Cuba, I thought about Starr, and wondered how I could come up with enough money to help her out—to say nothing of that raise we still had to make for George Curry. At the same time I kept mulling over the Winters woman . . . and Ab Winters, and his bounty-hunting relation—Frank Canton.

"Three days to go," Sundance said one morning as we were rolling up our blankets and downing a last cup of Arbuckle's. "Three days and we can amble down for th' meetin' with Walt and Lonny—that is if this is th' fifteenth of August." He thumbed at his *New Home Gazetteer.*

"So why wait three days?" I was getting tired of lounging about—and wondering how Walt Punteny and my brother were making out. We'd planned to meet them about August twentieth at Sheridan, Wyoming, and if we got in a couple of days early, what was the difference?

That would put us within a hundred miles, or so, of the Hole, but we wouldn't go near that place until we had something to bring back.

We traveled long each day, getting up with first light and threading our way through wild, hilly land, too timbered and stony for good cattle country. Keeping the black, wooded humps of the Big Horn Range to our right, we crossed the Montana line ten miles west of the Crow Reservation on the eighteenth, and rode down into the lush, and still green, bowl-shaped Sheridan Valley.

A line of willows rambled in a curve to our left, marking a water-course—Little Goose Creek. We headed for it, crossing a stretch of prairie, the grass spattered with blood red masses of Indian paintbrush. Nearing the river road, we loped through a golden blanket of evening stars.

"Must be gettin' on for suppertime," Sundance pointed out the yellow flowers. "They allus come open in late afternoon."

"Got that from your Gazeetter, eh? Well ask it if we'll get ourselves a lawman's welcome or a plain howdy-do from Walt's shirt-tail relation—because that looks like some sort of tavern or big house out beyond those cottonwoods."

Sure enough, when we came around a bend of the road, there was a big two-story, frame building, with a huge pair of antlers nailed up on the slanting porch roof. *Elkhorn Tavern and Saloon Bar,* read the green letters on a board under the decoration.

We rode up slowly, keeping our eyes peeled, but nobody seemed to give a rap that we were there. In fact, I had to get down and jiggle the door handle, before I roused anyone.

There came the sound of bolts being shoved. The door creaked open. And I was looking at the *Winters Woman!*

I just stood there dumfounded. She was some thinner than she'd been at Ab's place, and her eyes were sort of dull-like, but she was as sassy pretty as ever.

"We're not open on Sundays, Mister." She appeared not to know me. "Mister Haynes, the proprietor, is off and won't be back until tomorrow, but you might find lodging over at

Sheridan to the new hotel. It's a fine, big place. Only been open a couple of years, they tell me."

"Ain't you from these parts?" Sundance came sashaying up, hat off, and grinning as usual.

"No! She's a good long ways from Ab Winters' place!" I couldn't help saying that. It made me hot around the neck to see her playing dumb with me.

She turned white then and I thought she was going to fold up in the doorway. Clutching the doorjamb, she leaned forward, hand shading her eyes, peering at me. "Harvey?"

"Used to be." I kept my hand on the butt of my pistol, watching her, and waiting for whoever might be standing back of her in the darkness.

"Used to be? Why, you *are* Harvey Logan! I couldn't see who it was, just coming out of the kitchen into the daylight. What do you mean, used to be?" Color was back in her face, and she looked more like her old self, eyes blazing.

"This is th' famous Kid Curry, ma'am," Sundance horned in. "You know, th' famous banker from Belle Fourche."

"Kid—Curry?" She backed away, looking at Sundance, who was also giving her a good looking over. He'd finally got her name— Winters!

"Who are you?" she asked. "You told—or Ab told me that you and your brothers were called Logan."

"Just a new handle we hung on him, ma'am." Sundance was bowing around like a chicken on a hot stove. "Th' Kid is—"

"This Kid is going to knock you out of date, unless you rein in a little!" I was getting mad about the whole thing. Here was Ab's woman . . . and Sundance shooting off his mouth at her.

"I don't know what you're doing off up here, Mrs. Winters, but we still need to bunk down here," I said, trying not to see her curves and getting warm all over. "We've got to meet friends here shortly, and that's just that."

Without a word, she led us through the closed barroom, with chairs tipped up on tables, and down a short hallway into an older section of the building. This part, built from logs, had no upper floor and only two rooms, one beyond the other, but with windows on the ground level. "This is all I can do for you, *Mister Curry.* As I said we don't open Sundays, but I guess if you want to put your horses up in the barn out behind, I can find you something to eat."

I tried to thank her, get a look from her, but she went out into the kitchen beyond the barroom and stayed there.

When we got back through the front door, with the horses rubbed down and fed out, there was a table straighted up with some good hot grub on it . . . but no one about and not a sound.

"Sorta on th' chilly side, your Missus Winters,"

Sundance tried a joke, "but she sure can rustle up hot steak and potaters to beat th' band."

I grunted and kept my nose in my plate, when I wasn't keeping an ear cocked for anyone coming through the door. All was still and though I didn't care for the setup much, we had to stay and wait for the boys. And what she was doing here, I couldn't guess, but it looked for all the world that she'd ran off from her husband Ab.

After we finished eating we went to our rooms in the log section of the tavern.

Mrs. Winters came to the door. "Harvey—that's what I call you, anyway." She hesitated, seeming to wait for me to speak.

"Yes?" I stood in the doorway, while Sundance, boots off, lay on the bed in the farther room, wriggling his toes and pretending not to listen.

"I just wanted to tell you I was terribly sorry about what Ab did to your brother. In fact, I left him that same week and came up to Sheridan. I had a friend in one of the saloons—but I didn't like the place . . . I'm not the saloon girl sort, I guess."

"I'd say you weren't, either." I tried to ease through the door, and close it behind us, but she stayed in place.

"Let me speak my piece, now!"

"All right," I said, watching her.

"I want you to know, Mister Haynes took me in to do the cooking, and make the beds—and that's all!" She turned away, went back down the hall and through the empty saloon. I could hear a door being bolted.

And that *was* all!

CHAPTER FOURTEEN

There was no sight or sound of the Winters Woman, nor anyone else, the rest of that night—though I pulled on my boots and scouted around as far as the river.

Sundance and I took turns beside the windows with our Winchesters, two hours at a crack, until after daybreak, but we might as well have turned in and slept solid.

She showed up about eight o'clock and announced breakfast, which was on a table in the saloon, then went back into the kitchen without another word.

"Can't say as she takes much to you," Sundance grinned as we sat out on the front porch after the meal, feet propped up on the railing, and saddle-guns handy by our chairs.

"She feels bad about what her husband did," I said shortly.

"Hold on, Kid," Sundance raised his voice. "Who's that?"

I looked up the road. All morning there'd been little movement, just a couple of buckboards and a horseman or two. Now here came three dusty-looking riders, pounding down on the Elkhorn Tavern.

"That ain't th' law, is it?" Sundance let his chair

slip down to reach for Frank Canton's needle gun. "Naw!" He leaped up.

"Right! That's Lonny and Walt—and who else?"

The three horsemen pulled up in front. Lonny and Walt were smiling at us as they dismounted stiffly, while the third man, square as a block of granite, came off his horse like a cat.

"Keerist!" Sundance stood grinning at that third man. "Ain't that th' Morman Preacher, Robert LeRoy Parker?"

"Say, is that th' Horse Thief from Sundance?" The man, Sundance called Parker, finished tying his big white stallion to the hitching post and came around to the porch steps.

Lonny and Walt, still smiling from ear to ear, followed *Parker* on to the porch. "Harve, this is Butch Cassidy," Lonny announced.

"Glad to get to meet you." Cassidy's steely-grey eyes twinkled from under sandy eyebrows as he gave me a shake that nearly bent my fingers.

"Likewise," I said, rubbing my hand on my shirt front.

"Where's th' boss of this shebang—Walt's cousin?" Cassidy asked.

"Nobody here now, but th' little gal who cooks," volunteered Sundance.

"My cousin Alf ain't here yet?" Walt wondered, looking at the Winters Woman, who'd come to the door to see what the rumpus was all about.

"Could you rustle us all some dinner?" I asked, trying to catch her eye and failing again.

"In a few minutes." She went back inside.

"We met Butch here north of Sheridan early this morning, and when I said Sundance would be here, he up and joined us," said Lonny, batting the dust off himself with his Stetson and sinking down into one of the extra chairs.

"Thought I'd see if he was still in one piece," Cassidy grinned, perching on the porch rail and poking Sundance in the ribs with his thumb. "However I ain't joinin' for long. I got a few gents interested in that horse of mine—they got some idea he belongs to one of them."

"And who's callin' who a horse thief?" Sundance drawled.

"Butch was tellin' us about that raise he made back in March at Castle Gate, Utah," Lonny reported. "That was th' way to pull a job. Slick! Over eight-thousand dollars in one haul. And I got an idea that we could pull th' same deal over at Red Lodge. Walt and me rode in and looked at her good."

"We'll talk about it after dinner," I said as I studied Cassidy, mindful that Sundance had told me that this fellow was going to be the top outlaw of the West—if his luck held out. And from where I sat, Butch Cassidy had a look of pure luck. The men who followed him, I figured, were in for plenty of money—and excitement.

But here I was, a man who didn't want anything, but a place to hang his hat and three squares a day . . . with half of two territories on the lookout for me. I'd never heard of Red Lodge, but maybe my own luck would change if we paid that bank a visit. There could be money for George Curry, for Starr, and enough left over to take my brother and myself down to New Mexico for a new start. And after that, maybe we could come back and straighten out that Pike Landusky matter.

Cassidy hadn't said another word, and Sundance seemed to be waiting for someone to pick up the conversation—but the five of us just sat there and smoked.

"Dinner." The Winters Woman poked her head out and back inside.

"There's another one without much to say," Sundance chuckled.

"Who is she?" inquired Lonny.

"Friend of th' Kid's here," Sundance said, up and heading for dinner.

"Where'd you meet her?" Lonny, the ladies' man, was interested.

"Never mind. She don't want to meet you—or me," I said. "What about that Red Lodge bank?"

Lonny went into a long-winded description of the bank's location, easy look, and, presumably, large amount of money.

Cassidy, head cocked on one side, sat working

his way through the grub, not saying a word—just grinning to himself.

"Butch? How about you? You want to throw in on this job?" Lonny asked. "My brother, here, will let you run th' show—if you want."

Cassidy shook his head slowly, and downed the last of his coffee. "Nope! Like I said I got to keep movin' on. I got just one question about that Golconda of yours, though."

"What's that?" Punteny wanted to know, while we leaned in to listen.

"Just this. How're you going to get away after your raise? It takes mighty good, grain-fed animals to outrun a big posse. We did it, Elza Lay and myself at Castle Gate, but we had th' best, and staked along where we needed 'em."

"Oh come on, Butch, no sour grapes," quipped Sundance. "Just because you ain't got time to go along—don't think we ain't able to pull off a good job!"

"Like Belle Fourche?" Cassidy laughed, getting up from the table and hitching at his gunbelt. "Seems I heard about some troubles there."

"There was plenty." The Winters Woman stood in the kitchen doorway, wiping her hands on her apron. "There was plenty and there'll be more. Harvey Logan here is in enough trouble now. Why don't you all leave the country—while you're in one piece?"

"Lady," Cassidy took off his hat, which he'd

just clapped on, "you spoke a'plenty. Don't know what you just heard, but I'm takin' your advice. And these boys here ought to ride on southward, not back up around Red Lodge. There's a power of law in that part of th' country!"

"I see you can talk when you got a mind to, eh?" Sundance glanced over at the Winters Woman, who was standing with her hands on her hips, staring at the bunch of us.

"When did you think Alf Haynes, that's my cousin, oughta be back?" Punteny addressed the Winters Woman.

"Tomorrow or Wednesday. He had to go into Laramie on business."

"You said he'd be here today," I reminded her.

"I say what I please—when it needs to be said."

"Yes, and you damn well do what you please— when you please!" I was getting my Logan dander up at this wrong-headed piece of calico.

"Yes, and you damned sure are doing what you please—you fool!" She whirled and flew into the kitchen with her apron held up to her face, slamming the door.

"I'd say that had all the sounds of a lover's spat—or a couple of old married folks a'goin' at it hammer'n tongs," laughed Cassidy.

"Who is she, Harve?" Lonny was looking narrowly at me.

"Just an old friend we run across," Sundance answered and changed the subject. "I sure don't blame that Haynes feller if he tried to wish this old white elephant onto some sucker, and maybe that's what his business is in Laramie. Them beds are enough to age a man twenty years in a night."

"No need to wait for your cousin, Walt," I said. "We can settle up with the lady now, unless you and Lonny plan to stay a spell, seeing we both are a day early."

"Lady?" Lonny snorted. "She's too pretty for a lady. Looks more like a dance-hall queen to me."

"Her name wouldn't be Winters, would it?" asked Cassidy.

"Winters! That's Ab Winters' wife?" Lonny jumped up, started for the kitchen—and stopped in his tracks as the door edged open and he was staring into the business-end of a Remington over-and-under Derringer.

"Nobody comes in here unless they're invited—and that means you most of all!" The Winters Woman cocked the wicked-looking little gun in a silence so still I could hear the boards in the floor squeak as Lonny shuffled his feet.

"My name's Logan, same as him." Lonny jerked a thumb at me. "Logan—get it?"

"I get it, but that doesn't mean you have to come roughshod at me, because Mister Winters beat your brother to the draw."

"Hold on," I said. "The way Lonny got it from the folks in Landusky, Ab didn't give Johnny a chance. And I thought you were so all fired sorry?"

"I am, Harvey." She lowered the nickel-plated little pistol. "But I'm sorrier for you, because you're just letting your fool brothers get you deeper into trouble."

"Wait a minute here, Calamity Jane!" Lonny, thinking her attention distracted, made a grab for the Derringer.

The big bullet ploughed into the floor at the tip of Lonny's right boot, giving him a whack on the big toe and splitting the leather. He nearly fell over backward getting out of the line of fire, while the rest of us froze in our tracks.

"We don't aim to trouble you, ma'am." Cassidy held up his hands and marched away, whistling out through the barroom onto the porch. The bunch followed, including my brother, who limped off, muttering.

"You got the other barrel for me?" I started for her, but she just stood looking at me, with a queer look on her face—until I took the gun out of her hand and tossed it onto the bar top.

"Harvey . . ." was all she said before I kissed her. Then for a spell we clung to each other, whispering. I learned she'd thought of me—even more than I'd thought about her. And though we'd parted that morning at Winters' ranch with curses, she'd hoped for the day we'd meet

143

again, just as I'd daydreamed about meeting her.

"I can't say a lot of fancy things, Annie. But if things work out, sometime, I'd sure like you for my own woman."

"I've not been anyone else's from that night. And I'll not be, either, come tomorrow or a hundred years—just yours."

From all the tramping back and forth on the front porch of the tavern, the boys sounded restless. Finally, someone pounded on the door and called me by name. A head poked in, very slowly, "Don't shoot, lady, but we ought'a get underway. That is, if th' Kid ain't kidnapped," Sundance called cautiously.

"I'd best be going," I told her.

"Yes." She walked behind the empty bar, and stood watching me. "You take care of your business, but I don't want to know about it." She took a slip of paper out of her apron pocket. "If you can't come back here, write to me at this address."

"How much do we owe?"

She named an amount, which I paid.

"If you'd hustle a bit, Butch'll show us a good trail into th' Red Lodge country." Sundance was back at the door.

"Red Lodge! You're going up there with that devil of a Frank Canton still around?"

I'd mentioned our run-in with Canton and was already sorry I'd brought it up. "Maybe, just

144

maybe." I tried to reach her hand over the bar, but she pulled it away.

"Go on. Get it over with. It's the only way you'll learn." She took the Derringer from the bar top, and put it into her apron pocket. "Go along with those wild men. Just leave!"

"All right. We parted before, with sparks flying, and things worked out. They'll work out again." With that I went out the door, without looking back at her, and mounted up.

All I knew, as we rode away from Elkhorn Tavern, was that she wasn't the *Winters Woman* any longer. She was Annie. And she was mine, if I wanted her . . . and I was mighty certain I did.

CHAPTER FIFTEEN

Cassidy rode with us, taking us over a piece of country wilder than the stretch we'd come through down to Sheridan. The trail led up through foothills of the Big Horns, skirted several sheer drop-offs that towered eighty or ninety feet above the silvery curves of the Tongue River, then veered away to the west.

By late afternoon we'd ridden down into a long, narrow valley between the shimmering blue bulk of the Fisher and Sheep Mountains, and then, gradually, gained a great, meadow-like plateau that stretched over toward the Big Horn River.

"This is where I point my nose in another direction," Butch said as we sat around a small fire at the base of a great, wind-shattered pine. "Y'got about a hundred miles or so as th' old crow flies, to Red Lodge."

"Beats me how you find your way around this neck of th' woods," Lonny marveled. "We must have come two hundred miles to cover th' same distance."

"Been over it more'n once, as far back as when Mike Cassidy was runnin' other folks' cattle over half th' territories, and me with him."

"He's th' jasper you got your handle from, ain't he?" asked Sundance.

"Yep! Took it from him, to sorta spare th' old folks an overdose of shame back home . . . like Kid here seems to have latched onto George Curry's name."

"Speakin' of names, how'd you know th' Kid's lady friend was named Winters?" Lonny asked as he looked down at his split-toed boot.

I started to call Lonny down for being so mouthy, but Butch raised a hand, laughing. "I was at Sheridan about a week before I ran into you all, and th' town was still buzzin' about a dance-hall gal called Winters that put a Derringer ball into a gambler who'd tried to get fresh with her. She got off Scott-free with th' court and came out to th' Elkhorn."

"Thought she was mightly handy with a firearm." Sundance glanced over at me.

"So's her damned husband," growled Lonny, glaring at his boot.

"Well, I wish you all luck." Butch arose and swung up on his big, white stallion. "But I think you'd be better off to head back south, or north—about anywhere but on west. I didn't want to bring it up, but there's probably a posse out lookin' for this horse."

"Horse!" We all stared at the animal.

"Yeah. It used to belong to old Liver Eatin' Johnson th' town marshal at Red Lodge. Old Johnson's got a reputation to hang on to—even though he couldn't hang onto his horse."

"I see what you mean. He's a fine horse," I said.

"Yeah, you got a dandy mount too." Butch kicked the big stallion into motion. "And you'll all need good horses if you go on to Red Lodge."

We sat at the fire and watched man and mount dwindle into the purple shadows that were welling up in the folds and dips of the mountain meadows.

"We got nothin' to worry about with that there fool marshal," Lonny observed as we rolled up by the fire for the night. "We ain't got his blamed horse, and we been in that burg once without any trouble."

I lay staring at the red glow of the fire and thinking, as usual, of Annie, and also wondering about the girl, Starr. I puzzled some why a man as sharp as Cassidy would be going around making more trouble for himself than he needed.

The only answer I got was that I was doing the same thing, and Red Lodge could be another Belle Fourche. We just weren't professional enough yet to swing the business.

Two days later we were standing right in the middle of the general store in Red Lodge, buying supplies, Sundance and I, while Walt and Lonny strolled over to take another look at the bank.

After we'd got the grub stowed behind the

horses in a couple of gunny sacks, we went up to the bank to see for ourselves. What I saw didn't look good. A big man, with a great grizzled beard, wearing a buffalo coat, was anchored in front of the bank, sitting on a bench and whittling at a stick with an over-sized Arkansas Toothpick.

"Don't tell me," I said to Sundance, as we got a twenty-dollar bill changed in the bank, ignoring Lonny and Walt, who were fiddling with pens and paper at a stand-up desk.

"Yeah, it sure looks like law—Liver Eatin' Johnson law! I read about him in a paper once."

"So you read more than almanacs? Well, I read too—and I read the signs of another foul-up. We're going out of town, while we're in one piece."

"Unhunh, any man who wears himself a buffaler robe coat on a sunny day is tough enough to make all kinds of bad medicine . . . though I wonder where's that posse Butch was worried about?"

"Probably trailing him, or someone else. Posses don't worry me much. But what muddies the water is that big buffalo out there. Looks like he thinks Butch might still be around and after more than his favorite horse."

"It sure puts th' frost over any work here."

We sauntered out of the bank, nodded to Liver Eating Johnson, who ignored us and went on looking up and down the street, possibly for his vanished horse—or Cassidy.

Gathering up Lonny and Walt, when they came back to the hitching rail in front of the Jordan Mercantile Emporium, we rode out of Red Lodge as easy as we could.

We went into camp along a bend of the Tongue, the afternoon of September 25th, two days after leaving Red Lodge. It was a mild, warm day with the cottonwoods and willows all red and gold with early Fall.

Walt and Sundance were down on a sandbar getting water for supper, and Lonny was breaking up dried driftwood to start the fire, while I was just moving Dan a ways to picket him in a good stand of grass when—out of nowhere, came the pounding thud of many horses.

Sheltered as we were in the small valley, without a look-out, their approach was a flat-footed surprise. Lonny jumped up and made a try for the saddle-gun on his bay, while Sundance and Walt crouched, six-guns in hand. By the time I'd yanked my Colt and cocked it a dozen horsemen had breasted the hill, all heavily armed.

"Posse!" Sundance yelled, diving behind a cutbank along with Walt. Unable to get his Winchester, Lonny scrambled after them. At the same time, some of the riders opened fire on us, without hailing or giving us a chance in any direction.

With the three boys pocketed behind the cut-bank, I was the only one out in the open. Several bullets whistled around me as I dropped the picket rope, holstered my pistol, mounted Dan in a hustle and gave him the steel.

We shot out ahead of the posse like a scared rabbit. I could hear shots and shouts along the river, but kept going, larruping Dan for all I was worth.

One of our bunch had to stay free, in order to bring possible help—though where I'd get any help this far from the Hole was anybody's guess. When I got out about a quarter of a mile, pounding over the rolling prairie, I turned and caught a brief, wind-blurred glimpse of all three boys—hand high, deep in a circle of horsemen. And about a hundred and fifty yards behind me, two riders were coming fast. As I stared, one lifted a long saddle-gun and fired, the bullet sizzling past my face.

I pulled my six-shooter and threw a couple of shots back to try and slow them down, but as I guided Dan around a small swale, fringed with willows, that high-powered rifle spoke again, slamming a ball into my pistol, spinning the weapon away and plunging through my horse's neck.

The poor brute stumbled, and began to slow

down. Though nearly pitched headfirst, I pulled enough leather to stay on board. But the old pardner I'd ridden for two years, in all kinds of trouble, was hurt to death.

There was just time enough to hit the ground, running for the willows, when Dan stumbled again and rolled over onto the edge of the marsh. Another couple of shots cracked out, one bullet exploding a spray of splinters and yellow leaves about my face. The next instant I was into the swale, but it was only a matter of moments before the riders loped up and shouted, "Come out of there, Curry! Out of there. You're covered, Kid!"

Unarmed—there was nothing for it but to raise my aching hands and come out to stand staring into the barrel of Frank Canton's needle gun, with that old side-winder on the other end.

"Dandy of that Sundance horse thief to hold onto my rifle for me," Canton gave a dry, gruff laugh. "I grabbed it off his buckskin and it came in mighty handy bringin' down your big race horse."

I looked over at poor old Dan, lying there motionless in the reeds and hung my head for a moment. It wouldn't do to let Canton or the other posseman see my tears. But I knew, for a fact, that if I ever got Frank Canton in my sights again, or within hands-reach when he didn't have the drop, he was a dead man. I shook my head a couple of times to clear the red fury of my Logan temper, and then shrugged.

"Nothin' to say," the fat-faced puncher with Canton snickered. "I guess these waddies ain't much when you got'm covered."

"Shut up, and get down and strip that there horse," Canton ordered. "We got to get this gang back to Billings. And you," he poked me with the needle gun, "you start a'marchin' back to th' river. We got a couple extry mounts just achin' to tote you to jail. 'Course Billings is jest th' first stop on your way to th' Pen. Deadwood is where you're bound. They got a foolproof jail there that'll hold th' wild bunch of you till th' judge throws away th' keys!"

CHAPTER SIXTEEN

Frank Canton was right—up to a point. Dead-wood Jail *was* foolproof, but the jailer, Si Mansfield, wasn't dealing with all the fools around, just the ones on the inside.

We hadn't been in his damp, buggy lockup more than a week when a note came in, on the sly, from nobody but Butch Cassidy.

That message of three lines, written on a bit of paper and stuffed, somehow unbeknownst, into the spout of a coffee pot, toted over by Mrs. Mansfield, let us know Butch was out there somewhere, ready to give us a hand.

Sundance, who'd fished the paper out of his tin cup, after nearly choking on the soggy thing, motioned me over to read: *"Four saddled horses at the head of Spearfish Canyon. Look near the Way Station of the B and M Line. Try for Sunday night, October 31. Butch."*

That particular Sunday was a good three weeks away, and we spent most of the next twenty-one days going over all sorts of plans on the Q.T., trying to keep the other prisoners from listening in. There certainly wasn't much for me to do, except think about Annie—and Starr; talk to get them off my mind—and eat monotonous grub.

For breakfast it was coffee and a plate of

hominy grits. Dinner was coffee, beans and hominy grits. Supper was the real splurge—coffee, fried beef and hominy grits.

Sundance, parted from his *Gazetteer* by Frank Canton, who'd taken it back along with his needle gun, usually did the most talking. "It ain't that this grub's so bad," he said one night, "but it sure has a heap of sameness. 'Course, you could get sick and tired of Delmonycoe's in Noo York, I guess, if you ate there every time."

"This sure ain't any Delmonico's," Lonny spoke up, "but our waitress could be worse."

Lonny was beginning to sound and act more like himself. His treatment of the Belle Fourche rancher's wife had been brought on by the jangle of the fight with that posse, I told myself. He was all right—except in a tight spot. Not that the bunch of us weren't in a pretty tight spot right now—with rumors around the jail, all the way from a plain lynching coming up for us—to life in the Deer Lodge Pen—and not one dime for a lawyer. So the secret break, with Butch Cassidy's help, had to be our ace in the hole.

Mrs. Mansfield, the jailer's wife, gave me an idea—at last. She was a mighty plain woman, with a bit of a squint, and freckles to boot. I thought about it for a spell and then called Lonny over.

Next morning when she came into the jail corridor with our hominy and coffee, Lonny got up off his bunk, and began to palaver with her. He praised her blue-checked apron, told her how starchy she was looking, and wound up with a bare-faced lie about her "tasty" meals.

It took hold right away. Along with the next dinner, she fetched over some soggy friedcakes, and tossed in a withered apple for each of us at supper time.

Every day she stayed around a little longer, while Lonny turned on his lady-killer charm. She bragged on her brats' school chores and laid it on about her husband and all his influence in town and at the Odd Fellows' Lodge. It didn't fool us much. We'd heard her in the next-door jail office hen-pecking old Si more than once, and carrying on about his shiftlessness at not getting out and getting himself a paying job.

So it happened that the evening of Sunday, October 31, when Mrs. Mansfield and Lonny were standing nose to nose, through the bars, passing the time of day, I motioned Sundance and Walt up to the front of our cell.

At my wink, Lonny grabbed the poor lady by the shoulders and hauled her up to the bars, while I beat on the steel door with a wooden stool.

Mansfield came running in from the outer office, unarmed, and then turned back as if he were going for a weapon.

"Open up, Mansfield, we've had one damned

chunk of hominy too many," I yelled, waving the wooden knife I'd carved out of the top of a cigar box lid with my spoon and covered with tin-foil from a plug of chewing tobacco. I stuck the tin-foil knife under Mrs. Mansfield's freckled nose, feeling low-down, but it brought Mansfield to a dead halt.

"Let Mazie alone, you devils! I'll turn you loose!"

I don't know if he thought I'd commit bodily-harm on his homely wife, or if he was afraid of what she'd pull on him afterward, but he fell all over himself unlocking the cell door.

Next minute the Mansfields were inside, with their hominy and coffee pot, and we were out, while a pair of sheep thieves and a whiskey-soak in the next cells yelled to get out with us.

"We got enough of penny-ante crooks," Sundance shouted, slamming the corridor door and following us into the Sheriff's office.

The uproar kept on, with prisoners and Mansfield squalling their heads off, old Mansfield using words his Odd Fellows certainly wouldn't have liked.

The jailor had been without a pistol, and our weapons were toted away by the posse when we'd been gobbled, so we hurriedly scratched around Sheriff Plunkett's office, but only turned up an unloaded shotgun. Unable to find any shells, I smashed the weapon over a corner of the desk before we opened the front door to make a break up the street.

It was full dark now, with only a few folks on the street, mostly on their way to church services. As they didn't seem to pay much notice to us, I slowed the boys down to a brisk walk. But I knew that racket back at the jail would fetch some trouble in damned short order. And Plunkett, who always packed a pistol, lived just a street away over on Sherman.

A block past the jail, we split, planning to meet at the B and M Way Station two miles out. Sundance and Lonny hustled up the Carbonate Road, while Walt and I headed for the railroad tracks along Carney. By the time we were past the freight sheds, I could see lanterns bobbing around by the jail.

We ran up the tracks, our breath puffing bright silver in the moonlight. Back toward Deadwood several dogs commenced yelping shrilly in the crisp night air.

"Damn them dogs!" Walt gulped, tripping over an uneven tie.

"Save your breath, you'll need it by the time we get to those horses."

"Yeah, if there is any."

About a mile out, we stopped to rest around a bend of the tracks, while the hullabaloo of the hounds kept up.

"Them damn dogs is close, and us with no

weapons at all." Walt was sweating like a hog butcher in fly time. "What's that?"

There came a crashing of feet through the underbrush, and Sundance stumbled down the embankment, followed by Lonny.

"Sheriff's got his trackin' hounds back there," Sundance huffed.

"We can hear. Let's go!" I started on up the rail line, the rest jogging behind. In about fifteen minutes the tracks swung around a tall, wooded hill and we saw the dark outline of the Way Station.

Back of us hounds were keeping up their steady racket, though I couldn't see anyone in the moonlight—yet!

"Ain't that th' horses?" Lonny gasped, motioning toward the rear of the dark building. Peering through the night, we saw a horseman ride up out of the gulley behind the station, leading a mount.

The man forked a big white mare and there was a familiar look about his stocky figure. Butch Cassidy!

"Hist there!" Sundance, nearest the station, called hoarsely. "If'n you fetched th' horses, where's th' rest of 'em, Butch?"

Cassidy and his big white horse came on toward us, the steel hooves striking red sparks from the rock ballast of the right of way. He reined in a couple of yards from us and cocked his head at the noise down the tracks. "Seems you boys are so popular they might be comin' to invite you back to Deadwood."

The racket grew, hounds baying shrilly, and now I could see the bobbing approach of yellow lanterns coming around the bend. It looked like half of the damned town was hot on our heels.

"Where's th' rest of them horses?" Lonny yelled, his face dead white in the moonlight. "We sure can't get far with five men and two gol-damned horses!"

"Go to th' head of th' class!" Butch swung down and handed the reins of both horses to Walt Punteny. "As you see," he told us, grin flashing in the moonlight, "you can't work th' *Chinese Trick With th' Hole in th' Middle,* real perfect each time!" He pulled his new saddle-gun off the saddle holster and jacked a shell into the chamber.

"Ain't gonna start a scrap here are you?" Sundance stared wildly at the oncoming mob. Now we could see, from a quarter of a mile off, a good half-dozen horsemen, in addition to a nigh score of men on foot. All came along the tracks as fast as they could travel—lights flaring and rippling, dogs baying, and men yelling—all making one hell of a lot of commotion.

"Regular damned coon hunt," Cassidy grunted, standing stock-still beside the silvered rails. "But

I reckon we'll stop it right about now." He raised the rifle to his shoulder.

"You might have rode with Mike Cassidy as a young'un, Butch, but his savvy didn't rub off too well on you," I said, grabbing at his arm. "You want to scare off our extra horses?"

"Yeah——." Butch lowered the saddle-gun and took the reins of his horse from Walt. He motioned Punteny to follow with the black horse, back down into the gulley behind the station house.

"Don't think they've seen us or the horses," I told Lonny and Sundance, "so both of you get out of sight and keep your heads down."

"We stayin'?" Lonny craned his neck at the oncoming mob.

"Doin' more than just stayin'," Butch was back beside us in the shadows. "Your brother and me are, maybe, goin' to get us some more mounts." He handed over a nickel-plated Colt's six-shooter, keeping the saddle-gun.

Sundance and Lonny took another gander at the hallooing, ominous-looking group down the tracks—now within easy rifle range—and darted into the protection of the darkness behind the Way Station.

"So what's your idea?" Butch pulled down his sombrero tighter.

"I'll show myself to 'em in a minute, sort of lead 'em on. They didn't spot us by the looks.

They don't know we've got any weapons, so they'll come on until they're between us, and then we open up. Not shooting to kill. Just wing a couple, and I'll bet they fold their hands damned fast."

I waved him back into the dark pools of shadow, thrown by some tall clumps of half-bare choke-cherry trees and walked slowly across to the other side of the tracks, lingering in the moonlight as if undecided over where to go, or what to do, in the face of the mob.

A bullet whistled over my head, but high. The racketing echo of the explosion cracked and banged around the rocky hills. Another gun went off, and several of the horsemen spurred yelling toward me.

I couldn't make out any words, but took off up the tracks about ten rod, then jumped into the shadows and worked my way back opposite Butch. The thunder and rattle of the horses' hooves drowned out what he was calling, though I saw him motioning me to get down.

The riders were almost on top of us before I could roll back from the right of way fast as I could scramble, and I knew Butch was also darting out of the reach of those pounding hooves.

At the same instant that I fired the pistol, I heard Cassidy's high-powered .30-.30 began to crack.

One horseman gave a yelp as he flashed past, and I saw reins dangling while he grasped at a punctured arm.

"Freeze! Freeze right now—or we'll let you all have it! Hold your fire, boys, till we say so!" Butch and I were whooping and shouting and throwing shots into the air like an army of liquored-up Modocs on the war path. It brought quick results!

Four of the five riders pulled up, two a good ten yards past Butch and I—elevating their hands. One horseman got away down the track, lashing his mount, the horse stumbling and pitching over the gravel ballast and wooden ties.

In the other direction, the foot posse had turned and was plunging headlong back for Deadwood, in a dark mass of yelping dogs, and dashing, dodging figures, lanterns flung away.

Not another shot was fired. The foursome on horseback sat rigid with hands raised straight at the moon. Cassidy, running back up the tracks, poked his Winchester at the farther pair, ordering them to join my two. They rode back slowly, the wounded man cursing under his breath.

"All right, you fire-eaters, off them horses! Pile off fast!" Butch ordered, waving the .30-.30 under their chins.

I came up with the six-shooter and jammed

it into the gut of the sourest-faced horseman. "This is the kind of posse I like," I told Butch. We closely watched the four riders as they slowly dismounted, but they made no moves toward their weapons.

Sundance and Walt came up out of the galley grinning like a pair of lobo wolves and helped strip the possemen of their gunbelts. Lonny followed, looking so pale around the gills that I thought for a moment he'd been hit.

The wounded man was in such pain that I let one of the riders bind his arm up with a couple of bandanas before we sent the four of them off down the tracks toward Deadwood. From the time we'd halted the gang until they left, there wasn't another word spoke, though I could see them eyeing us mighty hard. But when they were about fifty feet on their way after their fleet-footed friends, we heard them cursing out Plunkett.

So it was the Sheriff, himself, that had kept on past us, heading for the safety of the high lonesome.

"He could be layin' in wait for us, or even roundin' up some more men down th' line," Lonny muttered. "And I've had damned-well all th' commotion I want for a good long time!"

The others looked curiously at Lonny, but he paid them no mind. Having picked out a black mare, he was busy tightening its saddle girth and rummaging through its saddle bags.

"Your brother's about right, Kid," Butch drawled. "I vote to put a lot of distance between here and th' next place."

"Where'd that be?" I asked.

"Oh, I thought you and some of th' boys might like to come along on a little expedition."

"Where to, Butch?" Sundance wanted to know. "Goin' back to get them other three horses that was supposed to be waitin' for us here at Spearfish?"

Punteny, who'd gone down into the gulley behind the way station, was back, leading Butch's big white mare and a smaller horse.

Cassidy climbed up into the saddle, rammed the Winchester into its boot and leaned toward Sundance. "What was I supposed to do? I'm not slick enough to be a good professional horse thief, like some folks I could mention. Guess I was just lucky gettin' old Johnson's White Wing here. Y'see I thought I had a rancher close by here who'd sell me a string of mounts, but when I was ready, he only had that brown mare there. And that one cost me fifty dollars."

"I'll take her," I said, "but you'll have to wait for your money. They cleaned me out completely when they tossed us into that damned excuse for a lockup."

"Sounds like you don't like sittin' in th' pokey," laughed Butch. "Well, neither do I. You know, they claimed to find some wrong brands on my stock back in '94, and gave me two years in th' Wyoming pen."

"Two years? I wouldn't stay cooped up that long. I'd break out some way, and you can bet on it!"

"Well, you sure did all right tonight, and that's certain." After telling us how he'd carried the coffee pot over to the jail for the jailer's wife that morning, slipping in the note, Butch wanted the full story of our break. And when he found how we'd worked it, he roared with laughter. "I wasn't wrong when I decided to take you boys into the firm."

Lonny, who was edgy, kept riding down the tracks, inspecting the silent landscape, while we tightened our saddle girths and inspected the weapons. We'd decided to leave the extra mount, a fat roan with a gotch ear, with all the looks of a wagon horse, tied to the end of the way station. Folks would be out in the early light to visit the battlefield and would find her.

"So where do you figger on goin' to?" Sundance quizzed Butch as we rode in single file up the long incline of the rocky-faced hills away from the tracks.

"Got any money?" Butch inquired from the head of our little column.

"Hell, no!" Sundance gritted.

"And you want some, and ain't too particular

where you go to get it—as long as you don't have to go back to Belle Fourche, or Red Lodge?"

He was answered by groans and muttered curses.

"I take it that means yes. A vote of confidence from all members of the Syndicate?"

"What in th' hell Syndicate?" Sundance spurred his bay up beside Butch's white horse as we crested a rise and looked out over the vast reaches of the ghost-pale plains, stretching on forever toward the starwalled horizon.

"Why—th' Train Robbers' Syndicate, of course!" Cassidy put the steel to White Wing, and we all went away from the black hills of Deadwood, loping free through the winey-cool air of the moonlit night.

CHAPTER SEVENTEEN

Heading directly for the Hole, hitting the blankets after dark, too tired to even think, and up before dawn, we reached the Red Walls late in the afternoon after a grinding three-day ride.

Once there, Butch went into a huddle with Flat Nose George Curry, and a bottle of whiskey, barely sticking his head out of Curry's cabin for several hours. When they did come out, Curry was smiling.

"Boys, you had a streak of bad luck—no doubt about that." He stood, hands on hips, looking us over. "That damned fool of an O'Day should'a been driv out'a here months back!" He spat on the ground at the mention of the name. "And that's just what happened to that trouble-some devil of a Bronco."

"Bronco's gone for good?" Sundance looked around at the crowd, which included that half-Mex kid, and two high-binders from Idaho, Red and Two-Deuce.

"Yep. We don't need quick-trigger saddle-tramps like him around, so I tole him to hit th' pike, a'fore you-all got back. He went off sommers towards Californy or Texas." He looked over at me. "I don't want th' Kid here gettin' into more gundowns. He could be valuable to Butch and me."

"Meaning, what?" I felt a prickle crawl across my backbone. But both Butch and George Curry kept on looking mild and calm-like.

"Oh, you think we'd hog-tie you fer that Landusky reward?" George laughed. "Hell's bells—you know half th' riders passin' through here are lookin' over their shoulders."

"Yeah," Butch spoke up. "And after that Belle Fourche job, with O'Day spillin' th' beans about th' desperate characters from *Curry's Gang,* old George here's on th' wanted list good and strong." He poked Flat Nose in the ribs. "So there goes George Curry, prominent rancher, right out th' door . . . and here stands George Curry— prominent owl-hoot!"

George cut out the smiling, for a minute, then shrugged. "What th' hell. They can't say I didn't try to keep my ranch, but them big, big bugs of *Cattle Kings* at th' Cheyenne Club, a'sittin' up on that mahogany porch with their spurs on, are th' jaspers who're to blame. They been tryin' to run us little ranchers out'a business, pullin' deals with them skinflint bankers to kite up th' interest until out we go, when we can't meet payments." He shook his head. "Too bad you boys wasn't able to raise enough cash, but with damn-fools like O'Day blattin' everything, don't make no difference now."

"Don't fuss, George," said Butch. "You damned well know that we're gonna make it back—and then some!"

"Yep." Flat Nose turned away and looked off up the valley where the shadows were commencing to herd in purple bunches along the walls. He turned back. "It means a long wait, and we're just about as busted as we can get right now."

"You sat it out here before, and until the right word comes along, I guess you'll have to sit it out some more." Butch winked, motioning me to come with him.

"I don't know what you're hatchin' up with Harvey and George, but I've got my own ideas as to what to do—and it don't include roustin' any more banks or doin' time in jail," Lonny stared at us, hand back near his six-shooter.

"Seems to me you're on them wanted posters, same as th' rest of us." Sundance grinned at Lonny, with an old-look in his eye. "Like it or not you're lumped in with us desperate characters. What do you say to that?"

Lonny seemed to sense Sundance was trying to crowd him. He shrugged and walked away to our cabin followed by Walt Punteny, while George and the others sauntered toward the cook house.

"That brother of yours thinks he can cut loose and turn honest-jake again," snorted Sundance. "From what he's said, buyin' a saloon and sittin' around playin' th' fiddle for dance-hall queens is his idea of success in th' world."

"At least he ain't listed on th' dodgers callin' him a penny-ante horse thief. And what do you say to that?" Cassidy snorted and took me by the arm, marching me off to Curry's cabin.

"I say that makes two of us," yelled Sundance as Butch shut the cabin door.

"What I wanted to tell you was this, Kid." Butch peered at me in the half-gloom of the cabin. "George and I think you done fine, in spite of some tough luck. You really use your head, though—like pullin' that jail break at Deadwood and gettin' up th' ambush of them boneheads afterwards. Flat Nose and I want you should come in with us on some real A-Number-One things."

"Hell, if I get any more law looking for me, I might as well give up trying to square things at Landusky and leave the country for good."

Butch eased himself into a battered chair at George Curry's one window. "Well, I think you're in more than just that fix. Remember th' bum deal I had over those brands back when I was sent up to th' pen? It was just a set-up by them cattle kings to squeeze out little nesters like me and George. Well, when I'd done time, I thought I was through payin' for someone's mistakes. But then th' law—*their law*—up and tried to brand me for everything that'd been pulled in th' past five years." He stood up and smacked one hand into the other, staring out at the growing twilight. "Right then I made up my mind I might as well be hung for a sheep-killin' dog as for a damned sheep." He gave that dry chuckle of his and shook his head. "And you'd best decide th' same thing sooner or later."

"I don't need to push my neck into any rope, shooting it out with some posse," I said. "And I think Lonny's got the right idea. We'd best just ride out and make ourselves scarce, somewhere."

Butch stretched cat-like, and taking off his grey Stetson, rumpled his sandy hair with short, thick fingers. "All I can say, it's gonna be a rough road to ride, with that Landusky murder warrant! Anyway, I been thinkin' about big hauls that are big hauls! Railroads, that's what!"

"And you want to try to tackle one with your Train Robbers' Syndicate?"

"Right." Butch breathed deeply. "There ain't been a real professional train job up here in th' northwest in years. Oh, there was a few tries back in th' early Nineties—one by a couple chuckle-heads, led by another—Charlie Hanks. All they got was bullets, and Hanks is still doin' hard time in Deer Lodge."

"Sounds like a mighty tough business," I answered, thinking I didn't want any part of Butch's *Syndicate*.

"Not if you got th' right man, on th' inside, to

tip you when to make th' strike," he laughed. "And George and I already know just where. So, what d'you say?" Seeing I was going to stay silent, he kept on. "You'll have plenty of time to make up your mind, if you stay here—and don't go off rampagin' around pickin' fights with posses. Though I got to say that's exactly why we really need you. You are one scrappin' son-of-a-gun. And real scrappers are mighty hard to come by. Besides you fight with your head . . . which is more than Sundance, or Walt can do." He sank back down on the rickety chair, a vague figure against the silvery-blue of the dusk-dimmed window.

"Plenty of time? What do you mean, plenty of time?"

"Oh, that? Well, it may be a month, or even six months or even longer before we get th' word that th' right cargo is comin' over th' rails—with just th' right set up, guard-wise."

"Guard-wise?"

"Yes sir. We're gonna operate this Syndicate with our heads. Businesslike! No pickin' a battle with a squad of riflemen. But, sooner or later, th' big boys at railroad headquarters'll get careless, and send out a shipment of cash or bullion, without enough firepower to hold th' fort. That's when we hit—and run. Make sense?"

"And your inside man will give you the right tip at the right time?"

"Right!"

"Well, I guess it does make some kind of sense—if you feel like tangling with the law."

"The railroad police are always holed up in Denver or Chicago, or some other damned place and send out trackers and trailers days after a hold-up. Nope! Th' things to be leery about are th' possibilities of some snoop ridin' in here all innocent, but ready to turn you in to th' nearest lawman, and just for th' reward."

As I sat there thinking about a chance at some real money to pay for Starr Jackson's operation—and what Annie had said to me when we parted at the Elkhorn Tavern . . . and what she must have thought when she heard of our fight and capture by the Red Lodge posse, I gritted my teeth.

Butch got up and lit George Curry's kerosene lamp. "Well? Do you want'a sit tight here with George and th' rest until we get that word. It'll pay plenty. Then you really could head for th' far places—with enough cash to tide you over for a damned long spell."

"Let me talk it over with Lonny," I said, just about certain what he'd say.

CHAPTER EIGHTEEN

Not only wouldn't Lonny go for Butch's plans, but next morning he packed his warbag, and bedroll and picked out his Black Velvet mare at the corral.

"No use, Harve! No use! I can't stay around here another day. This place is startin' to fidget me—even worse than Deadwood Jail." He sat on his horse and looked at me. "I just don't know what you think you're up to. Don't know, but it seems you're gettin' in deeper than you figure."

"Deeper?"

"Deeper into a world of trouble."

"Deeper? What about George Curry and that big debt you kept harping about us owing him? Remember that?"

"Yes. And we damned near got killed, tryin' to pay it off. Far as I'm concerned, it's paid. We tried." Lonny glanced over at the corral rail where Sundance and the Mex-kid, Billy Rogers were perched, looking off toward the tops of the Red Walls, but keeping their ears cocked. Cassidy, Curry and the others were still in their cabins.

"But where'll you go?" Lonny was my brother and I was worried for him. And he had stuck up for me, even come to the Hole to share my troubles—but it had just got too much for him. "Are you going to try to get back to our place?"

"Oh, no. But don't fuss. I'll write Jim Thornhill, tellin' him to keep hold of our old Four-Tee for us—if that's all right?"

"All right, but what are you going to do? You know they may have your name and description on wanted posters in half of the territories by now."

"That's all right, I'm gettin' plumb out of this neck of th' woods." He lowered his voice. "Didn't tell you before, but I got a letter before I left th' ranch from that shirt-tail cousin of ours, Bob Lee, who's been runnin' a gamblin' layout down at Cripple Creek in Colorado. Been thinkin' about it off and on for weeks. He wants to go into th' saloon business, and I'm goin' to look him up and talk some."

So, Lonny had his secrets, like the rest of us.

Sundance, whose ears were keen as a coyote, called out, "Be sure and take along your fiddle!"

"Hell!" Lonny leaned down and shook hands. "Harve, I wish you were comin'. I'm some worried about you. I think you should ride out of here, before—"

"Before?"

"Before you get so much taken up with this kind of a life you can't shake it. You were th' hardest workin' one at th' ranch. It's not just natural for you to lay about doin' nothin' for weeks on end."

He headed his black horse out of the corral, while I raised and lowered the bars. "It's like gettin' a taste for whiskey, this life."

"I've got that now."

"I mean th' excitement of this owl-hoot raidin'. I seen how you lit into that posse at Deadwood . . . and at Belle Fourche. You blamed well enjoyed it. You'll get like a sheep-killin' dog. And wherever you go—they'll be gunnin' for you, th' way they're gunnin' for Butch."

"He seems to thrive on it."

Lonny shook his head. "Sooner or later it's gonna catch up with him—*and you!* But you still might be able to beat that Landusky warrant."

"Landusky! I'm sick and tired hearing about him or his town. And that goes for everyone up there—but Jim Thornhill."

"Write him, when you can."

"Write him, yourself—and we'll keep in touch." For some reason my voice was getting raspy.

Lonny spurred his mount, without another word or a backward glance, and rode down the track toward the Hole's main passage in the Red Wall, a mile away. There would be one last man there to bid him goodbye—George Curry keeping a guard out in most weather.

When my brother had dropped out of sight over a hill, I turned to find Butch Cassidy standing waiting.

"Didn't hear it all. Didn't mean to—but I guess we scratch your brother off our Board of Directors."

"I guess. He's got an idea to put a lot of distance between himself and the Hole."

"Ain't a bad idea—for him." Butch cocked an eyebrow. "Not faultin' him, but he don't seem cut out for this kind'a life."

"And—I am?"

"I'd say so," grinned Butch. "Come on, let's get some mornin' grub. I want to fill you in on a couple things, because I'm joinin' Brother Lonny in hittin' th' trail."

Cassidy spoke the truth, for that same afternoon he was gone—on his way south toward New Mexico aboard Liver Eating Johnson's stallion.

"What give them fellows such an all-fire anxiety to leave here?" Sundance asked, leaning out of his bunk in our cabin.

"If it's any of your goldummed business, which it ain't, Harvey's brother's got business out'a th' Territory—and same goes for Butch," George Curry grumped.

"Ah-ha," Sundance, broke and out of credit, climbed back into his bunk, while George, Billy Rogers and I went back to our game of poker.

All through the evening, when I wasn't thinking about Lonny, and the others . . . Annie, Starr—and Ab . . . I kept recalling Butch's talk:

"Got a top hand, Elsworth Lay. We call him Elzy. He's down near Alma, New Mexico. He's sent word for me. We got several ways. He says there's a sure thing waitin' for th' two of us. So, I'm on my way to take care of things. You just sit tight. Th' big one's bound to be comin' up."

"How soon?" I'd asked.

"Can't say," Cassidy had answered. "What'd you care? Ain't goin' any place special are you?" He'd slapped me on the back and grinned. "Hell, if you really feel caged up—and want'a ride for a spell, you come on down after me. Tell you what. Stop off at Greenriver, Utah, and ask for any mail at th' general store under th' name of—uh—oh, Tom Capehart will do. That way, I can tip you off what's doin'—then it's up to you."

Two weeks after his exit, I followed Butch southwest. The bunch at the Hole, especially Longabaugh, let on I was losing my wits, heading out on the trail, with damned little cash—and not much of a way to make it, except one. And that way, according to George Curry, who wanted me to stay close, was bound to get me dry-gulched or plain hung.

But I felt like a kid out of school, drifting along. Lonny was right. Camping month after month in that damned Hole had just been swapping one prison for another.

I kept on a southwest tack, day after day,

traveling through the sage and across grassy open plains. It was late November, but the days stayed warm and the nights, though getting nippy, were still comfortable.

Following the rough map Butch had sketched out for me, I veered toward Casper in Natrona County. I knocked over a brace of prairie chickens with my six-gun within two miles of town and baked them over a fire of dried sage while a red half-moon floated up over the dark, pine-studded slopes of the Caspar Mountains.

That was my last look at a big town, or any town for that matter until I fetched up at Rock Springs. And I only stopped there long enough to buy a couple of dollars-worth of supplies and coffee. With the grub slung back of the saddle in a grain sack, I rode on past the large timbered towers of the coal mines south of town. Black-faced men were coming, like gophers, out of one of the shafts that ran back into a large hill. It seemed to me that working for someone else, down in the earth, was also like being in prison. I put the steel to my brown horse, Nancy Hanks, and went away from there.

Another half-day's ride put me just to the west of Brown's Hole. But I'd had enough of holes, and was beginning to want to get to Greenriver, so I kept on, being forded across on a flat-bottom barge at a crossing of the Green, northwest of its meeting with Red Creek. I had just enough to pay the boatman, a rough old Swede, who looked me over from top to bottom all the way across that wide muddy.

I stayed clear of Vernal, Utah the next morning. Butch had warned me that a mighty narrow-minded sheriff, by the name of Jeff Carr, had been holding down the job there for the past year or so, making his living mainly from fees slung onto strangers who rode into town showing a pistol or even a saddle-gun. I didn't want any hard-nose lawman prying into my background. That snoopy flatboatman had made my neckhair stiffen enough.

Real winter was bound to come, yet the calls of the evening grosbeak and killdeer rang out long after dusk, and mingled with the cries of the kingfishers along the streams at earliest light.

Those wandering little, willow-lined creeks and water-holes were beginning to thin out, along with the vegetation. The land was taking on a different, sandy, parched-yellow look, though the grey sage flats were still studded with fading color of the bluebells and wild mustard.

I'd been on the way an easy-going three weeks and was deep into Utah now. The Green River, I'd crossed back near Red Creek, had meandered along until it was now running due south toward the little village of Greenriver itself.

Reaching the banks of a good-sized stream, stretching east and west, marked Price River on Butch's map, I staked out Nancy Hanks near the water where there was plenty of good bunch grass, and made camp in the shadowy dusk.

I figured to be within a morning's ride of Greenriver, and was satisfied to be so close. It was getting tiresome with no one to talk to but Nancy Hanks, and she never answering.

After a slim meal of the last of the beans and a half-pot of coffee, I rolled up in my blanket by the fire and listened to the ripple of the stream, and the lonesome quaver of the coyotes off on the sage flats.

Before I closed my eyes, I pulled out the *other map*—the one old Frank Jackson had given me before he died. I'd studied it for the hundredth time since, though never when anyone was about. I'd not told Butch, or even Lonny about it.

I thought of it as my "ace in the hole"—though I couldn't say why.

Where, I wondered, was Star Valley? That creased and folded piece of paper gave general directions, but the place could be in any of the territories. The map, drawn in indelible pencil on the back of a blank withdrawal slip, had probably been snatched up during a bank raid when Jackson hadn't the time to fill out the right forms. It showed a trail coming "from springs," running along a river and through a gap, lettered "pass." Beyond the pass, the trail followed the river between mountains into the center of the valley. There three crosses marked a "settlement." Across the mountains another large river ran beside the valley on the right-hand side of the map. This could be on the east, if the way through the pass and valley led north.

There must be someone, somewhere, who could read the map for me, someone who'd heard of the place. But who could I show it to—or trust? I folded it and put it away in my shirt pocket, along with Cassidy's trail map. Maybe I'd ask Butch, after all, if and when I found him—again.

Next day, about noon, I rode down the cottonwood-shaded main street of Greenriver and hitched in front of the Greenriver General Store.

According to Butch, there was another hard-case lawman in town, so I'd stuffed my belt and holster into my bedroll and stuck the six-shooter under my coat. I hoped I had the look of a law-abiding cattleman just passing through. My saddle-gun had to stay on my horse.

I seemed to pass muster, for the fat, wheezing storekeeper tipped me to the best of Greenriver's two eating houses, and offered to have his clerk take Nancy Hanks around to the livery stable.

I thanked him, but decided to leave my mount hitched in the shade. Unless I came up with a windfall, I'd have to settle for one hot meal—and a pound of dry beans and coffee for the trail.

I got down to the real business after clearing my throat. "Any mail for me?"

"Fer you?" The old man pushed his specs up and poked his head around a string of wicker baskets and tin pails. "Post office, she's two doors down th' street."

"Tom—Tom Capehart."

"Whyn't y'say so?" He rummaged in a drawer under the tobacco case. "Here's one. And that's funny."

I took the soiled, unstamped envelope and saw it was addressed in Butch's handwriting. "Funny —because it didn't come through the post office?" I wondered what the old gent knew— about Butch, or me.

"Jest funny you should march in a' lookin' fer a letter from . . . who some-ever. And it only hand-deelivered half hour back." He leaned back against the shelves, folding hands across a big bay-window while his keen little eyes looked me over.

"The man that brought it still around?"

"Could be. That is, if'n he ain't got filled up with grub and rid off already. But by the looks of th' big feller, it'll take plenty."

"He's still at the restaurant?"

"Said he was goin' there. That'd be th' Bon-Ton." He gave a sharp yap of laughter. "We call it th' Bum Tum. Still th' best place for vittles."

I thanked him and went back out, heading down the street for the restaurant. Several hacks and spring wagons, plus a half dozen cow ponies were lined along the Bon-Ton's hitching rail. A good dozen punchers and townfolk were tackling such vittles as antelope steak, mulligan stew and beans and soup. The only customer not eating was a tall, broad-shouldered cowboy, who sat staring mournfully at a menu soaped on a mirror over the cash register.

When I edged myself in and sat down at his table, a thin, little waitress, in a white apron, stepped up for my order.

I glanced at the scrawled menu on the looking glass. "Steak and eggs."

"Same here," the cowboy slowly spoke up.

The waitress turned away toward the kitchen with a quirky look at the cowboy. "Couldn't you make up your mind any sooner?"

The big fellow rubbed a thumb across a three-day growth of whiskers and glanced sideways at me.

"You wouldn't be the one-man mail route?" I asked.

He studied the mirror as if he'd just discovered it. "And who're you-all?"

"I'm the fellow that got your letter."

He turned back and extended a big paw. "Howdy, Mister Capehart."

"The name's Lo—, Curry—that is."

"Well, mine's Kilpatrick, Ben Kilpatrick from down in th' old Lone Star. But I sometimes answer to John Arnold, or even Big Ed."

After I got my hand back, and rubbed some circulation into it on my pants leg, I asked, "How's Cassidy?"

The waitress returned with our order, and placing it on the table, walked off, looking over her shoulder at Kilpatrick.

"She thinks I'm kinda stupid," he drawled, "but I got trouble sometimes to make up my mind."

"And—Cassidy?"

"Oh, he was fine when I seed him a week ago."

In spite of my hunger, I pulled the envelope out of my coat and tore it open as Kilpatrick commenced to wolf down his meal.

As usual, Butch came right to the point: *Kid, on the chance you got itchy feet, I'm sending this billy-doo your way.*

"I'm camping out at the WS Ranch here at Alma, New Mexico. A Mister French is the gent what owns it. We just about run the whole shebang for him. Elza and a big ox from Texas name Kilpatrick has been riding fence, making themselves useful as well as ornamentul for me, as I'm sort of straw-boss foreman.

"That piece of business we'd planned misfired and we're waiting for a better layout, which should be coming around the corner soon. Should you come on down, follow the map I gave you. But for the time being I'd steer kleer of most New Mexico as there's a bunch of wile cats name of Ketchum that have been hitting trains and

banks and driving local law right up the gully.

"Watch the papers and check either at Greenriver there, or at the Basset Ranch at Brown's Hole. You can leave messages the same way. Send them to yours truly, Jim Lowe."

"Say anythin' important?" The man Kilpatrick was sopping up his plate with the last slice of bread on our table.

"Just that you've been doing a good job at the WS," I said, and putting the letter away, dug into my food.

"Take your time," Kilpatrick drawled. "Unless you wanta get outa town today."

"I guess not," I answered around a mouthful of steak.

"Just so. Then if you want, we can bunk down at th' hotel and ride on tomorrow."

"Who said anything about riding on—or bunking at the hotel?"

"Wall, I seed you countin' your wad comin' in th' door and it appeared mighty slim."

"What's that got to do with anything?" This sleepy bear of a man was a bit shrewder than he seemed, but then Cassidy wasn't the kind to ride with complete dim-wits.

"My poke's filled up pretty good right now. Seein' as how you're tight with Butch, I'll stake you to a grub-sack, and split a hotel room fer th' night."

"All right, if you don't snore. I could stand

to lay over . . . seeing I don't know where I'm traveling from here."

"Well now," Kilpatrick slowly turned his big, handsome head, looking over the ranchers and townfolk, "let's us go to th' barber and spruce up some. Then we can make talk over bottle'a beer." He lowered his voice. "Think I might could throw some interestin' work your way."

CHAPTER NINETEEN

After we'd sat it out in the stuffy, fly-crowded Greenriver Tonsorial Parlor, getting sheared and scraped to a fare-thee-well, Ben Kilpatrick paid the Barber, and we went out to fetch our horses, both of us smelling as if we'd been sprayed with sheep dip.

I picked up Nancy Hanks at the General Store, while the Texan unhitched his big buckskin gelding from the rail in front of the eating house.

With our mounts stowed away in the livery barn, behind the General Store, we spent the rest of the afternoon in the shady quiet of the Greenriver Saloon. And it didn't take long to find out Ben Kilpatrick—for all his simple-minded ways, was a man who had a fondness for money—just about anybody's. As soon as we'd taken a table in the saloon he began leading up to a way to get some of that money.

"Y'see, Butch was fixin' to pull couple jobs, includin' one down on th' railway, but he got word th' Arizony Rangers was coverin' the territories." Ben took another swig of his Golden Grain beer, polishing off the bottle in two gulps. "That trouble about them damned Ketchum boys from Texas. They're plumb crazy about bustin' trains . . . and you know Texans when they go bare-headed for a proposition!"

189

"I know a few," I said, as Ab Winters, his rattlesnake relation—Frank Canton . . . and Annie, all came to mind.

"Now I'm from Texas, myself, but I think things out, maybe slow-like, but pretty good." He ordered another couple of beers, and sat back on his rickety chair. "And what I cipher is that Butch is just plumb corralled for th' time bein' at th' WS, where him and Lay is workin' th' honest dodge. They ain't in no shape to handle any bankin' business for some spell."

"What bank business?"

"Down at Clifton, Noo Mexico Territory. Th' bank Butch'd planned to visit, but ain't able, it seems." He stared at his empty bottle. "But we shore can."

"You're saying you want to go and take a crack at one of Cassidy's own jobs?"

" 'Nother couple 'a beers here, you-all." He shifted his six-shooter under his vest as the barkeep came over with the bottles. "Now, I got that ciphered out too. So Butch won't be mindin'."

When we'd bedded down in a room in the Greenriver House that night, I could see why Butch wouldn't mind. The big, slow Texan, with his hazy plans, just didn't have a prayer of pulling off a raise. And I couldn't seem to get nerve enough to tell him all he'd grab from the

Clifton Bank was about a six-foot hole in the New Mexican soil.

"When're you-all turnin' in, Curry?" Kilpatrick, peeled down to his long-johns and socks, raised up in the creaking brass-bound bed, rubbing at his eyes. "It's nigh on to nine o'clock, and we orta be ridin' as soon's we buy us supplies in th' mornin'."

"I'll be there in a minute." And I went on winding up my letter to Annie Winters. It was just a page or so, telling of our trouble at Red Lodge, and the getaway from Deadwood—trying to laugh it off in so many words. I knew she'd be saying to herself that *she'd told me so.* But that was a woman for you . . . and she was certainly one hell of a woman!

Then there was Starr. She was woman a'plenty, too. But I'd not write her any kind of words . . . at least until I had some money for her, money that snoring Texan over on the rumpled bed thought we could walk in to the Clifton Bank and help ourselves to all we could tote off.

I wound up the note to Annie, putting it aside to mail from the Greenriver P.O. in the morning, blew out the smoky oil lamp and piled into bed beside the Texan.

Morning seemed to roll into the hotel room, before I'd really closed my eyes. Not only had Kilpatrick snored like a Lone Star twister, but

191

he'd pitched around like a fresh-branded long-horn.

"Slept mighty good," he announced when we sat down to early breakfast of eggs and wheat cakes.

"Glad one of us did."

"Oh, you-all went and stayed up too late—and that's about why you tossed around so blamed much." He munched away and stared into space for all the world like a contented ox.

Before my Logan dander could get started, I changed the subject. "Just what makes you think you'll be able to crack that Clifton Bank?"

"Not me, myself—y'mean ourselfs, don't you?"

Stalling, I looked out the window and caught a glimpse of the morning sky. Damned if it wasn't about the same shade as Starr's eyes. And the minute she came to mind, again . . . I knew I was going to pitch in and help this big, likeable long-rider.

Polishing off our coffee, I pumped Kilpatrick as to why he'd come away up to Greenriver with Butch's letter instead of staying on the WS and riding fence with the other cowpunchers.

It seemed that he'd got enough of riding the fence and begged off, so Butch had let him loose with the promise to get back as soon as he'd played postman. And now he was ready to head back—but with plans of his own. I cringed a bit to think of Butch's comments if we didn't pull off the raise at Clifton with precision. Well, maybe it could happen, and at least Tom O'Day wouldn't be around—or Lonny.

We were on the southbound trail by ten a.m., with supplies enough for a week—and Annie's letter mailed at the Greenriver Post Office.

"Why'd Butch use that big fat gent at the store for his private postmaster?" I asked to get Kilpatrick talking again. He was showing a habit of dropping off into what some folks called "wool gathering"—a mighty bad habit for a working cowboy.

"Oh, plenty riders along th' owl-hoot trail use Charley Gibbons as a go-between. He had you spotted th' minute you walked in. Charley was a real bad actor in th' old times before he got fat. Rustlin' and th' rest." Ben let his buckskin slow down to an amble as he began "wool gathering" again, probably about his Clifton Bank.

"Well, let's get to doing some hustling on our own . . . that is, if you ever expect to get to your damned Clifton before it dries up and blows away, which is what this whole country looks best at doing." We'd veered away from the river basin, with its fringes of willow and cottonwood, and were riding through some of the most God-awful land I'd ever seen.

"Them runty lookin' peaks over there is th' start of the route into Robbers' Roost country."

Kilpatrick swung an enormous arm toward the south, where three flat-topped mountains loomed low and misty-blue, like chunky clouds on the horizon. We'd already crossed the San Rafael River, a tributary of the Green, catching it when it was low, due to lack of rainfall, and were slogging along over the barren wastelands, heading up the forty-mile, gradual climb to the top of Sam's Mesa.

The least said about those forty miles, the better. I was too hot and tired to talk, and Kilpatrick was able to "wool gather" to his heart's content. It was plain forty miles of riding and walking beside the horses through blow-sand and over rocky ridges with the grinding monotony broken from time to time by the grey-green of the scrubby serviceberry bushes.

At sundown we'd reached the point on Butch's map I'd been aiming at—a place Kilpatrick called The Tanks. Red, orange and dark brown sandstone rock reared up in wild shapes and lay scattered about the gravel-firmed, sandy soil for a quarter of a mile.

We went into camp here, refilling our canteens, and letting the horses drink their limit of the brackish, but clear-colored water that seeped up from underground into a long, shallow pool at the foot of a lofty sandstone cliff. There was bunch grass for the mounts and some corn from the sack Kilpatrick carried slung behind his buckskin.

The following two days were a repeat of the trip across the barren wastes, and by evening we neared the Dirty Devil River crossing, miles to the west of Hanksville, the last town in that part of Utah.

By firing off our pistols we managed to rouse the boat-man, who came following the cable across the wide, sunset-flamed river, like a water-spider reeling in after a tug at his web. That night we slept with the great, saw-toothed ridges of the Henry Mountains etched against the star-filled eastern sky. Kilpatrick, in his own blanket, tossed, turned and snored his head off, but I was too tired to care. One more day would see us in Arizona. And exactly one week after leaving Greenriver, we crossed the line at Lee's Ferry.

Then we rode, as near as we could, on a crow-flight route for two-hundred miles across one giant mesa after another as they swept upward, rising in huge steps across a land so barren that even the slowly drifting cloud shadows were a welcome relief in that huge emptiness.

But at last we pulled into Globe, Arizona Territory . . . one day's ride from Clifton and its bank.

CHAPTER TWENTY

For about a week we laid around Globe, spending most of the day at the Globe Saloon, not doing much drinking, but a lot of listening. As the county seat of Gila County, Globe was mainly a mining town. The talk was generally about ore, mother-lodes, schist and the rest. But what made Kilpatrick's and my ears prick up one day was the mention of the banks. Both Globe and Clifton had considerably good-sized banks. And the money was stored there on the first and fifteenth of each month to pay off the miners.

One main feature that decided us on behaving ourselves in Globe was the fact that it held a hefty population of law officers. In addition to the Sheriff and his Deputies, there was a good sprinkling of Arizona Rangers—the ones that had given Butch second thoughts. They were big, tough appearing men, who looked as though they'd just as soon shoot a man down before breakfast as not.

One of them, Jeff Kidder, a well-set-up, young fellow, with a low-tied-down six-shooter, took a drink with us several times. Though he looked Ben over, he paid myself—*Tom Capehart*—little mind, except to talk cattle . . . because of my story that I was on my way to New Mexico to buy range stock near Silver City, and was just relaxing after my trip down from Montana with *John Arnold,* alias Ben Kilpatrick.

On Wednesday, the fourth day after our arrival in Globe, Kidder dropped into the saloon and bought us a round of beer, Ben and I not taking anything stronger. The Ranger was on his way to help bring down a payroll to Clifton, and would see us in a few days.

"See what a little neighborliness can do?" Ben asked, sticking a thumb in his vest. "Now what do you-all think of me and Butch's surefire Clifton scheme?"

"I'll like it better after I get a look at that bank!"

"It's only three days to th' fifteenth. Whyn't I saddle-up tomorrow and ride over?"

"No, I'll do the riding and the looking." I'd had one bad time with other folks doing *my* looking.

"What if you-all run into that Kidder feller?"

"I'll buy him some beer."

I was gone next morning before Kilpatrick had roused up in our dingy, third floor room at the Silver-Strike Hotel. But I left him a note with instructions to follow the next day, meeting me on the fourteenth, back in the town's main saloon . . . which seemed to be about the best place for an office.

I got into Clifton as the sun was going down. Shadows were running long down the streets, and

I was dead-dog tired and hungry, but I rode on out of town a mile looking for a certain landmark Ben had told me about.

There it was, a long slash in the gravelly, cactus-studded landscape, now filled to the brim with dusky-blue shadow—a deep arroyo, two miles long . . . with no crossings.

When I got back to Clifton at last light and put up at the Clifton House, damned if about the first person I saw wasn't Jeff Kidder! The Ranger sat out on the broad verandah, boots cocked-up on the railing. And hunkered on a chair beside him on a chair sat a tall, thin-faced man, with a five-pointed silver star on his vest.

There were introductions.

"And haw-long you intend stayin', Mister Capehart?"

"Oh, Capehart here's goin' on to Silver City, a' cow buyin', ain't you?" Kidder shifted his low-slung gun.

"Day or so, as soon as my friend joins up."

"He means as soon as that sleepy pardner of his wakes up," Kidder laughed, while the Clifton Sheriff looked down at the gun on my hip. I'd forgotten to take the belt and holster off, and tuck the Colt in my waist-band under my coat.

"Ain't supposed to pack firearms inter town. It's an ordnance. If'n you didn't know Jeff here, I could'a run you in."

"Hell, Tom's all right. He done come down here from Montanny to pay good money for southwest beef . . . and y'know them Ketchums, High Fives, Bronco Jack and th' whole pack of rascals are all out there in th' bresh," drawled Kidder. "Let'm be, he'll unheel himself."

"Sorry. Where I come from, we still pack equalizers on the trail," I said, with a sudden feeling of wariness. What if this damned lantern-jawed Tin Star threw down on me? I didn't think I'd be match for both of them. I held my breath for a long moment. But the Sheriff stood up and stretched, smiling thinly. "Let's see you on th' streets without firearms, next time, or it could cost you ten dollars in fines." He turned to Kidder. "I'm goin' back to th' office." He nodded and left.

"Did you say Bronco Jack?" I was hungry, with my eye on a restaurant down the street, but that name popped out.

"Yep." Kidder arose, facing me. "There's been hell-to-pay for th' past six months, what with one bunch of coyotes after another hittin' banks and trains and runnin' back into th' bresh again." He shifted his gun, looking at me in the pale-yellow light streaming out of the open hotel doorway. "Bronco? You know that there damned vinegarroon?"

"Heard about him, somewhere. A rustler?" Before Kidder could stand me to a drink, I excused myself and went down to the restaurant after checking in at the hotel.

Following breakfast next morning, I got Nancy Hanks from the livery, behind the Clifton House, and rode out to the deep arroyo. The air was still cool and the wintery sun gleamed down, burnishing the desert.

Overhead a red-tailed hawk circled the blue, screaming at the climbing sun.

By the time I'd ridden two miles down the lip of the great wash, three things were set in my mind. One—we couldn't outrun the law, or whatever makeshift posse they threw at us, along the arroyo and get away with it. Two—we didn't have firepower to stand them off. So—three . . . one of us would have to jump that yawning crevasse.

Riding back up the wash, I thought I'd found a section where a good, strong horse, ridden full-out, could take a jump. After sweeping the horizon with my glasses, without seeing a soul, I put them away and tightened my stirrups.

Circling Nancy back about a hundred yards, I turned her around and gave her the steel. We tore straight at the edge, and then she straightened out and with arching muscles . . . sailed over onto the opposite bank, landing on all four feet without a hitch.

The hawk, overhead, screamed once more and bore away to the east, and as I rode down the arroyo to the northern end of the cut, a little covey of brown quail darted ahead of the horse, before melting into the grey scrub.

Back in town, I hitched Nancy in front of the hotel and went down to the bank. My gunbelt and holster were tucked away under my horse's grain sack, on her back. The six-shooter was in my waist-band out of sight.

I cashed a bill at the teller's wicket in the bank, and casually took in the particulars. There were a couple of shotguns leaning against the wall near the vault. A half-open door, leading into the building's rear area, allowed me the sight of at least one drowsing Guard, tipped up against the wall in a chair, Winchester cradled in his lap.

Though the next day was December 15, that was all I could see of any effort to protect a payroll, which had to be in the bank that minute. Three clerks, or tellers, were behind their counter, one sitting at a desk, scratching away at some papers with a pen, while the others were busy inside their cages.

I caught a bit of talk between the Clerk at the desk and one of the others: "like to see them try! A bit of excitement around this darned place would do wonders for my constitution."

I filed away a pale face, gold-rimmed specs, and thinning hair—for future attention.

I sauntered up the alley and looked over the rear of the building. The windows and back door were covered with bars, as was the front. In the glare of the white sunlight, all was flat planes and darker slabs of shadow. The sun, which was now about ten o'clock high, burned down like late September instead of the middle of December.

On the way back to the Clifton House, I looked over the streets. I didn't run into the Sheriff, which eased my mind. I wasn't about to be searched for a weapon this late in the game. I never caught sight of Jeff Kidder either, and wondered what had called him out of town, especially when the mine payrolls rested inside that bank vault.

After dinner I checked out of the hotel and sat back down on the porch, along with several sleepy drummers. About one o'clock I was mighty relieved to see Ben Kilpatrick poking past. I hailed him with some remark about it being a hot day for a ride, and he pulled up and hitched in front of the place.

Kilpatrick mumbled about being on the haul since six a.m., and plopped down into a cane-bottom rocker with the sigh of a bull turned out to pasture. Tugging his chair nearer to me, he muttered, "that damned Kidder and a couple other Rangers come out from behind some rocks back there five miles outside town and threw down on me. And then he laughed about it, and we both went on our ways."

"What?" I stiffened in my seat.

"Yeah. You must'a not heered about it, but they was called out because some damned fool tried holdin' up a mine office south of here. But you and me—" he lowered his voice even more—"we know where th' real sponduliks is at!" He batted the dust off his Stetson. "We sure do, don't we?"

I looked down the hotel porch. The guests snored on. A Mexican hotel hand leaned on a broom. "You're right. We do. And now's the time to go get it." I went over the bank set-up, as I saw it, and spelled out our route of retreat at the arroyo. Kilpatrick agreed, rubbing his hands like a kid hearing of an unlocked candy store.

We got busy. I rode slowly on out of town to the east—Ben following in ten minutes.

By two-fifteen, Kilpatrick was riding along the Arroyo to get into the far side, while I was already on my way back to town. He'd offered to give me a hand at the Bank, but I had pointed out that both he and his big buckskin were too hefty to make the leap with safety. He'd stay on the far side to give me cover.

As I trotted up the sandy street of Clifton, I looked for Rangers, but saw few folks at all—as the Mexican says it was "*La Siesta*."

I'd taken off my coat, tied it behind the saddle in place of the empty grain sack, and was wearing my gunbelt and holster when I reined in behind the Bank in the alley.

A big Seth-Thomas clock, on the dingy, yellow

wall, stood at quarter-to-three. Just fifteen minutes to take care of my business. In the drowsy afternoon that clock's tick-tick-tick was about the loudest sound in that place. The door leading into the back room was shut tight, with only two clerks in sight. A beefy, red-faced man, with hair parted in the middle and a big, ox-horn mustache, was waiting on a customer who looked like a mining man. The other clerk was the pasty-faced, bespectacled fellow who'd been honing for excitement. Both gave me a casual look as I came in and went on with their paper work.

The bank official at the desk had a change of color to match his pale-faced friend, while the customer stared with bulging eyes as they all got a look at the Colt in my hand.

"Everybody hit the floor!" I spoke up harsh and mean-like, with my eyes on that closed back door. "Forget about your gold dust and get down into some plain dust," I told the mining man. Clerk and customer flopped face-down. I ran a hand over them, but found no weapons.

"And you over there," I raised my voice a might, still watching that back door, "looks to me like you need some excitement—so get over here!"

The Clerk, paler than ever, joined the pair on the floor, while I stepped around and picked up the two shotguns in the corner. I broke the scatter-guns and tossed the shells into a waste basket. Then I thought of the front door, a little too late. As I turned to flip the lock, in walked the Clifton Sheriff.

The lawman's jaw dropped longer than ever as he got a good look at the cocked six-shooter in my hand, but he made no move at his own pistol.

"A friendly face, at last. Get around here and take an Arizona siesta with the boys." I plucked the officer's Frontier .45 out of its holster and stuck it into my belt. "Hold on there!"

The Sheriff halted, with his hands shoulder-high, scowling like thunder-spoiled milk.

"Almost forgot. Think I owe you something." And I pulled out my last ten-dollar bill and stuffed it into his vest pocket. "Like you said, there's a ten-dollar fine for packing firearms on the street!" I waved him down with the others. "And you, get back up." I nudged the bespec-tacled clerk with my toe. "Where's the keys to this place?" I should have felt mean to be bulldozing these folks, but I thought of Banker Peck back home and how when his money couldn't buy our ranch, he'd backed that damned Ab Winters play—and Johnny had died. Bankers all seemed to have gold for blood, and by damn I meant to have some now for myself—and Starr.

"Where's those keys?" I gave him another boot and he scrabbled up and fished into a cash drawer, while I watched him closely.

"Here," handing over a batch of keys, while the

Banker with the ox-horn mustache growled under his breath. "Th—the brass one's to the vault. The big black one's to the front and back doors."

"All right, get back down! Looks like you got enough excitement for one day." I locked the front door, which was reinforced strongly with vertical rods every half a foot like the windows. "I'm going to be busy making a withdrawal so don't wiggle around too much, or you'll bite some of that dust," I told the bunch on the floor.

Hustling back around the counter, I rapped on that closed door to the back room. With another siesta spoiled, a sleepy voice answered, "Whaat?"

"There's a little problem out here," I shouted.

"Who's that?" The door cracked open and a boozy-red face poked out along with a rifle barrel.

I gave him a good wallop alongside the head with my pistol barrel, catching his Winchester before it hit the floor. The guard who rolled out through the door, sat up rubbing a thatch of tangled hair. He wasn't a Ranger. He looked and sounded like a plain barroom loafer to me as he sat on the floor cursing a blue streak.

So the Rangers still weren't around, but I didn't know how long it would be before they lit back in the middle of things. All I wanted was to be long gone before that happened!

Glancing into the empty back room, I saw a roll-top desk, several chairs and the usual office bric-a-brac, but no more guards.

"Stay on the floor, tin-horn!" I poked my six-shooter into the guard's big ear. He gentled-down, joining the others in their enforced siesta.

Yanking the grain sack out from under my coat, I went through the cash drawers, grabbing all bills in sight, and then backed over to the steel vault, tried the key and stepped into the inside of the chamber.

The shelves were stacked with gold piece, like piles of shining yellow poker chips, all twenty-dollar double-eagles. The sight of all that gold made my throat tighten and my face burn—as if I stood over a bonfire. But after I hoisted a handful, I knew that even a thousand-dollar stack would stop me from clearing that twenty-foot-deep wash. It was a weight that could kill dead!

I stuffed a double fistful of eagles into my coat pockets, and began to fill the grain sack with paper money, all in Tens and Twenties from the bundles on the shelves above the gold coins. By the time I had what I figured was ten thousand, I was down to a basket of Fives and Ones.

There was no sound out front, but the jingle of the Sheriff's and the customer's spurs as they shifted their boots, and the guard's non-stop curses along with the tellers' whispers. And that damned clock was getting louder and louder until I began to be leery that it might cover the sound of anyone trying to get into the bank. All at once it began to strike three.

"To hell with it!" I came back out with my grain sack, leaping over the people on the floor and ran straight for the back. Outside, I locked the door behind me, heaving the keys and the spare Winchester onto the roof.

Untying Nancy Hanks from a corner of the building, I could hear the devil of a racket beginning inside the Bank. Windows were being smashed and the Clifton Sheriff commenced to bellow through the window, glaring out the bars like a regular jailbird.

I strapped the bag of money behind the saddle, mounted up and rode past the Bank, tipping my hat to the Sheriff, and left town on the lope. My Logan blood was up, and I felt just like singing— if I could have remembered the words to any sort of a song.

Looking around, I could see several people saunter out of a nearby store and stare at the Bank and the noise coming from it, but nobody raised a hand or a gun to stop me. It was surely mighty different from Belle Fourche!

By the time I neared the lip of the crevasse, things had changed considerably. I heard a gun crack out, and taking another look saw a bunch of horsemen racking along through the green spears of the forest of saguaro and organ pipe cactus, about half a mile behind. How they'd got saddled and organized so fast, I couldn't tell.

Another gun cracked and then another. But the

sound came from in front of me. And there across the Arroyo, on a rise of ground, two riflemen stood beside their horses, firing over my head at the oncoming riders. One was Ben Kilpatrick. The other was a stranger.

I pulled up and waved my Stetson at them to hold their fire—then with the Posse a mighty scant quarter mile away, and coming hell-for-breakfast—I spurred Nancy straight at the Arroyo's yawning brink.

CHAPTER TWENTY-ONE

A spine-jolting thud—and Nancy landed on all four feet!

We were across the Arroyo, while the Posse pulled up short on the brink in a cloud of sand and dust.

"Look out, Kid—them's Rangers fixin' to fire!" Ben Kilpatrick ran up, smoking saddle-gun in hand . . . as I sat on Nancy Hanks, patting her, and staring at—Bronco Jack Caldwell!

About three rifles cut loose from the far bank, and I piled off in a hurry. "Get those horses around this sand-hill, and stop shooting. That looks like Jeff Kidder, and he's mad enough now!" I tugged Nancy Hanks by the bridle, Ben and Bronco following suit.

We hunkered down, staring at each other behind the slight hill, while rifle slugs kicked sand, gravel and bits of shrubs over us. "Where in hell did you come from," I asked Bronco, while I batted sand off my Stetson.

"Made me a try at a mine office over other side of Clifton this mornin' without much luck," Bronco gave me a hang-dog grin. He was turned out in better shape than back at the Hole. His checked pants were tucked into mighty fancy, calfskin "Cattle-King" boots, sporting scalloped tops. But he was still Bronco Jack, with a couple of buckshot holes in the crown of his dove-grey Stetson, and a red splotch on the sleeve of his double-buttoned, wine-colored navy shirt. A patch of blood trickled from his forehead, and his hair was wild as ever, though he'd shaved down to a decent enough mustache. He reminded me of someone.

"Said he knew you," Kilpatrick grinned, and standing up, stooping-shouldered to stay out of the line of fire, ran a hand over the half-filled grain sack. "This it?"

"Yes. Near ten thousand, I reckon."

"Ten thousand!" Bronco's dark eyes narrowed, then opened wide as he stared at the money-sack. "Ten thousand, and I didn't get ten cents."

"Tough luck old sock," Kilpatrick laughed, ducking as a rifle slug screamed just over his head. "Kid here, and me are obliged to you for gittin' them damned Rangers out'a town—for a while."

I edged around the base of the sandy mound and squinted across the wash. Two Rangers stood behind their horses, Indian-fashion, with rifles leveled dead at us over their saddles. The remaining three were lashing their mounts along the Arroyo, two riding north and the other south—to cut us off.

"Mount up. Hit east!" I yelled, swinging up on Nancy. "We've only got twenty minutes on Kidder, and that's not much!"

Bronco ran up on the little hill, and in spite of the rifle fire from across the crevasse, poured a hail of shots at the north-bound riders. "Th' son-of-a-bitch on that black horse emptied a double-barrel scatter-gun at me when I was high-tailin' it from that mine office. Didn't fetch me, but he sure rooned my new hat!"

While the guns across the Arroyo cracked out, Kilpatrick and I spurred our horses off, bent low in the saddles, while Bronco hustled to his bay and followed us down through the saguaro thickets.

We were headed toward the blue-green ridges of the Peloncillo Mountains, with the Arizona–New Mexico Border just twenty miles to the east.

We rode hard as we dared push the horses in the afternoon heat, stopping every ten minutes to blow them and look back. About five-thirty we'd crossed the line, marked by a hulking rim of mountains to the north. Ben held up his hand, and we dismounted. "Them's th' Bullard Peaks. Th' Noo Mexico Border, and them damned Rangers might as well go trailin' back, if they ever get here."

Ben was right, there'd been no sign of pursuit since we'd left the Arroyo, and it didn't look as if there would be now.

"These horses need water," I said, rubbing my hand over Nancy Hanks' quivering flanks.

"Well, right around here there's gotta be a seep,

accordin' to Butch's say-so," said Kilpatrick looking about at the scattered boulders and rolling hills.

While Ben and Bronco poked around for water among the boulders and outcroppings, I led Nancy Hanks down the trail between the upthrust foothills and climbing onto a great, brick-red slab of rock, scanned the country with my glasses.

The westering sun stretched long shadows from the boulders and tumbled rocks across the gently rolling desert country. The only movement was that of several road-runners darting in and out of the scattered salt bush and catclaw. All else was still, and lonesome. There was not a sign of Rangers or Posse, nor any tell-tale drifts of dust from faraway riders.

"Knew them damned fools couldn't get within hailin' distance wunst we put th' steel to our horses," crowed Bronco as he slowly watered our mounts in the seep he and Kilpatrick had found up a draw.

"They didn't have to," I said. "All Kidder had to do was trot back into Clifton and telegraph every damned town along the border to keep an eye cocked for three riders on broken-down horses. And that's going to be us unless we hole up for a spell to rest them."

"Then I figure th' best place fer us to head for is th' WS," Ben Kilpatrick drawled as he sat, leaning against a boulder, hat tipped over his eyes.

"That so? And Butch will welcome us with open arms when he finds just what we did to his pet bank," I said, loosening the saddle girth on Nancy Hanks, but tightening the rawhide thongs on the grain sack.

"How far are we from the WS spread?" Bronco glanced over at me as he squatted by the seep, peeling off his shirt to doctor his wound.

"About thirty miles, but she's rough country all th' way up there," Kilpatrick mumbled from under his hat. "So if Kid here wants to give th' plugs a breather, we'd best camp for th' night."

Bronco, cursing a blue-streak, as usual, twisted and tied a bandana around his arm and got up. "Big man's right. It's comin' on fer dark soon . . . and if we shook them Rangers, why not camp right here? We got water and I got some grub in my saddle bags, which I'll split."

"All right. I don't think they're coming, and this is pretty well sheltered." I looked at the looming walls that surrounded us. The sun had sank far into the west, and the shadows had spread.

"Here you be." Bronco rummaged in his saddle bags and came up with a small, iron skillet and some fat-back wrapped in waxed paper. "I plan ahead. Gotta travel light sometimes." He gave us a lop-sided smile, reminding me of nothing so much as a fawning cur-dog showing its teeth. For a lot of reasons, I couldn't warm up to him . . . and probably showed it.

214

"All right. Ben, you hustle the water. You've got our coffee pot in the grub sack, and we'll sample Bronco's hospitality—if I don't get us any game." I staked Nancy Hanks near a small patch of gamma grass and taking my Winchester, walked back down the rocky trail toward the big, red boulder. "Rustle that grub, I'm going back to take one last look-see before dark."

"When're we gonna split up that bag of sponduliks?" Bronco called after me. I could hear him laugh, a sharp yap-yapping like a coyote.

"Don't be a damned fool," I yelled over my shoulder. "That money's going to better places than your pockets." I looked back when I went around a bend in the rocky-faced hill. Ben was putting together a small fire, while Bronco Jack Caldwell, frying pan in hand, stood watching him.

In fifteen minutes, I was standing on the rock, sweeping the horizons with my glasses. The shadows seemed to well-up from the rolling desert floor, spreading in purple pools of darkness as I watched. Over on the western skyline, the sun was going out in a mass of fading orange and tawny lemon streaks.

The first quavers of the coyote serenade began as the last gleams of sunlight turned the acres of cactus into hundreds of golden fingers reaching up from the smoky haze of the desert floor.

Watching the saguaro vaulting their golden spears at the diamond-like stars that were commencing to blaze out in the darkening sky, I thought of the money in the grain sack, and what the money . . . no matter how it was come by . . . could do for old Frank Jackson's daughter.

The way that money came to be strapped up behind my saddle just wasn't right and nobody knew it better than I did. None of us Logans had been raised up to such things by our old Aunt Lee in Missouri. She'd never understand such things—and neither for that matter would Starr, or Annie. But the one that was going to get the most of the money was the one I wouldn't tell, and the other . . . well, Annie would settle for a small stake to get us out of the country, I was certain.

Yes, I'd split that ten-thousand right down the middle with Ben Kilpatrick. Four thousand, at least, would go to Starr in the name of her dead father. So what did it matter where the money came from, if it could work its good? And, besides, there was plenty more back in the ground for those miners—all they had to do was dig a little harder.

I took a last look around in the twilight. All was calm. There was hardly a chance that we'd get jumped as we had at Red Lodge. As I'd told Bronco, Kidder had probably wired the little towns along the Arizona–New Mexico Border

. . . and loped back to Clifton, expecting some lawman would be waiting for us when we hit a town.

I walked up the trail thinking of where Annie and I might go. We could head for the Pacific Northwest. There was a country you could lose yourself in. Timber, cattle, or whatever, I'd take a fling at it. No matter what I did, I'd be a long way off the Owl-Hoot Trail, and be making a new life for the two of us. Though I had to admit to myself—that it had been a hell of a lot of fun. But it was a fun that could turn deadly as lead commenced to fly.

When I got near to our camp, it looked as though the fire hadn't been started yet, but as I turned a bend, I saw it burning brightly, throwing red and yellow tatters of light against the surrounding cliffs. Everything seemed right. The horses were bunched together—and yet it still didn't look natural.

There were only two horses! And damned if Ben Kilpatrick wasn't curled up at the fire, napping. I started on the run, yelling, "Ben!" But he didn't answer.

Then I knew! The grain sack was gone, and so was Bronco and his horse. "Ben!" I gave Kilpatrick a good boot with my toe. "Get up! You've gone to sleep and that damned Bronco Jack Caldwell's run off with our money!"

"What?" Ben groaned and raised up slowly,

rubbing his head. "What'd he hit me with?"

"Hit you?" I looked closely at him in the firelight and saw a good-sized lump on the side of his head.

"Don't know. Last thing I was sittin' and listenin' to Bronco gab about his troubles. How everybody back at the Hole in th' Wall did him dirt. And I was gettin' ready to pour us some Arbuckle, when he musta' walloped me with that little iron skillet of his'n." And there it was—the little frying pan that Caldwell was going to cook up the fat-back, lying in the ashes of the fire.

"Here's a hell of a note! Bronco's gone and all he left was his skillet and a knot on your head."

"Hell!" Ben staggered up, rubbing his head. "What'll we do?"

"Nothing tonight. Too dark now. And he's probably long gone. We couldn't trail him on this rocky shale. But tomorrow we'll cut his trail, though I doubt we'll fetch him."

"If we don't, then what?"

"I guess we make a stop at the WS."

We were in the saddle next morning as the sun was painting the eastern sky with red streaks. I didn't want any posse sitting up on the cliffs, riddling us in our blankets—the way they'd dry-gulched a rustler named Joe Walker back in Utah.

"Where'd you think that polecat of a Caldwell is by now?" Kilpatrick wanted to know as we rode over the grassy mesa, with the Mogollons rimming the southeast skyline with a solid wall of brutal-looking, snow-clad peaks. After three hours of riding we were now out of the desert, but had given up on finding any sort of trail.

"He'd better be in Hell—because that's where I'm going to send him if I ever do!" I grated. "It'll save him a trip!"

Seeing my temper flare up, Kilpatrick changed the subject. "Oncet we git beyond th' San Francisco River, she's named for thet big town in Californy, and th' bends of her ought be in sight beyond them hills—then we'll be about a hour's ride from th' WS Ranch."

In the early afternoon we crossed the muddy streak of the San Francisco, and riding across continually better grazing land, at last came to a three-strand wire fence, marking the southern end of the WS range.

"Here, let me handle this bob-wire. I've cut me a heap back home, which is one reason them Texas Ranger boys wanted me to stay with 'em at Huntsville Pen." Ben swung down from his buckskin, with a pair of wire-cutters in his hand.

Before he could do more than snip the top strand, a horseman rode out of a hollow to our right and loped up, saddle-gun at the ready.

"Ben, if I was you, I'd wait and see what this fellow's got on his mind," I said, loosening my six-gun in its holster.

"Howdy, Ben." The man, a pleasant-faced young fellow in a checkered shirt, stained ten-gallon hat, Levi's outside scuffed boots, with jangling rowels, and forking a pretty little chestnut, lowered his Marlin carbine.

"Well, Elza, howdy yourself." Ben put away his clippers and got back into the saddle. "I done forgot th' way to th' main south gate."

"Looks like you forgot more'n gates." The man, called Elza, stuffed the carbine back into its boot. "Come on, ride up this way to th' Texas gate— and let's git you galoots into th' ranch before th' hull world knows you're here."

We galloped after him, skirting the three-strand fence, with its sturdy cedar posts, holding the wire tight and ship-shape every thirty feet.

"Spent a hell of a lot of time puttin' this blamed fence up a couple months back, with Butch bossin' every move," Ben yelled. "We must'a replaced twenty good miles of it down here."

"And you'd cut the damned thing just like that?"

"Oh," Ben grinned at me as we racked down a slope, coming up to the Texas gate, "sometimes I just get absent-minded about things."

"Yes," I answered as we pulled up, "especially when you're dishing up coffee to a poison-pup like Bronco."

The man called Elza got down and unlatched the long pole, swinging the makeshift gate open until we'd passed through. He closed it, remounted and we headed north over some miles of good pasture land, past several windmills, with big iron tanks, and at last crested a long juniper-studded hill, and rode down into a pleasant bowl-shaped valley holding a group of ranch buildings and corrals, all in first-class shape.

"This WS is sure a tidy-looking spread," I said as we dismounted and turned our horses over to a fat Mexican stable boy.

"Been that way since Butch's been comin' down here," Elza said, looking me over good.

"Butch around?" Ben asked, hitching his gunbelt and gawking toward the red and green bunkhouse.

"Needn't get spooked," Elza motioned toward the main house, a big, two-story, white building, with a gallery running across its front and back. "Mister French, th' owner, is one straight gent. He don't ask no questions, long as we cut th' mustard and do a day's work." He gave a wag of his head. "And you'd be lucky if'n you don't run into Butch until he cools down. He rode into Alma to fetch back supplies, and hit a couple of saloons, it bein' Saturday."

"Butch on the prod?" I asked, while Ben looked away and shuffled his boots.

"C'mon over. Let's us eat," Elza jerked a thumb at a long, adobe building on the corral side of the bunkhouse. "Crew's t'supper. And to answer your question, Butch ain't much happy over Ben and you beatin' him in th' bank business."

We found out how downright unhappy Cassidy was when he burst into the bunkhouse late that night, half tight yet quietly furious. The dozen-odd hands, settled down for the night, never roused up as he yanked the blankets off Ben and me in our separate bunks and lit into us like a sore-tail grizzly.

"But Butch," Kilpatrick shoved the hair out of his eyes, squinting at Cassidy in the lantern light, "we thought you'd be all roped in down here at th' WS and in no shape to tackle any banks."

"I don't know where you ran into this churn-twistin' candidate for th' hoosegow," Butch ignored Ben. "I guess you must'a got together when I let him out'a my sight long enough to peddle some letters. And that wasn't just any bank—*it was my bank!*" He slammed his fist into his palm. "But I do know one thing for damned sure. Both of you had better be long-gone before sundown tomorrow!"

"There's trouble if we stay?" I asked.

"Trouble for you two, and for Elza Lay there, and for me too, dammit!" Butch grated, while Lay held a smoking kerosene lantern and looked quizzically at us without speaking.

"Law right close?" Ben sat up on the edge of his bunk.

"They ain't close—yet!" Butch motioned at Elza and they went back up the aisle, weaving slightly. "Thought you had more horse-sense, Kid." He stopped at the door. "They grabbed a pardner of yours named Caldwell at a variety saloon in Silver City with a sackful of money. He sure sang loud and strong. And our local law could get somewhat nosey about new riders out at th' WS—so you've got to hit th' pike before Mister French gets involved . . . along with Elza and me. This is too good a hangout to blow apart. We'll figure out what to do in th' mornin'."

"So that damned Bronco Jack wasn't so blamed smart after all, and you might know he'd peach on us, th' varmint!" Ben piled back into his bunk, groaning to himself. "I can allus let myself in th' backway down at th' family ranch in Concho County, and stay out'a sight, I guess."

I settled down, replacing the pistol I'd held beneath the blanket back under my pillow. "You hit for the brush country and I'm going on north. This country just don't seem too hospitable."

The slip of paper Annie had given me when we left Elkhorn Tavern was still in my pocket—and it gave an address at Colorado Springs. A telegram there could fetch her to Denver, if she'd come. I rolled over and forgot all about that vinegarroon of a Jack Caldwell, and an icy-eyed Cassidy.

There wasn't any money for Starr, after all, but there was Annie and I . . . and in just a week or so . . . and then, we'd go—where?

CHAPTER TWENTY-TWO

I was ready to get off the train, at least an hour before it pulled into Colorado Springs.

Butch had trailed north to Albuquerque with me in order to fetch my Nancy Hanks horse back to the WS, leaving me free to travel like a solid citizen on the cars . . . just my .44 in my alligator traveling bag. We'd camped out in the local hotel and next morning bought me some duds, sent Annie a telegram at Colorado Springs, and got my ticket.

He'd not mentioned Ben and my raid on that Arizona bank, after his first blow-up at the WS. But that was Butch, no rehashing things after he'd made his point.

Seeing Cassidy was ready to talk about most anything, I brought out Frank Jackson's map of Star Valley while we sat in the Albuquerque Station waiting for the up-train.

Butch pointed out landmarks, and gave me a compass heading from *the springs,* which was Rock Springs. "If you get into that place, you might as well be in Chiney," he'd said. "That don't mean one or two of th' Owl-Hoot Society don't know how to get there. But Matt Warner and Blacky Jackson was th' first and last long-riders to spend any sort of time there . . . and they done got themselves snowed-in for th' whole winter, back in th' early Nineties. So, besides visits from Morman Elders of th' Church they wasn't a new face around for nearly a year. Plumb desolate, they said."

Before I'd got aboard, Butch had told me there would be no raids upon the railroads for some time. He looked for big trouble to come from the Cuba hullabaloo. "If they start up a shootin' war, this whole country'll be crawlin' with soldier boys—and they pack a hell of a lot of fire-power. So we'll lay low with our Syndicate for a while and see. But I'll get in touch with you when the time's right."

I hadn't said yes or no. It wouldn't do to let Butch think I was going off with Annie and leave him flat when he needed me.

Though I'd spent a day and a night on the cars, and had plenty of time to think what I'd say to Annie when I saw her, I was just about tongue-tied when I'd swung down onto the station platform amongst a crowd of travelers and drummers.

I saw her almost at once coming toward me through the first light snow of the season—just about the nobbiest looking young woman on the station platform. In her stylish blue suit and broadcloth cape, and perky little hat with its red ribbon rosettes across its black brim, she sure was mighty different from the down-at-the-heels slavey at the Elkhorn Tavern.

We were both pretty formal, shaking hands and making small talk as we hailed a hack to take us over to the Windsor Hotel.

Once inside the big, red-brick hotel on Blake Street, sitting in the dining room over a lunch of mountain trout and mighty good coffee, Annie leaned back in her chair and looked me over.

And I couldn't help looking at her. Her dark hair was piled up on her head and the little, plain gold necklace at her throat seemed to just set off the blue velvet dress. "My," I said, polishing off my third cup of coffee, "if you ain't a picture, then I never saw one. Guess in the books, they'd have to call you—ah . . ."

"A grand lady, I hope," she laughed outright for the first time, and she was the Annie I'd been dreaming about for months on end.

I put down my cup, but before I could take her hand in mine, she drew it back. "This isn't the spot to sit around too long. There'll be time for hand-holding, *and the rest.*" Her face suddenly colored up.

"I'm not planning on taking any health cure here at the Springs. I figure we should be moving on."

"I wonder where?" She leaned closer, and her breath was sweet as twinberry blossoms on my cheek. "From what I've managed to pick up from all the folks around the variety houses—gamblers, high-rollers, tin-horns and even lawmen—the word is out that your friend Cassidy has got his sights set on the railroads." She squeezed my hand tightly, her eyes wide with interest. "The Pinkertons have been in and out of the Springs, so Cassidy must be up to something pretty big out this way."

"Well, when Butch does something it generally turns out pretty big," I said, wondering if I should tell her about that bank in Arizona, and seeing that Bronco had taken me in for a sucker, decided to change the whole subject. "But I don't think they need hang around waiting for Butch to oblige them. He's gone under cover the same as us. Can you get away from here right soon?"

"Yes. After I got your wire, I quit at the Casino in the Springs, and my grip is packed and upstairs in my room."

I paid for the meal, while Annie went and checked out. We didn't wait to buy any extra traveling duds. The clothes I bought in Albuquerque were good enough. A rough-and-ready, round cut, brown sack-suit, had set me back ten dollars. Along with a wide-brim, black wool Planter hat, and my own boots, worn under my pantaloons, I had the look—I hoped—of a cattleman, or a miner, and not some travel-worn long-rider.

An up-train was due at the Colorado Springs Station at three p.m. And just an hour-and-a-half after landing on the Denver and Rio Grande platform, I was on my way north, again . . . this time with Annie.

She rode in one car and I in another of the four coach Denver and Pacific train. It had been her idea to keep apart until we were well out of Colorado. I saw her at a distance at supper time in the dining car, but we stayed clear of each other in our own coaches until the big Baldwin eight-wheeler pulled out of Laramie, Wyoming in the morning after breakfast.

"This seat taken, Miss?" I'd come through into her coach from my end of the train and settled down beside her with a copy of the Rocky Mountain News. Without another word, in case anyone was watching, I opened the pages and began to read—but all the time I could feel the warmth and curve of her body close to mine.

"There's a lot of seats taken in this particular car." Annie tipped her head slightly, and I spotted a man, three seats up who seemed mighty interested in what was going on behind himself. He was peering at the train window beside him and every so often getting up, seemingly to rearrange his grip on the overhead rack—but, all the while, sneaking looks back down our way.

"Frank Canton!" I said.

"So that's his name? I've seen him around the Casino at the Springs, generally with some tin-horn or other."

"Yes, that's his name, and besides being a law-

229

man, he's a mighty near relation of yours . . . that is if you still claim kinship to that gander-eyed husband of yours."

"I'd not mentioned Mister Winters, because you hadn't," she bristled, "but since you bring it up—I'm never going back to his place. He got me by false promises . . . and if any man ever plays false with me—it's the end." Her eyes flashed and she turned to stare out at the passing country, then turned back to me. "You say he's a lawman?"

While I kept my eye on Canton, who'd seemed to have settled back down, I told her about our run-in with Canton and his posse, and the events that followed, making it as funny as I could— particularly our break-out of the Deadwood Jail. I did a pretty good job of it, for at last she relaxed and leaned back on the scuffed yellow plush seat, smiling at my joshing.

I thought Annie might try to read me a lecture about my escapades, and get me to promise to stay away from harum-scarums like Butch, Sundance and the rest—but she only watched the sun glinting on the patches of new-fallen snow as the prairie rushed away past the car windows . . . and smiled to herself.

We'd rattled over a long, winding river and were curving toward the sunset while a range of mountains rose in blue waves across the skyline. "That's the Medicine Bow Range," I told her. "And we've crossed the Platte, so we'll be getting into Orrin Junction in about an hour—and that's where we leave this rattler."

"But our tickets are good to Casper?"

"And that's just about where Frank Canton will try to get the drop on us. I think he's learned not to try tackling me, unless he's got himself some help." I kept an eye on the old sidewinder, who looked for all the world like a drummer in a checkered suit and bow tie. His wide brimmed hat was stuffed on the overhead rack along with his small grip. There was no gun in sight, but I knew he had a six-shooter on his person. He'd settled back and seemed to be dozing like many others in the coach, but I knew he was waiting patiently, like an old panther, for the right time to move. How he'd got next to us at Colorado Springs was beyond me—but someone must have been watching Annie, while she was watching everyone else.

Annie didn't seem to want to talk, and as I took her hand and held it, it didn't seem like words were necessary.

The car was filled with silence, broken from time to time by the snores of a bald-headed rancher across the aisle, and the rumble of the coach wheels spinning over the rails—that and the tap-tapping of a sudden snow storm we were running through. The engine whistled once, and then again, and I could feel the train begin to slow down, though the swirling storm outside blanketed all sight of what must be Orrin Junction.

"Get your grip and get off the other end of the car," I whispered. "I'm going on up to my car and get my stuff. If we work it fast, he'll fall for it—Canton's not the smartest one in the world . . . runs in the family." I winked and getting up, sauntered down the aisle slowly, but when I turned to wave to Annie, she was already gone.

"Should be in Casper before eight," I told her empty seat, ignoring Canton, and went out into the next coach.

The storm, blustering around Orrin Junction, was blotting out the sun and even any sight of the train as it pulled out, bound for Casper . . . with Frank Canton and the rest.

It was nearly dark when we rode down the single street of the Junction, headed for—Star Valley, halfway across the Territory. We'd spent the past hour buying three horses, and stocking up on supplies. Those Clifton gold double-eagles, the only money Bronco didn't get from me, were coming in mighty handy now.

I'd told Annie about the Valley back in Colorado Springs and while we were eating an early supper at the Orrin Junction Restaurant, we'd gone over the map Butch Cassidy had unraveled for me.

We bedded down that night in a sheltered

canyon about ten miles out, wrapped up snug as could be under our blankets and a piece of canvas tarp I'd bought. I was back into my range clothes now and Annie was togged out in a split riding-skirt, wool shirt, mackinaw and a pair of neat little red boots—plus some ladies-sized long-johns. She looked so downright fetching, I tacked her with a handle—"Cattle Annie."

Each day we traveled along at a good pace, but not hard enough to wear down my saddle pardner, who was ready for bed each night in our one bedroll. I don't think we really knew when it was raining or when it snowed,—though the weather stayed unusually fine for mid-winter.

According to Annie's pocket calendar it was January third, 1898 when we sighted the wooded humps of the Snake Mountains to the northwest of Rock Springs. Another day's ride, now following the map closely, brought us through jagged walls of rock, paralleling the brawling and still unfrozen Snake River. By late afternoon we'd made our way through the pass, and with the Snake to our right, come down into the quiet depths of Star Valley.

The valley, running about five miles across, was rimmed by great rugged peaks and ridges stretching northward for nearly fifty miles. It was a vast and completely isolated hideaway from the rest of the world and even from the Territory of Wyoming.

Riding down into the broad brown meadows with our pack-horse tagging behind, we'd passed several cabins, where curious eyes watched from behind doors and out of small windows, and just before dusk came to a scattered cluster of about twenty houses, ten miles from the valley entrance.

We stiffly dismounted to stand looking up and down the lonely street, lighted by the last of a cold sun, sinking behind the blue walls of the distant mountains.

"Welcome to nowhere," I grinned at Annie as a brisk wind puffed whorls of dust around our boots.

"Strangers, mighty welcome to Afton." A big man with a friendly face came walking toward us along with several other men, all calm and easy looking. "You surely are mighty lucky."

"I'd say so." Annie smiled at the men. "Might there be any sort of a hotel in this—ah—town?"

"Don't find many folks passing through our Valley, Missus," another man spoke up. "Come to think on it, you'll probably be th' last until next spring." He motioned southward where the valley was blotted out in a sudden swirl of snow that came rolling toward us. "She's held off for weeks on end, but that there snow'll block th' passes tight." He laughed deep into his long beard.

"Guess you will need to put up somewheres. We've no hotel, but I got a prime, empty cabin."

Before full dark, with our three horses bedded down in a nearby barn, we were settled into a neat, clean three-room cabin at the south end of the little village—and there we were to stay for over four mighty pleasant months.

CHAPTER TWENTY-THREE

Star Valley was the most peaceful place one could imagine. And Annie was there with me.

The valley was a good three times as big as Hole in the Wall, and many cuts over any other spot I'd heard of. Robbers' Roost, to all accounts, was a regular sandy, dry hell stuck out in the middle of nowhere, and even Brown's Hole was a cramped up place next to Star Valley.

But the best thing I found about it was the easy-going pace of the life there. The folks seemed to have enough to keep them going, without much worry about anything except some fresh meat from time to time. And that's where I seemed to fill the bill.

One of their best shots had been scooped up by the law on a trip to Salt Lake City—too many wives—and wasn't expected back in the valley before his jail term was over.

After one look at my weapons, and a little talk with the Mormon "Fathers," including Mister Preston, my landlord, I'd taken on the job of providing meat during the winter months.

As far as any of that tight little community of Mormon folks knew we were just a rancher and his wife who'd been caught off guard by the snows and bottled up in the valley 'til spring.

Having their own ideas of personal freedom and being pretty much at odds with the Territory, I don't think Preston and the rest gave much thought to what had fetched us so far off the beaten trails—nor cared much, one way or the other, it seemed.

Most of that winter I spent in hunting, when I wasn't doing odd jobs around our cabin, such as fitting up the doors and windows and building shelves for Annie. Old man Smith, who lived down the road near the one general store, had a fine set of tools, and I used them to a good advantage.

About the only time that Annie ever spoke of what had fetched us into Star Valley came one day after I'd put together a neat, little bin in the kitchen to hold kindling for the small, iron cook stove.

"I just don't know why you couldn't go East and make good wages as a carpenter or mechanic. You're just about the handiest man with a hammer and saw I ever knew. Yet—when we leave, whenever that comes, you'll ride away from all this."

"We'll see," I answered, taking down the Winchester and a box of shells, getting set to jaunt out toward the eastern foothills of the valley.

"You'll see? You are still thinking of scouting around with that brazen Sundance and grinning Cassidy . . . and winding up in jail for life—or something worse!" She flounced off to the small bedroom. But I didn't follow right away. I knew better.

"Thought you liked it here—being together," I called after her.

"I love it, and you know how much. *But I know you!*" Her voice came low and muffled through the closed door. "It won't last."

Right then I made up my mind to open the door.

The weather broke early that year, with a lot of runoff from the mountains. The creeks and the river fairly boomed for a while. By the first of February the pass to the south was open and commencing to dry along the little rutty, trail-like road that sneaked out of the valley.

By mid-month I'd talked Annie into the idea that it was safe enough to ride down to Rock Springs with an extra pack horse and fetch back a supply of canned goods and the like for the General Store. Mister Preston, our landlord and store keeper, had said that his stock was just about fizzled, which Annie found out for herself when she tried to buy some baking soda. The old Mormon drummer, who generally packed in the grub, wasn't due yet for some few weeks.

The morning I left I took my pistol, which I'd not worn all the time we'd lived in the valley, and a good stock of both rifle and Colt ammunition. In spite of what I'd told Annie about an easy trip,

I wasn't taking any chances ever again . . . if I could help it.

"I'll be back within the week," I told Annie as I kissed her and swung up into the buckskin's saddle. "I don't think you'll have any visitors, but if you do, tell 'em to wait and I'll be back."

"The only visitor I want to see is you," she frowned, and then laughed. "And I don't think you're any sort of a visitor—not after all these months."

When I rode down the rutty, little road and out of sight around a bend, I looked back. There she stood, straight and all alone in front of our little cabin home. For some reason I had a bit of trouble in swallowing as I gave her a last wave, before hitting up the horses for the bottom of the valley.

Once past the foothills along the wide elbow of the brawling Snake River, I headed through patches of snow and small drifts for mile after mile as we traversed one foaming, mountain-fed creek after another, coming, at last, to the iron bridge over the Green south of the little hamlet of La Barge. I was well on my way toward Rock Springs when the sun flattened out in a flurry of fire-tinted clouds beyond the limestone cliffs to the west.

I made camp that night in the shelter of a towering, red rock rampart, well out of the wind and rolled up in my blanket before a crackling fire of dry greasewood. Before I'd turned in, I had a look at the carvings on the soft limestone of the cliff. The trail here seemed to have been used by many of the old-timers as they traveled on toward Idaho and the Northwest. The earliest dated inscription was 1822, and the most legible—*James Bridger 1844*. Old Jim had put his brand on several of the rocks.

In the morning after feeding the horses and cooking up some bacon and coffee, I saddled up and took the route over the sand flats, crossing a branch of the old Oregon Trail. Several small herds of elk drifted along ahead of me but I didn't have the heart to pull the trigger on any of the bucks—beside I was traveling light and wanted to make time. I'd had some thoughts about my destination during the night.

With each hour, the stubborn south-west wind seemed to grow in strength, buffeting the drying grasses as I headed on toward Rock Springs. The birds were returning on that wind, and I counted six flocks of geese heading north. Game, which had been plentiful back in the valley, now was mighty scarce and I began to regret not getting an elk when I had the chance. I wasn't ready to live on bacon and beans again. Annie had spoiled me for that—among other things. And yet, I still found myself thinking of Starr . . . and her deep blue eyes.

Yes, I just might take a trip on up to Miles City.

The roads were o.k. for the jaunt. If I worked it right, I could make the circle in little more than a week or so. And besides I needed to stretch out after being cooped up in the valley.

Though I hadn't heard from Lonny since he rode out of Hole in the Wall, I was sure that I could reach him by wire down at Cripple Creek, Colorado. He was bound to be there with our cousin, Bob Lee, in his gambling hall saloon, working at being a businessman—of sorts. At least it was just about the safest place for him . . . and he was out of the country.

I wanted Lonny to hear that I was in one piece, and needed to know what was going on with Jim Thornhill and our ranch back home. It seemed safer to use the telegraph from some place like Miles City, rather than exchange messages so close to Star Valley. At least that was the reason I gave myself for a ride that would take me up a hundred miles and more into Montana—and to Starr Jackson.

It was along toward supper time when I rode down winding K Street in Rock Springs and tied up at the local livery. The evening shadows were running long from the neighboring sandstone cliffs along the Green River and the streets were full of miners going home to their hodge-podge of little shacks on the outskirts. The Rock Springs coal mines, owned by the Union Pacific, and about the largest west of the Mississippi, employed hundreds of laborers—and the payrolls were also about the heftiest west of the big river.

As I sat with one leg cocked over the saddle of my buckskin and looked over the shambling parade of black-faced Irishmen, I wondered just how Butch Cassidy would size up the possibilities of a raise. Would he go for the paymaster's office as he'd done back at Castle Gate, Utah about a year ago? Or would he lay for the UP train itself, out of the town around some long wall of sandstone cliffs, where it could be bottled up tight as a snake in a jug?

With a dry chuckle I dismounted, turned the horses over to the stable hand, and headed for The Rock Springs House on Front Street. Here I was, not two days gone from Annie, and already sniffing out trouble. Lonny had been right on the money when he told me that this sort of life could get into a person's blood. And I was damned if I wanted to turn into a shiftless owl-hoot, like old Frank Jackson—and go the way he did!

By noon of the next day, I'd up and sold off both horses to the local liveryman for a decent sum, and was sitting on the scuffed, yellow-plush seat of the Union Pacific Flyer, heading for Rawlins and a transfer to the Montana Central. I'd made up my mind, overnight, that it would save time and trouble to pick up a mount and another pack horse in Miles City—after I'd seen Starr. It just wouldn't do to gallivant around so long, and leave Annie alone in the valley. It was one way, I reasoned, to have my hot-cake and eat it, too. I was becoming a regular jailhouse lawyer at arguing myself into all sorts of crooked corners—though I swore by all that was holy I'd backtrail to the straight-and-narrow as soon as I could . . . because of Annie.

When I arrived on the Montana Central at Forsyth, Montana, the evening of February 16, 1898, not wanting to get off at Miles City, all the talk was of some U.S. battleship being blown to smithereens down in Cuba.

That, said everybody, meant a shooting war—and about time, as those damned Spanish needed a good thrashing. But what that would do to Cassidy and his Train Robbers' Syndicate, with troop-trains rushing every which way—filled with soldier-boys and rifles—was anyone's guess.

I gave up trying to figure out anything, except that I wanted to see Starr . . . just to find out how she was . . . so I told myself.

I was able to pick up a good horse, a chestnut with two white forefeet, at the C.T. Horse Camp on the outskirts of town, and rode the thirty odd miles over to Miles City, passing down a road that paralled the Bozeman Trail of an earlier time. It was a cold ride, but the moon was up and the horse racked along easy-like, and we got to Miles City with the dawn of a frosty morning.

Once there, I put the mount up at Ringer and Johnson's livery barn, and checked in to the commercial hotel for a few hours rest.

I got my money's worth at that place, because I slept the clock around, rolling out the next morning hungry as a lobo wolf.

Once up and around, and shaved in the barber shop next to the Chinese laundry, I walked over to the telegraph office on Front Street and sent a wire to Lonny, care of the Big Strike Saloon, Cripple Creek, Colorado.

> *"Everything ship-shape here. Spent the winter in that valley. Will be here for a day or so. Let me know what you are up to. May see our friend Jim Lowe one of these days. Answer."*

I went over to the same Can-Can lunch room where Sundance and I had visited back in July of the past year. It seemed a life-time away already, and my face burned to think of seeing Starr again. It also burned, somewhat, to see the fat town marshal, badge and all, sitting in a corner of the place, blowing away at a bowl of soup. But he paid me no more attention that one of the flies around his head.

When I finished with my mulligan stew and peach pie, and paid my bill, with one eye on the busy marshal, my pistol felt mighty comforting as it nestled in my mackinaw pocket. Frank Canton had followed Sundance and myself out of town on that last visit, but the old side-winder wasn't around—probably down on his Johnson County Ranch—and the devil with him!

I walked in to the Yellowstone Journal office about noon, but there was no one behind the counter except a brindle cat asleep on a chair at the desk. The cowbell over the door seemed on the fritz and no one answered my hello.

I was thumbing through the last issue of the paper, and grinning at a box on the front page signed by old man Gordon, the editor.

"If the Journal is a little thin this morning, just bear in mind that the telegraph office was closed for repairs yesterday, the mail from the East hadn't come in on time and there wasn't anybody in town who had enough accommodation to die, get married or have a baby."

The door opened behind me, and I turned to see Starr coming in with a paper parcel. I stepped aside and closed the door after her.

"Thank you, Mister." She placed the sack on the counter, leaned her wooden crutch against the wall, shooed the cat out of the chair, and took off her bonnet—then her face brightened as she seemed to recognize me.

"You!" She held out her hand, and I took it. "Oh, Mister—Nelson wasn't it?"

"Yes, ah—*Bob Nelson*." I'd near forgotten my alias at that. I was about to say something when—damned if old man Gordon didn't come out of the back room, ink on his chin and glasses up on top of his bald head.

Starr broke in on him. "Uncle, here's Mister Nelson. Remember him? He's the gentleman who brought us news about . . ." And her voice trailed off as her mouth trembled.

"Yep!" Gordon pushed his glasses down on his red nose as he looked me over—then they narrowed, and I had the feeling he knew more about me than I wanted known.

Sending Starr right on into the back room with her purchases, he turned to me and didn't mince words. "Young man, you have just got to be the most unique, double-barreled, iron-plated numbskull of the past decade! Here you come back to the same town that saw you and that other saddle-pirate commit bodily mayhem upon one of the meanest, most vindictive dry-gulchers that ever breathed the pellucid air of old Montana— Frank Canton!" He rubbed his nose, getting a smudge of ink on its tip. "No!" He raised his hand to cut me off in mid-air. "Don't explain. I was young, some time back, and it doesn't take the wisdom of Solomon to see you're pretty smitten with our girl. But—!" And his face took on a rock-ribbed look. "You just aren't the sort of fellow I want calling on our little lady. You are just too damned dangerous—to yourself, and to her both."

"Well—" I finally got a word in edgewise, but only one.

"Well, indeed! Frank Canton has those Belle Fourche reward notices around most of the counties, plus half of Dakota and Wyoming. Only thing he hasn't got on the things is your picture. But I know who you are. I read the other papers. The Pinkertons don't seem to be involved as yet, but those shenanigans over at Belle Fourche, plus your Deadwood jail episode, could land you right in the middle of a lot of trouble—and I just don't want Starr hurt anymore!"

Starr came back into the office, but I don't think she'd heard any of Gordon's rantings, which he'd quickly changed to general conversation regarding the affairs in Cuba.

"Well, thanks for your time, Mister Gordon. Goodbye, Miss Starr, see you later, I hope." I laid down a nickel for the paper and went on out.

I sauntered up the street, keeping my eye peeled for any law, but the only one I saw was the same fat marshal still perched in the lunch room, his nose in another bowl of soup—just the way I'd left him.

By the time I'd got back to the telegraph office

there was an answer from Lonny, addressed to Ike Rose (I'd borrowed the name of the town drunk back at Landusky, but I saw my brother had got the slant).

"Things o.k. here. Standing pat. Hope you don't go for any sucker play with Jim Lowe. Keep in touch and watch out for too many stars."

Lonny had recognized Butch's Jim Lowe alias, all right. And I got the message about stars—*tin stars* and Star Valley . . . but I thought he could have kept his remarks to himself concerning Starr Jackson.

I walked away, muttering to myself—and turning the corner back onto Main Street came near to bumping right into Starr, herself.

When I rode out of Miles City later that afternoon, heading back to Forsyth, I kept running over the brief time spent with Starr, as she'd stood in front of the saddle shop, the wind tossing and teasing the ribbons on her perky, little flowered bonnet.

"I saw that Uncle Gordon seemed upset." She'd hesitated, then gave a defiant little tug at her bonnet strings. "I just had to follow you and see what brought you back." She colored a bit. "I was glad to see you, anyway, because . . ."

Because? My blood started to race—as if I were face to face with some sort of danger—and realized, suddenly, *that danger* was in her blue eyes. Yes, old man Gordon was right. *Smitten!*

"Because, I suppose, you were brave enough to come back here after your trouble last year with that detestable Frank Canton."

I must have stared pretty hard, because she smiled at the look on my face. "Yes, I read the other papers we exchange at the office. We get almost a dozen a week. That's one of my jobs, clipping and pasting up items from other towns for our Journal. I'm our exchange editor as well as ad taker, part-time compositor and printer's devil." She came a step nearer and I caught the faintly haunting odor of her perfume—like a gentle breath through the lilacs back home when I was a young'un.

"I'm mighty sorry you had to learn such things, Miss Starr." I was at a loss as to what to say to this lovely, young girl. And I could sense that she somehow seemed to feel what I was feeling—bewilderment and longing.

"I don't mind a bit. I know, whatever trouble you are in, it wasn't of your making." She glanced around at the folks passing on the street and then suddenly leaned forward and kissed me full on the mouth. "There! That will let the whole wide world know what I think of you—*Harvey Logan!*"

To say I was flabbergasted puts it easy. I couldn't have replied one word if Frank Canton had a shotgun right on me. I took off my sombrero and ran my hand through my hair, letting the February breezes cool my head.

"Don't say anything, Harvey," she grasped my other hand. "I don't know if Uncle would be so downright mean as to inform on you to Seth Rand, our fat, old marshal, but it isn't safe to stay around!"

"You asked what brought me back here?" I yanked my hat back down on my head and took both her hands. "It was a couple of things. One, I had to tell you that there'd be money coming from—your Pa's estate . . . money to get your foot taken care of, and that's gospel."

"And the other?" She was very near now, seeming to lean toward me out of the sudden chilly blasts of February wind that was chasing bits of paper and assorted tumbleweeds up the dust-filled street.

"The other?" I took her by the arm and she came with me into the shelter of a doorway. "The other was—that I couldn't get you out of my mind. But maybe this will help." And I took her in my arms, held her close and kissed her a good, long one!

Riding on toward Forsyth I kept thinking of Starr—and could see then and there I wasn't going to get her out of my mind. It seemed that she was there deeper than ever as I recalled her last words before I turned and hurried away for my chestnut at the livery.

"This white ribbon is for you—like the favors the knights wore in *Kenilworth*. Do you like Scott? Anyway, wear it and write me when you can. I handle all the mail that comes to the office."

When I kissed her goodbye, she whispered, "white stands for faithfulness."

As I looked down at that white ribbon, wound around my mackinaw button, when I rode in to Forsyth that evening I wondered about that word—*faithfulness*.

CHAPTER TWENTY-FOUR

I had just one piece of business left to take care of before I rode out of Forsyth with a full stock of supplies lashed to the pack horse. The wife of the proprietor of J. P. Webster's Staple and Fancy Groceries helped me pick out a stunner of a doll, complete with curly yellow hair, open and shut eyes and dressed up in a satin gown. "As good as any in a mail order catalogue," she said as she took down the address of Viola Clay, the little girl at the Three Vee Ranch, Belle Fourche.

Little Viola, who'd lost her own doll in the feed lot, when a horse stepped on it, now would have a new one. Santa might be coming a month or so late—but it would be all right. Besides, I owed Viola some sort of present to pay for her fortune telling the night we'd been holed up there at the Three Vee. How had she said it? *"This King of Spades means you, and you're going to meet surprises . . . the Queen of Clubs is a lady coming back into your life (Annie) . . . and another Queen—a Queen of Hearts is also coming into your life."* Was that Starr?

I got back to our valley five days later without excitement of any sort, camping out on the trail each night as the weather warmed, actually meandering my way southward. I'd wanted to be on my lonesome for a spell—to sort things out. Much as I loved Annie, and I had to admit it, that I really felt that way about her—I was puzzled how anyone could still have the same sort of feelings for another woman, or girl. But then I'd never been a ladies' man like Lonny. I wished I could sit down and get some advice from him, but he was stuck away in Colorado and I didn't dare open up a line of communication with him by the U.S. Mail. What old man Gordon had said about Frank Canton's posters and the possibility of the Pinkertons getting on our track made me leery of sticking out my neck—or Lonny's. He knew where I was, and I knew he was out of the Owl-hoot Trail for good, I hoped. If I wanted to get in touch with him there was always the telegraph.

So I drifted along, taking my time, and thinking. But no matter how much I thought things over, I couldn't see how I could get money (a lot of money in a hurry) from any means except through Butch Cassidy and his Train Robbers' Syndicate. So there it was, I was still on the hook, thanks to my so-called chivalry. Looking at Starr's white ribbon reminded me. Yes, I knew a little about old Sir Walter Scott and his damned chivalry. That was what got the South into such a deep hole it still hadn't clawed out it, yet.

"Mister, you're one damned fool," I told myself

a dozen times, but I just couldn't see any way out of it—for the time being.

Annie welcomed me back like I'd been gone for two years, instead of two weeks. She didn't even ask why it had taken me fourteen days when the trip to Rock Springs should have occupied no more than four. All she said was, "Harvey, I missed you bad." She didn't even ask about the new horses, though she must have wondered.

I tried to make up for lost time, and I think Annie was satisfied, but there were many nights over the next months when I woke up and lay in the dark thinking of Starr.

We stayed in Star Valley for the rest of the year of 1898, the longest stretch that I'd remained in one spot since the night I fought Pike Landusky. If, as I think many times, that I'd known of a place like the valley when Pike died, I'd have gone straight to it and never would have strayed to such spots as Hole in the Wall. But then I'd never have met Annie—or Starr.

The winter of 1897–98 had passed as a happy dream, but 1898 beat those months hands down. There had been some cattle running wild up at the upper end of the valley, real wild stuff, and it took every ounce of my ability to round them up, plus one hell of a lot of rough riding. But, at last, I had a brush pen filled with over twenty head of stock five miles up the valley. And there I was—a rancher, again.

I was more proud of that scrubby bunch than if I'd become a millionaire, and I think that Annie was just as proud.

"You see, Harvey, that you can make all the money we'd ever need, just with your rope and—."

"And running iron, you mean," I joshed her. "It's just my good luck these Mormons don't know whose cattle they are or I might get that rope—around my neck."

But I fattened the stock up, and using the poker from Annie's cook stove, ran hair brands on all the beef. My brand (unregistered) was an A on a lazy H, and one day in the early fall, Annie, in her cowgirl gear, and I headed the little herd out of the valley to the whoops and shouts of every Mormon kid in the place. You'd have thought that we were Colonel Teddy Roosevelt's Rough Riders back on parade from Cuba according to the ruckus that exploded. Dogs barked, kids whistled and even the old folks came out of their little houses and clapped their hands until I had visions of a stampede.

The long and short of it was that I sold every head to a small-time stock buyer down at Rock Springs, who asked no questions, but turned around and got himself papers, somewhere, and called my brand The Pine Tree.

We did it up proper after I collected that four-hundred dollars for the stock, putting up at the best hotel (which wasn't that special) and dining at first one and then the other of the two restaurants. It made me feel good that the money I was tossing around I'd come by in a, more or less, honest manner. Annie was mighty quick to point that out, also, but I only nodded and ordered her another champagne cocktail.

It wouldn't do to stay around any place too long—and after two days we pulled freight back for the valley, Annie talking every minute of the good time she'd had and making plans to come back to the place—for all the world as if it were New York or Chicago instead of a rough-and-ready mining town stretched along the U.P. tracks.

In a way I was actually looking forward to returning to Star Valley. The place had got to me. I must have been feeling sort of poetical about it—thinking that, nestled within its protective walls, it was sort of a Garden of Eden for the two of us. We had everything we needed there. Food, friends when we wanted them, and safety.

But there's no Garden of Eden, worth its salt, that doesn't boast of some sort of serpent. And when we rode up to the door of our little cabin—who should step out to greet us but Butch Cassidy!

• • •

After supper of antelope steak that evening, Butch and I strolled down the dusty, little street of Afton, him pointing out the cabin where Matt Warner and Blacky Jackson had run their saloon while hiding out from some high-rolling. "Think of it," said Butch, rubbing his chin and looking at the desolate old cabin. "They hit it so big at Telluride, Colorado that they didn't know what to do with the money. Besides they was snowed in for the winter, like you and your lady."

"What do you mean they didn't know what to do with the money?"

"Well, what could they spend it for in this forsaken place? And besides it was in whopping big bills. A couple were even one-thousand-dollar denomination. And how in hannah do you change one of those?"

"It seems they might have planned better," I said, and knew what was coming as soon as I opened my mouth. So far Butch hadn't said a word about what had brought him all the way from the WS Ranch down in New Mexico.

"You're right! Plannin' is th' thing. And just to remind them to plan better th' next time, Matt and Blacky up and papered one end of th' saloon with hundred-dollar bills—and put those two-thousand-dollar bills right in the middle." He coughed and rubbed his chin, squinting at the evening sun. "Yep, plannin' is th' thing, and

I got a few dillies planned, myself." He turned his head, his eyes glittering in the red light. "Interested?"

I nodded, thinking of Annie and what she would say—but also thinking of Starr. I'd been thinking a lot of Starr lately. Here it was months since I'd seen her, and yarned about the money coming to her—from her share of a ranch that had been. Here was opportunity knocking at my door in the form of Butch Cassidy. But it could be an opportunity that might be downright deadly—if things happened to go wrong. But, as Butch said, planning was the thing.

On the way back to my cabin, Cassidy filled me in on the whereabouts of the old gang. Sundance and big Ben Kilpatrick were working the range down at the WS Ranch, along with Butch, who had been handling the spread as foreman. Walt Punteny had gone back to George Curry at The Hole in the Wall, and Peep O'Day was still in jail.

"And your brother, Lonny is over in Colorado?" Butch mused. "Well, that's all right. He's a pretty edgy fellow. A little rest will do him good."

Cassidy bunked down in the kitchen that night and I'm sure his ears were cocked at what went on in our bedroom, which was one lot of talk . . . Annie hot after me to keep out of Butch's schemes, and myself trying to justify the risks involved in taking part in the raids.

• • •

Before Butch left next morning, he pulled me to one side as we were getting his white stallion out of the corral up the street. "Ever see these before?" And he unfolded a pair of reward posters.

The one with a photograph took my eye. I stiffened as I read: Photograph of *JOHN W. CALDWELL*: And there staring out at me was a face that looked mighty familiar, then I realized it was Bronco Jack Caldwell. I glared over at Butch and then back at the other sheet. Then I did tighten up. It was a new reward dodger for *KID CURRY!* It was issued by Frank Canton, offering $200 for my capture.

"Didn't want to upset any applecarts last night. Didn't think you wanted your lady friend to get a gander at that one." Butch took the sheets back and looked at them. "Y'know, it never hit me at first, until I got a good look at Bronco's mugshot, and then took another look at you."

"Talk some sense."

"No offense, but I think you'd see somethin' sorta familiar in that picture of our mutual friend, John Walter Caldwell."

"Familiar?"

"Y'know I thought that picture was you— *Harvey Logan,* when I spotted th' dodger on th' Vernal, Utah post office wall. But then I knew it wasn't when I read th' print. And your own greeting card from Frank Canton was sorta buried down in the stack. Yours was older." He tightened his saddle girth and then looked up sideways. "Those posters are nothin' to get hot under th' collar about. Small time rewards. Only get anxious like when you see your name and tintype on a Pinkerton poster. Those babies play rough and for keeps."

I took the sheets back and stuck them in my shirt as Annie came out with some food for Butch's saddle bags. All the time he'd been with us, she'd been distant but much more polite than the last time Butch had bumped into her back at the Elkhorn Tavern. Giving him a little nod, she went back inside, blue-checked apron whipping around her.

"Whew!" Butch swung up into the saddle. "Well, if Bronco Jack Caldwell ever comes around, and he's reported to be back up this way, I only hope she's as accommodatin' . . ." Then he was off down the valley road, followed by half-a-dozen Mormon kids and a dozen dogs. He'd been his usual generous self, with a lot of pennies for stick candy at Mister Preston's General Store. He'd also been mighty free with his plans for the rebirth of the Train Robbers' Syndicate.

His words came back to me, many times over the months to come. "Stick around here if you can, then I know where to reach you—because, when th' time is just right . . . *We'll make train robbin' history!*"

CHAPTER TWENTY-FIVE

We set out another winter in the valley, and Annie seemed just as contented as if she were living in a Knob Hill mansion instead of a two-room cabin on the edge of nowhere. And—to tell the truth and shame the devil, I was getting into a regular rut of respectability. That poster of Frank Canton's was a joke as far as I was concerned.

We made one trip down to Rock Springs for supplies and came back in a couple of days, having done the bright lights along the U.P. tracks again.

We brought back the latest papers, but there was little happening, though the war dragged along in the Philippine Islands. They were still swamping out gold in the Alaskan Klondike and striking it nearer home in the Nevada hills. Nothing much seemed to be happening at Cripple Creek Colorado, where Lonny and Bob Lee were running their saloon dodge. One story had the silver mines there about petered out.

The only news hitting close to home was the fact that, while the shooting was over in Cuba, Governor Wells of Utah had been offering a hefty $500 each for the rustlers at Robbers' Roost. Among these named were such hard-cases as Jack Moore, Silver Tip, Blue John—and *Jack*

Caldwell. And, I thought, Bronco, old fellow, if ever I get you in my sights, I'll sure pull your stake rope!

Sitting out on a stump behind our cabin, I re-read the reward posters Butch had left: *JOHN W. CALDWELL, alias CHARLIE MARLOW, alias BILLY REED, alias MILT RUSSELL, alias TAP DUNCAN. AGE, 33 years (1898). WEIGHT, 166. EYES, dark. HEIGHT, 5 feet, 11 inches. COLOR OF HAIR, dark brown, NOSE, prominent, long and straight. COMPLEXION, swarthy. OCCUPATION, Cowboy. CRIMINAL OCCUPATION, Horse Thief, Cattle Rustler, Highwayman and Bank Burglar.*

The reward of $300 was offered by the Cattlemen's Protective Association of Denver, Colorado.

I cursed to myself. Butch wasn't too far off in spotting our descriptions as matching. But as far as I was concerned, even with that $500 reward added to the $300, Bronco Jack Caldwell was still a penny-ante thief.

The other poster offered a pretty penny-ante reward, itself, for the arrest and conviction of one *HARVEY LOGAN, alias KID CURRY, for the participation in the Belle Fourche Bank holdup of June 26, 1897, and the escape from the Deadwood Jail in July, 1897, along with the felonious assault upon a peace officer (Canton!).*

Sundance, Lonny and Walt Punteny weren't

even mentioned. It looked as if Canton was trying to tree me all for himself. Well, the old panther was welcome to try!

But reward dodgers weren't the only things I read as fall drifted toward winter in Star Valley and the hillside aspen changed their silvery leaves for a flame-dipped mantle, and the choke-cherry thickets along the streams bowed heavy with pea-sized, dark red cherries, drawing wandering bears as well as many Mormon wives, with plans for making up jelly for the long winter.

I'd borrowed several Sir Walter Scott novels from a nearby Mormon, *Kenilworth* and *Ivanhoe* among them, and read these by lamplight on the long evenings. And as I read the deeds of derring-do, I wondered if Starr was reading the same books, and if she thought of the little white ribbon she'd given to me when I rode off from Miles City. That ribbon was safe and sound in my wallet.

Annie matched me for a great reader, devouring every last issue she could find of the *Overland Monthly* and holding forth on the many tales she'd read, including some from Alaska by a fellow named London.

With the coming of white winter, I took up my chore of hunter for the settlement, bringing in deer, elk and even an occasional bear, who'd forgot to den up in the mild weather.

From time to time we'd visit one or other of the

families in Afton, with Annie exchanging recipes with the Mormon wives (sometimes two or three in one house), while I talked over the weather and crops with the husbands, and whittled toys for the kids—whirligigs and cornstalk fiddles, along with jumping jacks and bows and arrows.

One by one the months passed and almost before I knew it, it was spring. And with the coming of spring, March 25 to be exact, came a message from Cassidy.

The messenger who brought the letter was no one else but Elza Lay, and he'd come all the way from New Mexico by way of Hole in the Wall.

He was the same easy-going, pleasant puncher I'd met down on the WS after Ben Kilpatrick and I had pulled the Clifton job—and lost just about every dollar to that underhanded sidewinder Bronco Jack Caldwell.

Annie put Elza at ease, and turned out a fine supper. But after it was over, she called me outside. "I know why he's here, Harvey, and if you ride out—for any reason—you won't find me when you get back . . . *if you get back!*"

I tried to reason with her, telling her that with one good haul we could get out of the country for good—go to California or back East, wherever she had a mind to. And I made a promise to myself to see some of that money would get to Starr Jackson.

I'd been hoping, part of the time, that Butch would leave me out of his plans, for I knew this would happen—that Annie would fly off the handle and give me an ultimatum I couldn't get around. But my restless Logan blood was beginning to tell, and I gave her a hell of an argument.

The upshot of that was to find myself bunking down on the kitchen floor with Elza Lay that night.

Next morning Elza and I cooked our own breakfast, with Annie barricaded in the bedroom of the cabin. I knew her too well to try to talk any sort of sense into her. I suspect, that having Elza Lay around to take back word to the bunch that Annie had me by the nose-ring, helped me make up my mind to ride out that very day.

Elza made himself scarce, after we'd got the horses saddled and our supplies lashed to the pack horse. Then I tried to talk to Annie—through the door, but never a sound could I get out of her.

I was mad clear through but wrote a short note and left it on the kitchen table:

"Annie, I'll be back just as soon as I can. Elza says that Butch gave his word to the Governor of Wyoming, when he first pardoned him, not to trouble any one in the Territory—so I've got to pitch in and

help the boys pull this off. Then we'll be able go where ever we want and live the way we should. Wait for me."

"Goodbye. I'll see you in a few weeks," I called through the door. But that was the last I saw of Annie for a long, long time.

CHAPTER TWENTY-SIX

It was close on to two hundred and fifty miles to Hole in the Wall, by the most direct route, and we made the ride in just under six days, taking our time and not putting a great deal of strain on the horses, for we'd need them when the chips were down.

Crossing the Continental Divide early in the season could have been a tough proposition, but a Chinook had been blowing for over a week and the passes were open but treacherous with rotten snow. Over the Divide, we crossed the Wind River by ferry at Riverton and skirting the Shoshone Reservation, headed due northeast across the high plains, keeping away from any settlements.

Sitting around the campfire at night, I filled Lay in on the story of my ups-and-downs, and he told me details of his own life to date. Like a lot of fellows on the Frontier, Ellsworth Lay came from the East, being born in Boston. With a good education, but sporting a great bump of wanderlust, he decided to go West, and lit in Denver broke. He took a job driving a horse car until he could squirrel away enough money to get back home, but one day a drunk tried to molest a woman on his car and Elza didn't do a thing but heave him out onto the cobblestones.

"I thought the damned fool had broken his neck and that I was for it," Lay said. "So I left the lady and the car right in the middle of Main Street and beat my way up into the mountains. Eventually I got to Brown's Hole, where I worked for some of the ranchers and fell in with Matt Warner and Butch Cassidy. And that was the beginning of a new way of life—to say the least."

"And you helped Butch pull off the Castle Gate raise back in 1897, which put you all on the map," I said. "Not bad for a out-of-work horse car pilot."

Elza spat into the red eye of the fire and watched it wink back. "Yep, but I guess Butch didn't fill you in on our Idaho outing. Matt Warner got scooped up over a shooting scrape with some prospectors near Vernal, Utah and heaved into the local hoosegow. Butch, always a soft-touch, decided to raise money for Matt's bail and so we hit the Montpelier, Idaho bank for over seven thousand."

"Do Warner any good?"

"Not much, he got two years. Matt's still in the can, some guys just aren't lucky."

"Well, let's hope we are by the first of June." That was the date Butch had set for the raid on the Overland Flyer!

• • •

Once in the Hole, we seemed to spend most of our time going over the plan of operation for ambushing the Union Pacific.

Day after day, we pored over Butch's notes. George Curry, as head of the Hole Bunch, had the plans from Elza and worried over them as much as if he'd been promoted General of the U.S. Army. Only his *troops* included just a half-Mex kid, Billy Rogers, along with Elza Lay and myself. But according to Curry, there'd be some extra hands on deck when we got to the rendezvous.

"But why so close-mouthed about our partners?" I wanted to know, looking across the cabin at Lay, who shrugged.

"I told you that I just don't know. Butch said he'd send a couple of good men to us at Medicine Bow at the right time."

"And you know Butch, he's got this figured down to the last detail," said George Curry, rubbing his growth of whiskers, but still looking worried.

"Guess this time you'll get enough cash to take your ranch out of hock," I answered, recalling our try to get Curry money to pay off his mortgage—only to land right spang in Deadwood Jail.

George rubbed his big, flat beak of a nose and grunted, "I sure say we'll all get a good stake out of this one."

"Then why are you so down in the mouth?"

"Hell, Kid! We got th' plans. We'll have th' men—but we still ain't got Butch."

When we rode down the branch of the Powder and out of the Hole through the winding cliffs of the Red Wall on April Sixth, 1899, though I didn't realize it, I'd started on the trail of no return.

Up until now, except for those two local rewards of Canton and the Belle Fourche Bank there was nothing to stand in the way of trying to square myself with the law over the Pike Landusky fight. There was nothing to tie me into that Clifton, New Mexico raid. So time was still in my favor as Annie would have said. But after the Overland Flyer—time started to run out . . . faster and faster!

For the following six weeks we camped out, staying away from towns and settlements, except to replenish supplies. It was just *General* George Curry and his long-riding cavalry.

By the evening of May thirty-first we'd still not made contact with the other men Butch Cassidy had promised to send us.

Sitting around our supper fire on the banks of The Little Medicine, forty miles north of Laramie, Wyoming, George Curry and Lay were playing a hand of cards, while I was showing

Billy Rogers how to clear a bent cartridge out of a Winchester—when there came the fast gallop of horses headed down the river bank in our direction.

"Kick out that fire, and take cover," George bawled, while we scattered.

"Hey, Flat Nose!" called a voice that sent a chill down my backbone.

It was my brother Lonny!

In a moment the horsemen had pulled up in a spray of sand and gravel, and were tumbling out of the saddle laughing fit to kill.

"Lonny, is that you?"

"Harvey? Couldn't see you there, but it's me all right and here's Bob Lee come along for th' fun."

"You damn fools could'a got a belly full of lead, poundin' down here like a pack of idjits," George Curry growled. But I could see he was pleased to have his reinforcements . . . even if it was my fiddling brother and some stranger.

Later that night as we lay blanket wrapped, with feet to the fire, I got the straight of the matter. Butch had come up short in the way of help. Sundance had wandered down below the border to call on some señoritas, and Sam Ketchum was off stealing horses, leaving Cassidy up a tree.

"Don't think Butch liked it too much, but he sent a wire to me at th' saloon at Cripple Creek layin' out th' proposition."

"Took a chance didn't he? As far as I know

you'd retired from the road agent business." I was still mad, clean through, to think Lonny would show up on this raid, particularly after lecturing me about falling for Cassidy and *his propositions*.

"No chance, at all. I jumped at it, and so did Bob Lee there." Lonny raised up on one elbow and looked around at the sleeping figures. "You see, Harve, we had just about gone bust. The mines petered out and most of th' high-rollers had already left for other camps. This is one chance for us to make a strike and get out from under our saloon."

"Well, you're one damned fool—but, I guess, it's the pot calling the kettle black. Everyone's trying to make a raise to pay off something."

"Not me," came Elza Lay's even tones. "I want th' money for myself, because I'm just a selfish crook."

Next evening as we sat on our horses in the moonlight, George Curry showed me the wire Lonny had fetched. I scratched a match on my saddle horn and read:

"L. Logan, Silver Dollar, Cripple Creek, Colorado.

Please round up one good man and meet Syndicate at Wilcox Station, Wyoming no later than June 1. Shipment arrives there 2 A.M., June 2. Luck, Jim Lowe . . ."

"And that's why we had to lay over for one more day," said George. "Butch must have got another message from his inside man that th' *shipment* was a day late." He turned his black mare. "Come on let's git up th' track, and git ready. And, Billy, be damn keerful of that dinnymite!"

Billy Rogers held up a gunny sack in the moonlight. "Got her!"

By the time we had ridden past the silent station (the town lay off to the east half a mile), the moon had clouded up, and the mutter of thunder rolled toward us out of the hulking dark shoulders of the Medicine Bow Mountains westward.

"Remember when old Aunt Lee used to tell us kids that was th' potato wagon, and th' spuds were fallin' off?" Lonny rode up close to me, with Bob Lee beside him.

"Yes, and I'll bet you wish you were back sitting on the front porch at Aunt Lee's right now," I answered, still disgusted with him.

"Come on, Harvey. I want to bury th' hatchet with you. I told you Bob and I have gotta get a stake somehow."

"We pay off that dyin' saloon and we're long gone," laughed Bob Lee.

"Butch sure was hard up," I replied and spurred on to the head of the column where George Curry was dismounting near the iron bridge over a branch of the Little Medicine.

George was squinting at his watch in the light of a sputtering match. "Two o'clock. Let's git ready. She's due any time now. Damn it!" Sudden falling rain had squelched out his match.

The rain that had been threatening, now came down in torrents. Then as suddenly as it began, the downpour was over, leaving puddles that gleamed and glittered in the glow of the pair of lanterns in Elza Lay's hands. "That's right, git them ready," said George. "In fact I think that's th' pay train comin' right now." And there came the faint whisper of an oncoming engine, then the shrill whooping of its whistle as it blew for a crossing. Suddenly, from up the track, rounding an intervening butte, a headlight cut streaming through the blackness. It lingered for a moment over the knot of horses along the right of way, swung to the left, and then back to touch the rails until they glistened like silver ribbons.

"Hustle down th' track there and flag her!" George bellowed over the oncoming roar of the transcontinental. And the red and white arc of the swinging lanterns flashed the danger signal as the big ten-wheeler stormed up, coughing sparks heavenward from its stack while the engineer slammed at the brakes. Iron wheels skidded, then gripped the creaking rails, steam hissed and crackled—The Overland Flyer was stopped.

"Come on," George shouted and we went on the run toward the cab.

A rifle cracked out high and brittle over the chuffing pant of the engine and I heard George's voice shouting, "Cut that damn firin'!"

Lonny came hustling along, followed by Bob Lee, both toting the new Krag-Jorgensen rifles they'd bought for the expedition.

George yelled in my ear, "That brother of yours is trigger happy. He just fired two shots into th' cars . . . could'a killed someone."

I aimed a kick at Lonny as I clambered up into the cab of the engine, but he was past me in the darkness, laughing like a damned loon. Spooked again! I cursed him out and then went on up into the cab Colt in my fist as George Curry and Elza Lay scrambled up from the other side of the engine.

We'd put on flour-sack masks at George's urging, and the eye holes were making it difficult to navigate, but I finally spotted the Engineer and Fireman, where they crouched by the firebox with hands in the air. "That's right, boys, keep quiet and you'll be all right. Now pull ahead across the bridge."

The Engineer threw his lever and the big engine picked up steam as George Curry leaned out of the cab. "O.K., so far. We cut th' cars and Billy's got th' stuff ready under the bridge."

"Where's the rest?"

"They're back mounted and headin' up th' line. Hey!" He made a grab at his flour-sack mask. The Engineer had tried to pull it off. "You try that again, and I'll pop you!" George connected with a solid kick to the trainman's rear end.

The Engineer turned back to his throttle, but he was a feisty devil. "Son of a bitch, you go on record as th' first fellow ever kicked me and got away with it." The Fireman looked as though he were going to fold up.

Suddenly there was a shattering explosion behind us. Billy's dynamite had done its work. The bridge was wrecked.

"Now let 'em try to follow us," Elza Lay chortled while we all peered out into the moonlight to see Bob, Lonny and Billy galloping along beside the bob-tailed train.

After we'd clicked along for two miles, George ordered the engine halted. "Pile out!" And we jumped down onto the cinders, Elza herding the Engineer and Fireman along ahead of us to where Lonny and Bob Lee were beating on the door of the express car.

"Get back, or I'll put six bullets through the first man who tries to get in here!" came a muffled yelp through the express car door.

"That's Woodcock!" The Engineer volunteered. "He's a bearcat."

"Well, by hell we'll pull his claws then," George Curry cursed and went to work helping Billy Rogers stow dynamite around the door and under the express car. "Fire her up, Billy!"

We retreated up the tracks from the crackling red snakes.

A massive clump of sound rocked the night, and we rushed back to find the Messenger staggering out of the shattered doorway. "Next time you get funny, we'll blow you to kingdom come for sure," George laughed as he shoved the gritty Woodcock along to join the trainmen being guarded by Lonny and Bob Lee.

In another minute the door of the iron safe was blown by the last of Billy Rogers' dynamite, this time making a tremendous explosion that hurled pieces of metal and papers through the air.

Dodging the rain of debris with the others, I crowded back into the smoking shambles that had been a Union Pacific express car.

"Here's a haul that is a haul!" George scooped up $60,000 in Adams Express Company banknotes out of the reeking safe and tossed the bundles into his gunny sack.

There was little reason to linger. We had what we had come for. And Butch Cassidy's Train Robbers' Syndicate was ready to declare a dividend on the spot.

Pulling off our masks and firing several shots into the air to discourage any trainmen from following us along the tracks, we rode north for a mile and divided the money—Lonny, Bob Lee and Billy Rogers taking $20,000 along with them as they rode off northwest toward Lander.

Elza Lay, George Curry and I put the spurs to our mounts as we rode full tilt in the direction of Casper. I'd not said another word to my brother after we blew the coach—and the days to come would find me regretting that I'd not taken him by the hand and wished him all the luck in the world.

But now, with the yellow glow of dawn streaking the eastern sky, we hurtled headlong toward the south—and the hope of safety, before the posses began to put out their inevitable dragnets.

CHAPTER TWENTY-SEVEN

Now began the roughest part of the Overland Flyer affair. Cassidy's plans had worked out fine, with one exception. The late arrival of the train at Wilcox had meant there would be only a couple of hours until morning . . . and we'd be riding over a lot of open country in broad daylight.

There'd been a bridge over the Little Medicine about an hour's ride to the east, and we'd pounded there first. Crossing the bridge we headed south again, riding hard. Turning the pack horse loose, we carried what supplies we could handle on the back of our own mounts.

By eight o'clock we were riding through the tall buffalo grass at the Big Medicine Bow River, searching for a crossing. The water was up and boiling muddy yellow.

"Well, Butch's plans didn't take in walkin' on water," Elza Lay offered as we stared across the foaming expanse of the river.

"No time for wisecracks," George grumped, wheeling his horse and loping down the bank, searching for shallows. We followed, peering over our shoulders. The posses had to be out by now and hot on our trail.

"There's some sort of bridge down there," Elza pointed out the spot.

It didn't take us long to lash our horses to a wooden bridge, now wobbling and awash with the rushing river. "Looks like she's gonna bust up any minute," George gritted, also looking back north.

"Let's go before!" I spurred up and went sloshing and skidding across the buckling floor of the structure, followed closely by Elza Lay. George sat forlorn and stiff on the other side for a moment and then giving a sort of despairing war whoop plunged across after us.

Looking back, again, we all saw the bridge splinter, twist and vanish.

For the next several hours we rode hard across the Laramie Plains, seeing nothing except a few deer and, once, a flock of butterflies, big yellow fellows, that hovered over the wet grass in a cloud of drifting gold.

"Look'it those bugs," Elza shouted, "gold enough for you?"

"I like the kind that's on paper," George yelled back, lashing his mount through the mass of fluttering wings.

We stopped for a quick breakfast about noon five miles outside Glenrock, the old Deer Creek Station of the Oregon Trail, and then headed off across the foothills near Hat Six Canyon.

That night we spent several hours in an abandoned hunter's cabin in the foothills, turning in early and taking turns at look out. But luck seemed to be on our side, for the time being, and we rode down the main street of Casper, Wyoming early Sunday morning.

We'd had some hot debates as we neared the town, but Elza and I talked George into going straight through the place. Casper, founded only about ten years past, was still pretty much of a typical frontier layout.

It had been raining, again, quite steadily since we piled out of the hunter's shack about one in the morning and ahead south. Now, swathed in our yellow slickers, and with no weapons in sight, except our saddle-guns, we didn't attract much attention from any cowpokes looking out of the open saloon's doors.

"So far, so good," George grunted as we trotted up the street about 2:00 a.m. "But what happens when we hit the bridge over that damned North Platt?"

"That we'll see when we get there," I said, knowing full well word of the robbery of The Flyer had to have been telegraphed to every town in the Territory—and that it stood to reason the lawmen would be waiting to stop our crossing of the only available bridge across the turbulent Platt River on our way southward.

The word was out all right, for as we passed the last of the noisy saloons, a couple of cowhands looked after us, joshing each other. "There's a chance to make a reputation. There go th' train robbers," one hooted, doubling up with laughter at his own wit.

"I told you so," George growled, reaching under his slicker for his pistol, but not pulling it out into sight.

"Just drunks being funny," Elza Lay said as we kept on through the downfalling rain. "Let's get some feed for these horses. There's old Bucknum's livery barn."

We pulled up into the stable yard and tried to rouse out the hostler, making so much racket that I got worried we'd wake up the wrong sort of people.

"Guess he thinks we're just some of th' town drunks," Elza commented when we headed north out of town toward the bridge we had to cross— each of us with one hand on his pistol.

But—there wasn't a solitary soul guarding the vital crossing.

"Guess they don't think we come down this way," Elza volunteered.

"You better be guessing right," I said, "or we'll hear blue whistlers sing a hot song before this party is finished."

"Cut th' guff and let's ride to hell out of this," George cursed, spurring his horse forward into the early dawn.

We stopped at broad daylight near a ravine on Casper Creek and cooked breakfast. The rain had ceased, and it was warming up pleasantly. While we downed a meal of bacon and bread, along with some mighty hefty coffee that Elza had boiled up, a rider appeared so suddenly we were taken by flat-footed surprise.

It turned out (before we could make any move with our weapons), that he was only looking for stray horses from a nearby ranch. We let him look and then waved him on his way.

George turned the air a blue tinge when the cowhand was out of sight. "By Hell, what a way to get rat-trapped! I don't know what's th' matter with us. He's bound to tip off th' law, no matter what he was up to in th' first place."

"Right!" I said, as we saddled up hurriedly. I was furious with myself for being so damned careless. It could have been a repeat of the ambush after Belle Fourche when I lost Dan Patch and we were gobbled up.

We traveled for a good twenty-five miles after that and went into camp on the rocky height of Tea Pot Rock, where we ate a hasty dinner. Then, after scanning the empty countryside with our glasses in all directions, and not sighting any movement, we mounted up and rode for nearly six miles through the shallows of Tea Pot Creek to throw off any trackers.

We had doubled back to within thirty miles of Casper, about five miles west of the old horse ranch on the Salt Creek Road and were debating over where to camp for the night when the balloon went up!

Elza Lay spotted the riders in the distance as they came up out of a draw—about a good dozen of them and armed to the teeth.

There was no running for it as that would put us in the open, astride three fagged-out horses. Fortunately we were within a hundred yards of a long line of bluffs and we headed there in a hurry, with the riders galloping after us, but without any shots being thrown our way . . . yet.

"Hey!" Elza Lay reached over and grabbed at me. "This looks like a box canyon we got into." And he was right.

The light was already dim in the narrow canyon, but there was enough to show us that we were bottled in tight—at least it looked tight to the posse at the far end of the towering walls of grey sandstone.

Off our horses, we continued to guide them down a rubble-filled track that led into a narrow opening, running off at right angles and offering just enough room for a man to wriggle through— but absolutely none for horses.

We stood stock still and looked at each other. "Damn it!" George rubbed his chin, while Elza began to haul off his saddle-gun and what supplies he had left lashed behind the saddle.

"As far as this car runs, folks! Take the straight

and narrow line to the promised land—and have your tickets ready," Lay stood by the opening with his hand out.

"Keep your fool horse car conductoring to yourself," I gritted, as I stripped all I could tote from my horse. George, without a word, followed suit.

Suddenly bullets splattered around us, ricocheting off with shrill screams, while our frantic horses plunged and reared, knocking us against the rocky walls.

"C'mon, git through there before we're all kilt!" George lunged into the opening, followed by Elza and myself in short order, leaving the horses to their wild cavorting.

"Hey look! Here's a hell of a port hole," and Elza dropped to his knees in the gloom and thrust his Winchester through a crevasse in the rock wall that gave a perfect field of fire. The echoes of his shots crashed out like a volley of artillery in the narrow space. "There, that fetched 'em! Got one of th' bugger's horses plumb center. Look'it scatter now. That'll stop some of their damn enthusiasm, I guess!"

Peering over Elza's shoulder, I could see half a dozen of the posse horses stampeding in every direction. The fool lawmen had left their nags standing while they opened fire on us—and their mounts had run off.

"Even-steven, I guess," George muttered,

rubbing at his ribs. "Looks like we're all on foot—least some of us."

It was now so dark that I could barely make out Elza's features, but I'm certain they reflected my own concern.

After the brief exchange of long-range shots, the posse settled down to wait—like cats at a mouse hole—thinking they'd sweat us out after our food ran low. But they didn't know us—yet!

As soon as it was dusk, Elza went slipping along the crevasse and was soon back with the report that it led to a blind draw about two hundred yards south of the main rock formation.

Come full dark, we felt our way through the passage, stumbling over small boulders and fallen shale, but not daring to show any sort of a light.

It paid off, for by midnight, with the sickly half moon down behind the mountains, we were five miles away, and approaching the piece of badlands north of Dugout Creek. It was now so rough hiking we were falling all over ourselves in the starlight.

"We'll kill our fool selves if we try to get across this stretch in th' dark," George panted, rubbing his ribs. "I'm just about stove up anyway with them damn cayuses kickin' around when that bunch opened up on us back there."

"How're we gonna get out of this one?" Elza

wanted to know, slumping down on the ground with a groan, Winchester clashing on a rock.

"We'll make it a lot easier when it's daylight," I said. "Let's bed down over in one of those coulees, and get some rest. We're just about all in."

"Yeah, maybe we've give 'em th' slip," George offered hopefully, looking on the bright side of things—for a change.

I've got to say sleeping on that rocky ground of the coulee didn't do anything to help my temper. When we crawled shivering out of our blankets, I'd just about made up my mind that we'd been pushed far enough.

"We don't need Butch one bit," I said to George, who'd begun to look on the dark side of matters again, and bemoaning the absence of Cassidy and his "strategies."

"Hang it, it's blamed near ten o'clock already," Elza shouted. "Here come them fools again! Don't they never quit?"

In the distance, the morning sun glinted on the weapons of a good dozen riders. They were heading our way, slowly but surely, looking over the ground as they rode, searching for our tracks. Suddenly a large man who seemed in charge, gave a shout and waved an arm. In an instant, the group had piled off and were dodging around the scattered boulders that lay about a hundred yards from us, where we crouched behind an upthrust rock formation.

Elza's Winchester cracked out dry and loud, and the big man leaped straight into the air, ran off ten yards and keeled over. George and I opened up on the dodging figures and the whole bunch, including horse-holders, squatted down behind any sort of rocky barrier and stayed there.

"No battle this time," George barked. "Guess we cut th' wind out'a their sails when you nailed that big bastard!" He was right. An almost eerie stillness fell over everything. The wind whined softly and high overhead a hawk circled on silent wings. It put me in mind of the redtail hawk that had flown over the arroyo back at Clifton. This bunch, hunkered down behind the rock formations, weren't the calibre of Rangers—but there were enough of them to wipe us out if they got up grit to rush us.

"The wind may be knocked out of those folks' sails for the time being, but they'll come on sooner or later. Let's get under way again," I said.

We threw a few shots in the direction of the forted-up posse, then scrambled down the coulee and, keeping out of sight, worked our way over into the nearby Castle Creek.

It was a long, wet hike, but by continuing to follow the left-hand draws for about two miles we stumbled onto a perfect, defensible position behind a long, ragged rocky cliff, miles to the north of Casper.

We sat behind that natural fortress, drying out in the afternoon sun, after our march up the river shallows, and frying the last of our bacon. When we'd downed the end of our Arbuckle, we looked over our weapons and ammunition.

I'd a beltful of pistol ammunition, and about a dozen shells for my Winchester, but George had dropped his rifle on our retreat from the coulee, and hadn't taken time to hunt around for it. Elza, always quick on the trigger, had shot away over half of his Winchester ammunition, so we weren't in a-number-one shape to stand off any determined posse.

"If they show up, we're in a good place to hold them back until night, but make every shot count," I said.

"Start in right now," Elza snorted, "for here's that bull-headed bunch, and by the looks of it, they've picked up some more on th' way."

We ducked, for the possemen had opened fire as soon as they spotted us. Bullets slammed into the rocks, with explosions of dust and murderous shards of spinning shale.

"Let 'em keep that up and git it out of their damned craws!" snarled George, hunkering down, with the sack of money clutched to his vest, for all the world like an anxious mother with an ailing offspring.

There we stayed, never answering the posse's sporadic volleys, except to shoot off a pistol every half hour to let them know that we were ready to fight if they got too close.

After the posse chief had fallen at the coulee, the rest of the lawmen had seemed satisfied to keep us pinned down—and wait until we starved out—or caved-in and surrendered.

At last the sun went down behind the black peaks of the Big Horn Mountains. Coyotes howled at the dwindling moon, where it rose in the east, while posse campfires bloomed out flame-gold in the gathering night.

There was no fire for us in our bleak fortress, while we waited for the night to deepen. At last, about midnight, we stole cautiously down the far side of the rocky incline, and right between the dying campfires. There may have been scouts out, but we never saw or heard them— nor did they see or hear us, as we limped past the sleeping figures on the ground, holding our boots in one hand, and our guns in the other.

Someone said luck favors the bold, for when we'd tramped along the Casper Road until we were about spring-halted, according to George, we stumbled on a freighting outfit bedded down for the night, out in the middle of nowhere.

It didn't take us long to unhitch the draught horses, big Conestogas, from the prairie near the wagons, and lead them down the road until we could rummage in the wagons for enough rope to make three bridles and snaffles.

I took three hundred dollars out of George's sack and left it in the tool box of the end wagon to pay for the loan of the horses—and all the while the drivers "sawed wood" as hard as the last posse had.

"Seems like everybody gets a good night sleep around these parts except us," Elza grumbled as we kicked up the wide-backed giants and went thundering up the dim-lit wagon road.

For the next week it was just a repetition of what had gone before, until I began to feel as if I were riding through some sort of never-ending bad dream. While no posse got close enough to us again for any exchange of shots, it was as though we were always just one jump ahead of them. As we rode this way and that, having swapped our draught horses for some decent horseflesh and gear, we put up at sheep camps, line camps and even some out of the way ranches, but always paying on the nail for everything we ate or used.

It was pretty obvious that most folks knew just who we were, but the unwritten law of the open range protected us—though we didn't stay around in one place more than a few hours, in case any of our hosts got second thoughts about tipping off the lawmen.

By Tuesday, June 13, we'd made up our minds

that all this doubling and redoubling of our tracks was only stalling for time.

"We got to either lay for one of them posses and wipe 'em out, or git straight for Hole in th' Wall and let 'em follow us there—if they dare," George gritted as we sat over our evening meal at Jim Thorn's sheep camp at the head of Buffalo Creek.

"Yeah, I heard that old Bob Devine, th' foreman of th' CY Ranch, brought a whole damned army of lawmen into th' Hole after th' Red Sash Gang couple years back," offered Elza, swiveling his head as he watched the sheep herders eating their own meal twenty yards off.

"Well, you heard right, but Devine didn't stay around th' Hole very long," said George. "I wasn't there then, but th' boys bluffed him good and plenty . . . told him he'd never git out alive and pointed to th' dozens of guns up on th' tops of th' Red Walls trained on him."

"And—?"

"Hell, t'was only a lot of sticks and dummy guns they'd stuck up there, but it did th' trick. That posse never did stop ridin' until they got back to Buffalo."

"Well," I said, "I vote for the dummy guns, if we have to try that again, but I don't rule out trapping a posse—if it gets too close."

"My, look who's gettin' blood-thirsty," Elza snickered.

"I hope we never have to do more than chase them off," I said, wondering what Annie would have said to hear me talk so. But we were worn down to a thin edge, and I don't think any of us were in our proper minds.

"Well, we're now within two days of th' Hole, and I do a little votin' on my own hook," Elza replied. "I vote we steer clear of any more shootouts, one dead sheriff is enough for my notch-stick. I also vote we steer clear of th' Hole for th' time bein' and ride straight for New Mexico, th' WS Ranch—and Butch Cassidy."

"What about Lonny, Bob Lee and Billy Rogers?" George wanted to know.

"I don't think they'll come back down this way," I said. "I'd guess they've gone over to Colorado to let things cool down. And, you know we haven't heard a single rumor of them in all this time." I didn't say that I'd worried and fumed over Lonny ever since the robbery—but there was nothing to do but hope I was correct about him leaving the Territory.

"I guess you're right," said George. "And I guess you're right too," he told Elza. "It's a hell of a long ride, but I think we need a change of scenery if anyone ever did. Let's get started."

CHAPTER TWENTY-EIGHT

Once we'd made up our mind to get clear out of the country, and away from posses buzzing around our heads like a swarm of deadly wasps, we rode long and hard for the WS Ranch near Alma, New Mexico.

We picked up a pack horse and supplies at Kaycee, Wyoming, just missing one posse, south of the Speed Stagner Ranch. That particular bunch of lawmen, not trusting their own noses to ferret out our trail, had brought in a pack of bloodhounds from Beatrice, Nebraska. But those four-legged lawdogs fizzled out in the badlands, forty miles from Thermopolis, and we were out of the Territory before we heard about that new wrinkle in western posses.

Following the Outlaw Trail, George, Elza and I bypassed both Brown's Hole and Robbers' Roost, because of the activity around those hide-outs, due to the Governor of Utah's new hobby of catching horse thieves. As we rode past the desolate face of Robbers' Roost, with its twin flat-topped buttes, facing north and south across the sandy wastes, I wondered if Bronco Jack Caldwell was back there with his fellow rascals, Silver Tip and Blue John, but there wasn't time to make a call.

A week's ride fetched us over the Colorado

River at Lee's Ferry and traversing the red sandstone canyons of Arizona, with the great blue-tinged Mogollon Mountains rimming the east.

By the time we'd ridden into New Mexico, we'd lost one member of our team. George Curry, ailing ever since he'd been injured by his horse, when the first posse fired on us at Salt Creek Canyon, had to give up, and hunt for a doctor at St. Johns, Arizona Territory. The Doc, took one look at George's cracked rib, and ordered him to bed for a week.

"And when I'm outa here, I'm headin' back home," George had said, as he sulked in bed in the St. Johns House, chewing on the end of a cigar.

"But there could be posses still out," I said.

"I got enough cash to grease two dozen palms at once," George grunted. "Besides they ain't gonna look for anyone headin' northwards. I got friends at th' Bear Paw Mountains, in the horse business. And I'll stick there till things cool off—like your fiddle-playin' brother and Bobby Lee over at Colorado."

We all three shook hands—and that was the very last time I ever laid eyes on Flat Nose George Curry.

The WS was still the same fine spread I'd seen, when I'd rode in with Ben Kilpatrick back in December of '97. The same big windmills turned in the hot wind and the same white buildings shone in the brilliant New Mexican sun. The place looked more prosperous than it had last time—and there stood the man who kept the ranch ticking with the precision of a fine Swiss watch—Butch Cassidy.

"Here's a sight for my old sore eyes," Cassidy practically pulled me out of the saddle and hammered his welcome on my back. "Two of th' three top members of th', ah—" he glanced around at several cowpokes busy in the corral—*"railroad fraternity!"*

"George is O.K.," Elza hastened to say. "Got bunged up by a horse, and went back home—with his share."

"Come on, let's get you two settled in th' bunkhouse." Butch clapped Elza on the shoulder, while a big, burly cowboy sauntered up and took our horses to the barns.

"Where's Sundance and Ben Kilpatrick?" I asked when we'd squatted down on the empty bunks with our gear.

"Sundance and Ben are over in Texas with a long-rider named Carver." Butch grinned slightly as he thumbed through the loot from our pair of saddle bags. "Lots left after all th' splits, eh?"

We agreed and were dumbfounded to see Butch scratch a match and set fire to a packet of the money!

"Hey—for pete's sake—hold on!" Elza made a

frantic grab for the burning bundle, then dropped it with a yelp.

Butch stood up, stamped on the flaming paper. "That's about th' hottest money you boys'll ever see . . . and about as worthless!"

"That money was hard to come by, and a hell of a lot harder to hold on to," I said, completely baffled by Cassidy's actions.

Like a father, talking to his erring offspring, Butch laid his hands on our shoulders. "It's money, all right, but only negotiable when it has the right signatures. I hope you noticed that batch of bills from the First National Bank of Portland, Oregon was unsigned—all five thousand dollars worth."

We nodded speechlessly, and glanced over at the remaining money bundles. There was at least ten thousand dollars—in regular currency and safe from Butch's matches.

"I know what you boys are thinkin'." Butch smiled sadly. "But that money there is goin' right back out of the Territory of New Mexico."

We gaped, and Elza slumped down on his bunk. "Hunnh?"

"This is th' way th' pie was split," said Butch. "Lonny, Bobby Lee and th' Mex Kid, took one share apiece, fair and square . . . five thousand each."

"And . . . ?" I had a feeling what was coming.

"And George took two shares as th' leader of

th' strike. That made ten thousand for him."

"That totals, so far, twenty-five thousand." Elza was counting his fingers.

"Correct. But we subtract five thousand in bad money from th' total. Forty thousand, wasn't it? And that leaves just ten thousand dollars."

"Right!" Elza brightened up, and looked fondly at the rumped pile of yellow backs.

"But, you say this money's got to go somewhere else?" I felt very tired all of a sudden. All that commotion and rough riding, and no money?

"Sorry to say, yes! Y'see I try to play a square game with everyone, even some crook on th' inside of th' express company. It was agreed long ago that his information would always get him one-quarter of th' total haul from any robbery of th' express company's cash-box."

"Which is ten thousand?"

"Yep!" Butch took us each by an arm and piloted us out of the bunkhouse. "There was supposed to be damn nigh double on that Overland Flyer. If there'd have been, it would have worked out fine. But it's just bad luck for you, me and Elza that th' rest of our bunch took their cuts first."

"So that's why George's back give out on him before we got here," Elza swore under his breath. "Th' damned old sidewinder wanted to get for home with his bundle before Butch whacked it up proper!"

"Ah, there's Mister French, th' owner of th' WS," said Butch, pointing out a tall, neatly bearded gent who'd come out on the upper verandah of the big main ranch building. "You didn't get to meet him th' last time you were here, Kid. Seems you got in and out of here in a hurry."

"Mister French is a right nice fellow," Elza volunteered. "Takes on anyone Butch vouches for, as long as they do an honest day's work." He gave a short laugh. "And I guess we settle down and do a lot of honest day's work—broke as we are."

"I don't mind," I said, thinking that I never would get up enough money to help out Starr— or get Annie and I out of the country for good, that is—if she were still waiting for me in Star Valley.

My stay at the WS was longer than my last visit, back in Ninety-Seven. I rode fence and helped cut hay for nearly a month, along with Elza and the big cowboy who had taken our horses to the barns on the day we arrived.

Butch had a way of keeping his cowpokes in special groups. The regular riders went about their chores each day, and the punchers (in on Butch's plans) worked as teams. Thus Elza and I worked with the big, burly Texan called Franks (though his real name was Sam Ketchum).

On the fourth Saturday of our stay, Butch called Elza, Sam and myself out into the far corral after supper.

"I've waited long enough for that loony Sundance and dim-witted Ben Kilpatrick, and can't wait any longer."

"Longer for what?" Ketchum wanted to know, while Elza and I sat there.

"Th' Syndicate is going to take another crack at th' railroads," Butch answered, and leaned over to poke me in the ribs. "And th' Kid here is going to call th' shots on this one."

Then in a few words Butch laid it all out for us. His information told him there'd be a tidy sum riding the Wells Fargo strong box and coming down on the southbound from Denver to Fort Worth on the night of July 11. The exact time the shipment would be pinpointed in a few days.

"So, I want you to draw your wages tomorrow and ride out, one by one, meeting in Cimarron by the ninth. That'll give you time to get supplies, and rest up for the big one. I'll send you word, and one more man, by that date. This should go to make up for th' balls-up deal of th' Overland Flyer. There'll be money to burn this time!" He laughed ruefully. "And I don't mean in unsigned bank notes."

We three met in Cimarron at the time set up by Butch. Cimarron took to strangers, according to

Elza. There were plenty of those on the streets and in the several saloons. In fact, Sam Ketchum spotted a couple recently chased out of Texas by the Rangers. We gave such hard-cases the cold shoulder, keeping to ourselves and watching the calendar. We all put up at the big St. James Hotel, passing ourselves off as cattlemen on the move across the Territory. Sam Ketchum had never been inside so grand a building in his life and spent most of the day gawking at the etchings on the walls, rubbing his horny hands over the polished top of the grand piano, in the big parlor, and making the most of the marble lavatories.

"Tom'll call me a double-damned liar, when I tell him about them Eyetalian marble thrones," Sam said. "Sure wish he could take a gander at th' bed in my room—what with them four posts a'rearin' up, you could corral a small-sized horse in th' thing!"

Sam's brother Tom, called Blackjack by some folks, was on the dodge out in the Big Bend country of Texas, and not likely to be riding our direction in the near future.

However, a peculiar-looking rider did come trotting into Cimarron the afternoon of July 9 that Sam spotted. "Hey!" He took his feet down from the verandah railing of the St. James, and reaching over, poked Elza awake in his rocking chair.

"Deaf Charlie!" Sam grunted. "So that's who Butch sent over. And now we'll know th' time and exact place."

The horseman kept on down the street, and pulling up in front of one of the saloons, tied his mount to the railing and ambled into the place, head cocked on one side like a road-runner looking for a meal.

"Deaf Charlie, all right," said Elza. "No one could miss that crooked neck. I heard he was just out of th' Deer Lodge pen. Butch must'a wrote him to come on down and join th' festivities."

It did prove to be Deaf Charlie Hanks, alias O.C. Hanks, alias Camilla Hanks, as well as Charles Jones. And he was a figure of interest to us for several reasons. While we waited for Hanks to wet his whistle and come back up the street—for we could tell he'd seen us as he rode by, Sam and Elza filled me in a bit of Deaf Charlie's history.

"Folks think Charlie got that wry-neck from falling off a horse, or he tips his head that way to hear better, and he is pretty deaf at that—but he's just about the only cowboy I know that was hung and lived to tell about it," said Elza.

Sam agreed. "Charlie rode with a bunch th' Mexicans called th' *Seven Devils*. They was horse thieves and cattle rustlers and operated along th' border. Charlie made th' mistake of runnin' off a spread of horses while th' Ruales was in the neighborhood. They run him down and stretched his neck to a nearby cottonwood."

"He hung just long enough for th' Mexicans to go on about their business, then the rope broke and down come Charlie—with a crooked neck," added Elza.

I watched Hanks come out of the saloon, wipe his mouth and walk toward us, head cocked off center. "Think he'll be of any use to us?"

"Well, he's got pretty good creedentuals," said Sam. "He's just finished doin' ten years at Deer Lodge for holdin' up th' Northern Pacific at Big Timber, Montanny along with Bill Madden, back in Ninety-Two."

"He doesn't sound too lucky," I murmured as Hanks came up on the porch and sank into a chair near us, cocking his head at all and sundry.

After, whispered introductions, and some small talk about the weather and the latest gossip about cattle prices (for the benefit of a pair of sleepy drummers), Deaf Charlie tipped his head, even further, and muttered: "Butch says ten thirty on th' S-curve at Twin Mountain, tomorrow night." His husky voice creaked, like an unoiled hinge. "You fellers ready?"

"More'n ready!" said Sam. "Come on in this here place, Charlie, I bet you never had beds like them in Deer Lodge."

CHAPTER TWENTY-NINE

The morning of July 11, 1899, we rode out of Cimarron and headed through the hot sunshine toward the Colorado and Southern tracks miles to the west, aiming for the way station at Ute Park to catch the northbound Colorado & Southern, which was due to take on water there at 8 p.m.

Charlie Hanks took off in a bee-line for the north the day before, with a string of saddle horses, ready to meet us at the right spot just north of Folsom, New Mexico. He had a long hard ride ahead of him, driving the fresh riding stock, and he had to be there promptly.

We arrived at the way station in plenty of time to board the train when it came through. And as we waited in the shadow of the water tank, out in the middle of just plain desert, Sam Ketchum and Elza Lay swapped stories. And the more I listened, the more I became convinced that the New Mexico Territory was just like a dry tinder box—ready to explode into a hell of a fire-fight with the law at the next train robbery.

The Black Jack Ketchum gang, with Sam's brother Tom at the helm, and boasting such hard-cases as Bill Carver, George Musgrove and Billy Anderson had held up the *Gulf Express* near the Taos Mountains on September 3, 1897. A month or so after that, another gang robbed the Santa Fe Train at Grants, New Mexico. And in December of that year the Southern Pacific's *Sunset Limited* was stopped at Steins Pass.

"It looks as if the Territory has had about all the train-busting it can stand," I told Elza. "I wonder that Butch didn't think it over before he sent us out here to pull another one."

"Butch wants to give us a chance at making up for that wash-out of a raid back north," Elza answered.

"Won't be nothin' to it, Kid. You'll see." Sam Ketchum drained the last of his canteen, and shifted his feet out of the sunlight into the shadow thrown by the water tank. "What's th' time?"

We'd checked the time over and over by the end of the first two hours of riding the scuffed plush seats of the leading coach of the Colorado & Southern.

Boarding the northbound express at the way station on schedule, we were now only half an hour from the target site.

Elza and Sam had finally given up digging out their watches, relying on me to rouse them out at the right time. And they'd told me with a variety of winks and nudges, that as Cassidy had made me chief of this raid, it was up to me to worry it through.

I sank back on the hard seat and looked around

one more time. The conductor had gone back down the train somewhere, leaving the usual bunch of passengers. Leathery-faced cattlemen in range clothes, flashy drummers in loud suits and one or two Mexican-Americans in wrinkled white cotton outfits, rode elbow to elbow with a scattering of farmers in bib overalls, and a few tourists—all nodding with boredom as the train rocked along, climbing up toward Trinidad, Colorado.

At last it was time. The express was rounding one curve after another. Out the window, the moon swung toward the train—a great silver Peso that hesitated and then rolled away again.

Poking Elza and Sam, I got them on their feet. Then leaving Elza to watch the coach, Sam and I went out the front of the car into the windy night, pulling our pistols out from under our coats. I stood on the swaying, creaking platform and watched Sam clamber up to the top of the tender and then followed him—six-shooter in hand.

"Pull back on that throttle," I yelled into the ear of a very surprised Engineer. After one quick stare over his shoulder, he jabbed at the throttle and slammed on his brake lever. The big engine shuddered, wheels squealed and skidded on the sanded rails and we gradually came coasting to a halt—within twenty yards of a stretch of flaming grass along the right of way, torched by Deaf Charlie Hanks to light our approach. Beyond the burning prairie, the headlight of the engine picked out the welcome sight of our horses on the offside of the great S Curve.

"Boy!" shouted Sam as he herded the train crew back to the express car, "this is just about the same spot we hit th' Gulf Express in Ninety-Seven. Git along there you!"

Deaf Charlie came stumbling and panting up with his Winchester and the bag of dynamite, and we began to pound and thump on the express car door. When there was no reply to our calls and demands, I fired a pair of shots at the very top of the car—and got results in a hurry. The door slid back and the Messenger stood with hands high.

Questioning the fellow brought no reply. He was either scared stiff or bull-headed, or both. Sam's hair-trigger temper went off with a bang. Leaping up into the car he grabbed the messenger by the throat, shouting, "Cough up what you've got and don't be foolish, or you'll find yourself shootin' skyward to your maker!"

"All right," I said, "we'll get those cheese boxes open. Hand me that dynamite, Charlie!"

In a minute the dynamite went off with a bigger bang than Sam's vocal explosion and we scrambled back into the smoke-choked car where the local and through safes lay on their sides, completely shattered.

Both were bone empty!

Sam and I stared at each other—then glared out

at the Express Messenger. "You heard what this man said before," I shouted at the Messenger, waving my six-shooter in Sam's direction. "He'll tear you apart unless we get what we came for— where's the money?"

"All the money was taken off at the last stop," he said, finding his voice, and using it loud and clear.

A pistol cracked out, back toward the coaches. Charlie Hanks ran toward the commotion, Winchester trailing in his hand, head cocked for any sort of action.

"Let's git out'a here," Sam yelled, still covering the train crew with his 45's. "They'll be comin' down on us . . . let's ride!"

A pistol exploded again, and then Elza and Deaf Charlie came hustling up to us. "Damn if there ain't some sort of a Tin Star on board—Sheriff from Chavez County. And he's hot to become a hero!"

A gun boomed, this time sounding like a heavier weapon. The bullet chirped overhead with a mighty wicked sound.

"All right, mount up!" I shouted. "Be damned if we're going to get into any shooting match over two empty cash boxes. Butch'd better can his squealer, before he gets us all killed!"

When we rode away, firing our six-shooters to keep that bristly lawman's head down, the patch of grass touched off by Charlie Hanks, now charred into a scattering of sparks, flooded to a silvery pool by the mounting moon. Our raid had taken less than an hour, and well it might. We'd probably raised ourselves a hornet's nest—and not taken a nickel!

Butch's plans for our retreat had left the field open to us. We could either ride a long circle and come back to the WS or go to ground in the mountains of the Territory until all pursuit died away.

Next morning we halted in the rocky wilds, north of Cimarron and sat letting our tired horses blow. I'd been riding lead, with Elza bringing up the end of the column. It had rained off-and-on during the night and I was bothered that our tracks might be easy to follow.

"Let's take a vote." I waved everyone up. "I say we circle around to the WS and trade off these mounts, then shake this New Mexico dust out of our boots."

Elza, Sam and Deaf Charlie outvoted me. "We'll stay in th' mountains!"

The next evening, Sunday, July 12, we were camped in one of the deep gorges of the Sangre de Christos. Sam, who'd been through before, called it Turkey Canyon. Whatever it was called, I didn't like the looks of the place. Though there was just a narrow trail to the bottoms, and plenty of underbrush and interlocking tree branches to screen us from any spying eyes above—there was also enough cover to let a man get up within fifty yards of us before we could see him.

When I'd pointed out the fact that we could be in a real bind if any posse ever got down into the gorge, both Elza and Sam laughed it off.

"Hell Kid, you're plumb jumpy," Sam joked. "Those Tin Stars couldn't get in here without us hearin' 'em comin' half-a-mile away. Besides, it's two-to-one they ain't even organized yet—if there ever is a posse!"

About five o'clock, while Sam and Charlie Hanks were playing High Fives and arguing about their cards, under the cover of an old tarp hung across a couple of bushes, and Elza was just coming back from a small spring with water for coffee, I got up and walked down to look at the horses. I was nigh as jumpy as Sam had said. If I'd had my way, we would still be riding toward the WS or in that general direction.

It had begun to rain again, and I was turning back to camp when a blast of gunfire crashed out of the underbrush with the sudden fury of a thunderbolt!

The posse had found us—and found us flat-footed!

Sam and Charlie tumbled over and made a grab at their weapons, while Elza and I dived for the bushes. But Elza was a bit late, and as he hit the ground a 30.30 slug tore through his shoulder, whirling him around.

"Look at me knock that one!" One of the possemen yelped.

Fortunately I was close to several large boulders, giving good protection from the continuous storm of bullets that whistled, screamed and smashed off trees and rocks. This posse was out for blood and firing to kill!

Leaping up, I made a dash for the rifles, and managed to grab my new Marlin 40-65, and roll out of the way behind a big boulder as another fusillade slammed around me. Off to one side, Tom was getting into action, firing his Winchester at the sudden puffs of smoke that broke out of the trees about 100 yards away. As I levered and fired, I caught a glimpse of Deaf Charlie Hanks crouched over, tugging Elza behind a heap of fallen timber, his head cocked with determination.

I yelled at Tom to take care, for he was rising too high to fire, then staying up too long to watch the effect of his shots.

From the number of rifles throwing out dark puffs of smoke, I guessed there had to be at least a good dozen in that bunch of ambushers. The way they'd opened fire, without a word of warning—filled me with a rage that I'd never known before—even with the posse up north.

My black Logan temper was struggling to get the upper hand and force me to fire my ammunition as fast as I could pull the trigger. And a stray bullet hurling off my sombrero, to give me a crease on the temple, didn't help my temper any. It was fire, yell, pull the trigger and duck the volleys of lead smashing against trees, rocks, and whistling over in a screeching storm.

Suddenly Sam took a rifle ball in the left arm and pitched back with a groan.

I grew calm and calculating. It was up to me now! From somewhere came the shouts of Deaf Charlie, but the firing broke out again, and I had to wait until it thinned down. Then squinting carefully around my great rock, I put three fast shots through a thick pile of brush. They took effect, for a distant figure lurched into the trail, threw out its hands and folded.

For a long moment there was dead silence. The rain continued to patter, and I could ever hear the distant stamping of our uneasy horses down the gorge. Then again the posse's guns rapped out their staccato hate.

I could tell from the shifting of the posse's fire that one or more were trying to work around to flank us. I waited until the next shots came and then pumped a pair of the big 40-65 calibre bullets at the group of trees to my left. The fellow, whoever he was, was a battler—for he returned the fire with interest. But now my blood was up and I was determined to stop him in his tracks or go down trying.

We fired back and forth for over 20 minutes, until I began to dread running out of ammunition. I could see the large pine tree that shielded my antagonist and I kept up a steady pounding away at it until I'd fired at least 12 shots into the splintering trunk.

Then all was still, as I paused and listened for the movement of the possemen off in the underbrush. I heard a groan from the pine and knew that I'd downed my man.

Somewhere I could hear the moans of other wounded, among them the voice of Tom Ketchum calling to me—then all was silent again. A stillness that seemed weird hovered above Turkey Canyon.

I waited and waited, but never another shot came my way, so I worked over cautiously to where Sam Ketchum lay crumpled, with Elza Lay propped against a rock trying to grin at me with a bloody face. Both were bandaged and had their weapons beside them. But Charlie Hanks was gone.

"Charlie did all he could," Elza grunted, waving a blood-stained hand toward Sam. "Then he got a chance to hit th' trail, and I told him to git while th' gittin' was good. Charlie sort of lost his taste for fightin' while he was sittin' it out in th' Deer Lodge Pen."

"Can you ride?" I asked, looking at my watch, noticing that it shook so I could scarcely read it. Six o'clock, only six o'clock and still time for the fight to break out again.

"I guess I can," Elza staggered up, and I put out my hand to warn him—but there wasn't a sound, except the drip, drip of the rain.

As it grew darker, still no sound of activity from the posse, nor any movement, I got Elza into his saddle, bringing up the horses from below . . . but try as I might, I couldn't get Sam on his feet.

"No use, Kid. It's no damn use," he groaned. "Here, leave me my guns and th' canteens and I'll come along after you boys when I get my second wind."

"He's right, Kid," Elza muttered from where he sat, bent over on his saddle, hanging on by sheer grit. "If we don't pull out now, they'll be comin' back in th' mornin' and we'll all go down together."

It was now too dark to do more than get into the saddle and move on down the twisting trail that led out of the other end of the box canyon. I felt low as a sheep thief, but it would do no good to stay and wait for the posse to brave-up or be joined by more trigger-happy lawdogs in the morning.

We shook hands with Sam, Elza leaning far out of his saddle to reach down to grab at Ketchum's trembling fingers—then we rode.

• • •

Lying in my blankets out in the rugged hills that night, I thought of what had happened. Not only had we fought off a hard-headed and determined bunch of lawmen—and fought them off to a standstill, we had also made that part of New Mexico so hot that we had to get clear away and as soon as possible. I would be a wanted man—and wanted damned bad, for I was certain that someone had been killed in that posse. Who killed who, I wasn't certain—and I didn't want to know, for I refused to think of myself as a coldblooded killer. I'd fought to keep my freedom, and I think any real man would have done the same thing, but it still didn't make me feel any better to think I might have cut the string on another human being.

When the sun gleamed up over the Taos peaks, I put Elza on his horse and we rode on across the hills toward the south—and away from Sam Ketchum's Turkey Canyon and any possible posses that might be ranging around trying to come up with us again. I was about certain that Sam had been picked up, for I couldn't see how he could have got out of there by himself. I could only hope they would get him to some place where he would be doctored up.

And as far as where Deaf Charlie Hanks had got to, neither Elza nor I could hazard a guess. "Charlie's probably put as much space between his hide and th' law as possible," said Elza, as we rode on down into the wild and lonely Seven Rivers country.

As gritty as Lay was, by the time we'd been on the trail for three days, and had traveled along the wandering Pecos and crossed the shallows of the muddy Rio Hondo, near Roswell, I could see that we had to call a halt for the time being.

Riding through the New Mexico Territory from time to time, in the past, Elza had made more than one friend at the small ranches along the Seven Rivers grasslands. At his suggestion, I dropped him off at the Double-D Ranch, close to old Fort Sumner and there he stayed to rest up, while I went on to the Lusk horse ranch about 20 miles from Carlsbad.

The Lusk place was one of the spots that Butch had mentioned in the past as a pretty good hide-out. Lusk, a penny-ante horse trader (and horse thief), seemed glad to have company, and we got along well for two weeks until Elza rode in to join me.

Elza was feeling pretty chipper, the wound in his shoulder about healed up, and we were making plans to ride on around to the WS when we went to bed that night of August 14.

"With a $1400 reward out for you and me—and Sam, if he's still alive—I think we'd better get on out of this country and head back north," I'd told Elza. "We can check in with Butch at the WS, on the way, and see what he's got on the fire."

"You bet. Funny ain't it? We seem to be worth more on th' hoof than we can collect for ourselves with all our shootin' irons!"

Next morning, while Elza got us some breakfast in the lean-to kitchen, and Lusk was out rounding up some strays, I went to the corral on the nearby hill and saddled up our mounts. I'd just led the horses out of the corral and was putting up the bars when I looked down toward the ranch house and saw a pair of horses in front of the place. One I recognized as Lusk's roan and the other, a dun horse, was unknown to me.

Something made me pause, then vault into the saddle of my gray pony, and keep a sharp watch on the house. It was mighty well that I did, for in a moment I heard a gunshot, then another and here came Elza, tumbling out of the kitchen door with a Tin Star hanging onto one leg and Lusk onto the other. The three went down in a heap in the dust and rolled over and over. A pistol went off again and the bullet keened over my head.

The Law had Elza and there was nothing I could do—save charge headlong for the trio and take a possible bullet in the process.

By the time I could turn my horse and prepare to head for the traitorous Lusk and the lawman, they had Elza hogtied and sitting on the ground.

I wheeled my mount again, stood in the

stirrups, waved *adios* at Elza, and galloped off at a fast clip toward Carlsbad. Just like that former member of The Seven Devils, Deaf Charlie Hanks, I was putting as much distance between myself and the law as possible. If I'd stayed and tried to battle that tinhorn Lusk and the officer, I might have won—but then I could have stopped a bullet, and where would the money come from to help Starr through her trouble? That is—if I ever was able to get my hands on any money. And I was beginning to truly wonder if I ever would.

CHAPTER THIRTY

That late summer, fall, and winter, following our fight at Turkey Canyon, seemed to pass mighty fast. After Elza had been grabbed at Lusk's and poor old Sam Ketchum was taken to Santa Fe, where he died on July 24, I had come back to the WS by roundabout trails.

Butch already knew about our defeat on the railway and our stand-off battle afterward. "Just th' breaks of th' game, Kid. Like my old teacher at horse thief'n Mike Cassidy, used to say, *'There ain't a horse runnin' that can't be rode, and there ain't a man ridin' that can't be throwed!'* "

For the rest of 1899, Butch and I stuck tight to the WS Ranch and stayed busy. We became plain working cowboys. Butch, of course, kept on as *Jim Lowe,* honest and efficient ramrod for the ranch. And I, carried on the WS books as *Tom Capehart,* rode the range, mended fence, punched stock aboard the cattle cars at the Alma railroad yards, and pitched hay into the big WS barns when time came to button up for winter.

We heard through reading the *Santa Fe New Mexican* and some local papers that Elza Lay had shot up both that tinhorn, yellowbelly Lusk and also the Sheriff, but as nobody died in the fracas, Elza was sent to the Santa Fe Pen for life.

"At least they didn't hang him," said Butch. "You know, once upon a time I'd have tried to bust him out, like I did you fellows, but I get wiser as I get older—you tend to live longer that way."

Unbeknown to me, Butch had sent a blind wire to Lonny at Cripple Creek, informing my brother that I was working at the WS.

Lonny's letter arrived Saturday, March 3, and never was a letter more welcome than that one. It put my mind at ease to find he'd gone back home to Aunt Lee's in Missouri, and was out of the saloon and the long-riding for good—I hoped. One Logan on the dodge was enough . . . or one too many:

Dear Harvey,

Glad to know you're working for a living down at the WS. Maybe I'll come down there sometime, when this dodging around is done for good.

After Bob Lee, Billy the Mex Kid and I left you at Wilcox we gave those Tin Stars the slip easy and hid out for a week in the Owl Creek Mountains. Billy Rogers left with his split a couple of days later, on his way south. Bob and I went to Harlem, Montana and bought a half-interest in a gambling saloon there, and made out o.k.

for several months, Bob traveling back to Cripple Creek every so often to try to peddle our Big Strike Saloon.

Early in January a pair of Pinkerton snoopers pulled into town on some crow-bail plugs and got the postmaster at Harlem to point us out to them. I hustled around and sold the place to a Mr. Ringwald of Great Falls, and wound up with $1,000 for my half, $300 cash, and a note payable to our old pal Jim Thornhill at our Landusky ranch.

I woke up Bob in our back room of the place and told him about the Pinks, who I hear are called Siringo and Sayles—good name for a music hall team, eh?—Anyway, Bob was all for fighting them, but I talked some sense into him, and we wound up shaving off our mustaches and catching the westbound Great Northern at the Zurich Water Tank, west of Harlem. We got to Shelby Junction, where we caught a southbound for Cripple Creek, Colorado.

While we were disposing of our Cripple Creek place, Cassidy's wire came, and as I was coming on to Aunt Lee's, I thought I'd write you from here.

Bob decided to stay in Cripple Creek, and try his luck as a dealer at one of the last saloons open in that ghost town.

I'd like to go back to the ranch and help Jim Thornhill run it—but I suppose, as long as Winters is around—there's be no chance. He's still on the warpath over me taking that shot at him, before I came down to The Hole.

I hope to stay here for the winter, and fill up on Aunt Lee's good home cooking. Write when you have some time. Adiós from Lonny.

On Monday, March 4, Butch had gone into Alma for supplies. When he came back, I could tell that he was upset about something.

"Did you run into some trouble—or see someone you didn't expect to?" I asked him, as we unloaded the buckboard, and carried the boxes and bags into the cook shack.

"Here." He handed me the Monday copy of the *Alma Gazette*. Right on the front page was a news item, datelined Kansas City, Missouri.

I took one look and sat down on a bag of potatoes.

Lonny was dead! Shot dead by a posse from Kansas City, as he ran from Aunt Lee's home at Dodson, Missouri, rather than risk a gun fight near the house. It was the same old story— they fired first and never even gave my brother a chance. Though he carried a six-shooter, he'd made no effort to fire at them. And it had happened just one week after he'd mailed the letter.

What went wrong, I wondered? Did Lonny, never the best of fighters, loose his grit and just run for it—like he'd been on the run ever since he'd followed me? As I looked at it, I was as responsible for his death as if I'd have pulled the trigger, myself.

Butch must have just about read my mind. "Worse thing you can do is to blame yourself, Kid! These things happen, sometimes. Someone tipped off somebody, and those Pinkertons fell on your brother like a load of bricks! They're downright deadly." He scratched his chin and looked off at the evening sky, then glanced back at me. "We'll have company in about an hour. Sundance and Ben Kilpatrick are campin' out on th' north range. Saw 'em as I was comin' back from town. They'll be ridin' in later. Then I think we'll all move out of here around midnight."

Sitting by myself on the corral fence after supper, and left strictly alone by Butch, and the other hands, I found myself taking my kid brother's death even harder than when Winters backshot Johnny.

As I sat there, I made one sullen vow after another to get some sort of revenge against the world for what it had done to us. We'd lost a profitable ranch (even though Jim Thornhill still held it down), and we'd been driven out into the wilds, hunted down and killed. Now I knew how the Indians had felt when they'd been cheated, hunted and killed off by the white land thieves.

We'd done wrong, Lonny and I, though Johnny hadn't harmed a single person. Yes, Lonny and I had taken money that didn't belong to us and at the end of a six-shooter. I wouldn't try to deny that. But we'd tried for money that belonged to the mortgage bleeding banks and land grabbing railroads and not from some poor rancher nor nester the way the banks and railroads had done and continued to do!

It *was* wrong, but I'd made myself a promise that I'd come by sufficient money to take care of Starr's affliction—and with enough left over to fetch Annie away from the lonely life she'd led . . . and I meant to do it.

The way those Indians had fought back, stuck in my mind. Now I was going to fight back as well, whenever I got the chance. The Indians had taken all they could from the white land thieves and then went on the war path. I had a touch of old Indian blood in me, as well. And I was going to take my own war path, whenever the situation arose. Let the next posse that tried to jump me—look to themselves.

I got off the rail and went to hunt up Butch.

CHAPTER THIRTY-ONE

Late in March, Butch, Sundance, Ben Kilpatrick and myself had been on the trail for several weeks. We'd given our notice to Mister French and collected our wages the same night Ben and Longabaugh had showed up at the WS.

Now we were heading toward the northwest, riding leisurely up through Arizona, with The Hole in the Wall as our final destination. Butch's *inside man* on the Union Pacific was on to a "good thing," and we meant to be ready whenever Butch got the signal. This time, we all said, *the third time is the charm!*

There had been a rash of posses out scouring the country ever since we left the WS. They weren't after us, in particular, but any of the gangs that still ranged the outlands. Sam's brother, Tom Ketchum, known as Black Jack, had robbed the Folsom train in late fall of '99, but his luck was about as bad as poor Sam's for they wounded him so badly he had to surrender before he died in the wilds. Now he was sweating it out in jail and ready to be hanged for train robbery. They were deadly serious about busting trains down there. And that was one reason we were on the way back north, where they only threw you in the pen for such tricks. Of course, they had to catch you first!

We'd heard from a sheep herder that two posses were out in the field, looking for some tin-horn badmen who'd robbed some stores and post offices down below St. Johns.

Camping out that night of March 26, about five miles north of St. Johns, we took turns at sentry-go, but nothing happened until we had eaten dinner next day and were headed out on the trail toward the Navaho reservation, west of the Painted Desert of Arizona.

"Hell!" Sundance yelled from where he rode along with the pack horse at the rear of the column. As one, we swiveled in our saddles to see what was eating him and discovered six horsemen lashing their mounts after us. It was one bad spot to be in, for there wasn't a bit of cover for miles.

"Let's go," Butch shouted and set the example by spurring up into a gallop, while Sundance dropped the pack horse's rope and took right off after the rest of us.

In a minute, the posse was close enough to begin firing. Though they let off plenty of shots, none came very close. Seeing they weren't the sharpest marksmen in the world, we slowed down enough to fire back. This kept them at a pretty respectable distance, and so it went for over fifteen miles—another retreat, but a retreat with some sense behind it. By fighting a rear-guard action with backbone to it, we'd tired out part of the posse's horses. They weren't a patch on the fine horseflesh we rode and it showed by mid-afternoon.

About four o'clock we'd got far enough ahead of the straggling pursuit to be able to pull up into some of the first cover we'd come to.

"I vote we keep on goin'," said Sundance, while Ben Kilpatrick slowly nodded his head and rolled a cigarette. Butch just sat on his big white mare and watched the trail behind us.

"And I overrule you," I said. "Last time I was outvoted by two of your friends that are now permanently out of action. We're going to stay right here and hold a reception for those gentlemen!"

Butch dismounted and signalled the rest to pile off. We took the horses up a trail that ran to the top of a bluff, covered with cedars and brush, staked them out, then scattered through the thicket and waited for the riders' approach.

"If we pull this off right, it could put the fear of God into the whole damn gang of posses around here," I said. "So make each shot count."

At five o'clock the first pair of possemen rode up the trail toward us, bold as brass, not taking the trouble to look for tracks, or consider the possibility that someone might be waiting in the rocks to have some target practice. I recognized the man on the lead bay horse as the strapping, big fellow who'd been at the head of the posse ever since it made its appearance. This was the chief, and the very man to knock out of the pursuit.

I lifted my Marlin, drew a bead on the middle of the big star on his buckskin vest, and then as the thought of old Pike Landusky and his tin star came into my mind, lowered the rifle and nodded to the boys. A volley of lead blazed out at the possemen. Both riders turned to dash their horses back down the narrow, rocky trail, collided with each other, and then fell sideways off their frantic horses.

We stood up and waited until the echoes of our rifles racketed around the hills and died away. Though we made no move for half an hour, no one else made an appearance. That posse had enough!

We walked down the narrow trail and looked over the downed men. Both were already stiffening in death. It was a sorry sight to see such brave, but foolish fellows in such a case. I picked up the hats and put them over their faces, while we rounded up the pair's horses, stripped the dead men of arms and ammunition and mounted up again.

"Well—," Sundance turned down his mouth, "I guess it's better them than us, eh?"

"That's what I was goin' to say," Ben Kilpatrick muttered as he rolled himself another cigarette. This was a trick he'd learned last year, while back in Texas with Bill Carver and his gang. Someone had told him that true-blue cowboys always rolled their own and he was determined to shine at it.

Butch pulled a pack of ready-mades out of his pocket, lit up and waved his arm for our column to get under way.

By April 1 we were deep into the Chiricahua Mountains and still on a trail that led northwest toward the Colorado River and the top of Arizona. We'd seen a quartet of riders at a distance, but were able to take a good long look with our glasses and discover them to be some Mexicans loping to the south.

"Those Greasers are up to no good," Butch laughed, putting up his binoculars. "Two-to-one they're on their way through the mountains at Rustlers Park to lift themselves some horses or cattle below the Mexican line."

We gave them no more thought and rode on toward Triangle Springs, a regular stop on the northbound Owl-Hoot Trail. It was late afternoon when we arrived and went into camp for the night. While Ben Kilpatrick and Sundance were scaring up greasewood for the fire, Butch and I took a walk up to the top of a nearby knoll.

"Well, here's another chance to snap the trap on some more possemen," Butch gritted, pointing out a pair of riders racking toward our camp from the southwest.

One look at them through the glasses brought us back down the hill on the dead run. "That's nobody else but George Scarborough!" Butch signaled Sundance and Ben to drop everything and get ready for a fight.

"Christmas, don't they never let go?" Sundance complained, while we bellied up behind some rocks and got ready.

"That's what I was goin' to say," blandly offered Kilpatrick, rolling his inevitable cigarette as he squatted behind a sage bush.

"And I was going to say, I wish I had a frying pan right about now," I told him, jacking a shell into the Marlin. "I know what I'd do with it—and so do you . . . get your tail out of sight behind these rocks!"

The riders loped up, pointing at our saddled horses. Then they caught sight of Ben, out in the open, like an ostrich with its head in the sand and its rump in the air. The man, Butch called Scarborough, had a pistol in his hand and he instantly opened fire on Kilpatrick, getting off three shots.

We fired back, Sundance becoming so over-heated, he jumped up and pumped shot after shot at the lawmen.

It was over before it started, for Scarborough folded up in the saddle and went over backwards as his horse felt a bullet and bucked him off into the sand.

The other man was also winged, for we heard him yelp as he took a bullet in the arm. He slid from his own animal, in the midst of the firing, and helped his wounded companion out of sight behind some rocks.

"Hold it!" I said in the sudden stillness. "All we want to do is stop these people in their tracks—not slaughter every mother's son!"

Butch tugged his sombrero off, wiped the sweat from his eyes and nodded. "Kid's right! We don't need any more posses out after our scalps just because we're trigger happy. Scarborough, over there, is as tough as they make 'em. Knocked over a rustler named McRose right in the middle of the bridge between El Paso and Juarez, Mexico. Damned fuss about it by th' Mexicans—but George Scarborough didn't care. Then he let daylight through old John Selman, the jasper that killed Hardin. George's tough, all right. And we don't want him on our necks all th' way to Hole in the Wall."

We led the horses down behind a dip in the sandy ground and mounted up. As we rode off north, Cassidy yelled at the two wounded lawmen. "No offense, Sheriff. We ain't no tinhorn bunch. We just don't like bein' followed too close. Take it easy, and we'll send back some help!"

"Did you mean that?" Sundance asked as we lashed our horses onward.

"That I did," said Butch. "And when we get within hailen' distance of th' next town, in you go and let someone know the whereabout of Scarborough. He's no tinhorn either."

After the two fire-fights with the posses in Arizona, the rest of our trip north was calm as cream. When we finally rode into Hole in the Wall on April 20 all tuckered out, we got some more bad news. In spite of the fact Sundance had actually risked his neck riding into San Simon to tell a saloon keeper that Sheriff George Scarborough had been shot and needed help back at Triangle Springs, it hadn't seemed to do very much good, for Scarborough up and died, anyway, just four days later.

Butch was down in the mouth about that death. "There's some fellows on both sides of the law you can admire, and poor old George Scarborough was one of them, even if he toted a badge."

"Not me," said Sundance. "As long as I'm on this side, I don't want anything to do with that other side."

"That's what—," Ben Kilpatrick started to remark.

"Here, have a ready-made," Sundance hastened to say, jamming a hardroll at Kilpatrick to change the subject.

The dispenser of this news was none other than Deaf Charlie Hanks, who showed us a newspaper with the story. Charlie had a large amount of explaining to do concerning his vanishing act after the Battle of Turkey Canyon.

With his head cocked on one side, more than ever, the ex-member of The Seven Devils, and star boarder of the Deer Lodge Pen, went into such detail over his retreat and subsequent travels that, at last, Butch and I both left the Hole in the Wall cabin to go on a hunting trip to the north end of the Hole.

"Let him tell all that to Ben Kilpatrick," Butch snorted, "and he'll see that Ben was just about to say the same things."

When Butch and I came back five days later to the cabins without one piece of game, we found ourselves really knee-deep in bad news. The Hole was jammed with glooms, and a good dozen long-riders. Charlie Hanks had been holding down the place all by his lonesome until we'd arrived from Arizona, for George Curry and Billy Rogers (who'd normally been in residence at the Hole) were off on some sort of scouting trip. Now the place seemed packed with horses and hard-cases.

Prominent among the newcomers was no one else but the half-Mex kid, Billy Rogers. He was going on at a great rate when Butch and I entered the cabin, waving his hands and jabbering half in Spanish and half in English.

"You hear that?" Sundance turned a mighty long face to us, when he saw us come in. "Seems open season on Georges, don't it?"

"Meaning what?" I asked, while Butch raised his eyebrows and looked over Billy and the rest.

"Poor old George Curry got it in th' head up these Green River. Ah, *nombre di dios*!" And Billy went into a flurry of Spanish, waving his hands in the air.

"Here!" Butch poked him in the ribs a good one, and wig-wagged for Ben Kipatrick to toss over a bottle of Old Crow. "Down a little belt of this and then talk straight."

Billy, tears running down his face, gulped a snort or two of whiskey, and then settled down to tell us of the last days of poor old Flat Nose George Curry.

Cutting through all of the hand waving and relapses into Spanish, George's finale went about this way: Both he and Billy had been in and out of the Hole since George returned from New Mexico. He'd gone over and tried to pay up on the mortgage the bank carried on his little ranch, but there was a new man at the top—and he'd shuffled so many papers George still owed more than that $5,000. It was still no deal, so George gambled and drank up most of that $5,000 in a regular fit of the blues.

When he sobered, he took up with Billy and they began to run off cattle from the ranches along the Green River. It got so bad that, at last, the ranch owners went to Sheriff Preece of Unitah County. Preece, not wanting to go after George alone, put in a call for help to Sheriff Tyler of a neighboring county. Between the two of them, they got up a posse and went after Flat Nose. In the meantime George had run out of supplies, and sent Billy to the nearest town for some grub. So Billy was out of the area when the posses caught up with George Curry.

It developed into a running fight that went on the rest of the day and began again the next morning on April 17. George finally holed up on the other side of the Green River and tried to stand the posse off. But Tyler happened to be on the same side of the river as George and shot him through the head at a great distance with a new, high-powered Krag-Jorgensen.

After Butch has heard all the particulars, and Sundance, Ben Kilpatrick, Charlie Hanks, Billy Rogers and the rest of the assembled long-riders were downing toasts to the fallen Flat Nose, he took a full bottle of Old Crow (his favorite drink), and motioned me back out of the cabin.

"Let's saddle up tomorrow and take a little ride for ourselves. Maybe you, Sundance and me." Butch sank down on the sandy soil at one corner of the Hole in the Wall cabin. "I think we ought to go out and kill a little time, now we know th' huntin's pretty poor in th' Hole right now. There ought to be better huntin' up around Green River."

I sat down beside him and took the bottle for a belt. "I'm not so sure I know what you're driving at."

"Oh, I think you do. You've been developin' into a champion posse trapper, ain't you? Well, I think, peaceable as I usually am, that we ought to try to trap just one more posse for ourselves."

I handed the Old Crow back, looked at him carefully, then nodded.

"And in th' meantime, as old Bill Shakespeare used to say, 'let's sit ourselves upon th' ground and talk about dead kings.' " Cassidy tipped the bottle long and steadily.

CHAPTER THIRTY-TWO

Good as his word, Butch led us out of the Hole the very next day on the way to Green River. We hadn't said anything about our talk to Sundance. I figured that if we did run into the people Butch was looking for, things would sort themselves out at that time.

As far as Sundance knew, we were out looking over the country for a possible strike—and that suited him.

So we camped along for the next three weeks, just taking our time, though Sundance had a puzzled look on his face as the days went by and we stayed on the trail. Butch had the idea that if we let ourselves be seen by enough people, word would get back to the men who had shot George Curry. We'd heard from time to time that both of the Sheriffs, responsible for Flat Nose's end, had made plenty of war talk about cleaning out all the territories of such trash as George Curry and his bunch.

"That remains to be seen, don't it?" Butch said, squinting over his tin cup of coffee when we ate supper on the night of May 26, along Hill Creek, fifty miles north of Thompson, Utah.

Piling out in the early morning mists arising from the creek, we took care of the horses, then came back to have a cup of coffee by the campfire. As it was still chilly, we sat hunkered over the fire, wrapped up in our blankets.

While we sat there, half-listening to Sundance digging nuggets of information from his "Pocket Cyclopedia"—and learning (against our will) that St. Petersburg, Russia had a mean summer temperature of 60.8 degrees and a winter mean temperature of just 17.2 degrees, Butch shifted around in his blanket and reached for his Winchester.

"It's going to be a lot hotter than St. Petersburg's summer in just a minute, if I don't miss my guess. Take a look at those fellows, Harry!"

Now, I sat up straight when I heard Cassidy address The Sundance Kid by his proper name—something he never did unless very drunk or very sober.

"Hunh? Oh—yeah! That's Jesse Tyler, himself—one half of th' Tin Star murder team."

"Sit tight!" Cassidy muttered. "Let's see if he wants to plug some more border trash."

"Now I know why you've been draggin' my carcass over half of th' blamed country," Sundance slowly lifted his six-shooter, under the blanket. "Y'knew I could spot th' big skunk!"

By this time, the Sheriff and one of his Deputies had dismounted and were walking straight for our camp, hands on their pistols.

"Hello boys," the big law officer grunted,

"thought you was a party of Indians, all wrapped up in those blankets. We're on th' lookout for some Ute hoss thieves."

"That so?" Butch grinned. "Thought you was out to shoot yourselves some more of George Curry's horse thieves!"

At the mention of Curry, both men yanked out their weapons and turned to run back for their mounts, where a third man sat on horseback.

We waited for them to turn and fire, but they were on their way!

"Plug 'em!" Sundance squawked. "They never give George any chance to ride for it!" His pistol banged off, while Butch's Winchester joined the fray. I was up on my feet, pulling the trigger of the Marlin, right along with them!

Tyler and his Deputy hit the ground stone dead! George Curry was avenged.

Our first stop after hurriedly leaving the camp at Hill Creek was at Jack Turner's Ranch in Hay Canyon, eight miles northeast. We'd left the pack horse and one of the mounts that had been favoring a foreleg, in order to make it appear as though we were still in the vicinity, when the second Deputy returned with reinforcements.

We dropped our horses off at Turner's, taking three fresh mounts, though Jack didn't like the swap very much.

"We're going up Hay Canyon and across the

White River," Butch grinned. "As soon as some money comes our way—you'll get enough to settle up."

Turner shrugged, as he watched us ride off with his best horses.

"You can bet he'll light a shuck to get to th' nearest lawman," Sundance shouted at Butch as we tried to catch up with a fleeing Cassidy.

"And that's just why we'll be going in the opposite direction," Butch shouted back over his shoulder. "My mother didn't raise any fools!"

Jack Turner's horses proved to be well-worth the time and trouble we had in circling back twenty miles to the east and then on south, as they fairly ate up the miles toward Robbers' Roost.

The flatboat man, an old hand at ferrying owl-hoots across the Colorado River, had all the latest gossip and got rid of it as we creaked over the wide, coffee-colored water.

"Don't know who you fellers is, and damn-well don't want'a know," the old man rattled on, adding brown spurts of his own tobacco juice to the amber river. "No, don't know, but suspect you might want'a hear they's plumb hell to pay since persons, unknown-like, up and riddled Sheriff Tyler and his Deppity. Yessir, they's at least twenty riders out after those unknown folks, and lots more comin' inter th' field each day."

"That so?" Sundance said. "Wonder how come

we ain't seen any of them super-posses in our travels. Seems we should'a seen some."

"Got th' idee that all those furious riders, a'ridin' around, could be hopin' they don't run inter any ambushes." The boatman paused as his flatboat grounded on the gravelly shoreline. "Yessir, fear of ambushes can be catchin'."

Though the Territorial papers made a great to-do over the shooting of Tyler and his Deputy, hailing the hunt for the "unknown assailants" as—"the greatest manhunt in the history of Utah," we were able to visit Robbers' Roost without sighting a single posseman or anyone fitting the description. As Butch put it, "Old Hirm Johnson was right, th' fear of ambushes could be downright catchin'!"

Robbers' Roost was just as dreary a place as I'd imagined. A great five mile circular flat, with lookout points on all sides, and broken by two huge, flat-topped buttes that faced north and east, it gave men, on the dodge, a place to roost in safety. Cut off as it was by miles of terrible desert and box canyons, only those riders who had the secret of the trail could hope to enter or ever leave.

While Butch, Sundance and I camped on the Robbers' Roost flats, there was only two of the regular *Roosters* in attendance: Blue John and old Silver Tip. Both of these hard-cases, looking much the worse for wear, welcomed us to a very rickety cabin near the north butte.

Silver Tip, a tall, old rascal with a black beard that had a peculiar white streak on the end, was loud in his dislike of Governor Wells' war on horse thieves. "Wells be damned and all sich politicians—tryin' to interfere with free enterprise! He tried sendin' in that bugger Tyler, and didn't git to fust base. We run him right back out. 'Course couple of our so-called patriots up here, includin' that double-damned Bronco Jack, up and run for it themselfs."

"And good riddance," Blue John winked a blue eye and then his brown one in pure disgust. "But we hear one good thing. Somebody pulled th' stake rope on Mister Sheriff Tyler!" He passed around some very bad whiskey. "Say, how'd you boys like some prime hosses? You wouldn't even guess th' brands been fixed a mite."

We left those two champions of free enterprise at the end of a week and rode for Brown's Hole on our own horses.

We cooled off, as Sundance had it, at Brown's Hole for over a month and a half. It was the longest we stayed-put the whole of 1900. There'd been some trouble earlier in the year, when one of the small ranchers, named Rash, had been dry-gulched one morning. The talk around the Hole was that a certain Tom Hix was doing the shooting, at long range, to drive out the little ranchers and rustlers. It didn't work very well. Everyone stayed on, even the Bassetts and Hoys, who'd been in the place for fifty years or more, but they looked over their shoulders each time they went visiting.

Butch and Sundance took a shine to the Bassett girls and spent about half of their time at the Bassett Ranch, while I batched out at Matt Warner's old cabin on Diamond Mountain, just above the upper end of Crouse Canyon. I still hadn't been able to ride up to Star Valley, and griped about it to Butch when he and Sundance rode over to check on me and my cooking one evening in August.

"Sit tight, Kid. I got a mighty big hunch we'll be pullin' freight in a week or so."

"Your squealer is making noises like a train again?"

"This one's gonna be th' charm, Kid," Sundance chimed in. "When we git cash enough to buy half of Californy, you and your lady friend can hit for th' tall timber for a month of Sundays."

"And you've got it all planned out, just like the last two times," I quizzed Butch.

"Like Sundance says, th' third time's gonna be th' charm," grinned Butch as he passed his plate for another helping of my mulligan stew.

By the last of August, we'd left Brown's Hole and stopped off at The Hole in the Wall for some extra hands, including Ben Kilpatrick and the Bill Carver I'd heard about.

Carver had come up the trail after Ben Kilpatrick, and both were regular saddle pals, riding for several Texas spreads before getting in dutch with the local law and hitting the outlaw trail. Carver was as quick and lively as Ben Kilpatrick was slow and easy-going, and he never failed to beat Ben at any sort of card game they played.

Sundance's explanation of Carver's winning style was simple and to the point. "Ben's just not much good at readin', and Bill's a top man to deecypherin' th' marks on the back of a deck." Of course, he didn't say this when Carver was around. But I noticed that neither he nor Butch cared to play with Bill Carver, always being busy when the cards appeared.

Butch's message from his "inside man" had arrived while we were still in Brown's Hole— carried by one rider after another, from somewhere along the railroad, to Cassidy. Whatever it said and in what sort of code it was written, for many had the opportunity to read the four lines, it galvanized Cassidy into immediate action. And now, two weeks later, we were camped just outside the old town of Wamsutter, Wyoming, waiting for Bill Carver to come back with supplies and the evening papers.

We sat around a fire near Barrel Springs, Butch, Sundance and Ben playing at Seven Up, while I strolled through the red light of the late sunset, looking over the remnants of the old Overland route. Here lay an oxen skeleton, its ribs a pale pink in the fading light, and there, God pity them, the bones of unburied humans, whether Indian or White, there was no way of telling. That old desert had taken its toll for every mile the pioneers had traveled, that was certain. In all that vast expanse of sagebrush and greasewood nothing seemed to live except for our little party of freebooters.

To my right, the fire wrinkled and flared its orange light; to my left the railroad stretched away into the blue wastes of evening, two scarlet lines linking our camp with the great, unseen Red Desert.

Faintly came the drumming of horse's hooves through the fading light. The sound grew with the moments and then we could see Bill Carver astride his dun mare, belting along toward us; and far behind came the sound of gunfire—only to be blotted out by the crashing thud of his horse's shoes upon the gravel ballast of railroad right of way.

Butch and Sundance sprang up, sweeping away the cards, while Kilpatrick ran forward and helped Carver dismount.

"Little fuss in there," Carver panted. "One of them natives was a real sore loser." He stood, rubbing his hand over his mount's heaving flanks.

"Don't seem to have come on out here though. Afraid of gettin' a couple of blue whistlers for his trouble."

"Readin' th' backs again, I'll bet," Sundance whispered out of the corner of his mouth, while Cassidy held out his hand for the papers, took them and walked away to the fire with a sad shake of his head.

In the morning while we rode on through the brilliant wastes of the Red Desert, Butch held forth on the latest doings of the "civilized" world as recounted in the Salt Lake City papers:

"Teddy Roosevelt was over at Deadwood, stumpin' for McKinley and himself. And it seems he was carryin' on a little when his train got to Medora in th' Dakota Bad Lands—said th' romance of his life began there where he had his old ranch . . . said it didn't seem right not to come out there and not stay."

"Don't get what he's talkin' about, here he's runnin' for President . . ." Sundance horned-in.

"Vice President, McKinley's runnin' for President—"

"Vice President, then—and he can sit around in Washington, eatin' and drinkin' and th' taxpayers will foot th' bill," Sundance snorted. "And here th' dumned fool wants to come back to some moth-eatin' ranch and punch cows. Some folks don't know when they got a good thing!"

"But he ain't elected yet. That takes place in November," said Butch.

"Well as far as I'm concerned, he can stay unelected. He don't sound in his right mind."

"And th' Dutchmen in Africa are still kickin' John Bull in th' behind," said Butch, changing the subject. "And th' Chinks are gettin' th' stuffin' knocked out of them down at Peeking. Seems th' Boxers, that's what they call th' Chinks, tried to take over everything from th' white folks and th' U.S. Infantry come through and whipped 'em good!"

"Seems everybody's mad at somebody all th' time," Ben Kilpatrick told Bill Carver. "Like them folks that run you out'a town last night."

"Well, I'm not a bit mad at anybody," chortled Butch, kicking up his horse. "I intend to be just as polite as Teddy Roosevelt wheedlin' for votes, when we flag down th' Union Pacific Train Number Three—providin' I can slip aboard without being heaved off when she stops for water up at th' Tipton water tank."

Cassidy left us on the outskirts of the shambling, nearly deserted, little burg of Tipton at 6 o'clock and riding around the tanks, waved us on up the line to the upgrade near Table Rock. I'd asked to take on the job, stopping the engine, but he laughed. "Next time, Kid! You'll get your turn. What with all th' posses you been shootin' up, you might not be polite enough with th' railroad boys. Lead th' bunch up to the spot, and light th' bonfire like usual . . . and we'll stop by and visit, old Number Three and me."

We loped along up the incline to Table Rock, a large, red sandstone pillar with a precariously balanced piece on top.

"Think we could push that thing over on th' track?" Kilpatrick asked.

"No, I don't think," I said, "get down and get a fire built, we've visitors coming and they'll be right on time."

We took the horses, including Butch's extra mount, off the line and staked them out, looked over our weapons and got ready.

While we stood around the fire of greasewood and chunks of old railroad ties Ben Kilpatrick had lugged up from a gulley, I watched my companions in crime. Sundance sat as close as he could to the light of the fire with his Gazetteer, intent on stuffing his head with more facts. Ben was losing, as usual, to Bill Carver, this time at Old Sledge. They all seemed little different than any group of passengers waiting for some local to stop and pick them up. The only difference was their weapons, gleaming in the bloody light of the bonfire.

I looked away toward the west. Over there, within a stiff day's ride, was Star Valley, and Annie? If I could get there this time, and we had a good take from the raid . . . then things would be different—I hoped.

I turned and stared at the blue-black dome of the night sky, with its glittering frosting of diamonds winking away to the north. Starr was there, still waiting and hoping for some miracle to happen, that she might walk as other girls walked. Was she also thinking of the fellow who'd raised her hopes and then rode away?

"There she comes!" Sundance stuffed the book in his pocket and the card game broke up in a hurry. "Hope Butch hopped his ride!"

A quavering moan filtered through the rising night wind, faded, arose again to blend with the distant serenade of the coyotes. It raised the hair on the back of my neck, as it always did. "Get that dynamite handy!" I told Sundance, and he hustled off toward the horses to fetch up the gunny sack of explosives. We might not need it, but if we did, we had to be ready.

Shortly the headlight of the train poked a hesitant, golden finger through the darkness, disappeared, then edged nearer and nearer. Now came the huff-chuff huff-chuff of an engine laboring up the climb toward Table Rock. The whistle shrilled again in the brittle night and then Number Three was upon us, firebox sprinkling the right of way with dozens of drifting red specks, its headlight now glaring yellow white.

The big engine hammered past, steam spewing, rails clicking and cracking, then the brake took hold—with the shriek of sanded wheels loud and shrill. She gave a couple of grunting chuffs and slid to a jolting, jarring halt that banged cars and coaches all the way back to the end of the train.

We ran, stumbling over the rock ballast, and saw Butch Cassidy, bandana over his face, poking the Engineer and Fireman out of the cab. "Gents, here's some of my welcome committee down there, hop off and join 'em!" And the trainmen swung down, with Cassidy right behind, his two six-shooters at the ready.

"Here comes th' Conductor on th' run," Carver yelped, whirling and tugging his own neckerchief up over his nose. Ben followed suit and so did Sundance and I, as we waited with leveled weapons for the trotting Conductor.

"Here, you!" Butch grabbed the man by the arm as he got up to us. "We'd take it kindly, if you'd hustle your tail and get these cars uncoupled."

There was a brief exchange with the Conductor, who we later heard was E. J. Kerrigan: "What are you tryin' to do there, climbin' back on board?" Sundance wanted to know. "You were told to disconnect—so dammit do it!"

"I'm going to set these brakes first. If I uncouple the coaches from the engine, with this train on a grade—they'll roll back down hill and kill everyone!" He stuck out his jaw at the lot of us.

"Go ahead, but tell those folks staring out th' windows to get their heads back inside before I shoot at a few top-knots!" I told him.

"Just what I was goin' to say," mumbled Ben through his red bandana.

With the brakes set, Kerrigan cut the train and herding the crew back into the back, we pulled on up the track a mile—while Ben and Bill rode after us with the string of horses.

"Now for th' prize package," Sundance whooped as we leaped from the cab and ran back past the tender to the express car.

"Open up in there or you'll go up along with th' damned safe," Butch shouted as we all pounded on the door.

It turned out the same Express Messenger was on board we'd had trouble with back at Wilcox. Kerrigan had to talk like a dutch uncle to get the man out of the car before the dynamite went off. Then with the crew held under Bill Carver's Winchester, and Ben Kilpatrick herding the horses, Butch, Sundance and myself went to work on the safe. It took six sticks of dynamite and two doses to get the thing open. It was about as stubborn as Woodcock, the Expressman!

When the door of the safe was blown, with half of the car in shambles, we squatted on the shattered flooring and stared at each other. "Hell!" said Sundance, waving aside the blue wisps of powder smoke.

"That's what I was going to say," said Butch, quickly glancing over his shoulder in the direction of Kilpatrick. "And I think I'll say it again . . . *Hell!!*"

I was speechless, for a minute, for there was less than three hundred dollars in the battered strong box!

Stuffing the meagre stack of bills into the gunny sack, we dropped off the car and walked back to our prisoners. Butch looked at them, and then shrugged. There no use trying to find out what the trouble was. We all knew his informant was going to get a damned small split this time, as we stood there muttering and kicking the gravel with our boots.

"What time is it?" Butch absently asked the Conductor.

"Nine-fifteen," said Kerrigan, holding out his silver railroad watch.

"Keep it," said Butch, pushing the timepiece back, "we're not takin' anything from th' railroad, boys!"

"Nothin' except a lot of trouble," Sundance grumbled as we mounted up.

"I heard!" Cassidy grunted, settling into his saddle. "So, oh ye of a damn little faith, I'm gonna take you visitin' over to Nevada, and try to show you a Chinese trick with a hole right in the middle."

And with that, Butch led us out toward the southwest as fast as we could pound.

CHAPTER THIRTY-THREE

We all knew there'd be one hell of a rumpus after the stopping of the Pacific Express—no matter how much we took, and it was a mighty piddling total, all of forty-five dollars each, after Butch's *star inside man* got his quarter of the split.

"A damned poor showing for any sort of Syndicate!" Cassidy agreed as he led us on a twisted, turning route that tended to confuse us almost as much as any of the posses sure to be tagging along behind.

"This ain't th' time to stand and fight for any measly three hundred bones," Butch said, heading us across the Haystacks, the badlands of southern Wyoming—and on into the maze of the Bitter Creek Mountains and Powder Springs, where we turned north again.

It was a long, dry summer and as the creeks dried up, the only water, if there was any, was in hidden water holes—when a rider knew how to find them in all the vacant expanse of the dusty mesas. I was certain that the makeshift posses wouldn't fare so well.

Butch had little trouble in coming across some spring or seep, just when we needed it most for our horses and our empty canteens. "Don't look so surprised that I'm a pretty good dowser,"

Cassidy observed when we'd halted to replenish our water supply. "Y'gotta remember that I rambled over this whole country for six years, taggin' after Mike Cassidy, my old rustler pal, movin' whole herds of horses from one station to another. It sort of gets burned into your mind."

It was a great vastness of withered sage, yucca, cactus and wild flowers. Fortunately there was plenty good bunch grass, which dried and cured into fairly good horse feed in the long drought.

We rode across a regular painted rock desert, with the wildest sort of spires, buttes and cliffs, rising above the mesa's emptiness, all worn down by ages of water and ancient winds into every sort of human and inhuman shape that one could imagine, and of every color, from tawny-brown and sullen red through delicate pink to bleached bone white. It was nothing less than the Devil's rainbow touching desolation, and the most savage land I'd ever traveled.

Small wonder the posses never got within miles of us.

But with Cassidy at the point, we were satisfied to ride on day after day into Nevada—and the town with the odd name, Winnemucca!

There were just four of us sitting our horses five miles outside Winnemucca, Nevada the morning of September 19, 1900. Butch had sent Ben Kilpatrick on down to Texas, with a message he didn't trust to the regular owl-hoots riding the back-trails.

He told us, after Ben galloped off south from Powder Springs, heading for Forth Worth, that Kilpatrick was "fine for trains but too clumsy around banks!" I thought he could have been hinting about our Arizona bank escapade, but kept my mouth shut.

The Winnemucca Bank carried a good amount of cash to pay off the nearby ranch hands and few odd miners, and, though it had never had any dealings with hold-ups, Butch thought it was about time it had some excitement and paid for it.

There was just one catch, Cassidy admitted. Only three men were needed for this particular job, or we'd meet ourselves coming and going, as some of us did back at Belle Fourche. And Sundance and I looked at each other when we heard that.

"One horse holder and two with *persuaders* will do it fine," said Butch.

He let us cut cards for the *old maid,* the one who'd wait out of town with fresh animals. We'd bought a good string of prime horses down the line from a friendly rancher, who asked no questions.

"Lessee!" Carver shuffled the cards, and dealt them face down on a blanket on the ground by a cottonwood. "One fer Sundance, one fer me, one fer Kid—and—"

"None for me." Butch stopped the fourth card. "This is my game today."

We looked at the cards. Sundance picked up a Queen of Clubs, Carver had an Ace of Diamonds—and I turned over the three of Spades.

It only was after I watched them ride down the winding road toward town I remembered Carver's games with Ben Kilpatrick.

I sat in the shade of the cottonwood at the edge of the Sloan ranch with our string of mounts grazing in a nearby field. I hoped we'd seemed to be a party of ranchers, dickering in horses— for that's what we'd told the ranch foreman when we'd camped out overnight.

Now, about half-past noon, the ranch hands stopped cutting hay and looked a little more closely at me and our string as a series of gunshots rapped out back toward Winnemucca. Butch and the boys had stirred up some excitement at least!

Mounting up, I trotted my bay mare out of the field, gawking away like the other hands around the Sloan barns. It wasn't long before I could see the Trio hitting toward us.

I rode down a piece to meet them, and was waved back, by Butch, toward the field where the string of remounts awaited. The other two were waving, as well—Sundance swinging a canvas sack, and Bill Carver flailing his hat back and forth in excitement. "We done it this time! We done it this time!" Sundance was whooping when they galloped up and piled off their heaving animals.

Changing the saddles and gear took only moments and we were ready to go, but already I had most of the story of the past hour. And as we rode out of the field, into the road, waving a hasty goodbye to the staring ranch hands, I asked Butch if I'd actually heard right in all the hullabaloo of changing horses.

"That's right as rain, Kid!" Butch grinned from ear to ear while Sundance kept up his caterwauling like an Indian gone crazy. "Thirty thousand if there's a copper cent, and it's all in that ore sack there in Bill's paws!" He held up his hand and we pulled to a halt half a mile south of the Sloan place, where the Winnemucca road dipped down into a slight valley.

A large sheep camp here stretched away to the northwest, some of the animals moving along as we watched, but the herder seemed to be farther off and not in sight.

"Hey Butch, you gonna stop and count them sheep?" Carver stood up in his stirrups and peered back toward town.

"Yep, I'm gonna do just that, Bill—come on everybody and follow th' leader." Butch swung his horse off across the rocky fields among the flock of woolies. "Gettin' thirty-thousand-plus out of that sleepy burg was a pretty good Chinese trick—but now I'm gonna show you that hole in th' middle!"

We rode back toward Winnemucca over some of the roughest pasturage I'd seen. How these sheep made out a meal, I don't know, but we all could see their hooves had torn up the ground so badly it would have taken an Apache trailer to follow our track very far.

After clearing the area, we paralleled the road and trotted over rock hard soil, baked out by the sun until it would have taken a stick of dynamite to mark the surface. And every mile we rode brought us up nearer to Winnemucca, until we had skinned its outskirts to the west and still kept going—with never the glimpse of a posse or even a single rider.

If the law expected us to head south, they were in for a big surprise, for Butch did nothing but lead us to the northwest, up into the foothills of the Tuscarora Mountains and through a pass fifteen miles north of Mardis. From there our trail led on among the Independence Mountains to the Valley of the Owyhee. Now there was little danger of anyone following, and no need to try to set a trap for the posses, as we rode through the wild and lonely country of the junipers. From there, by easy rides, we went over into Squaw Valley, picked up supplies from a rustler friend of Butch's and headed westward.

Sixteen days after Winnemucca we rode down into Star Valley.

There was a dry lump in my throat as I reined up before my little, empty cabin and looked down the village of Afton's one dusty street. "Peers like no one's home, Kid," Butch said, while the others lounged on their horses and exchanged banter with the Mormon kids and their folks.

"Mister Capehart!" It was my old landlord, Jacob Preston. "Right proud to see you again, after all this time. Light down, gentlemen, light down—and we'll see if we can't scare up some vittles for you."

When we'd dismounted and turned in our horses to the younger Mormons to feed and water, we all walked up the street to Preston's home. On the way he stepped close to me. "Sort'a hoped that you'd be back before this. We don't get hardly anyone over here, as you well know . . . and we downright missed you and your handy hunting!" He looked quizzically at me for a moment. "And we were mighty sorry to see your fine lady-wife leave so sudden."

I'd not gone in our cabin, but had looked back at it several times on our walk up the street. Yes, there'd been no mistake. It *was* boarded up tight!

"I guess she had some business of her own," I said, thinking that if I could have come back months ago, Annie would have been waiting there for me. "Did she leave any message?"

Preston waved us into the front room of his fine big cabin. "She said pressing matters took her away. And she caught a ride with the first peddlar wagon that came in here two days after you left." He reached up on the mantel of his fireplace and handed me a letter.

I stuck it in my pocket away from the curious eyes of Sundance and the others, taking a look at it after supper.

It was short and not very sweet: *"Harvey, you'll find that I've got just as stubborn a streak as you! I hope you watch out for yourself, and you'll know I'm doing the same thing for me. I've loved this place, but it's just too lonesome now. I'm going back home to Kennedale, Texas for a while. Annie."*

We stayed with the folks at Star Valley for several days, resting up and then, with Butch's O.K., we split up for the time being. He and the bunch going south—"to see if that chuckle-head of a Ben delivered th' letter to th' right address," as Butch put it.

The right address, so Cassidy'd told me, was Fanny Porter's Saloon in Fort Worth, Texas . . . and I was to join him there when I had my own *business* taken care of.

So I rode directly across the Territory for Miles City, with a pack horse that I picked up at Rock

Springs, half-expecting to run into someone who'd seen my face on a Pinkerton poster—for Butch said they were out as thick as flies around hot cakes, but there was no trouble at all, folks being busy about their own affairs and not interested in Billy Pinkerton's bill-posting.

From Rock Springs I rode for Casper, put the horses up at the Brown and Kelly Stables on a side street and took the northbound express for Miles City directly—as the rail line ran up through that place now and on into North Dakota. Before I caught the train on the morning of October 14, I bought a complete outfit of store clothes. With slightly more than $6,000 in my saddle bags, I bought a grain-leather gladstone bag and transferred the money to it before I went shopping at Schafer's on Portland Street. There I picked out a dark brown, all wool suit in a good fit for $6.00. I topped off the outfit with a fine pair of calf peg boots for $2.00, a western fedora for $2.50, and a plain grey overcoat for $11.50—plus the rest of the rig-out.

The clerk who handled the sale, and got rid of my old range duds, assured me that I looked as nobby as any stockman that had ever graced his store!

It was a blue and gold day when I arrived at the Miles City's depot. About the first person I saw was the fat city marshal, but he was elbowing himself through the noontime crowds—headed for the restaurant, and never glanced my way.

I walked to the local livery, hired out a fancy, leather-topped buggy for the day, and drove the high-stepping black mare over to the Miles City Journal.

I swung down and tied the rig in front of the building. My face burned as though I'd been riding through a windstorm, and my throat was dry as if I'd gone a week without water. But I picked up my traveling bag and marched up the steps and into the office.

There she sat! Yes, Starr was working at the same old desk, with the same yellow cat glowering at me from the desk top.

I'm certain she didn't recognize me, in my city clothes, yet she seemed, somehow remote, and withdrawn—even more than the first time I'd met her. She was lovelier than ever though, but with a distant look in her blue eyes.

"Miss Starr?"

She'd risen as I entered, and stood with pen in hand, waiting. Then her face flooded bright scarlet, and I thought that she was going to pitch over with the shock.

"Harvey? *You,* here? But—I don't."

"Miss Starr," I found myself babbling, words stampeding over themselves so I knew I was making a complete fool of myself. I dropped my bag and grabbed her hands. "Shouldn't have busted in here. Sorry to have flustered you . . .

and apoligize for that! Should have dropped you a note . . . been busy . . ."

Then I sat her back down at the desk and hurried to tell her that her father's ranch had been sold and I had the money for it right there in the grip. Looking around and not seeing anyone, I opened the traveling bag and deposited $5,000 in bills on the desk.

"But this . . . what am I to do with . . . ?" Starr's face was now white with some unknown emotion. "Oh!" She wrung her hands together, biting her lip, eyes wide with tears. She suddenly smiled, rose and coming over to me, put out her arms.

We kissed, and we kissed long and hard, I'll tell you. It was as if I'd waited for this for the past long months—dreamed about it, even when Annie had lain by my side in the dark nights.

"Oh, I want you!" Starr murmured. "I want you, want you—" Then she arched away. "Can you come back tonight? I'll be working late, and Uncle won't come in during the evening—as he's got to cover a council meeting."

I had that buggy standing out in front, all ready for a ride in the country or—*whatever,* but I nodded and agreed. "That money should go into the bank! And pronto!" Then I had a thought. "How's the law here? You have plenty of bars on that bank?" If some owl-hoot tried for that money—I'd!!!

"Oh yes, yes! Even Marshal Rand keeps an eye on the bank—and that Frank Canton comes into town almost every day." Then her face paled again. "Canton could be in town today with receipts for the bank from his ranch—do you—?"

"Don't fuss. I'll go over to one of the saloons, sit quiet and read the papers." I pointed a finger at the pile of $5,000. "But get that out of sight. You've got money enough now to fix every one of your ten little toes. And you'll be able to toss that thing into the kitchen stove." I jerked my thumb at her wooden crutch, propped, as usual, in a corner by the desk.

She stepped over, kissed me on the cheek and then sat back down. "Tonight at eight o'clock. I'll be waiting for—for my knight of the range." Then she clasped the bundle of yellowbacks to her breast, eyes wide and strangely glowing.

I'd had about three shots of rye and was, actually, thumbing through the Cheyenne paper, bemused by the whiskey, the nearness of Starr at last—and the latest reports on the U.S. political campaign by Peter Finley Dunne's "Mr. Dooley," who was going on:

> *"Well sir," said Mr. Dooley, "if thayse anny wan r-runnin' in this campaign but me frind Tiddy Rosenfelt. I'd like to know who it is . . . It ain't Bryan . . . 'Tis*

Tiddy alone that's ru-runnin', and he ain't runnin', he's gallopin'."

Teddy wouldn't be the only one running—I'd be running too, and damned fast, if I bumped into Frank Canton in this town! It was foolish to sit there in that saloon like a clay pigeon, but I'd promised Starr we'd get together after dark—and I burned to think of it—*think of her*—

The hand on my shoulder brought the Colt out from under my coat so fast the person who'd touched me—without warning—fell back with a gasp. Then I saw it was Mister Gordon, who'd collapsed into a chair opposite me, and was making motion with both hands to put up the gun.

It didn't take him long to fill me in on the facts that Canton *was due to come into town* before the banks closed, and that there were at least two Pinkerton reward notices up in the city hall with my picture on them, along with Butch Cassidy and other members of his "Wild Bunch!", put up by no one but Frank Canton!

"And don't blame young Starr for not telling you—I think you've thrown her off balance, showing up this way." He waved at the wall clock. "Don't waste time trying to talk. It's good of you to bring over that money, no matter how it was come by. I'll see it goes to help Starr walk straight again, as she was meant to! I think justice may be done, after all—with men like you and

Frank Jackson allowed to make amends for the sort of lives you've led."

He stood up, and put out his ink-smudged hand. "Don't think I'm a sanctimonious old fool—but you'll see what I mean, if you live long enough." He grasped my hand. "And now get out of Miles City as fast as you can!"

"Thanks! Tell Starr, all the luck—and I'll see her again." I went out, got into the buggy and drove out of town, wondering what he'd meant when he shook his head.

When I left Miles City—and Starr, I made up my mind, then and there, to get back down to Texas the easiest and fastest way I could. I left the buggy at the next town down the line, paying for it—and giving the livery man there enough money to see it got back. I also sent a wire down to the Brown and Kelly stables at Casper, authorizing them to sell my two horses and gear, including my saddle-gun—the new Marlin, and send the money to Mister Gordon at Miles City.

Then I bought a ticket on the railroad straight through to Fort Worth, Texas on the Montanan Central, with a change of trains at Denver for the Texas and Pacific. I took a pullman, and meant to have a high old time in the dining car, and eat as I'd not eaten for months. With almost $1,500 left in my gladstone bag—plus my six-shooter, I was going to travel first class.

I still was puzzled about Miles City, and

somehow down in the mouth, because Starr and I had not been able to be together . . . but there'd be more times, if things went right. And with Butch and I knocking around, things were bound to go the right way. At least I told myself so.

What if Annie had walked right out of me? Who could blame her? Well, there were plenty of wild fillies to rope and brand—if I wanted them! But I still wondered where Annie really was.

CHAPTER THIRTY-FOUR

I landed in Fort Worth and took a horse cab to the address that Butch had given me—at Fannie Porter's, over the tracks in the "hi-jinks" section of the town. Butch and Sundance were out, but Bill Carver was there, dressed up in a suit that made him look like a Presbyterian Deacon.

"Great place to hang out, Kid," Carver puffed on a fancy stogie, tipped his hardbrim derby over one eye and lifted his boots up on the wicker settee. "Better than a cornshuck mattress at Hole in th' Wall, eh?"

What was enthusing Carver wasn't the furniture, the thick rugs or pretty pictures on the wall of the saloon; it was the curvesome ladies that drifted around from table to table and perched on the arms of the chairs like bright-winged birds.

"What better way to spend some of them hard-earned railway sponduliks?" Carver patted a red-headed waitress and ordered up a round of champagne for us. "Guess you got plenty to toss around yourself, eh?"

I admitted that I had a *little* left in the poke.

By the time I'd got settled down in one of the rooms upstairs in that combination saloon, hotel and gambling den, with my boots off and the daily papers over the bed—Butch and Sundance were back.

When the rough-housing was over and a little high-yellow maid, in a starchy French outfit, was straightening the place, Butch took me by the arm and led me out into the hall. "Know you're down in th' mouth over your lady friend, but don't let that raise your hackles. I just got word that she's been in town from her folks' place over at some wide spot in th' road—and I told Fanny to hire her!"

Fort Worth was, as Carver said, with the pride of a Texan, "plumb bustin' at th' seams!" And it had certainly come a long way from the time when it was so quiet some old timers swore they'd seen a mountain lion lying asleep, and undisturbed right on Main Street.

There was plenty of law around, but they left folks strictly alone, especially those from the west side of the Trinity River section, and that took in Fannie Porter's along with many of the lower-class grog shops.

Every day we four would roll out of our big mahogany beds and begin to do the sights. We rode hacks to look at the new packing plants going up at Main and Exchange out by the stockyards, took the electric cars downtown to play cards in the back rooms of the El Paso Hotel, and watched the girls in tights kick up their heels evenings at Holland's Theater.

We also did some drinking to pass the time, and the Sazarac Bar on Dagget was one of our favorites. It was while I sat there with Butch, waiting for Carver and Longabaugh to join us, that Cassidy spilled his plans for the new year.

"I might as well tell you, Kid, that I've been doin' considerable thinkin' right along with all our drinkin'—and I begin to see some sort of handwritin' on th' wall."

I looked around—but he went on.

"I mean this hold-up dodge is gettin' all played out. If you just want to think about it for a minute, look at this." And he stuck an evening paper in front of me. *Millions Made Overnight On Wall Street,* was the headline. "And squint at this one!" *One Oil Well Made Him Rich!* another headline ran. He turned a couple of pages—"and lookit' this!" *Rapid Communications Spell End of Western Badmen!*

Butch downed his rye and looked at me, without the slightest hint of a grin. "Well?"

"What are you driving at?"

"I thought you were smarter than that! I mean just this. Here some pen pusher in New York sits at a desk and makes his pile without takin' off his coat. Some other jasper pokes a pipe down in th' ground and sits around while his fortune just pours out into barrels—and all without him battin' an eye." He pounded his fist on the table.

"And look at us! We ride th' skin off our rear ends, trade bullets with half th' lawmen in th' territories—and just about take in enough to keep us in grub!"

"Well, your Train Robbers' Syndicate hasn't declared many dividends yet, but we made it back at Winnemucca."

Cassidy scribbled on the table with a pencil for a moment. "I don't think $6,000 each for two years' work figures out too well. And you're ignorin' that last item in th' paper there."

"End of Western Badmen?"

"Right. We're bitin' off more'n we can chew if we keep on playin' tag with Old Man Time! Where's Flat Nose George? And Elza Lay, my old pard? And those crazy Ketchums, as well as your poor kid brother? All behind bars or six feet under. And they don't never seem to run out of posses—no matter how many you trap!"

"You want to retire?"

"Actually I'm for foldin' my tents like th' Arabs and stealin' off to where I can get back into the cattle business, without half th' Pinkerton agents in th' country diggin' their chins on my shoulder. Can't do it here anymore, so I'm for tryin' it south—way south—*South America!* What do you say to that?"

"Sounds like sense, for a change. But how are you going to finance such a long range move as that?"

"When th' time's right, say next early summer, we hold one last meetin' of th' Syndicate—probably in Montana. This time th' fourth has gotta be th' lucky try. I've got positive information from my inside man—don't grin at me—that there's over $100,000 coming through in early July!"

"And until then?"

"We watch our P's and Q's, and stay out of trouble until time to ride!"

That very afternoon when I got back to Fannie Porter's I found myself in more trouble than I'd been in for months. For, when I walked in the front door with Butch and the bunch, who should sashay up but big, busty Fannie Porter, herself, and *with Annie at her side!*

She introduced Annie to each of the bunch, and then came my turn.

"Mister Capehart (we'd kept the old monikers), please to meet *Miss Annie Winters!*" And damned if Annie didn't smile at me all frosty-like and nod her head as if I were a complete stranger.

My Logan blood began to heat at such treatment, after all that time. I could see Annie noticed the symptoms, for hurriedly excusing herself, she made off into the barroom.

While Butch and the bunch grinned like a pack of baboons, I yanked my derby down on my head and went after that frigid little piece!

"Now Harvey!" was all Annie had time to

say, before I scooped her up, tossed her over my shoulder and went charging up the stairs to my room. Down below I could hear Butch and the boys holding Fannie's bouncers at bay. Then tables began to crash, mirrors smash, and all the curvesome, bar-and-bed ladies start to scream in a dozen, different keys. But by then I'd tossed Annie into the middle of my big, empty mattress and locked my door!

It took a considerable portion of Butch's cash, plus what was left of mine, to square ourselves with a very distant Miss Fannie Porter. In fact, we moved out the next day to another less gilded dive down the street. And Annie went along with me, having dropped her last name—again.

Everyone took it and all our antics in good humor, including the harness bulls on the stretch, and especially the ladies at Fannie's and along the street—for Butch had discovered that he was a seven-day-wonder at riding on the new bicycle. Sundance tried it, and thrown badly onto his head quit, declaring that four-legged critters were bad enough—but anything on wheels was "plumb untrustsome!"

I'd been telling Annie I was looking for a chance to get away with her and travel back to Star Valley—or off into the Pacific Northwest. We talked about it every night, weighing our chances to buy a small ranch someplace and settle down under another name. We both felt that it could be accomplished—but differed on how to do it. I thought that one more good strike with Butch would do the trick, but Annie violently opposed such a method—and argued that I should just go to work out on some ranch while she worked in some restaurant or decent saloon until we had a small stake. Then she said, we could make our move—even go to South America if we wanted.

I had just about come around to her plan, when Ben Kilpatrick came back from Concho County, and Butch had a little blow out for him at the Sazarac.

By three o'clock we were feeling mighty mellow, and out strolling along the sunny December streets of Fort Worth—congratulating ourselves that we weren't knee-deep in snow at some hell hole like Hole in the Wall. "Yessir," Sundance crowed, "here we are where the weather suits our clothes!" He paused and gawked around at us. "And clothes! Why we're th' best dressed bunch of train-busters in th' business!" Unfortunately, at that very minute we found ourselves standing in front of Schwartz' photo gallery, and nothing must do but we all march in, and let old John Schwartz line us up and take our picture. Ben Kilpatrick was the rose between two thorns, Sundance and Butch, all three sitting down, while Bill Carver and I stood up in back, as solemn as a brace of church deacons, trying not to bust out laughing.

But no picture taken in Fort Worth ever played so much hell with one bunch of cowboys!

About six a.m. three days later, Butch came pounding on our door. Old man Schwartz had stuck one of our group photos in his front window, and some Pinkerton snooper, who knew Bill Carver, had spotted it—and was asking questions in all the right places.

By ten a.m., we'd shed our store-bought duds, and were loping down the road for San Antonio, togged out as regulation cattlemen.

Annie was to stay in Fort Worth—until I could send for her. It was awfully hard to part with her, again, but it had to be.

And it was another mighty long time before I saw Annie again!

The next few months brought enough trouble to our bunch to last the rest of anyone's natural life.

After laying low in San Antonio's *Hell's Half Acre* (the town's tenderloin), from the end of December until the first of March, and really minding our P's and Q's as Butch had demanded, the word filtered down that the Pinkertons were around with that damned picture and asking for *The High Fives*. Now though we had no idea where they'd stumbled over such a dime-novel name (except out of the yellow press?) Butch decided we'd better go on the scout out in the back country, until time to ride north to the Hole and try for that $100,000 bonanza, which was due to come down the Great Northern rails.

Butch and Sundance rode for New Mexico and left me to travel with Carver and Kilpatrick. We headed out beyond the Pecos, and it was mighty fine country to ride across. Thousands of sheep and cattle grazed among the brush and cedar hills. And all about, the open spaces of the great south-western plains reached away to the dreamy blue haze where the Rio and Old Mexico began. The first flags of the blue bonnets nodded in the warming breeze, and dozens of the busy speckled-brown cactus wrens were nest-building in cholla and mesquite.

Spring was moving through the vast land, and we moved along with it—until we rode down into the valley of the East Fork of Devils River.

There Bill Carver's luck ran out on the evening of April 4, 1901.

We were four riders, Ben picking up his younger brother, George, as we passed through Concho County. A good-looking, slender boy, he was pleased as punch to ride with his dashing brother—and all of us. I'd been dead against taking him along, but Ben and Bill got around me by swearing that they'd send him packing back to the Kilpatrick spread when we went north.

Carver had been cussing his luck at losing his cushy life at Fannie Porter's, wishing he was back there instead of rolling up in a threadbare saddle blanket alongside such hard-cases as Ben and myself each night. He ragged young George as a pitiful tenderfoot, but I could see that he cottoned to the boy—even letting him win at the Carver brand of cards, though he continued to stick Ben Kilpatrick each and every game.

Nearing Sonora, Texas found us low on supplies. So, when George begged to ride in with Carver to replenish our grub and feed, I let him go.

Ben and I sat our horses on the edge of the sleepy, little cattle town and watched Bill and George lope away. But neither of us knew that Carver was wanted for several warrants in the neighboring county. It was about eight o'clock when the pair moved out of sight—and twenty minutes later a burst of gunfire shattered the peaceful twilight haze.

There was nothing we could do. We rode for it! And Bill Carver and young George Kilpatrick died on the streets of Sonora for some horse feed and baking powder.

As Butch said—playing tag with Old Man Time was a losing game!

CHAPTER THIRTY-FIVE

After the shooting of Carver and Ben's kid brother, Kilpatrick and I lost no time in getting clear of Texas, riding north through the Guadalupe Mountains, using a pass that Ben was familiar with, hitting the blazing White Sands for a stretch before turning toward Albuquerque.

We rode close enough in to Albuquerque to buy supplies at P. Everman's out in the sandhills on South Edith, then swung to the west and caught *the trail,* north of old Fort Wingate, crossing into Arizona. Following the outlaw route (traveled by owl-hoots and rustlers since the Civil War), we ranged up across Arizona, forded the Colorado at Horse Head Shallows and were in Utah at Hanksville by April 21.

As I expected, there was a short note from Butch, who'd passed through the week before:

"Kid and Ben, Heard about Bill and the brother. Rotten luck! Come on up to The Hole as soon as you can, as I think we'll be taking some revenge on the railroad barons in a couple of weeks. Ran into that terror of the Mexican Border—Charlie Hanks, over near Alma and he's with us as well as The Mex Kid—who we now call

Billy Rob, as he thinks that sounds sort of desperate. Keeping riding! Butch."

We pulled into Baggs, north of Browns Park, on April 24, had our horses re-shod, then took on some more supplies and headed for the Hole, arriving there in a heavy rainstorm the night of April 29.

While I stood in my long-johns before a crackling fire in the fireplace of Flat Nose George's cabin, drying out, Deaf Charlie Hanks held the floor on how he, Harry Bass and Bill Madden had stopped the Northern Pacific up in Montana in the Fall of '93, taking a total of $45,000!

"How long did you get to keep that bundle, Charlie?" Butch asked, winking at us as he passed the jug of corn around the circle at the fireplace.

"Just damn long enough to feel like a million-aire, before th' posse up and shot Bill and Harry out of th' saddle and run me fifty miles," rasped Charlie, cocking his head. "But why'd you always want to know? You heard all about it before, ain't you?"

"Yes, but I like to hear a millionaire—even a short-term millionaire speak his piece, then point out th' error of his ways!" Butch pulled out his maps, called us over to the table and began to chart out our campaign for the second time since supper. "I know this kinda bores you boys some, but I want this one to go like clock-work. Then we can take our money, and be long-term millionaires wherever we want to go. Now look here!"

By early June we had eaten and slept the upcoming raid so many times that we were about ready to hold a full-scale mutiny and chase Butch out of the Hole for good and all. Sundance put it the most strongly: "No matter how much money we make on this deal, I'd about give twice as much to have Mister Robert LeRoy Parker shipped off to his infernal South America, parcel post immediate!"

But Butch only grinned at us and went over the plans again. "Cuss and fuss, I don't care! If this is gonna be th' Syndicate's swan song I want it to be sweet and strong. Because, by Nelly, we'll show 'em that train bustin' can be a profitable enterprise! It's a matter of pride in th' American system."

When the word arrived from Butch's railroad contract on June 12, we got ready. Our little unit was made up of Sundance, Billy Rob (the Mex Kid), Deaf Charlie Hanks, Butch and myself. We rode our best horses, and led another remuda— along with two pack horses. As Sundance said, we were loaded for bear this trip!

Two of the second string, Bill Cruzan and Joe

Chancellor, stayed back in the Hole to watch things, though Butch told me privately that he hoped he'd seen the last of the place. "We pull this th' way I think it'll go—and it's excuse my dust, all th' way to South America. Sundance is makin' plans on takin' a tootsie he got friendly with down in Texas. And you do the same with your lady, right?"

I told him that it was something we could think about when the time came, providing I could get word to Annie without tipping off any law.

"It's this way, Kid. When we knock off that train, there'll be Pinkertons out in platoons. Billy Pinkerton will have to put up or shut up this time—and, I'm afraid, it's gonna mean every man for himself. This is 1901 and not 1895— remember that newspaper story about th' doom of rascals like you and me? Old Man Time's on Billy Pinkerton's side. So you do more than just think about your vanishing act. You better do it!"

It was nearly 450 miles up to Wagner, Montana but we took our time as The Great Northern Express Company's shipment of gold and currency wasn't due to come over the road from Milwaukee, Wisconsin until early in July, passing through Wagner, (which Butch had picked as the robbery site) on the night of July 3, 1901.

As truth is always a mighty lot stranger than fiction, Cassidy had actually decided to halt our train at the same place that Deaf Charlie Hanks and his saddle pals robbed the Northern Pacific. You might guess that when Hanks found that out, he was so puffed up with pride that his head was just about straight for days.

When we neared Wagner, we split up until the first of July. Butch and Sundance went into a hidden camp along the breaks of the Milk River, while I took Ben Kilpatrick, Deaf Charlie and Billy Rob with me to an old abandoned cabin about five miles south of the Great Northern tracks in an out of the way draw.

I was now less than thirty miles from our old 4-T Ranch on the Crimson and how I wanted to saddle up and ride there as fast as I could. Jim Thornhill was still there holding down our place—until, I, the last of the Logans could come back and take it over. But when that would ever be—only the good Lord knew!

On the morning of July 2 Butch rode over to our hidden camp and dropped a complete bombshell, calling me out of the cabin for a private talk.

"Took it on myself, again, Kid . . . and hope you won't think I'm buttin' in on your private affairs, but I damn well want you to come down to th' Argentine with me and Sundance, and I knew you'd want Annie with you."

He paused and I just looked at him, wondering what he was driving at.

"So I sent a wire down to Fannie Porter askin'

her to get your lady in touch with you—" He paused again, then handed me a folded telegram.

"Jim Lowe, care of Battle's Saloon, Malta, Montana—Annie Winters gone back to husband. Signed F. Porter."

Then he dropped the *other shoe!* "Don't want to rile you too much, and I'm certain you can get her back—if you want to—but we've got our work cut out for us tomorrow. That money box is comin' thru special delivery, marked don't open 'til th' Fourth of July—but we'll get it on th' *afternoon* of July 3!"

I was still mad clean through next day when I left the bunch on the road below Malta and rode right on into town. I was taking the biggest chance of my life, and Butch and the rest knew it. If I ran into someone who recognized me, though I'd been out of the Territory for almost four long years, it could be another Sonora, Texas! Bill Carver had been quick on the draw, fast with horses and women—and deadly with a deck of cards. But the great gambler—Fate—dealt him a hand he couldn't handle when someone spotted him on the streets of Sonora!

Butch's plan called for me to board the blind baggage of the Great Northern *Coast Flyer* as it stopped at the flag station of Malta for water before proceeding west toward Havre, Great Falls, Missoula and on to Spokane.

I looked at my watch when I reined up in front of Shade Denson's Saloon on the main street, across from the one-room depot. There was just about time for me to grab a drink and then watch for the train.

Malta was as sleepy as I remembered it. While there weren't any stray mountain lions dozing in its dusty street (as those Fort Worth old timers had remembered), there were at least three hound dogs, dead to the world, on the saloon porch.

The barroom was empty except for a cowboy named Campbell. Johnny and I had some dealings with him when we were raising horses, but I could see he wasn't certain who I was. Well—after I caught the Flyer he'd have another horse on his hands. While I nursed my shot of Old Crow, I fished up a pencil stub from my vest and scratched out a bill of sale on the back of an old reward dodger I'd carried in my pocket:

"To whom it may concern, I hereby assign and deliver one horse, clay bank in color, with white mane and tail; weight about 1100 pounds; branded with a double slash on right shoulder. This horse I give to one George Campbell, free and clear. Signed Robert Nelson, Malta, Montana—July 3, 1901."

Campbell might as well have the horse as to leave it hitched out front, all by its lonesome. I tossed off the rest of my whiskey, tipped the bartender and went out through the batwings. My six-shooter was under my coat, and my saddle-gun on ahead with Sundance and the bunch.

By the time I'd finished tucking the bill of sale under the horse's saddle blanket, the Flyer was clanking up to the Depot water tank across the empty street. It was just 2 p.m. Several people ambled out of the buildings, and stood watching the Fireman drop the long-neck water spout to fill the engine's tank. Even the three hound dogs sat up and scratched a little.

I crossed to the Depot, keeping my eyes open for any trouble. And when the train gave a couple of short whistle blasts, I ran alongside and pulled myself onto the front platform of the baggage car next to the coal tender. I'd hardly got stationed—with the train pulling out—when the Conductor hurried up and ordered me off—mistaking me for some hobo, riding the blind baggage.

I pulled my six-shooter and told him to get on board, for I was there to stay! While the train picked up speed, I climbed over the coal and slid down onto the deck of the engine.

I told the surprised engine crew to keep her moving until I wanted them to set the brake. When the Engineer whistled for the Exeter Siding, up the line, and the Conductor signalled for him to stop the train. I advised him to keep on, if he wanted to stay healthy. "I can run this train if you won't!" I couldn't handle that machinery, but planned to bring the Fireman over to run the engine—if I had to wallop the Engineer.

He chomped down on his cud of tobacco and motioned for the Fireman to keep throwing in the coal, and we roared along, with the Milk River bottoms to our left.

At 2:30 we were coming up on the Wagner siding, just a section house for tools and a few sheds. Butch and the rest were there with the horses. "Stop right now!" I emphasized the order by a poke in the ribs with my Colt .45. The Engineer yanked on the brake and the big Baldwin Mogul 4-4-0 engine steamed down to a halt within twenty yards of the gang.

There was some brief confusion from the passengers on board the express, many thinking there'd been some sort of wreck or disaster. Heads began bobbing out of the windows, but went back in when Longabaugh and Billy Rob started shooting over the top of the cars. Butch swung aboard and hurried through the coaches warning the passengers to stay inside.

While this was going on, I marched the Engineer and Fireman over to cut off the coaches. When we'd moved the shortened train with the baggage car up the tracks a ways, Butch sent the crew back to the engine, keeping the Fireman to help carry the sacks of dynamite and help him blow the way safe open.

While Butch and his *volunteer* were setting

the charges, Ben Kilpatrick and Charlie Hanks guarded the train crew, leaving Billy Rob and I to watch for interruptions from any quarter.

There was really little excitement, though someone in the last coach fired at us with a pistol. Sundance opened up on him with his high-powered Winchester, and the shooting stopped as quickly as it started. We heard later that it had been Sheriff Grifith of Great Falls, but he'd not seemed to be in any mood to press matters.

Just before Butch touched off the dynamite, a rider appeared on the bluffs to the south and sat watching the commotion. "Say Kid, I don't like th' looks of that son of a gun," Billy Rob shouted at me. "I guess I'll take a shot at his knob!"

"All right, but don't hit him," I said. "Hit the horse!"

The Mex Kid's rifle cracked once! It was a perfect shot, just creasing the animal on the hip, and sending the snooper off on a wild ride out of sight.

When the explosion of the way safe thundered across the open country-side, its echoes rumbling out to the distant Bear Paw Mountains and back again, all the bunch whooped and cheered, while the trainmen scowled—but we were just a little optimistic—for Butch and the Fireman had to give that tough-nut of a safe two more charges before it cracked. In the process, Cassidy about demolished the baggage car—but emerged from the smoking wreck with two gunny sacks full of money . . . to the tune of over $75,000!

And that was the last full-scale performance of Butch Cassidy and his (so-called) Wild Bunch in the West!

Following the robbery at Wagner, we rode long and hard for the safety of our first hide-out at Morton's sheep ranch on the Trail of the Little Porcupine, south of the Missouri Breaks, where we picked up the first relay of mounts that Butch had set up beforehand. Here was shared the proceeds of the last meeting of the Train Robbers' Syndicate. A real dividend at last, with each member getting a whacking $12,000!

It gave me a mighty odd feeling to think we might not get together again, for Butch and Sundance were determined to head down for Fort Worth as soon as the trails were safely open—and Ben, Charlie and the Mex Kid had some plans of their own regarding certain banking business in Arizona.

But in the meantime we played tag with the half-dozen posses out in the field after us, splitting for a few days and then rejoining at some pre-arranged spot in the wilds.

Sitting around the campfire one night in early July, I asked Butch about the generous division of the Wagner loot. "Wouldn't have been quite so much—if your railroad spy got his, eh?"

Butch spat into the fire and winked. "You'd make a good book-keeper! But you're right. I decided to let him whistle this time. I know it's not very ethical of me to cut him out—but then I never could stand a sneak. Besides I don't plan on doing any more such work in this country." He leaned over and tapped me on the knee. "Look at them." He pointed at Billy Rob, Charlie and Ben, all with their heads together muttering. "Some of them can't quit. They'll go on until it's too late, grabbin' somebody's money and ridin' two jumps ahead of a posse." He rubbed his chin and grinned at me. "But I guess that's th' thrill of matchin' your wits against th' other side, and gettin' away with it. That's th' lure of th' outlaw trail. It's a game for real men . . . maybe fools— but men!"

Criss-crossing the country, still around the Little Rockies, we became pretty hard-pressed by a bull-dog posse. Instead of setting a trap for them, I suggested that we give them a problem in tracking the way Butch had over at Winnemucca. We rode into the George Knowlton Ranch, got the drop on the night-herder and tied him up—then drove about 200 horses south to the Muscleshell, culled the herd, and turned most of them loose. Our tracks were completely lost in that maze of hoof prints.

Following that we split again, with Butch

taking Hanks and Kilpatrick along, and leaving me with Sundance and Billy Rob. We were now heading south, away from the Little Rockies and the Wagner posses. We'd stopped once and exchanged horses at Coburn's Circle-C Ranch on the way down, not seeing anyone but young Walt Coburn out in the horse pasture. I'd known him ever since he was a sprout, as our ranches were pretty close. I was also mighty near Winters' place—but, with Sundance and the Mex Kid along, didn't have time to swing over there.

But as soon as we parted—I'd be back. I hadn't gotten it out of my craw that Annie had gone back to the very man that killed my brother, Johnny! Yes, I'd be back!

CHAPTER THIRTY-SIX

The morning of July 25, 1901 dawned red and threatening with storm. I rolled out of my blanket and saddled up my big brown mare for instant action. Sitting by my small fire with my cup of Arbuckle, I reviewed the happenings of the past few days—and found nothing to be pleased about.

I'd brought my own crew of long-riders down to meet Butch's at Cherry Creek, below the XIT Ranch, south of the Mountains Sheep Bluffs on July 19. Here we split up for good the next day, with Butch and Sundance riding south to Fort Worth, and Kilpatrick, Hanks and Billy Rob off to sample the hospitality of Robbers' Roost.

We'd shaken hands, and Butch had slipped me several addresses where I could reach him, before he planned to dodge out of the country for South America. "I'm countin' on you usin' your head, Kid. Get that social butterfly of yours and follow us. You've got th' names and numbers there, plus money to burn. Remember what I told you before—you just can't play games with Old Man Time!"

Next morning, after they'd become tiny specks bobbing on the prairie to be swallowed away into the blue maw of the horizon, I rode hard for Miles

City. It was little more than fifty miles down the Fort Keogh-Bismark Road to Starr Jackson—and I meant to see her, once, before I went anywhere . . . even with Annie!

Riding up the main street from the east, and just passing the Huffman Photo Gallery, the first man I saw, leaning against a post by the meat market was Bronco Jack Caldwell!

He saw me at the same time I spotted him, and guided my mare over to a hitching post. "Caldwell, if you make one move, I'll blow a hole in you!"

Bronco pulled himself off the post with a jerk, then dropped his hand from his holstered gun, and gave me his usual, kicked-cur smile. *"Kid!* Gawd, you gimmie a turn! You ain't gotta worry about me one bit." And he flipped back his vest to display a silver badge, half the size of a small saucer. "I'm th' new Marshal, since two weeks. Someone let daylight inter' th' old fathead who was Marshal one night."

I watched the fellow closely, but made no moves. "And you wouldn't know anything about that?"

"Hell no! Just thanks heavens fer small favors! And thanks to your old friend Frank Canton, too. Yep, knew Canton back in Texas when he was plain Joe Horner and always one jump ahead of th' Rangers fer rustlin'. When I left them chuckleheads over to Robbers' Roost and drifted up this way, Canton got me this job—after th' late Marshal went to his reward. Old Frank's a big man in this County and he either had to shoot me on th' sly or gimmie work."

"Well, I just left another of your Texas friends by the name of Ben Kilpatrick, and he'd be more apt to shoot you on sight!"

"Ah yes, heard all about you, Ben, Butch and th' rest. That was sure a fancy Fourth of July party you boys had with th' fast mail up to Wagner!"

I yanked the horse's head around and started on down the street. "Bronco, I swore I'd pull your stake rope the first time we met again, and if I don't move on, I'm liable to do just that!" I turned in my saddle to see him leaning against the post. When he saw me look back, he lifted one dirty hand in a salute.

I rode on over to the Miles City paper and went into the office. Mister Gordon peered up from his desk. "Curry! Now I know you haven't a lick of sense! Don't you know Frank Canton and a dozen men rode out of here not two hours back on the trail of Cassidy's Wild Bunch!"

I shrugged. "How is Starr?"

"Starr has gone to the Cordova Clinic in San Francisco. She had her operation one week ago, and thank God, it was perfectly successful. She'll come back to us an apparently whole girl." He got up and came around the desk. "But I must talk to you about Starr. You should know that—"

But here the front door crashed open and Bronco Jack Caldwell leaped in—both empty hands held before him. "Kid—Jest in time! Y'gotta ride, and ride like hell! Canton's men are comin' down over th' bridge at West Main Street. Be here in five or ten minutes."

I pulled my six-shooter and covered both Caldwell and Gordon as I went out, untied Brown Beauty and vaulted into the saddle.

"Told you we'd make up that little trouble we had," came the voice of Bronco Jack as I loped down the street and around the corner, heading northwest toward the Winters' Ranch—and Annie.

Now with the blood-red sun drowned out in a smother of grey, wolfish-looking clouds, as it arose on that Thursday, July 25, the growl of some huge beast rumbled through the darkening sky.

It was a hell of a day to go calling on Annie, but it had to be done.

I was riding up to the Winters' ranch building at 6 o'clock when the first few drops of the oncoming rain began to lash bullet-hard down onto the parched ground.

I got off the horse, tied her to a rail, and was walking to the front door, when Ab Winters came out—with a double-barrelled shotgun pointed straight at my belt-buckle.

"Get to hell out'a here, Logan!" He waved the

scatter-gun in the air and there was froth on his mouth, like a rabid animal. "Y'took my Missus and I'll kill you on sight if y'ever show up here again!"

"Where's Annie?"

"She ain't here. Was here about half-an-hour, weeks ago, to pack up th' stuff she left last time. Said she was leavin' th' whole damned country— and you do th' same!"

So Annie had come and gone! I should have known she wouldn't stay. I turned to get on my horse and, suddenly bending to untie a knotted pair of reins, missed the hellish blast of the double-barrelled scatter-gun. Some buckshot winged Brown Beauty slightly, and she screamed and plunged as I pumped three Colt slugs into Winters before he could reload.

"God! Don't shoot anymore. Don't shoot!" And Winters' foreman, Abe Gill, ran out and bent over the fallen rancher. "Tried to get you like he did your brother. Y'got him fair and square, but y'better ride!"

"Where'd Annie go?"

"Somewhere back East. Could have been Tennessee, maybe. Ride!"

And I forked my big brown mare and rode through the crashing downpour of the worst electrical storm of my life. It was as if the entire West, that I knew, was exploding into hell-fire and thunderous damnation.

CHAPTER THIRTY-SEVEN

When I left the Winters' Ranch in that driving storm, my only thought was to find Annie. If I didn't find her, there was no use following Cassidy to South America. As for Starr, she was cured, according to old man Gordon, and that was that as far I was concerned. It was only Annie that mattered now, for if I didn't have her what had it all meant? What had all the riding, robbing and shooting been about? I knew Annie hadn't approved of my life—but if I found her, I knew she'd go with me to wherever we could start over. And that meant one hell of a woman!

I rode south to Billings, Montana, arriving there Monday, July 29. I sold my Brown Beauty mare at the Billings Livery, along with my saddle and gear, then went over to the Billings House and took a room. I slept the clock around, as I had before after a tough ride. Getting up, I breakfasted and went out to send a wire to *Jim Lowe* in care of Fannie Porter, Fort Worth, Texas.

Three hours later I had a reply:

"Annie Rogers has distant relation in Memphis and may be working at Corinne Lewis' Gambling Palace there. She also might go to work at Ike Jones' Crystal Hall in Nashville, Tennessee. One thing

Porter says is that Annie can take care of herself! See you do the same—and join us at New York address before January 9, 1902. Signed, Jim Lowe."

So Butch and Sundance were leaving New York in early January! Well, I'd have to find Annie and talk her into such a move before then. I went uptown and togged myself out as befitted a prosperous railroad man set on traveling far and wide, then bought a ticket for Denver, Colorado. The first stop in my search for a runaway lady.

It was sunny and pleasant in Denver when I got off the Denver and Rio Grande, August 1. With my alligator bag held tight, and filled with over $11,000 and two six-shooters, I strolled up town, enjoying the brisk air and the many fine buildings.

Away to the sides mountains reared up in great sugarloafs of purple, topped by white snows along some of the highest points.

Many of the homes I walked past were built of handsome redstone, with green grass lawns between. Downtown, some of the most elegant stores I'd ever seen stretched along Larimer and Curtis. *Daniels & Fisher* had one plate glass window after another filled with wax models in derby hats, pointed shoes and the newest pegtop pants. Their wax lady friends looked like a bunch of wine glasses turned upside down.

Thirsty from my hike, I went into the Larimer Saloon for a drink, and read the slogan over the long stretch of mahogany: *Wilson Whiskey—That's All!* I downed a couple of Wilson's before going over to the Curtis Street Theater to watch the musical show there—all about those new-fangled "Horseless-Carriages."

On the way out of the theater, that Wilson's still working, I joined the rest of the citizens in singing the hit of the show:

"*I guess I oughtn't auto any more . . .*
"*Oh, I guess I oughtn't auto any more . . .*
"*For there's seven doctors mighty busy*
"*Taking splinters out of Lizzy . . .*
"*So I guess I oughtn't auto anymore!*"

I stayed on in Denver for a week before taking the Denver & Pacific for Omaha, Nebraska—I'd had such a downright fine time of it.

Though I missed Annie like blazes, and was looking forward to finding her again, the sudden change from a hunted owl-hoot, on the dodge, to a man of means was just mighty easy to take!

I got into Omaha a couple of days later and set out to *do* the town, but found the local *Blue-Stocking Party* was in office and always pulled in the sidewalks after 10 p.m. at night, and most saloons were shut down tight.

So I spent my time, between trains, rubber-necking like any other tourist. As the terminus for three of the country's largest railroads, a powerful lot of people were coming and going. The waiting room of the Union Pacific Depot (where I changed for Chicago) was jam-packed with crowds of people . . . some of the strangest looking humans I'd ever seen. Men in alligator boots and loose overcoats, with shaggy hair and beards, like old buffaloes, prowled around between trains—tagged along by women, with handkerchiefs over their heads, in place of hats, all surrounded by herds of chubby children who tumbled and frisked in and out among the boxes, baskets, bundles, bedding and babies' chairs, piled waist high on the platforms.

Emigrants—someone said, and bound westward as far as California. So, some were still heading west for fame and fortune?

But I was on my way Eastward—maybe as far away as South America!

By the time my train pulled into Chicago, on August 12, I was a veteran of train-travel. I ate mighty well in the spick-and-span dining cars, and slept each night in a fancy berth. And I had to admit it seemed to beat bunking down on the cold ground, all hollow.

Chicago was a wonderful but noisy place, filled with chimney smoke the gusty winds off the great, sparkling lake couldn't drive completely away. The busy streets were alive with drays, electric trolley cards, buggies and even here and there, a chugging, sputtering, smoking "Horseless Carriage." These were driven by desperate-faced fellows, eyes glaring from behind big goggles and filled with women in big hats and trailing veils.

I could have stayed in Chicago for weeks, dining on Great Lake whitefish, peas from New Orleans and drinking fancy liquor from France. The stockyards were huge, and the Palmer House worth a trip from anywhere, but I still missed Annie!

Leaving Chicago on the 21st of August, I rode the Memphis & Louisville all the way south to Memphis, Tennessee, arriving there the morning of Saturday, August 24.

The air *was hot,* and I could see why the local folks moved so slowly and talked in that same slow tempo. But at night Memphis lit up like a Christmas tree, with bars and dives going full-blast until sunup. I made every grog and hook shop in that town by the levee, but never a line on Annie! She'd never appeared at Corrine Lewis' Palace—nor had anyone ever heard of her.

Memphis had a lot going for it, for someone with money to spend, and time to spend it. And it wasn't long until I found myself putting off going on to Nashville. I liked the bars and, especially, the places up and down Beale Street with the ragtime piano-players. I'd never heard much music but I liked to sit back in a corner of The Monarch, light up a fancy cigar, sip some brandy and listen to such ivory-ticklers as Benny Frenchy. He certainly beat anything I'd heard in Fort Worth. His long, brown fingers seemed to gallop over the keys when he rattled out such lively tunes as the *"Peacherine Rag"* and *"Lily Queen."*

With one thing and another, it was the end of September before I got around leaving for Nashville. And I told myself that if Annie wasn't in Memphis—then she'd have to be in Nashville.

Nashville had a different feel to it than Memphis, with its easy-going, play-all-night atmosphere. The mountains, and the many rolling hills around the town were already turning with the color of fall. Here the folks stood up a little straighter, and talked a bit more briskly—and so my hunt for the vanished Annie went on. No one had seen her, and not even Ike Jones (a personal friend of Fannie Porter) had any sort of line on her.

I was puzzled, but decided to hang around the "tenderloin" and wait for some word. It was a wait that went on, day after day, and night after night. I knew Butch and Sundance (and Sundance's filly, Etta Place) were already making plans to move to New York—and points way beyond, but I couldn't think of joining them—yet.

Then on Saturday, November 22, I got word from Ike Jones that Annie had been seen working in a gambling saloon in Knoxville. I packed my two alligator bags (one for the money and pistols, and the other for my razor, and extra clothes) and caught the Gulf Coast Flyer for Knoxville.

It was Sunday morning when I got in and so took a room at the Knoxville House on Mountain Avenue.

On Monday I prowled the streets until dark and then went down to the Dryades Club on Central Avenue. The usual ragtime pianoman was working on the keyboard in the bar and the usual drink-and-dance girls circulating. But I pushed past the feathers and fans and went into the back room.

There Annie was! Sitting at a table and dealing cards to a group of intent gamblers. I eased in and took a seat. "Deal me in!"

She glanced up—and the cards exploded out of her hands in a fountain of pasteboards. "Harvey!" Then I was around the table, brushing one cardshark out of his seat onto the floor—and had her in my arms.

She took the rest of the night off!

For the next three weeks it seemed we duplicated our idyl at Star Valley—back there we'd been surrounded by the everlasting walls of a hidden valley closing us in, guarding us from all the outside world and its troubles, yet, somehow, I felt the same about Knoxville. Here we were in the midst of thousands of people who passed us on the streets and never gave us a backward glance. It was a time of contentment.

Annie kept on at the Dryades, where she was rated as one of the most valuable and straight dealers the club had ever had. And no one got out of line with her, for her reputation had preceded her.

I agreed to her working from eight until midnight, as we had to mark time until we could meet Butch and Company in New York City on Monday, January 5, 1902, and this seemed about as safe a place as we could possibly imagine.

During the days, that remained unusually mild for December, we took long buggy rides out into the country, traveling over the hills and down into the hidden valleys surrounding the city, just glad to get away, and actually escape from the swarms of faceless hundreds that made up Knoxville.

Of course, we were completely by ourselves all through the long nights after I picked Annie up at the stroke of midnight and took her home, by cab, to our rooms in the Tennessee Arms of Central Avenue, eight blocks from the club.

I was so satisfied with the way things were going I sent out several letters, one to Butch in

Fort Worth, another to Jim Thornhill at Landusky and a third to Starr at Miles City, all without a word to Annie. The last was just a card to wish Starr an early Merry Christmas and Best Wishes for 1902.

I didn't sign the notes, nor leave any address. I was sure each would know who the letter came from.

Every evening after I took Annie to work, I went on down the street to the Old Central Bar at Commerce and Central, and lounged around, killing time and picking an occasional game of cards or pool with some stranger—and nine-times-out-of-ten beating my opponent. I was pretty strong with a cue!

The evening of December 13, just after I'd left Annie at the door of the Dyrades and was going down the steps, Annie hurried back to the door. "Harvey! Louis Chauvin, the upstairs piano-player just said there were men asking questions about Bob Nelson or Tom Capehart this afternoon—all up and down the street. He thinks they might be Pinkertons."

"Well, let them ask for Mister Capehart or Nelson, we're registered as Mr. and Mrs. William Wilson, if you'll recall!" I laughed, gave her a squeeze and went on down the street to the Old Central. Yet on the way I got to thinking. If the Pinks were snooping around, it might be just as well to take Annie and travel on to New York ahead of Butch. Tomorrow was Sunday, and a good day to get out of town.

Once at the Old Central, I sat down, ordered a brandy and looked around for some sort of action. At about 8:30 p.m., I got more than I'd bargained for!

I had been playing a game of eight ball with two strangers, who I took to be a pair of tinhorn drummers, when the shorter of the pair began, very openly, to cheat. I called him on it, and his pardner, a big, beefy-faced fellow in a rusty black suit, suddenly hauled off and swung the butt end of his stick right at my head!

I was turned the other way to make a shot, at the time, and his cue gave me one great whack that buckled my knees for an instant. I staggered back against the wall, and then the old Logan temper flared up in roaring fury!

In a moment I'd downed beefy-face with a hell of a crack on the jaw with my own cue, and was going around the table, scattering loafers left and right, as I tried to catch that little cheating weasel—when a pair of harness bulls came running out of the back room, drawn pistols pointed straight at me!

I knew right there I'd been set up!

Before they could fire a shot, I'd drawn my Smith & Wesson from its shoulder holster and bored both dead center!

I knocked the bartender out of the way, kicked

two card-players off their chairs and was out the back door before the echoes died.

It was black outside the place, but I didn't wait to look around—and took a fall of 15 feet in the dark. I got back up, still ready to fight, but had dropped my six-gun and couldn't find it. As there was no sound behind me yet, I ran off into the night, determined to get from town before the Pinkertons called out the rest of their army.

Two days later I was sitting in the Knox County Jail!

Ever since Saturday night, I'd been trying to live off a land that had turned cruelly cold and inhospitable. With my head wound, I'd been half out of my mind, part of the time, as I limped along the railroad line. I'd thought I was back on our ranch, and held long talks with Johnny and my kid brother Lonny.

"We may be dead, Harve, but you're in worse shape than we are," Johnny laughed at me from the other side of the little, spindly fire I'd managed to start down in the bottom of a dried-up sinkhole. He grinned at Lonny, who crouched on the other side of the feeble blaze—ignoring the bullet hole in his own head.

"Johnny's right, Harvey. We don't feel a thing, but you'll freeze if you don't get in somewhere and thaw out!"

"He'll thaw out in Hell same as us," and

Johnny doubled over with a shadowy laughter that seemed to turn him into wavering smoke.

I roused up, rubbed the smoke from my eyes and saw other phantoms shimmering across the red glare of the fire. They pointed shining guns.

Then I knew that the Knoxville law had found me.

The local police, I must say, were mighty decent fellows—in spite of the fact I'd sorely wounded two members of their force. Their prison doctor bandaged my head and the department ordered some good meals for me from Billy McIntyre's restaurant across in Market Square—steak, potatoes, eggs, hot rolls and coffee . . . even some passable cigars.

Though I still refused to admit anything or my name, they hustled me over to the court of Squire Sellers, charged as being a fugitive from justice and also with felonious assault. My bond was set at a thumping $20,000!

"What is your name?" the old bald-headed Justice wanted to know.

"Charles Johnson." And Charles Johnson I was known—for the time.

Sheriff Fox allowed me the freedom of the jail corridor, which wasn't just what I had in mind— but it had to do for the time being.

I believe Fox and the local police felt rather

hangdog about being connected with the Pinkertons and their methods.

Naturally the press showed up as fast as word got out that "the shooter" had been captured. A *Sentinel* reporter described the scene as he saw it:

> *"The shooter (Johnson) was on the alert and saw every move that was made. Every time the jail door opened, his eyes traveled to it as would the eyes of a lion or some other terrible beast that had been entrapped . . . he heard every noise and saw every motion. One of the officers handed a pistol to another, and he saw it. The coveted look he gave it was something wonderful."*

There was more in the same vein. It was a field day for the newspaper hacks. I wondered what Annie would think, when she read such yellowback stuff.

It wasn't long until the Pinkertons showed up, in the person of one Mister Lowell Spence of the Chicago office. When I'd gone through the lineup with half-dozen ringers and hoboes off the street, Spence came to my cell.

"Is there anything I can do for you?" He looked like the cat that just gulped down the bird.

"Not that I know of," I said. "Unless you have a cigar on you."

Spence left, promising to send me a box.

And to give the devil his dues, he did just that. It was the only good thing I ever knew of Billy Pinkerton and his tribe. But then I must admit being prejudiced.

For weeks after Spence, of the Pinkerton Agency, identified me as Harvey Logan, and not Tom Capehart, Charles Johnson, William Wilson, Robert Nelson or—Kid Curry, I put in a monotonous period of time—made indescribably longer by the bars around me. I'd not heard from Annie or had any idea what had happened to her—yet I could imagine all sorts of disasters. And I knew that Butch and his traveling companions must be ready to leave the States. Except for some sort of bad break (I couldn't yet think how the Pinkertons had pulled it off), we'd be traveling right along with Butch and Sundance.

Christmas came and went, and then I heard both policemen I'd hit were on the mend—and that was the best present I could have had. There'd be no man with the rope in my immediate future— the way poor old Black Jack Ketchum got his down in New Mexico back in April, 1901.

When it came time for the court to get into action, it started out as a regular three-ring circus. In the meantime Ben Kilpatrick had wandered down South, like myself and got himself nabbed for passing off some of the Wagner money, all with crudely signed and misspelled signatures. They threw the book at Ben, and he got 15 years at Atlanta pronto. And yet my case dragged on and on—with half of the lawyers in the state having the time of their life in the fight.

Where the money was coming from for my defense puzzled me, until I received a visit from Mr. Reuben L. Cates, chairman of the Knox County Registration and Election Commission. He told me quietly that he and half a dozen other powerhouse legal minds had been retained by "parties unknown," except that the money, to handle my case, was good as gold and deposited in the Knox County Bank—and that there was "more than enough." I knew Annie was out there!

In May I went to court with my attorneys, Cates and Houk. The Great Northern Express Company was there breathing fire from the mouth of Attorney Walter B. Roberts. John B. Holloway, assistant prosecuting attorney, represented the state of Tennessee. And nothing was decided, again.

As usual the papers had their field day:

"Logan showed no evidence of feelings. Already the jail pallor was on his coun-tenance. His eyes were constantly moving around. There were officers and deputy sheriffs all about him, ready to checkmate

any move he might make. He was not handcuffed while in the courtroom, and did not make any false moves, though he seemed to size up carefully every door and window as an avenue of escape."

That particular reporter had mighty keen eyes!

On September 4, 1902 (when Butch must have been in South America for nearly a year!), a Judge Sneed ordered that the federal courts could get into the fray on a "concurrent jurisdiction" of my case. Federal warrants were slapped on me containing 19 counts "in the main for receiving, possessing passing and exchanging unsigned as well as forged(!) bank notes." All other charges would be continued as well. Then the case was postponed again until November 18, 1902!

When court reopened, the parade of witnesses was something never before seen in the entire state. And, to say the least, I'd have been mighty glad to have half of them stay home.

There were A.L. Smith, vice-president of the National Bank of Montana; Fireman, Mike O'Neal; Express Messenger, C. H. Smith; R. F. O'Neal, former sheriff of Chouteau County, Montana; Ed Bryant, railway money clerk out of St. Paul; Lowell Spence, Pinkerton operative; and even two treasury officials from Washington, D.C.!

My legal counsel entered a plea that I had

412

been in France from June until August, 1901 (showing great imagination, if nothing else), and so couldn't have taken part in the Great Northern hold-up in July.

Fireman Mike O'Neal and Express Messenger C. H. Smith testified that I resembled the man who blew the safe—and that they recognized my voice . . . which had to prove very keen ears, as I'd not said three words.

Horace Burnett, the bartender I'd upended the night of the row at the Old Central, testified I'd been drinking brandy just before the shooting of Patrolmen Dinwiddie and Saylor. Of course, the two officers had no difficulty in pointing a finger at the man who beat them both to the draw!

But the Pinkertons never did trot their pair of decoy weasels out; perhaps they were too bashful to let the public in on such methods.

When all the long months of argument and legal sparring were over and Annie had spent every bit of that $11,000 (and who knew how much more)—I was convicted of ten counts and sentenced to 20 years at hard labor in the federal pen at Columbus, Ohio.

In a particularly powerful burst of spleen, the Pinkerton Agency announced they'd wait the 20 years and then see that I was rearrested at that time and charged *with other crimes!*

And yet again, the newspapers had to have their "day in court":

"His career was like unto the dime novel hero. Logan's striking features, his great, straight nose, his Napoleonic (!) forehead, his strong jaw, his bold eye, and his physical endurance, indicated by his movements and assured by his past record, are everywhere cause for comment."

What can I tell about the next long, weary period of time that crawled by, grey day, followed by grey week, then grey month.

It was just a taste, I told myself, of that 20-year stretch that was coming, as surely as each day fell off the calendar and autumn withered away into blustery white winter.

At first as I sat or lay in my steel cage, on the isolated second floor cell block, watched more closely than if held in some death cell (due to the urging of the Pinkertons that extra guards be stationed around my cage), my very spirit withered with winter.

But the spirit that had withered, began to move and bloom again with the coming of spring. What sky I could see, from beyond my bars, was blue again, filled with white clouds that herded along from the west.

When I saw those clouds racing free across the blue of heaven's bright pastures, I made a vow.

Once before I'd made a vow but it was for

revenge for the deaths of my brothers, revenge against the system that killed them, took my ranch—and destroyed such free spirits as Flat Nose George, Sam Ketchum and Bill Carver. Perhaps that vow was wrong. I would admit that it could have been wrong. I'd never believe it was *completely* wrong! But now there was no revenge in my soul—just a burning, a longing greater than anything I'd ever known . . . *to be free!*

And when I made that vow to myself, I gave up eating the bread of despair along with my prison fare. I began to think!

CHAPTER THIRTY-EIGHT

Though the Pinkertons kept up their harping to have me moved out of Knoxville and up to Columbus, Judge Clark at Chattanooga telegraphed Marshal Austin, ordering that I be held where I was until my appeal could be heard.

That appeal was finally heard on June 2, 1903 by the Circuit Court of Appeals at Cincinnati and it upheld the decision of the lower court in the case of the *United States vs. Harvey Logan.*

Soon the Pinkertons would have their way. Soon a steel-lined mail coach would be brought up the Southern tracks. Soon there'd be Secret-Service Men and Pinkertons on hand to serve as an escort all the way to Columbus.

Soon—but not quite yet!

From the time I knew the appeal would be made in June, I began to put together (what I hoped would be) my own Chinese Trick with the Hole in the Middle.

Instead of sitting moping on my bunk, or reading the daily papers and laughing (once in a while) at the antics of *Happy Hooligan* and *Si and His Mule, Maude*, I began to exercise as if my life depended upon it . . . and it did.

The first key to my problem was discovered,

when I was chinning myself on a three-inch pipe that ran through my cell. It broke apart and I saw it was merely an air vent. The guards had not noticed, and I replaced it at once, before they saw what had happened. Now I had a place to hide whatever tools I could lay my hands on.

My regular guards were Irwin and Bell and they each worked 12-hour shifts. I found that the day guard, Irwin, was the most friendly, and I began to butter up to him. There was another unusual thing, I'd noticed. Bell went on at midnight and worked until noon. Irwin came on at 1 p.m. and worked until midnight. *There was an interval of one hour from noon 'til 1 p.m. without a guard on duty!*

The jailer let the guards in and out as neither had a key to the outer jail door. Irwin only had a key to the inner cell door. When Irwin came on duty at one o'clock I always stood by the open cell grate looking through the south window of the outer jail wall, down to the Tennessee River. When Irwin came into the corridor, I watched him and noticed that he looked straight at the left corner of the cell out of my sight and went there first.

I decided to find out what he was going there for, and by holding my pocket mirror out through the grating, saw a pasteboard shoe box on a shelf, and a revolver on top of the box. The shelf was about five feet from the end of the cell grating.

417

By watching Irwin, when he was not looking my way, I found that he always took the revolver from the top of the box. Then by listening to the guard Bell's movements, decided that he put his revolver inside the box.

My plan was simple from then on. I had to lasso Irwin and get his gun, get the other gun by some means, get the jailer to open the outer door at the right time and take the purebred saddle mare Sheriff Fox always kept in the barn next to the jail. But it had to go like clockwork, as Butch would say.

In order to get the gun, I needed a stick, at least five feet long, to reach that box! A broom stick was too short, and the jailer would soon miss his broom. Then I discovered the west window had some three feet of sash that could be split and spliced to make a five-foot stick. But how to get that sash? Then I got the idea to complain about my meals (which were really quite good) and told the jailer I'd tear the place apart unless I got better grub. Next day between noon and one o'clock I took the broom, poked it out of my cell and pushed out every window pane. Then I hooked the broom over the three-foot sash and pulled it out into the corridor. I hid the sash in the three-inch vent pipe overhead, and threw the broom handle and what was left of the broom out through the window, but I had to do it in a hurry as the jailer Bell came storming up the stairs.

"What are you up to, Logan?" He was furious, I could see.

"Give me better food and this won't happen again. I told you what I'd do to this place unless I got proper grub," I growled, watching him closely.

As I thought, he searched high and low for the rest of the sash and the wire off the broom—but couldn't find a thing.

Then I secretly went to work on the sash. The only tool I had was a small penknife, but I split the sash, morticed and grooved two ends to make a strong six-foot stick (Annie had said that I was handy with tools). This took a long time as I had only one hour a day to work (from 12 'til 1 p.m.!). Then I made my plans on how to get a metal hook to fasten to the end of the stick.

One day I threw another fit and kicked a bucket apart, and took and hid the pieces I needed in the overhead pipe.

And every day was one day nearer to the time when the Pinkertons and their friends from the Secret-Service would be coming with their steel baggage car to take me north to that 20-year stretch!

I'd heard, through the friendly guard, Irwin, the talk about the prison (on the occupied levels) was that I'd be gone north before the end of the month of June. And as I had great faith in grapevine news, I decided right there and then that I'd make my move the next day, June 27th.

There'd been a lot of rain that past week and the Tennessee was rising. Standing in my cell, on June 27, I lowered my voice, as I talked to the guard Irwin, and he stepped nearer to hear what I had to say. I pointed out what seemed to be something floating on the river and he turned to look!

Right then Irwin felt my wire noose around his neck, and tightening!

"I've got you! And I'll kill you if you make a sound. I'll choke the life right out of you, Frank! I don't want to, but it's a case of life or death with me! It's all right as long as you do just what I say," I told him all in one breath. "I'm going to get out of this place—and you're going to help me!" I took his revolver and put it in my belt.

I had him turn around and extend his hands through the bars, then, with the end of the broom wire lasso in my teeth, I tied first one hand and then the other to the bars, with rope taken from my hammock.

Then I hustled and got the sticks from the overhead pipe, put them together and slipped the metal hook in the end. I lay flat on my back, reached out through the bars of my cell and hooked the shoe box with the other pistol. It took one long minute to drag the box over, but

I breathed a great sign of relief when I got my hands on both those six-shooters—loaded in every chamber!

Looking at the watch I pulled from Irwin's pocket, I saw it was 4:30, just about the time Jailer Bell always showed up. I waited, but no Bell! Time dragged on, then I rapped on the bars and called him. It was taking a chance, but now chances had to be taken.

I heard footsteps on the stairs, and Bell appeared—to find a loaded six-shooter pointed at his head. He came right up like a lamb. Leaving Irwin tied up, I went and got my coat, razor, shaving brush and bar of soap, leaving behind most of my old clothes.

Bell and I went down the back stairs. The first time I'd been down them in months, but I stepped along mighty lively—and so did Bell.

As we came out into the alley behind the jail, the Italian handyman showed up with his mouth open. "Fall in line!" I told him and we went to the stable to get the Sheriff's mare. We had her saddled and bridled in short order, and then I was up in the saddle. With the mare's shoes clashing and ringing out on the cobblestones of the alley way, I had them open the Prince Street gate.

It was getting on toward evening, and the sun was already burning away into crimson ashes behind the mountains as I rode along Prince Street.

Pulling down my old crush black hat (long a prisoner like myself), I turned east on Hill Street at a rapid trot, then crossing the Gay Street bridge at an even gallop, plunged onto the Martin Mill Pike. The last of the summer sun went out and the stars of the evening sky were clouded grey from the dust kicked up by my swift and powerful mount.

I was heading west—and God help the man that stood in my way.

CHAPTER THIRTY-NINE

Two months after I galloped out of Knoxville, I was hiking up the moonlit road to my ranch at Landusky. If ever a man looked and felt the part of plain and simple hobo, it was me.

I'd left Sheriff Fox's mare tied near a mountaineer's cabin, ten miles out of town, then doubled back and caught a freight train north that same wonderful night. The few vagrants and tramps, riding the empties, left me strictly alone once I'd showed them the muzzle end of a six-shooter, informing them I'd heave all and sundry onto the speeding ties unless I had my corner of the box car to myself.

Several grew friendly after that, as dangerous kicked dogs fawn on an abuser. They initiated me into the mysteries of their scrawled symbols . . . that *A-Number-1* on a fence or tree signified the inhabitants of that particular farm or home were good for a handout . . . and NX-U meant a vicious cur lurking to sample the leg of some hopeful knight of the road.

So town by town and state by state, I worked my way homeward, riding the rods, blind baggage and, when in luck, the *side-door-pullman cars.*

It was a bitter contrast to my journey of those two long years before. Then I'd been in search of Annie, now every effort was strained to get back to the safety of the wilds. Annie had vanished with my arrest, though she'd lingered long enough to arrange for the most competent legal aid she could—and pay for it on the nail. Somewhere she waited in the West, I was certain. It might be Star Valley anywhere, but I knew I'd find her again!

Now, as I trudged the last miles to my ranch, the moon began to fade as a lamp is trimmed down, and the rim of the sun glittered on the horizon. I hobbled up to the door, hammered on the panel and sat down on the step. I'd come back to where it all began.

I stayed under wraps at the ranch with Jim Thornhill for a month. Though there was a rumor around Landusky that I'd been seen crawling off a freight down the line, I wasn't bothered. The talk around was that I'd got Winters—and it was good riddance! Abe Gill never let on who shot his boss, and so he took over the Winters' ranch. It was a stroke of luck for him.

Jim Thornhill had greeted me like a ghost from the past, and as I sat around our place, resting up and putting some meat back on my bones, I felt like a ghost. But gradually, as back at Knoxville, I got to thinking. And Jim could see the change.

"Itchy feet! You're gettin' itchy feet, I can sure see just that!"

"I've got to move on again, Jim," I told him one night at the supper table. "It's not fair to you—camping here and putting you in jeopardy . . . hiding out a fugitive. Beside, this place is barely making it—and you don't need an ex-hobo eating you out of house and home!"

There'd been rumors circulating around the area that the law was still sniffing on my heels—and I wasn't going to let the last of our "family" go down with me. Besides, I had to get out and get some money—*the only way I could* and then find Annie once more. Butch was long gone, and the old days were two years and more in the past. We had to vanish our own way. But first I needed some help and I thought I knew where to find it.

The day before I rode out of our ranch—for the last time, I happened to get a letter. It was so unusual I just sat looking at it after Jim fetched it from the mail box. It was addressed simply to me at the Four-Tee Ranch, Landusky, Wyoming. It had gone straight through the mails to Harvey Logan, Esq. Though it had been delivered all right, I knew the Pinkerton tribe would hear of it—and be around to visit. But they'd be too late!

It came from old man Gordon at Miles City, Montana and was a brief as a bullet: *"Logan, this is to inform you that Starr was the means of your capture in December of 1901. I just discovered this. She told us that she'd learned that you had been responsible for her father's death, and that she'd turned over your holiday card to Frank Canton, who is now Marshal again, and he'd noticed the Knoxville, Tenn. postmark and wired the Pinkerton office in Chicago. I don't condone such conduct, particularly after you financed her successful operation. She has got to be a handful and I am afraid she'll up and fly the coop someday. Hope this gets to you. A. Gordon."*

For several weeks I rode the old *Outlaw Trail* looking for recruits, but everywhere the story was the same. The men with spunk had left the Territory or were in jail, or worse. Hole in the Wall harbored a few petty rustlers and Brown's Hole was no better. And there wasn't a soul left on the lonesome heights of Robbers' Roost!

So I crossed and re-crossed the wild lands. Just happy to be free to ride under the great arching blue dome of the sky and sleep wherever I chose to at night, and that hard ground was mighty soft to me.

But the year went along and, after wintering in New Mexico, under an assumed name at a small ranch—working for my money, I rode back north. Though I'd not got to Star Valley or found Annie, I'd spotted a likely looking railroad that might be the answer to my need for a large getaway stake.

Word was whispered in the barrooms along the trail that the Denver and Rio Grande carried payrolls large enough to satisfy anyone. But, said the barflies, "who's around any more to take away that sort of money?"

I knew just one person!

In the spring of 1904, I moved out of my cabin in the wilds of the Green River country (a place I'd found on one of my lonely rides), and went looking for some backup men in earnest. It was getting late to try a train busting with the growing network of telephones, telegraph and constantly improved roads—but despite what Butch had said about Old Man Time, I was determined to pull it off and I found my first rider in a saloon at Green River. And it was Bronco Jack!

After debating whether to shoot him on sight, or buy him a drink, I did the latter and (sitting at a table in the saloon corner) learned he was on the dodge, *again!*

"Tried to stick up a bank in th' County, all by myself, and it didn't take, as usual. So I had to hightail it! Picked up myself a wild and woolly tenderfoot, couple towns back. That's him over there!" And Bronco nodded his head at a fresh-faced young fellow, dressed in an outlandish cowboy suit of woolly chaps and a big ten-gallon hat, who sat in the other corner of the saloon, watching us with wide eyes. "Told him I'd show him how to make a fast buck. He's from back East some'rs and honin' to see some of the wild West!"

It was against my every instinct, but I had Bronco, who was going by the name of Tap Duncan, fetch *The Tenderfoot over . . .*

※ ※ ※ ※

—Harvey Logan no longer tells his story! The rest of this tale is the responsibility of myself, who I'll continue to call *The Tenderfoot.*

Following our meeting at the Eagle Saloon in Green River, Wyoming, on May 16, 1904, we rode south toward Colorado at an easy gait. Arriving in the vicinity of Grand Junction, Colorado on June 1, we went into camp, presumably in the guise of wandering prospectors. Tap Duncan certainly looked the part of a desert vagabond, and Harvey Logan, while dressed with more care, in decent range clothes, could play the part. I had my work cut out for me with my pristine white hat and chaps.

Logan ragged me about my looks, stamped my hat in the dirt and made me get into some old trousers, that had seen better days. Then we sat it out waiting for the arrival of the money train (Train No. 5) of Denver–Rio Grande Western Mail.

We waited for nearly a week, with Logan riding in to the town of Parachute to keep his ears open. Several times he sent Tap Duncan on the same errand, to learn the exact time of the arrival of

No. 5, and Tap returned considerably the worse for wear. Logan read him the riot act and went into town himself from then on. On Tuesday, June 7, 1904 he rode back into our camp, in the hidden draw, and tossed the Denver Post at me.

A story on the front page told of $150,000 coming down the line on *Special Train No. 1.* "And we forget all about old Number Five," Logan laughed. "So get ready for some hot work!"

We'd gone over and over our exact schedule and knew to the minute what to do. I gritted my teeth and wished (in my most secret self) that I'd never run off with that $500 from my Uncle's Boston Bank—and was back safely in Beacon Street that very moment.

But by 10:30 that night I was too busy to do anything but follow our schedule. When the *S.K. Hooper*, the fast Denver-Salt Lake City flyer pulled into the darkened hamlet of Parachute and put off some express packages, then started up again—it had an extra passenger!

Logan had hopped up on the blind baggage, crawled over the coal tender and brought the train to a halt, opposite our bonfire on the tracks half a mile from the station.

Between Tap Duncan and myself, we covered the train crew and Logan got to work with our dynamite in the express car. The humming in my ears had hardly subsided when Logan was back with a half-filled gunny sack.

It had all gone off with professional precision. The only trouble arose when Tap Duncan took a shot at the Conductor as he ran toward us. The fellow went down with a bullet in his right leg, and we hesitated for a moment but there were no fireworks, and so we mounted and rode for it.

And I can tell you that the thrill of it has never left me. It was piracy on horseback. But there's nothing like it on this green earth!

There wasn't as much money in the strong box as we'd been led to believe, and Tap Duncan cursed the railroad, the penny-ante banks and his usual round of bad luck.

The disappointments were real for Harvey Logan as well. He was broke and had expected to send at least $1,000 back to his friend Jim Thornhill, to help out with the ranch. He also had wanted money for some other matter, though he never spoke of it.

As we rode through the night and into the morning, Logan tried to keep up our spirits, telling us it was a bad break but he'd been through too much in the past few years to be downhearted about it.

With a posse hard on our heels, we came up to the Stowell Ranch about 10 a.m. and found some fresh horses in the corral, which we exchanged for our own played-out mounts.

About noon we reached the head of a narrow

ravine, with timber on both sides. Here Logan stopped and said, "Boys, here's our chance to get even. We didn't get much of their money, so we'll get some of their damned hide off the tenderest spot!"

We lay out there in the timber until supper time, but that posse never showed up. Now, we had wasted half a day, and there was nothing to do but go on and make our getaway . . . if we could pull it off.

Next day, about noon, riding on toward Grand Mesa, we came up to a small ranch house. Tired and hungry, we decided to impersonate a posse. And when the rawboned housewife came out the side door, Logan said to her, "We're looking for those train robbers. Have you seen anything of them?"

The woman just stared at him coldly. "Why, *you're* the train robbers!"

I could see Logan was baffled, but he lifted his hat to her and said, "Boys, we better get going. We'll get little help here."

We rode on and were grazing our horses and resting them with the saddles off in a small opening, in the timber near Divide Creek, when that Posse finally showed up.

Then, my word, how the lead did fly! I'd never been in the army, nor heard much shooting, but I got my fill that day. We exchanged over 200 shots with the men in that little valley. Our luck was bad right from the start. The horses stampeded down into the posse's horses, leaving us on foot. But right then we were too busy to think about riding or even walking.

Just as the fight started, I heard Logan give an exclamation. *"Canton!"* It seemed he'd recognized the leader of that determined mob.

Tap Duncan gave Logan a most odd look, and crawled off twenty yards before commencing to fire at the posse. And it seemed to me, from where I crouched, that he was shooting high—but then I was not the sharpshooter of our trio.

Just before dark, Duncan began to work his way down the hill toward the posse. I saw Logan lift his head and break off firing his high-powered Winchester. "Where you going, Bronco?" I heard him call—and Tap Duncan's answer came back, muffled, but still discernible. "Pickin' th' winnin' team as usual—so goodbye, Kid!" Then Duncan stood up and pointed his pistol right at Logan—but, so fast, that I thought I was seeing things—Logan drew a six-shooter and shot Tap Duncan!

The posse began firing again just then and the exchange, in the dusk, between Logan and Duncan, went unnoticed by all but myself, where I crouched behind a boulder with a very bad case of the shakes.

Tap didn't die at once but lay there, breathing blood out through a lung wound, and cursing continually. He lasted for about an hour and just before he breathed a rattling last breath, he laughed, choked on blood and wheezed loud enough for both Logan and I to hear: "Yours truly, Kid. Told you, way back, that I'd get you someday. Blew on you to that little blonde filly up at Miles City when I was lawdog. Told her you kilt her pap in th' Hole." He paused and wheezed once more. "And wired your pal old Frank Canton down there in th' Posse, to come an' pull your stake rope. He'll do just that!" He gave a convulsion and rolled over.

Logan stood up slowly, and put a bullet through Tap's head. "That's what you do to snakes, to make sure they're dead!"

He came over, reached for my hand, shook it and gave me the best directions for getting out on foot to the Colorado River. Then he was gone in the enveloping night.

EPILOGUE

Can there be an epilogue without a proper prologue? However, some of my final words may be of interest in the summing up.

My life since the summer of 1904 approximated that of any other *useful* citizen. I returned to Boston in August of that year, an apprehensive prodigal, to find my father had made certain arrangements with Uncle and the proper authorities. My little peccadillo (as he termed it) had been squared, as they used to say in Wyoming. That fall I went into the office of my stockbroker cousin, as junior clerk. By 1908 I was a junior partner and married to another distant cousin.

The remainder of my existence, as with countless others, blended into periods of war, peace, prosperity, depression, births, deaths, and at last retirement—unwanted, but forced upon a rich widower with a wealth of time and memories on his hands.

And always there was the haunting memory of the man that I thought of as the last of the larger-than-life Ishmaels of the plains and mountains—going his way regardless of any man or group of men, and most certainly not the villainous brigand, or blood-thirsty gunhawk of Butch Cassidy's Wild Bunch, as the Yellow Press and a half-hundred hack writers would have it.

This past summer of 1965, I again returned to the land I'd known during the month I rode stirrup to stirrup with Harvey Logan.

Traveling comfortably, and accompanied by my youngest daughter, an English Instructor on holiday from a fashionable girls' school near Philadelphia, we made our tour of the *back-trails.* Sleeping late in one or another of the omnipresent, mass-production motels of the latter day West, and taking our time, we visited Wyoming, Montana, Utah, Arizona, the Dakotas, New Mexico and Colorado.

Wherever we journeyed, whether it be lonely Hole in the Wall (now devoid of even a cabin site); Brown's Hole, with its cloud-swept vastness; the arid and God-forsaken reaches of Robbers' Roost—or, at last, the wind-haunted slopes of Kid Curry's *last stand* at Divide Creek, I could almost physically feel his presence.

Sitting upon a boulder, that I identified from its peculiar squared top as the one providentially sheltering me from the fierce fire of the Divide Creek posse, I looked out through the stands of timber toward the blue wall of the Grand Mesa and puzzled again the insoluble problem.

Logan's journal, studied many times, since I'd recovered it from his saddle bag that fatal night on that very slope, had not revealed any firm clues as to his intended destination. That is, indeed, if it were actually Bronco Jack Caldwell, alias Tap Duncan (thief and cold-blooded informer) and not Harvey Logan who lay in the little cemetery at Glenwood Springs.

One can only speculate what motives Spence, of the Pinkertons, had in positively identifying the cadaver, exhumed from the Glenwood Springs grave as that of Kid Curry—without the benefit of fingerprints or even Bertillion measurements. Was it because of the unsuccessful campaign Billy Pinkerton had waged upon Cassidy and his gang? Was it a means of closing the books upon one of that agency's thorniest cases? Several years later, the Pinkertons again attempted to use the same method in the matter of Butch and Sundance, after their reported demise in South America—only to be dogged, for years, with strong rumors of the return of Cassidy and Longabaugh.

Accepted as fact, backed by newspaper reports, and, apparently correct, police bulletins, was the alleged reformation of Tom O'Day, Walt Punteny and Elza Lay—the latter after years in the New Mexico Pen. Accepted, also, by the public, when they thought of it, was the end of Flat Nose George Curry, Deaf Charlie Hanks, and Lonny Logan, and the eventual demise of Ben Kilpatrick (back out of jail and not thinking fast enough), killed in an attempted train robbery in Texas in 1912.

So it went, Cassidy's Train Robbers' Syndicate, all scattered to the four-winds of the West, and accounted for—except, possibly, for Sundance, Butch—and Kid Curry?

Shortly after I became an executive in our firm, I'd enough money to hire some investigators (not Pinkertons; that would have been too ironic), to follow any leads as to the whereabouts of Annie Winters. My sleuths drew a completely cold trail. Annie had vanished, and never was there mention of her again in the shady, sporting world of the Old West.

My investigators had an easier task with that of Starr. She was found to have married a Miles City Businessman in 1905, and was living a fairly easy existence, though I couldn't believe a particularly happy life. Logan's Christmas card to her, which she gave to the devious Frank Canton, is still in the files of the Pinkerton office.

And where *did* that anti-hero (a phrase much in favor these days); where did that anti-hero, Kid Curry, get himself to? My investigators never knew. If he returned to Annie Winters, which could explain her complete disappearance, did they ride into the still isolated fastness beyond Star Valley? Or did they go on to the Pacific Northwest? At this late date, these are questions of interest to few.

Now nearly a lifetime away, it seems a legend recounted of mythical figures—remote as the stars that still burn their frozen fires above the jagged horizons of the Little Rockies . . . remote and fathomless as the winds wandering over the long abandoned camps along the Outlaw Trail.

Center Point Large Print
600 Brooks Road / PO Box 1
Thorndike, ME 04986-0001 USA

(207) 568-3717

US & Canada:
1 800 929-9108
www.centerpointlargeprint.com